THE RETURN OF THE
MOTHER SERIES: BOOK 1

DAUGHTERS OF NRI

PRAISE FOR DAUGHTERS OF NRI

'Oh . . . my . . . goddesses! This book is something special. There is so much myth, fantasy and genuinely great storytelling packed into the pages of this novel. Excellent writing, brilliant book.'

Dorothy Koomson, Best-selling author

'From a rich and deep culture, Amayo weaves a world of literary magic. Daughter's of Nri is a beautifully written novel paving the way for a powerful collection to follow.'

Buzzfeed

'A phenomenal debut from a brilliant writer which kept me on the edge of my seat from the first page. This is a beautiful story full of heritage, passion and bravery that every young black girl should read.'

Black Girl Book Club

'With Daughters of Nri, Reni K Amayo conjures a magical world that truly centres black sisterhood. Combining lush prose with a fast-paced plot, this is one read that everyone – but especially black teens – will struggle to put down.'

Alex Sheppard, Author of 'Oh My Gods'

'This book is a love letter to black women. It is beautifully written and its message is so powerful and incredibly important. Every black woman needs to read. We deserve this story.'

WCAN

THE RETURN OF THE EARTH
MOTHER SERIES: BOOK 1

DAUGHTERS
OF NRI

RENI K AMAYO

ONWE
PRESS

ONWE
PRESS

First published in Great Britain in 2019 by Onwe Press Ltd
This paperback edition was first published in 2019

The rights of Reni K Amayo to be identified as the author of
this work has been asserted by her in accordance with the
Copyright, Designs and Patents Act 1988.

Printed and bound in Great Britain by Clays Ltd, Elcograf S.p.A.

A CIP catalogue record for this book is available from
the British Library.

Paperback ISBN 978-1-9160429-1-9
eBook ISBN 978-1-9160429-2-6
Hardback ISBN 978-1-9160429-3-3

To my sisters, you deserve the world.

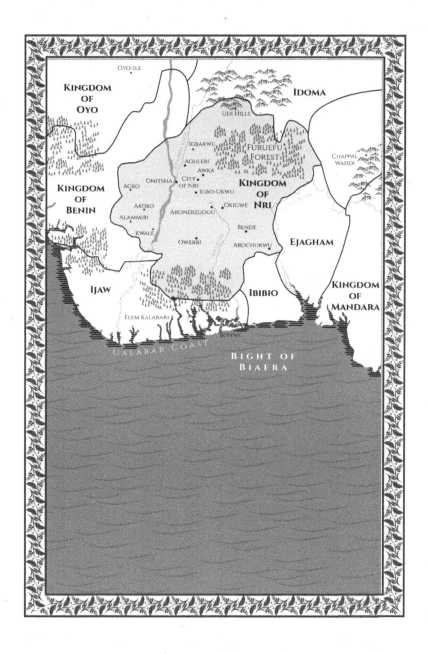

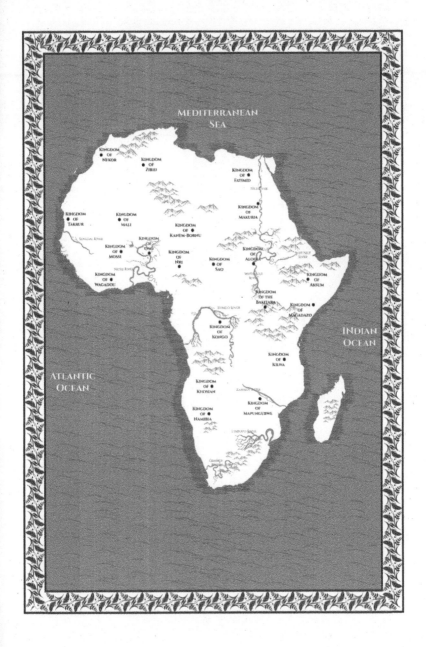

THE TRIALS TO ALA

Nsibidi of Soul
Trial: She has seen her inner God
Igbo translatiom: Chi

Nsibidi of Ground
Trial: She has spoken to the earth
Igbo translatiom: Àlà

Nsbidi of Air
Trial: She has been carried by the air
Igbo translatiom: Ikuku

Nsbidi of Love
Trial: She has given herself for another
Igbo translatiom: Ihunaya

Nsbidi of Death

Trial: She has taken breath

Igbo translatiom: Ọnwu

Nsibidi of Life

Trial: She has created breath

Igbo translatiom: Ndụ

Nsibidi of Creation

Trial: She has moulded beauty

Igbo translatiom: Okike

Nsibidi of Peace

Trial: She has found freedom

Igbo translatiom: Udo

Nsibidi of Ala

Trial: She has returned

Igbo translatiom: Ala

CHAPTER 1

THE BLACK AND GOLD ORACLE

Akoko

He stood outside the cave and took a deep breath, but the fresh night air did nothing to calm him. He tensed as the vine-covered entrance drew him closer. The hair on the back of his neck stood up as low, inhumane sounds from the creature within filtered through the moonlight. The Eze was not completely sure why he had chosen to leave the comfort of his *akwa* nest to wander into the starless night. He was neither intrigued nor was he curious. When the blubbering village chief had spoken about the mythical creature that his people had supposedly found earlier that day, the Eze had been filled with nothing but contempt.

He had watched as the old chief's eyes had grown larger with greed; the man's tongue had hung over his chapped lips and his fingers had rattled agitatedly. Chief Akunna was clearly hungry for recognition and thirsty for fame. His reckless rumour had brought the great Eze, the ruler of the entire kingdom, to his humble village, and now the chief's palms were laid open for a reward.

If it is a reward you are seeking then you shall receive it, the Eze had thought as he'd considered killing the man right on the spot. But he had not. Instead the Eze had ended the conversation abruptly, with his right hand raised dismissively in the air. The chief had lowered his eyes, visibly withdrawing into himself as he recognised his mistake.

The Eze's eyes had glazed over the wide-eyed village folk. They'd stared back at the large, powerful man with whispers of the *umu ada ogu*, the lost goddesses, stuck in their throats.

What did they know of the umu ada ogu? the Eze had reflected inwardly. He had regarded their simple expressions and frayed clothing, dulled by the red sand. They'd seemed to him like shadows of people, with no thought or life behind their eyes. He had found himself clenching his fists.

'What a waste,' he'd murmured as the village chief had cowered before him. The Eze had been certain that not one of these dull-eyed people had wandered further than the ten cubits of forest that enclosed them. It was simply impossible to believe that these were the same people that had somehow stumbled across one of the most majestic beings that had ever walked this earth. No living soul had laid eyes on the umu ada ogu in centuries. They,

2

like all of the magical entities, had died with the Mother. He'd been certain that whatever the villagers had found and locked away was anything but an umu ada ogu.

Yet here he was, standing alone outside the cave.

He had closed his eyes to sleep that night but something strange had lain heavy on his soul. A low and inexplicable sound. It had drawn him from his nest and compelled him towards the cave. Now it crept, thick and dark, over his black skin. It tasted like fear.

'Remember who you are,' he said under his breath. 'Remember what you have *done*,' he added quietly. He stared blankly into the cave's veiled mouth and took a deep breath.

The Eze descended like a shadow, blending seamlessly with the deep black that met him. He hesitated in the nothingness for a brief moment, before taking another step forward. He waited. He could still hear the leaves rustling in the wind outside the cave, but everything was still within. He shook his head. What was he expecting to find here?

'Nothing,' he muttered.

Just as he turned to leave, the air shifted.

The Eze stood deathly still. Hushed whispers suddenly bounced off the walls like birds dashing through a summer sky. The sounds started slow and low before growing in intensity and speed.

'*Ke iso Ala.*'

'*Ikenga.*'

'*Ekwensu.*'

'*Amadioha.*'

'*Anyanwu.*'

'*Agwu.*'

The whispers crept closer and closer to him, until they suddenly stopped and the cave fell back into silence. The Eze turned around as a heavy sigh was released into the air, and watched as two shadows materialised before merging into what appeared to be a woman seated cross-legged on the ground. Her eyes were shut and her bare black skin was outlined by a golden glow.

'So it's true,' he said, bewildered.

'Aljaneṣu-ojọọ. You have finally come.' Her voice was strange, both low and high, as if she had two souls trapped inside her, both struggling to be free. She opened her large eyes and they darted across the room before settling on him, shimmering with the same brilliant golden glow that coated her body.

The Eze stood frozen as he gazed with astonishment at the creature. She had spoken in the forgotten language.

'An oracle?' he gasped. A crippling shock overtook his body. Seconds passed as a cold sweat trickled down his forehead. The Eze sank into a sickening combination of anger and fear.

Stay strong! The phrase pounded harshly though the Eze's head as he shook himself, before falling into a defensive warrior stance. He forced himself to focus on his one strength: the enchanted crystal that lay hidden within his garments.

Oracles were said to be marked goddesses amongst the umu ada ogu, uplifted because they were not bound by time or space. They were the only beings with the power to utter words in the forgotten language. Oracles had always been a rarity, even during the time of the Mother, when it was commonplace for gods to roam the earth. Many considered them to be myths even back then. Only a select few students of the magical realm knew the true extent of their power. The Eze felt a cold chill run down his spine. Despite the fragile smell of mortality emitting from her bare skin, he could still feel the pulse of that intoxicating power.

'What are *you* doing here?' he said, his voice so low and deep it sent vibrations through the small cave. The oracle opened her mouth, as if she were going to speak, but stopped and settled back into herself. Confusion suddenly flashed across her beautiful, dark face.

'I don't know,' she finally replied, lowering her bright eyes and staring wildly at her hands, as though she had never seen them before. 'I was nothing for a long time, but then the black birthed me, and I remembered. Once I remembered, I knew I had to wait for *you*.' Her eyes, smouldering softly in the night like dying stars, flicked back to him. The Eze shivered.

'Be careful, witch; I have no qualms about slitting your throat tonight,' he spat, allowing his fear to fuel a vicious rage.

'That is not how you will do it,' she replied.

'I said be careful!' the Eze roared.

'Why?'

The Eze felt exposed and raw. He didn't want to open his mouth, lest she stole whatever was left of him.

'I asked why, Aljaneṣu-ojọọ.'

'Stop calling me that,' the Eze said sharply, taking a measured step closer to her.

The oracle cocked her head in confusion. 'Do you not know what you are?'

'How dare you?' he spat.

'Do you not *know* what you are?' the oracle repeated as the Eze stalked closer until he was towering over her seated body.

'I . . .' he started, before pausing abruptly.

'Yes, Aljaneṣu-ojọọ?'

'I am not Aljaneṣu-ojọọ! I am not a demon. I am Eze Ochichiri, son of Amobi, Keeper of Justice!' he proclaimed.

The oracle recoiled in disgust.

'Justice,' she murmured wearily. 'You dare to utter that word. After what you have done? You who blindly followed destructive greed under the guise of Amadioha's false *justice*. You robbed the earth of its greatest treasure and you dare to call yourself *just*? Once you took the Mother's life, you were and will always be Aljaneṣu-ojọọ; that title will always follow you.'

The Eze breathed heavily, his head swirling. With resolute determination, he used his brewing rage to burn up any traces of fear. *Oracle or not, the wench is mortal now, as mortal as those foolish villagers,* he thought coldly as he bent and pulled her up by the neck.

'My name is Eze Ochichiri and I *am* the Keeper of Justice,' he said, deliberately sounding out each word for emphasis.

'You are Aljaneṣu-ojọọ,' the oracle noted, her voice slightly distorted by the Eze's squeeze on her neck. The Eze's eyes opened slightly before narrowing in anger.

'Yes, you will kill me tonight,' she continued, as the Eze dropped her to the ground before turning his back on her. The thought of such a creature filled him with revulsion.

'Stay out of my head,' he bellowed into the hollow cave.

'I'm not in your head. You have lost your grip on your thoughts. They wander like ants all over your skin, the walls, the floor,' the oracle said, her two voices intertwining in a soft dance. She lifted her head up, 'do you know who you are?' she asked abruptly.

'I am Justice,' the Eze said once again. His voice remained solid, but lacked its prior strength.

'No,' the oracle replied, and her voices sang. 'You are the murderer, the thief, the corruptor of justice. The Mother's killer, and therefore the corrupter of souls. You stole hope and promised joy. You took everything, and you don't even know it. You don't even have shame. If I could, I would rip you to pieces over and over again for all of eternity, and let you soak in the evil that you have caused—' the oracle hissed as her body rose weightlessly from the ground and drifted towards him before settling down to a stop. 'But I cannot. Your fate is waiting for you and my fate is to tell you it.'

'You threaten me, wench?' the Eze asked.

'No, I do not need to. I have seen.'

'Hmm,' he grunted as he turned to stand squarely before her. The oracle's large eyes glowed even brighter. The Eze couldn't help but look away.

'I suppose you want me to ask you what you have seen,' he said quietly.

'You will ask, Aljaneṣu-ojọọ,' she stated.

He could feel the pull of the forgotten language and his hand found her neck once again.

'Tell me,' he murmured, as she shivered in his arms.

'Eze Ochichiri,' she said, her two voices more distinct than they had been previously, ringing loudly with a muted melody, rising slowly. 'Aljaneṣu-ojọọ, your time is coming to an end.'

The Eze held his breath in anticipation.

'Time will birth hope back to the earth; it will be brought forth by the daughters of Nri, brought forth by Ala—the Earth Mother's twins!' the oracle screamed as the Eze clamped his hand down and squeezed with all of his might until her golden glow dimmed into oblivion.

'Lies,' the Eze breathed as sweat appeared on his forehead. He shook his head violently. He must have been mistaken. She was no oracle, just an umu ada ogu driven mad by the snakesweed.

'Ala has no daughters,' the Eze whispered, as the shadow of death covered the cave.

CHAPTER 2

THE WHITE MAHOGANY TREE

Igbakwu

Naala allowed an army of red dust to swallow her whole, as she lay cocooned in the swirling cloud she had created. She squinted her deep brown eyes to prevent the particles, and speckles of bright orange sunlight, from irritating them. She'd held her breath but she could still taste the heat of the dust particles as they danced around her. Once they had settled, she exhaled loudly and closed her eyes, allowing herself to be washed by a wave of serenity.

For a moment, she was only aware of the hot sun caressing her and the feathery particles of earth lying against her body. As sweet as that moment was, it did not last. Slowly, images of her future marched unceremoniously through her mind. She saw starless nights spent pounding yams, bright mornings by the river washing Chinedu's clothes, wistful days waiting for something to happen, tiny feet rushing towards her eagerly, faces awaiting her instruction. Chinedu would make a good husband. He would build them a stable life, and Naala would teach the young ones the ways of a world she had never really explored for herself. Pressure began to swell in her chest; it was becoming increasingly difficult for her to breathe.

Naala drew her feet up against the floor and spread her arms wide against the earth. She tapped her feet and swayed her long arms, creating yet another frenzied cloud of dust. As she waited for the particles to settle around her, a strange feeling whirled within her, a slight tug that caused her to cautiously open her eyes. Naala's heart skipped a beat as she saw millions of tiny particles hanging weightlessly in the air. They drifted above her head, as though offering up a dance of worship to her.

'What the—' Naala started, before the dust suddenly all settled down towards her. Naala huffed thoughtlessly and dust scratched against her throat. She sprang from the floor and coughed violently. *I must be mad*, she thought, shaking off what she'd just seen—what she *thought* she had just seen.

Naala often found that her mind played tricks on her. Strange, sometimes delightful, tricks. Her grandmother had once told her that dwelling on the minute oddities of life was a sure way to lose one's mind. Naala rarely stuck to that principle. The oddities of life usually sparked an endless stream of thoughts and questions for her; she would gladly spend hours trying to get to the root of all obscurities. Only these peculiar occurrences that happened around her did not exactly feel like oddities to Naala. More like the facts of her life: her hair was black, her toes clicked occasionally, strange things occurred around her at a whim.

Naala looked down at her once-vibrant bridal garment, now dulled by the blood-red dust.

How in all of heavens am I going to explain this? she thought, as she slowly rose from the floor. Her throat still tickled slightly.

'Esinaala!' a voice shrilled behind her. Naala whipped around so fast that she created yet another thin cloud of red dust. She coughed again. Small but firm hands smacked her back, encouraging her lungs to clear.

'What in heaven's name is wrong with you?' Gini cried, as Naala's coughing fit subsided.

'*Ndewo*, Gini,' Naala managed, bringing her crossed palms to her chest and letting them fall towards her closest friend. Gini looked down at Naala's open palms and said nothing. She couldn't even fathom returning the greeting.

Naala dropped her arms to her side as she regarded Gini standing squarely with her hands on her hips. Gini was a small girl, almost half the size of Naala. She was short and plump, save for her waist, which was cinched in to give her enviable curves. The girl may have been small, but she was also mighty, and with her teeth clenched and eyebrows increasingly slanted, it was clear that Gini was seething.

Naala gulped.

'Okay, okay, I admit it looks bad, bu—' Naala started.

'Bad?' Gini cut in. 'The ceremony is in an hour, Naala! This is not bad . . . it's catastrophic!' Gini paced dangerously towards Naala. She stopped sharply before she crashed into her, shaking her head in disbelief. Naala rolled her eyes at the dramatic display, before throwing her hands up defiantly.

'Okay, fine . . . it *is* bad,' she replied. Her voice remained steady but her cheeks felt warm with shame.

'What's wrong with you? Why would you do this?' Gini exclaimed; her fury grew stronger due to Naala's obvious disregard. While Gini felt as though she knew her friend inside and out, at times it would dawn on her that she didn't understand Naala's behaviour at all: a realisation that never failed to make her even angrier.

'I just needed . . .' Naala started, as Gini looked up at her expectantly, but she couldn't find the words to truly express why she had spent the morning before her wedding rolling around on the dusty ground. Naala felt herself getting even warmer under Gini's gaze. 'Look,' she said indignantly. 'You are acting as if this is your wedding. It's not; it's mine. And yes, *this-*,' she said, pulling at her stained garments. 'This is bad, but it's bad for me. I'm the one that will deal with the repercussions, not you, so please calm down.'

Gini glared at Naala with raw anger.

12

'It is *your* wedding,' she cried out. 'But it was *my* hands sewing those beautiful stones into your garments and helping you plait your hair –both of which are now ruined!'

Naala opened her mouth in protest before settling back down. She knew she was wrong.

'It's this!' Gini continued. 'These moments when you . . . it's exactly why they say . . . this is why they say . . .' she trailed off, shaking her head and biting her tongue before she could say something that she would undoubtedly regret. After a pause, Gini eventually settled for reaching up to brush off the dust from Naala's shoulders.

'They say?' Naala asked, as she tried to follow Gini's gaze, but the girl only looked away awkwardly. Naala knew that Gini would never finish that sentence, and she didn't even have to, but Naala wanted to ask all the same. Naala had always loved her village and the people in it; warmth, laughter and playfulness had always flowed effortlessly through the small settlement. However, it had never felt like home. Naala had never felt like she belonged, and, while no one had openly admitted it, she knew that she was considered *strange*. Her impending marriage to one of the most sought-after men in her village was a complete shock to everyone. No one understood why someone like Chinedu would choose someone like *her*.

'Despite your *efforts*, we may have a chance to salvage this,' Gini said softly, as she took a small step back and began to inspect the damage.

A smile spread over Naala's plump lips. 'So I haven't completely ruined it yet?' she murmured, as a strange mixture of relief and disappointment coursed through her blood.

'Hey, hey, stop that! Stop feeling sorry for yourself; it's your wedding day, for heaven's sake,' Gini snapped, as she slapped Naala lightly on her arm.

'I know,' Naala said, trying to keep her face straight and sombre. 'I'm just sorry that I ruined your hard work . . . truly.'

'Mhmm,' she huffed, as she avoided being sucked into Naala's guilty glistening brown eyes. Gini, like most people, had always found it difficult to stay angry with Naala. Even now, Gini could feel her anger dissipating into the afternoon air, but she desperately wanted to hold on to it, if only to teach the cheeky girl a lesson.

'Come,' Gini muttered, as she grabbed Naala's slender hand and dragged her towards the Anambra river. It lay towards the east side of the village, where the trees began to thicken and grow tall. Aside from a few disgruntled grumbles from Gini, the two of them said nothing on the short walk. When they eventually reached the riverbank, Naala sat on a smooth rock and dipped her feet into the lukewarm water, creating an unfurling, red-orange stain. The smell of moist rich soil, hippo grass, and desert rose wafted through the air and the birds were in the midst of their afternoon song.

'Are we going to talk about this?' Gini said in a tone that

14

appeared harsh, but she failed to fully mask the concern in her voice. Naala paused and looked up at her friend.

'I want to marry him,' she replied.

'You should.'

'He is very handsome,' Naala continued.

'Éh.'

'. . . and strong,' Naala added.

'So?' Gini asked, with her arms outstretched perplexed.

'So . . .'

'What's the problem?' Gini exclaimed in frustration.

'There is no problem,' Naala said, before pausing.

Gini sighed, but rather than continuing to probe, she gathered a handful of banana leaves and clumped them together. She didn't say a word as she lightly ran the damp makeshift sponge over Naala's dusty garment. However, to Naala, her silence was louder than her most verbose speeches.

'He's . . . Chinedu, and he chose me, and that's good. He's . . . I know this is good . . . I really do, I'm just feeling, feeling unsettled,' Naala tried, pausing to look for validation in Gini's expressionless face. 'Didn't you feel unsettled when you married Tito?' she asked, but Gini said nothing as she continued to work away at her garment.

'Gini,' Naala said, exasperated, as she grabbed the small woman's hands. 'I'm really asking, didn't you feel . . .' Naala couldn't find the words. She sighed in frustration and dropped her hands.

'I felt scared? A little scared. Well, more than a little. Naala, it's normal to feel . . . strange before your wedding day; it's the day that you become a woman. That's a hard burden to bear. But we must all do it! Even pretty, loud, troublesome girls like you,' Gini teased with a smile; try as she might, she could not hold onto her anger.

'I . . .' Naala started, before looking away, ashamed.

'What is it?'

'I don't feel scared. I feel restless,' Naala muttered, as she looked out at the tall foreboding trees. She stood up abruptly, almost knocking Gini into the lake, and smiled as she saw Enwe, a little grey mischievous monkey that had taken a liking to her when she was a child. He swung freely from branch to branch in the huge white mahogany tree a few steps away from the riverbank.

'Look, it's Enwe; I haven't seen him for a while,' Naala commented, as she watched him soar. Gini kissed her teeth in irritation.

'You better not call that stupid monkey over here; remember what he did to my *nkwobi*? I spent so long on that dish and that little—if he comes near me I'll skin him alive—I've warned you.'

'I don't know how many times we have to go over this. He's a monkey, he didn't mean to knock it over,' Naala snapped, before turning back to the leaping monkey. 'Wow, look at him go. Do you remember when we used to chase after him up those trees?'

'I remember. But I remember *you* climbing trees to avoid playing normal games with everyone else.'

'Nonsense, you used to climb too,' Naala teased, as Gini rolled her eyes.

'What now?' Gini sighed, as Naala gestured at the giant tree in front of them. The dark green leaves rustled musically in the wind.

'Should we do it?' Naala said.

'No.'

'Gini, come now; you haven't even heard me out yet.'

'I don't need to; I'm a big woman now and so are you!'

'I think we should climb the tree.'

'Of course you do! Because you are mad.'

'Gini.'

'Esinaala.'

Naala regarded Gini quickly, before forcefully grabbing her hand and attempting to drag her towards the mammoth tree.

'Ai! Listen, we are married women . . . we can't climb trees like your monkey friend,' Gini protested. 'Ah-ah, there're barely any branches at the base . . . what is this nonsense? Naala, there's just no way—'

'We've climbed harder trees, Gini, and what does being married have to do with anything? We can do what we want; being married doesn't make us dead.'

'Well, I don't want to climb this tree.'

'Aren't you afraid?'

'I am—that's why I don't want to climb it.'

'Not of the tree . . . of being stuck and restricted, not being able to breathe under the never-ending heap of duties.'

'Duties are good.'

'So is freedom. The problem is there is no balance. Let's *create* some balance.'

'By climbing a tree? Naala, listen to yourself.'

'I know you think I'm crazy,' Naala said quietly. 'And maybe I am . . . but try and understand . . . this is our time, our moment, and it just feels as though . . . we're missing it. We're just standing here, trapped by . . . customs, watching life go by. I think that, sometimes, we should indulge ourselves in a little silliness.'

A loaded silence ensued before Gini finally said, 'We should head back; I think I've got as much of the dust off your garments as I can.'

Naala nodded in reply, her eyes cast downwards to hide her burning disappointment.

Gini began to walk back towards the village. Naala almost followed but a short, sudden screech from Enwe hit her squarely in her heart. The grey monkey leapt joyfully through the air and, before she could think, she rested one foot against the trunk before hauling herself up.

'Hey! Naala! Come on! We said that we would leave!' Gini exclaimed, but Naala was already too far up.

Naala felt completely calm as she climbed that tree. Her muscles were stretched and bursting with energy.

'You've had your fun, Naala!' Gini called from the ground, but all Naala could hear was the wind rustling through the green leaves.

Naala stopped for a moment as she almost neared the top of the gigantic tree. She closed her eyes and took a deep breath. She was at peace. She thought briefly about having to say goodbye to the child she had been, and the life of adventure she had never lived.

A bitter taste entered her mouth. Why should she give up these simple pleasures in life? Sure, she may not be able to explore the world and reach the moon as she had once hoped as a child, but she could always climb a tree and dream. Marrying Chinedu would not be the end of her life; she wouldn't let it.

Naala smiled as she felt Enwe settle onto her shoulders. She opened her eyes and took in the beautiful scenery before her. The lush green trees bent back and forth and the crystal blue lake cut through the sparring forest, creating intricate patterns. The birds floated gently in the hot afternoon air and various beasts wandered lazily through the shrubs and bushes. Naala's smile suddenly vanished as something else caught her eye.

Her body instantly tensed and she squinted. Something big and fast was moving in the bushes to the far north. She leaned outwards from the tree, and her heart skipped a beat. *The Eze's army*, she thought, almost falling off the limb in fright.

CHAPTER 3

DEATH AT THE WINDOW

City of Nri

Several miles away from Igbakwu, a girl with the same face as Naala stared blankly out of an oval opening in a bright, sand-coloured wall, overlooking the waking city of Nri. The sunrays cut the morning sky with deep red slashes, and chased away the darkness of the previous night.

The window that Sinai stood by was far larger than she was. Her bare feet curved at its base and her toes poked out into the open air. Sinai's heart fluttered as she felt the promise of death reach out its cold hand and brush her skin as the wind played softly with her long, thick, moss hair. She rarely wore it down. It was usually tied away in muted braids or hidden under one of her wrappers. She preferred it not to attract unwanted attention. However, this morning her mind was fixated on things far more disturbing than glaring looks and chuckled remarks from delusional men.

'What does it all mean?' she muttered. She closed her eyes and felt she could still feel the remnants of her dream hanging over her like dead skin. It wasn't a bad dream; in fact, many would argue that it was a pleasant one. She had fallen into a different world where the colours were brighter than she had ever seen them. The food was delicious and rich. The sky shone like the opening to heaven itself. It was her world, only different. She could sense something in the air that she had never experienced in her life; it seemed like true freedom. In her dream she had met a girl that she knew, but had never met. A girl who was exactly like her and yet nothing like her at all. There was something eerily familiar about that girl, and yet Sinai could not recall her name. Still, they had greeted each other like old friends and walked hand in hand, with one focus—the bright red light.

Sinai shook her head in frustration.

'What does it mean?' she groaned, as she looked out onto the golden clay city. It sparkled before her. The buildings curved and bent in submission to the ever-changing sun, creating art, not only in their design, but in the shadows they created. The bustling sounds of the stirring people had already begun to surface in the early morning; she could hear songs of the strange *nnunu* women; the rumble of the hagglers and the children's shrill laughter drifting slowly in the sweetly scented warm air.

Sinai felt as though she was viewing Nri through a thin veil. A veil that she had grown accustomed to, so much so that she had forgotten it existed –until that dream. Something was wrong. Something was missing, but she had no idea what this something was. She felt as though she had forgotten a word, her favourite word. It hid somewhere in the corner of her mind. Sinai was frustrated, and ashamed; how could she have lost such a beautiful thing?

She closed her eyes and felt the wind against her warm face. As the sun emerged from a cloud, it bathed her legs with a warm crimson light.

Sinai's eyes suddenly sprang open.

Something had changed. She swivelled around, but before she could register what was going on, something hard hit her head. She yelped in shock, drawing her hands up. The blow was not strong enough to knock her out, but caused her to lose her balance. Sinai swayed back and forth against the edge of the window. Her heart plunged to the pit of her stomach as she realised that death was no longer a quiet onlooker that she could wilfully ignore. It was a real and unstoppable force that had come to stake its claim.

Those brief seconds were both painfully short and disturbingly long. Her head turned and she caught a glimpse of the long fall that would certainly break her neck if she lost her footing. Sinai forced her gaze away from the sickening view and back into the room that was no longer empty, but held three or four people who watched from a distance.

She stretched out her hands in a plea, but this action inspired no movement from the inspectors; it only worked to throw her further off-balance.

Sinai screamed as her weight dropped into the open air. Her arms swung high above her head before scraping along the same ridged window ledge that her feet had hung from not too long ago. She clawed her fingers in desperation, trying to cling on to whatever she could. Suddenly, her descent towards the ground stopped. Her hands had found a grip along the window ledge. She screamed in pain as the weight of her body pulled against her armpits; she felt as though her arms were being ripped viciously out of their sockets. Three dark figures looked down at her with shadows cast over their faces.

'Help! Please!' she shouted in desperation, as she raked her toes against the grainy wall. But all Sinai heard was a short snarl in response. A sense of doom washed over her bruised body as it dawned on her that her fall was no accident.

'Oh, look girls,' Ina sneered, as she stepped into the morning sun. 'The little rodent has learnt a new skill.' The two other girls, Ebun and Lebechi, laughed nervously. For as long as they could remember, Ina had been their queen, their *Lolo*. She was intelligent, cruel, and breathtakingly beautiful. Her large dark eyes glowed with formidable power, her striking broad nose and thick lips captivated attention from anyone with a heartbeat. Ina walked through life with the intoxicating confidence of someone ordained by the gods. She brazenly wore her ankle-length hair in thick locs, a practice typically reserved for only the senior lords; she swore that she was a *dada* and her hair simply grew in that fashion. No one disputed her claim; after all, she was the daughter of the King of Oyo.

Whilst Ina was not born of Nri and her links to the Eze were obscure at best, no one could deny that she *belonged*. That said, neither of Ebun nor Lebechi had ever played a part in anyone's death before, and as they looked down, they could see Sinai's eyes begging them for mercy.

'Maybe we should help her . . .' Ebun said quietly, her heart quickening when she received a cold stare from Ina. 'I—I mean . . . she seems so . . . um . . . pathetic.'

Ina sighed, irked; she hated weakness and she could hear it in the cracks in Ebun's voice. It was clear that Ebun was afraid that the girl might die. *It definitely looked like that might be the case,* Ina thought, as she looked down on Sinai's quivering hands; they would not hold on for much longer.

Sinai's thick hair shimmied in the morning wind and her dark sepia skin looked beautiful against the gold walls. *Even now, frazzled and dishevelled, this girl looks like she stepped out of the god's quarter,* Ina thought in annoyance.

Ina was not afraid that Sinai would die; in fact, she was far more afraid that the girl would live. For months now, Ina had been fantasising about ways to get rid of the girl that threatened to take everything from her. Now here she was with Sinai's life resting at the tips of her very own toes.

A series of flashbacks burnt through Ina's mind: the first time Obi Ife had looked past her to catch glimpses of this girl; or when she had watched him follow Sinai out of the Mmanwu festival, or when Ina had caught him laughing with the girl in the corner of the west courtyard. She had fainted after seeing that; thankfully she had her wits about her and had blamed it on the heat.

Obi Ife, one of the highest lords in the Kingdom of Nri, second only to the Eze himself, belonged to Ina. She had known this since she was a child, and she used to watch him win against the other boys at *dambe*. As his body grew, so did his power, and Ina's interest. Until one day he did the impossible: he took a position amongst the high lords whilst he was still a young man. It was unheard of, but the Eze has granted him the position all the same. From that point on, Ina just knew that he was her promise. She knew with every fibre of her being that she was destined to be his first wife, perhaps even his only wife. This was the narrative she'd created for herself, and she was so *close* to living it. At least, she had been. Over the past few months she had started to feel that promise slipping away like water through her fingers. Obi Ife grew more distant from her with every passing day and Ina grew more frantic. She knew she was pushing him away; she felt him recoil as she grew more and more neurotic. *Look at me! Play with me! Love me!* He hated it, but she couldn't stop herself. Some days she thought it would be far easier to claw her own eyes out, than to watch his attention turn increasingly towards Sinai, who grew more beautiful, more alluring, and more interesting.

'Lebechi,' Ina said, stepping closer to the window as Sinai attempted fruitlessly to lift herself up. 'Do you also think we should help the rodent?'

'I—I—I. . .' Lebechi stammered, as Ina pressed a foot against Sinai's right hand. Sinai let out a blood-curdling scream and Lebechi looked around like a startled goat.

'Lebechi!?' Ina demanded.

'N—no, we don't have . . . to save her, I mean . . . she's so . . .' Lebechi mumbled quietly, her eyes wide with fear.

'Ina, please,' Sinai whimpered. Her eyes filled with thick tears and her throat was constrained with sorrow. Sinai didn't want these to be her last words. She didn't want to be a subjugated beggar in death. She wanted so desperately to die with dignity. Be strong, she wanted to tell herself; be dignified. But all she could hear was a quiet voice whispering in her head, *I just want to live.*

'Shut up, whore!' Ina snapped in anger. 'How dare you address me; we all know about the vile disgusting things your *kind* does to get attention from men who will never wed, never lo—' she spat furiously, as Ebun nudged at her forearm.

'Ina,' Ebun pleaded.

'What?' Ina shouted, as she turned towards the frightened girl.

'People are coming,' Ebun moaned, lifting her hands towards her head in angst.

Ina paused, taking stock of the shocked and disturbed expressions crossing Ebun and Lebechi's faces. They had never seen her act this way before; why would they have? Ina spent most of her life striving to maintain composure at all times. Self-control was power, she reminded herself as she stilled her shaking hands. She glanced down at Sinai, taking in her bruised fingers, tearful eyes, and pitiful expression. In that moment, the petrified girl held up a mirror to Ina, and she saw a monster reflected back.

Ina was suddenly overwhelmed with an intense desire to flee. *I shouldn't be here*, she thought. *I can't be here.*

'Let's go,' she said coldly, before turning to walk away calmly, as if nothing had occurred.

'Help! Help! Please help!' Sinai screamed frantically. She tried once more to lift herself up but her arms were too weak. She didn't want to die like this; there was so much more, more to see, more to discover and learn. That dream, as ridiculous as it was, was a testament to that. She needed to hold on.

'Please,' she gasped, just as her hands slipped, and she plummeted into pitch black.

CHAPTER 4

THE BIRTH

Alammiri

In later years, the people of Alammiri village would often recount the events of the night when the twins entered the world, but only ever in passing, and with eyes downcast and voices low. Different versions of the same story would be retold routinely. Whispers would spread, like thin golden threads, adding magic to the village's historical tapestry. People would speak about the night with an air of forced nonchalance, desperate to hide what it truly meant to them. When a villager could no longer resist the urge to discuss their experience on that miraculous night, no one would reply, no one would comment, but neither could anyone interrupt.

On that night, Ijemma looked up to find that the moon was double—no quadruple—its size. She stumbled backwards as she gazed at the large, heavy, pale moon peering through the clouds as if it too was eager to witness the magical birth. Ugo blinked in wonder as she stared up at the stars, so bright that it seemed as though the whole world was coated with sparkling silver. Obi gasped when she had reached the Akwụkwọ Ndụ lake. All her life she had known Akwụkwọ Ndụ to be a deep emerald colour, stained with lush green vegetation. However, when Obi had come for her usual evening swim that night, the lake was as clear as air. So clear, in fact, that for a brief moment, she thought that somehow the green murky water had been drained. She jumped when she saw the lake creatures swimming with frantic excitement.

Ezinne did not scream when she gave birth to those girls. Her smooth, deep skin was dripping with sweat, her eyes were clamped shut, and her teeth clenched. She was in incredible pain and her husband, Chief Obifune, knew it. He sat behind her, holding her trembling body. He shouldn't have been there. He could hear his father's gruff voice in his head, telling him that a man had no place in his woman's childbirth, but Obifune was no ordinary man and Ezinne was far from an ordinary woman.

I need to be there, he thought, as he pressed his face into his wife's soft, cotton-like hair, as slow tears ran down his cheek. *Something is not right.*

'Zy,' Chief Obifune murmured into her ear. His heart squeezed mercilessly as he called on the lost gods to hear his silent prayers. *Zy, please.*

29

He could feel her hot skin shake uncontrollably, and hear her short gasps. The birthing *osigwus* brushed away their tears and stifled their cries. They knew that his *nwunye* was dying. They loved her. He loved her more.

Obifune had been strolling with his father to an elders' meeting the first time he met Ezinne. He had yet to see nine full years, but his little, round face was very serious and etched with a soft frown he had stolen from his father. He knew, even back then, that he was going to be the next chief of his proud people, and that responsibility weighed heavily on his small shoulders.

Ezinne had interrupted that evening's stroll with the launch of a soft, ripe *udara* fruit. Obifune had felt it splat on the back of his head, and had swivelled in surprise. Only then had he gasped. Five or so cubits ahead, he'd seen a girl. Obifune had seen many girls before, but none like Ezinne. Her small face had hung upside down from a tree and her thin, black legs dangled from a fragile branch. He still remembered her smile, the same smile that could cause his heart to flutter so many years after. The smile that had beamed as bright as the high sun on that warm dry day.

At first, Ezinne would protest that it had been an accident.

'The udara just slipped from my hand,' she would shrug coyly. But after several years and a few glasses of palm wine, she had confessed that it was all a ploy to knock that foul frown from his little face.

She had been climbing the trees scattered across the village, a hobby she would secretly carry into adulthood. She had seen them approach and watched them curiously for a while, before plucking the udara and throwing it at the small boy.

'Sorry, little prince,' she had said that day, after leaping down from the tree, still smiling. She had approached them before crossing her palms across her chest and letting them fall as she greeted him.

'Ndewo,' she had murmured. Her large almond eyes had followed him intensely like a feral cat's. Chief Esomchi had grunted disapprovingly, and his rough tone brought the two children back to reality almost immediately. Ezinne had jumped nervously before bowing deeply to Obifune's father. The elder chief had paused, taken aback by the small girl's nerve. He had sneered, causing the girl to run off, leaving a trail of burnt red sand. Obifune had desperately wanted to run after her, but his father's mutterings told him to stay put.

Soon after that day, Ezinne and Obifune would discover that they were best friends. Her fiery passion was beautifully balanced with his cool tranquillity. Almost a decade after this, they would discover that they were lovers.

Eventually, after a series of tear-filled protests and high strong threats, they took sacred vows before their village. It had been a miraculous day. The village had collectively breathed a sigh of relief when the ceremony had ended, and erupted into an infectious excitement.

Ezinne and Obifune's love was so delightfully pure that no one could bear the thought of them being apart. Even Chief Esomchi's public disapproval held little weight; after all, Ezinne was the daughter of an equally prestigious family from their sister tribe, and Obifune had sworn he would neither marry nor bed any other woman. It was an abomination, but Chief Esomchi could not afford to gamble his legacy; he had seen the way the boy looked at that girl.

The world was silent when the first twin, Esinaala, was born. Esinaala broke this silence with one shrill scream, high and sharp, and with an echo that seemed to resonate through the village. Ezinne gasped as she brought the second twin, Sinaikuku, into the world. The little princesses cried loudly as they were taken away from their mother. Their wrinkly tiny fists punched the air in protest. They still longed for the safety of their mother's womb. The osigwus inspected their small bodies before taking a step back, stunned. The girls were beautiful and strange. Twins were a rare sight in the village; healthy twins were an even greater rarity. But these twins looked up at them with such purity, such innocence, such desperation to live, one might forget that they were already marked for death by the Eze's law.

Obifune looked at his two healthy daughters, and broke into a short laugh as his eyes filled with tears of joy. He then looked down at his beautiful wife and her soft smile made his heart leap to his throat, but something in her eyes made it sink back down to his feet.

'Zy,' he murmured, his voice cracking with tears. But nothing could be done. Ezinne was dead.

The Eze's law was clear: any woman that bore twins in Nri would be stoned; the children slaughtered within the first week of their birth. Their remains were to be sent to the palace for spiritual cleansing. Then, and only then, could the village be free of the inevitable curse that such an unnatural birth would bring about. Breaching the law would result in the death of every man, woman, and child in the village that those twins called their home. Alammiri was far away from the city. So far that the Eze and his obscure laws seemed as distant as the forgotten tales of the gods. However, the army's routine visits and crippling taxes were all too real. The Eze may have seemed like a fable, but the consequence of defying his orders was anything but. Stories of villages burnt to the ground for refusing orders had filtered through to Alammiri and no one wanted to test the mysterious Eze.

However, the people of Alammiri were overcome with grief; they had lost their beautiful queen.

Ezinne's burial service was held seven days after the twins were born and no one dared to mention the cruel law. Instead, they allowed it to drift over them like a small grey cloud against a clear blue sky. The Eze was the ruler of the kingdom. He oversaw the workings of every village, and if the gods had not abandoned the earth, he would have been the liaison between them and the people. His law was unshakeable. But Obifune was their beloved chief. He held their hearts. The villagers had seen him grow into a kind and fair leader. They had witnessed as his love for Ezinne flourished. They had placed so much hope into their relationship, and the life it would yield. With Ezinne gone, how could they destroy the only remnants of their profound love?

So they didn't. The seventh day passed, and then the eighth and ninth. . . until one day Obifune awoke to find his girls were gone. Snatched in the middle of the night. The village woke one morning to Obifune's cries. Those girls were the only thing he had left of Ezinne; without them he was broken. He died not too long after. It was an uneventful night and he had not fallen ill. He simply went to sleep and did not wake up.

CHAPTER 5

THE NAMIBIAN COOK AND THE EFUỌLA GIRL

City of Nri

Sinai felt the light before she saw it. Suddenly her world was bright yellow. A dull pain hit the middle of her head, and she grimaced and tried to reach for it, but found that every inch of her body throbbed with pain.

Am I dead? she thought curiously, but before she could answer, she was distracted by an overwhelming sensation. She knew this place. She recognised the smell, the air, the sounds, but she could not put it all together. Sinai shifted her head to the right, and the yellow light dimmed. She cautiously opened her eyes, but clamped them shut and groaned. Her head spun.

She didn't know where she was or how she'd got there. All she could remember was the intense fear coursing through her body as she fell. That, and Ina's cruel eyes.

Sinai had never understood Ina. The girl was smart, beautiful, and could navigate the complicated political scene in Nri with an appearance of ease and calm that Sinai could only dream of emulating. There were even rumours that Obi Ife, by far the most accomplished of any of the senior lords, was set to propose. Ina's life was perfect; it had always been perfect. She strolled through it effortlessly, given endless compliments, opportunities, and admiration. Yet, for as long as Sinai could remember, every time she was in Ina's vicinity she would feel the girl's eyes burning furiously into the back of her head. Ina would even, at times, peel off her subdued persona and openly sneer and mock Sinai.

When they were younger, Sinai had thought Ina's hatred stemmed from the fact that Sinai was illegitimate. Sinai had never known her parents; she was one of the unclaimed efuọla children. It was likely that her parent's union was impure, this being one of the few logical explanations as to why they would discard her when she only a few weeks old, if that.

Sinai repeatedly told herself that she was fortunate, particularly when the sneers and mistreatment stemming from the shame of her illegitimacy became almost too heavy a burden to bear. She was lucky, she would say to herself; after all, her parents could have left her for dead, or sent her to a squalid slum where no further questions would be asked. Instead, they'd sent her to the City of Nri, wrapped in fine clothes and with a parchment pleading for the council of elders to determine her fate, and sealed with insignia reserved for royalty.

Fortunately, the elders declared that Sinai's blood was far too noble for her to be anywhere other than amongst the members of high society. So she remained within the palace at Nri, placed grudgingly in communal care alongside the other noble children. She was blessed with rich food, comfortable quarters, and beautiful clothes. She was free to attend festivals, and school with the legitimate children and, when she came of age, she was likely to marry a low-ranking noble. Sinai was blessed to live amongst the highest in society, but she felt cursed to never belong. She spent most of her time alone, with most parents reprimanding their children for getting too close to the efuọla girl, less the shame of her illegitimacy rub off on them. Her life was so strikingly different to that of Ina, who belonged to an enviable family, had a herd of loyal friends enamoured by her very presence, and a future brighter than Lolo Obioma's largest jewels. Sinai never understood why a girl who had everything would bother wasting so much energy on a girl who spent most days struggling to stay afloat.

Ina's seething face flashed in Sinai's mind once again, and she was suddenly overcome with weariness. She wanted nothing more than to get away from that bloodthirsty girl.

Sinai lifted her eyelids again, bracing for the painful bright light. She blinked a few times before seeing that she was in a small room, narrowed by rows of cabinets against three of its walls. Sinai was positioned on the fourth wall, by a little window, her body slumped across what seemed to be a small wooden akwa nest. Sinai noticed sets of pestle and mortars scattered across the room; some were as large as a child, and some were as small as an apple.

I must be in the kitchen area, she thought incredulously. Or perhaps in a storage room, or maybe one where the cooks would rest between preparing extravagant meals for the nobles in the palace.

'So you're awake, I see,' a low voice at the far end of the room murmured.

Sinai ignored her pounding head, and peered in the direction of the voice. An old woman stood in the doorway, her eyes magnified by the dusty transparent glass circles she wore on her face. They sat in thick wooden frames, giving her the appearance of a beetle bug.

Meekulu Kaurandua? Sinai thought.

Meekulu was the head cook of the palace. She oversaw all the major festivals, and, most importantly, she cooked directly for the Eze and his wife. Meekulu's near-perfect meals and extravagant character preceded her. The old woman did not originate from Nri and insisted that this fact be known throughout the kingdom. Her title, Meekulu, was a term of respect used for elderly women in Namibia, her birthplace. All the nobles knew of her, but very few had been in her presence.

'Please, where am I?' Sinai asked, her voice hoarse and raspy.

'Surely you already know the answer to that question,' Meekulu replied, as she walked over with a warm smile. 'I've seen you wandering about here a number of times.'

Sinai noticed a playful glint in the old woman's eyes.

Meekulu suddenly stopped mid-stride before placing one finger in the air, as though she had just remembered something important. She swivelled on her heels before busying herself with something on one of the shelves.

Sinai stared at the old woman curiously. She had never laid eyes on Meekulu before, but whispers about the old woman had filtered through the palace walls for longer than Sinai could remember.

Meekulu was not only known for her impeccable meals, but her unique appearance. She was small and thin, and those flat crystal circles on her face supposedly helped her old eyes see even the most minute grains in the dishes that she prepared. Her hair was native to Namibia, several thick bundles of hair coated in a red waxy *otjize* paste, all but the ends, which were soft puffs of white hair that nearly reached the ground.

Her dark-leathered skin was a powdery reddish-brown colour, and Sinai felt inexplicably drawn to it, as though it promised stories of times past. Looking at the peculiar woman, Sinai felt a sense of familiarity, which came as a surprise to the girl who had spent her life feeling like a perpetual stranger.

'You . . . know who I am?' Sinai said quietly.

'Mmhmm,' Meekulu replied, with her back still turned.

'But . . . how?' Sinai asked incredulously.

'The same way that you know who I am,' Meekulu said, as she turned around with a pale pestle and mortar in her hand, both of which she placed on the wooden table by the foot of the akwa nest that Sinai lay on. She then scoured the room for a collection of various spices, bottles, and dried fruits before drawing up a chair and sitting by the table.

'Well, no. Sorry, I just mean . . . well, I don't think . . . well, it's just different. I'm not—I'm not *known*,' Sinai struggled to explain her thoughts.

'Neither am I,' Meekulu chuckled. 'But people tend to discuss peculiar things.'

'Peculiar? But I'm . . .'

'The strange efuọla noble girl who skips lavish events in favour of wandering, seemingly aimlessly, around the palace,' Meekulu said, dipping her chin so low that it almost touched her neck. Her glasses sank to the end of her wide nose, and her wrinkled eyes peeked over the top as she glared openly at Sinai. 'And I am the Namibian cook with the strange eyewear and extravagant hair,' she continued, with another light cackle.

It was true that, on several occasions, Sinai had roamed around the crooks and crannies of the palace. At times, she had even visited the kitchen quarters, but she had always been quiet and unassuming. She always slipped away before she could grab anyone's attention. It was considered uncouth for a noble, particularly a woman, to be in areas dominated by the common folk. After all, what need, other than something sinister, did a noble woman have to be in such areas? Sinai had always found it surprising that curiosity or even boredom had never been considered legitimate reasons.

Sinai reflected briefly on the old woman's words, and suddenly became increasingly warm. Rarely had she ever felt so *exposed*. She had always imagined herself to be someone who blended into the background. Nothing about her was loud or distinct enough to draw attention; she kept to herself, and lived mainly in her own head. She found it disturbing that while she had been hiding in her mind, people were discussing and scrutinising her. She didn't like that at all.

'It is quite curious that that was the first question that popped into your mind after a near-death experience, but each to their own,' Meekulu added, her lips stretching into another cheeky smile.

The weight of what had happened suddenly tugged at Sinai's core. Meekulu was right: she had nearly died. In fact, she was certain that she should have died; no one could have survived such a high fall.

Whilst her body felt like it had been dragged through hell, it was still, for all intents and purposes, in one piece.

'How am I even alive?' Sinai pondered aloud.

'This will help with the pain; recipes are very powerful, like potions,' Meekulu said. 'You can make people do almost anything if you have the right type of ingredients. I could give you something and you'd sleep for days!' She smiled as if she had just told a joke that only she could understand.

'Yes, I . . .' Sinai said, as she tried to get the old woman to hold her gaze, in the hope that it would focus her. 'Meekulu, how did I survive the fall?' she asked again, when she finally locked eyes with the woman.

'You fell on *Afọ*, the third day of the week.'

'Okay, thank you, but that's not . . .'

'Do you know what the cleaning ladies do on Afọ mornings?'

'Well, no, I was actually wonde—'

'They dry the akwa nest blankets. Rows of thick fur spreads from window to window. You must have seen it?' the old woman implored, as Sinai shook her head before opening her mouth to protest once more.

'Really? Hmph—so you nobles really never notice anything, eh? Guess that makes sense with your heads always floating in the sky,' Meekulu chuckled, before Sinai could say a word. 'Well, in any case, you fell out of a window that was on the corner of the Ọnwa building, which you *must* know is right next to the Anyanwụ building. What you *might* not know is that it is one of the most ideal places to hang sheets! Which is incredibly lucky,

42

because it seems as though those series of sheets broke up your fall! Now, you still ended up badly hurt—you definitely have some broken bones here and there, and let's not forget that the fur cloths were unsalvageable—but you lived all the same. Sergeant Olu found you on the ground and brought you here. Lucky he did, too. I don't think you would have survived without some proper seeing to, and the palace doctors are incompetent, if you ask me!' Meekulu poured the ingredients one by one into the mortar before proceeding to grind them together to create a beige paste.

'I don't remember seeing the fur spreads,' Sinai murmured with a deepening frown.

'It's funny what we remember and don't after such events,' the old woman replied. with yet another glint in her eyes. 'But I assure you they were there; how else could you survive such a fall?'

'Yes, it makes sense . . . I suppose . . . I just, I don't remember this at all.' A wave of sadness washed over her. It was by far the most dramatic thing that had ever happened to her, and it disturbed her that she couldn't recall what it had been like. She recalled the veil from her dream, and sighed audibly. Sinai quickly caught herself and was reminded suddenly of her surroundings. She cleared her throat uncomfortably.

'I must thank the man. Sergeant . . .?' Sinai continued. Meekulu did not reply. Instead she dipped a white cloth into the pasty substance and brought it to Sinai's head without warning.

Sinai backed away instinctively. She was not used to anyone touching her head; in fact, it almost felt threatening. However, almost as soon as the cloth touched her skin, she relaxed. Sinai sank back into the soft furs that lined the small akwa nest. She knew that she should feel outraged, perhaps even scared, but she didn't. Sinai's painful headache started to subside into nothing.

'Hush, child; you have a long journey ahead and so much to learn,' Meekulu murmured.

Sinai was about to ask her what she meant, but everything suddenly felt heavy. She was being pulled into a deep sweet sleep. She momentarily tried to resist, but a wave of tiredness overtook her body and suddenly she gave up, sinking into darkness.

CHAPTER 6

THE VISITOR FROM THE CITY OF NRI

Igbakwu

A dense silence accompanied Naala and Gini on their brisk walk towards the village.

Naala had practically fallen out of the tree when she'd caught sight of the approaching swarm of bloodthirsty men. In their hands were weapons that had shone brightly with the gleam of the Eze's enchantment. The stench of impending death that had trailed them had been undeniable. Even from her great height she had been able to see the swirling coils of power coating their large *abaras*, a deadly weapon synonymous with the Eze's army. Not only could it slice a man's neck as though it were soft yam, but it was also known to cripple its victims after even the slightest of grazes, causing a wave of intense pain that would ripple relentlessly through his soul. Naala had hit the ground hard with an expression as fierce and distant as thunder brewing on a warm night. Gini had instinctively known that something was terribly wrong.

'Aii!' Gini had gasped. 'What's going on?'

Naala had felt trapped between wanting to find the words to fully explain the situation, and the undeniable fact that, if her suspicions were correct and there was indeed an army marching to wreak havoc on her home, she was already running out of time.

Finally, she had managed to say, 'We have to go!' before pushing past Gini and pacing ahead.

Gini had run after Naala, pivoting in front of her when she'd eventually caught up. She'd held up both hands, hoping to halt her friend.

'Wh—'

'We have to go, I don't have time to explain it—they're coming!' Naala had said exasperatedly, as she'd attempted to bypass Gini, but the smaller girl had firmly stood her ground.

'Who is? Naala just—' Gini had started, but stopped as Naala had thrown her hands up in frustration.

'*Gawa!* I said move, Gini. We don't have time for this. The village is in danger. We *have* to go!' Naala's voice had been stern but tense with fear.

Gini's breath had caught in her throat. Naala had never been easily frightened, and yet now she appeared terrified. Whatever had happened in that tree was far more serious than Gini had imagined.

'Let's go,' Gini had replied softly.

Now, as Naala traipsed through the woods, the voices in her head ran rampant:

You're overreacting.

No, I'm not.

You're letting your imagination run wild.

No, I'm not.

What reason would the Eze have to attack the village?

The last statement was not her own, but she let it ring loudly in her head. It had been the words of her uncle, the night he had spoken to the man with reddish-brown woolly hair, who had eaten noisily at her grandmother's table.

The rumours had started slowly but they had grown relentlessly, like a spider's web weaving out until it finally reached Mama Ugoulo's home in Igbakwu. Mama Ugulo, Naala's grandmother, was a hard and stubborn woman who vowed to never leave Igbakwu. She gave birth to an equally hard and stubborn girl, who vowed to never stay. One day the headstrong girl left the village, never to return. Mama Ugulo would wait every night for the grey hamerkops to flutter into the village with a message from her lost child nestled in their long beaks, but all she was met with was disappointment. Years later, a visitor came with

Naala cradled in her arms, claiming that the baby was the lost girl's child. Mama Ugulo looked down at the sleeping child and allowed her hardened heart to soften. She took the baby in her arms and vowed, this time, to never let go.

Naala adored her grandmother. She followed the old woman everywhere and always made sure to take the seat closest to Mama Ugulo during meals, particularly the evening dinner, which was by far the most intimate within their home. Those nights, Naala would sit amongst her family and, at times, guests, contently hidden under the cloak of the night. Each one of their black faces would be illuminated by the warm glow of the floating *okụ* lights, small balls of fire that hung weightlessly in the air, remnants of Anyanwu, the lost fire goddess.

In the deep of those evenings, with her grandmother's warm food and fresh palm wine settled in their bulging stomachs, visitors would whisper animatedly about the Eze's madness. It felt like blasphemy. It *was* blasphemy. The Eze was their hero. The man who saved the world from the Mother's wrath. He ensured order when the gods left the earth. His heart was pure enough to hold the Mother's crystal! It was simply inconceivable that such a man could be unfit to rule. Yet the stories enthralled them all. While the tales felt too distant to be real, the thrill of hearing such scandal about the people in power was undeniably addictive. People would lean over the table as the conversations gradually escalated from nervous whispers to loud debates.

Naala, however, had never enjoyed these conversations. Her mind twisted and turned, collecting snippets of information and placing them cautiously into a bigger, frightening picture. The problem was, she had paid too much attention to the visitors' stories over the years. She remembered all the seemingly small but truly unjust laws that the Eze would throw into the mix of his loyal subjects' lives before dashing them away without reason or cause. She recalled the stories of the once-praised senior lords, who disappeared suddenly, with nothing left of them besides a bad taste in the mouths of those that used to sing their praises. She had spent too much time thinking about the Eze's wife, Obioma, and how no one had seen her in years.

These thoughts swirled in her mind and made the salacious rumours so much more than frivolous dinner table gossip; for Naala the rumours were simply too real for comfort.

Worse still, they were increasing. It seemed now that every visitor who strolled through the village brought new whispers about the almighty Eze's indiscretions. 'Something bad has happened,' they would say. 'Come, hear what the Eze has done.' And Naala would shudder with her eyes closed.

'Again with this nonsense!' her uncle had exclaimed across the table. His fingertips had been pressed together and a perfectly formed ball of pounded yam sat on top of them.

Her young cousin had waited until the main course to unleash the stream of questions that he had bubbling up inside. It was finally their turn to host a guest, and little Eddy had been saving his questions for weeks now. He had waited patiently for a new guest to arrive, paying mind not to disturb his mother with his usual questions; after all she always had the same response: 'I don't know, bobo, ask your father'; which, of course, he would never do.

When the tall funny visitor had finally arrived, Eddy had almost yelped with excitement. The man had been wrapped in fine barkcloth, strips of softened, patterned wooden bark that rippled as he moved. He had travelled into the village on the back of a huge bejewelled rhinoceros, which meant that he must have come from one of the grand cities. Eddy had waited at the edge of his seat for the kola nut welcoming ceremony to end, and had even sat through the man's boring reasons for passing through their village. Like nearly all the visitors, he was using it as a place to get a decent meal before embarking on his travels through the vast and wild Furuefu forest.

Finally, in a brief moment of quiet, Eddy had seen the perfect opportunity to ask about the latest news of the mighty Eze. Only to find himself being scolded by his father.

'Please, Father, how often do we see a visitor from the city? You saw his big rhino; he'll *know* things!' Eddy had replied with wide eager eyes as his mother had tried to pinch him under the table, muttering insults under her breath.

The man had laughed heartily at the brewing commotion, his

copper hair swaying as he'd shaken his head, and the series of raised line scars across his cheeks had lit up in the warm ọkụ light.

'It's fine, it's fine. He's not the first and he won't be the last!' the man had rumbled. 'First of all, I'm not from the city, and Kubwa, my *big* rhino, was a . . . gift of sorts. I'm from a village like this but in a place much further away. Do you know of a place called Kongo?' he'd asked the boy.

Eddy had shaken his head as a look of confusion had spread across his small face.

'Well, that's a shame, it's a remarkable place—in any case, it's a good thing that I'm from there and not the aforementioned City of Nri. I'd advise you not to have this conversation with a real city dweller . . . they are, how can I say it, built differently to us?' He'd winked. Her cousin's eyes had widened further as he'd turned back to his parents.

'See! He knows things,' he'd whispered enthusiastically, before turning back to the man.

His father had grunted disapprovingly as he'd looked down to grab another ball of pounded yam.

'So . . . you've heard of this nonsense too?' he'd muttered, before popping the ball into his mouth.

'I've heard stories on my travels . . . silly fanciful stories about the Eze, and if I were to be completely honest, I've always found them to be baseless . . . although there was this one thing—bah!

I don't know, it seems silly to even bring it up now . . . I think it just felt too close to home because it was about a village—'

'The villages? But I thought the Eze is the king of the city, not the villages. We had a visitor once who said that the Eze chopped a man's elbow off because he didn't bow low enough.' Eddy had bent his elbow to demonstrate, before catching a deathly cold stare from his mother and settling down quickly. The visitor had started a small smile that died before reaching his eyes.

'Well, he is king of the whole kingdom, little man, not just the city,' the visitor had replied softly. 'And as gruesome as that sounds, it's also unlikely; even if you believe these stories then you would know that the Eze is never so open with such acts. They say everything *sinister* gets swept under the table. Your one-handed man must have been dreamt up during an afternoon nap.' Hidden in the corner of the guest's smile had been a chill that had suddenly made the conversation seem far too real. The table had become still, and Eddy had shifted towards his mother, tugging at her cloth until she'd embraced him.

'Edo bobo, please settle down,' she'd murmured into his soft cushion of hair.

'What was that you said of the village?' Naala's uncle had asked after a moment of reflection.

'Well, it's nothing, most certainly more of these silly embellishments, but still hearing about it did . . . unsettle me somewhat.'

'Out with it then!' Naala's uncle had exclaimed impatiently.

'Well . . . apparently, he—they say he ordered the *removal* of a village near Bende. For no reason! Out of the blue, the Eze's army marched through and slaughtered all of those peo—' the man had stopped, taking heed of Eddy's mother's glare as she'd signalled down to the impressionable child in her lap.

Eddy's father, however, had seen nothing wrong with exploring the subject further, much to his mother's dismay.

'That's rubbish,' he'd exclaimed. 'A whole village? Why would he do such a thing? What reason would he have to attack the village?'

'Bah! I don't know, it makes no sense,' the visitor had replied.

'Maybe they did something bad,' Eddy had murmured under his mother's breasts, still clutching her in fear.

'Hush now, it's not true, I tell you, it makes no sense,' Naala's uncle had reiterated.

'You should listen to your father,' the visitor had said jokingly; the atmosphere had gotten far tenser than he had intended.

'He's a demon. Demons do strange things like that,' Naala's grandfather had said suddenly. He'd rarely spoken to anyone; the countless years that he had spent on earth had started to catch up with him, and his mind had begun to drift away. Nowadays he just seemed to blend in with the furniture; Naala would sometimes forget he was there.

A light laughter had bounced around the table. Naala had not joined in.

'We need to watch you around the tax collectors, old man,' her uncle chuckled, whilst shaking his head, 'you'll get us in trouble! We're talking about *the Eze*—the champion—not a common man.'

'Yes,' the guest agreed. 'I'm sorry to have even brought up all this gossip around the table. We travellers tend to get carried away; someone will whisper something to this person, and that person will whisper something slightly different to the other, until suddenly we're blaspheming against the man who saved us all! While it's clear that the Eze's actions may be difficult to explain from time to time, without him where would we all be? Not here sharing this wonderful meal, that's for sure. The Mother would have surely annihilated us all by now . . . sorry, *Ozo*,' he'd said, bowing his head respectfully towards Naala's elderly grandfather, who had already lost interest in the conversation. 'But I think it is wrong to call him a demon. The man is simply . . . something else.'

'Is it really wrong though?' Naala had blurted. 'You said it yourself; there is no sensible reason why he would murder an entire village. There was no sensible reason why he would round up siblings that look too similar and chop off their heads for all to see. Every year the taxes increase, the people get hungrier, and the palace gets richer; surely where we are now is bad enough without envisioning some alternative realm where the Mother won the god's war. I just . . . we keep hearing all these awful, inexplicable things about the same man; is it really wrong to question if he is indeed the saviour that we have held him up to be?' The words had tumbled one by one out of Naala's mouth before she could stop herself. Her heart quickened with angst; she had not meant to say that. She had not meant to say anything at all. However, the story of an entire village slaughtered at the whim of the Eze's mood had left her perturbed.

She'd dropped her shoulders in shame and shifted her dark-brown eyes down. The visitor had cleared his throat awkwardly; he was not used to women, especially ones as young as Naala, speaking so boldly in the presence of men. The talk around the table had quietened and they'd all gone back to eating their food.

Now, as she hurried to the village with Gini, the conversation at the dinner table melted away from her mind. She was walking so fast that her breath was ragged. Another image flashed through her mind: the dozens of soldiers that she had seen approaching her home, armed with long sharp knives and pointy spears that gleamed brightly in the daylight, thirsty for blood. Naala broke into a run through the fertile forest, her deep brown legs pounding hard against the shades of vibrant greens.

CHAPTER 7

THE CHIEF'S FATAL MISTAKE

Igbakwu

Naala felt a hot pulse ripple through her body; sweat trickled from the nape of her neck and down her spine. She had run as fast as her feet could carry her, and she was paying dearly for it. She struggled to keep her heaving breaths under control. Naala took another gulp of air just as Gini finally caught up to her.

'What is the meaning of all of this?' Aunty Yagazie, Chinedu's mother, asked with one hand on her hip and the other gesturing at Naala. She was already a large woman, but her extravagant wedding attire made her seem even more intimidating. Naala was standing in front of every man, woman, and child in her village, a total of 157 people from twenty-three families. They had gathered for her wedding, wearing their best clothes, bursting with various shades of colour. They were all looking at her as if she had lost her mind. Naala took another short breath.

'Army coming . . . we all need to leave now . . . please,' she tried again; her voice was stronger but still faltered with breathless heaves.

'Hay! She's mad, you see,' Aunty Yagazie exclaimed, as she turned to her son. 'Didn't I say this from the beginning? *This* is who you chose to bear your first child.'

Chinedu looked back at Naala in bewilderment. He had never experienced this level of humiliation in his entire life. He had no one to blame but himself; he had been warned after all. It was no secret that Naala was *peculiar.* She was far too outspoken for her age and sex, constantly questioning and pushing for answers for which she had no use. She would often neglect her chores to wander off deep into the lustrous forest for hours, emerging with strange and beautiful flowers or grains that she would use to appease her grandmother's fury. He had been warned several times that she was not the wife for him, but he had chosen her anyway. How could he not? Her energy was infectious, her smile bright, and her face exquisite. He had spent countless hours either watching or fantasising about her beautiful deep brown skin shimmering in the heat.

He had never been deterred by her oddities; after all, he was a man. Chinedu prided himself on his strength of mind and body; he strove to command and protect. He knew exactly who he was, and he was resolute in the fact that he could get exactly what he wanted out of life; and for now, that was Naala. The prospect of moulding a woman like Naala into exactly what he needed her to be did not make him nervous; if anything it made her more appealing. To him, Naala was a challenge. However, in that moment, with the whole village eying him as Naala stood heaving and dripping in sweat, her clothes torn and hair rough, his mother's word weighed heavily on him.

'We have to go now,' Naala tried again, looking around at the friends and family that she had grown up with, their eyes soft with concern and confusion. A quiet murmur buzzed through the group, but it quickly settled down when Chief Eyiuche raised his hands in the air.

'Girl, what did you see?'

'Men—an army of men approaching the village. They were armed. Please, Chief . . . we need to go now, a visitor recently tol—'

'The tax platoon is scheduled to arrive soon; that is what the girl has seen,' the chief concluded, before Naala could finish, his deep bass voice rippling through the crowd.

Naala had always known the chief to be a kind man; his eyes were small and slanted and gave him a smiling expression. Naala watched as his small round face crunched into a tight smile, and her heart filled momentarily with scorching hatred. Fear and fatigue spiralled through her body, creating an overwhelming and intoxicating rage.

A tax platoon?! Naala had spent her entire life confined within Igbakwu. She had spent years watching the tax platoons come and go. Why would she mistake them now? The blood-red sun hung high in the sky, large and ominous. A bead of sweat trickled into Naala's eye; she brushed it off hastily and then turned to Gini. She needed help, she needed someone to take over, but Gini remained silent.

'No, it was not a tax platoon,' she said in a small voice. The mood instantly changed; Gini inched towards her, slipping her small hand into hers and giving it a tight squeeze.

A burst of whispers erupted from the crowd; speaking out at family dinners was one thing, but this—defying the chief—well, that was something else entirely.

'What did you say?' Chinedu's mother gasped, her eyes darting between the chief and the girl. Aunty Yagazie feasted on gossip, stories of other people's weaknesses or, even better, their downfalls, which filled her with great excitement. Naala shuddered as the woman's eyes widened gleefully. Her expression was triumphant; she was certain that Naala would not be able to weasel out of such an indiscretion.

'She doesn't mean—,' Gini blurted.

'It was not a tax platoon,' Naala repeated. 'It was the army and we need to leave now.' Her breathing had begun to stabilise and every word she used was deliberate.

The crowd quietened in silent disapproval. They all liked

Naala; she was an exciting and curious girl. She was pensive and moved with a quiet but fierce love for life. They liked her so much that they brushed aside the occasions when she spoke out of turn or questioned the sacred customs that they felt bound to uphold. However, this was far beyond their comprehension. No one, least of all an unmarried girl, could defy the chief. Naala's back was straight and her gaze unfaltering; she had no shame. The birds flew higher into the sky, their wings beating hard and fast, fleeing the scene as if they too could taste the souring mood.

'I said we need to go now! Why are you all just staring at me?' Naala exclaimed, growing more and more frantic as a cold stillness swept through the crowd. 'We heard just the other day of a village burnt to the ground by the Eze and now an army is on its way—an army with weapons—and . . . please! We need to go!' A wave of hot anger rippled through her, followed by a loud crack, as a branch from one of the trees crashed to the ground. The noise jolted the crowd and whispers began to erupt once again.

The chief felt something similar to fear simmering beneath his skin; had he just seen golden speckles dazzle across the girl's eyes? He blinked furiously, but saw only her dark irises staring boldly. He shook his head, perturbed.

'You better watch yourself, girl,' he said in a low voice that vibrated through the crowd. 'You are clearly angering the gods.'

'The gods?' Naala murmured. 'The gods are gone! They've left us! But the army is coming now and they are coming for blood.'

The chief's mouth gaped. He quickly gathered himself, and sighed.

'The girl is not well,' he muttered, to no one in particular.

Naala's heart beat so loudly that she could hear it in her ears. *I am well.* The crowd hushed to silence and a strange melancholic mood spread like wildfire.

'Take her to the *mgbapu*,' the chief said sternly.

'Mgbapu? No, please, you don't understan—' Naala started, as she flung an arm towards him, pleadingly.

'Take her to the *mgbapu*!' he repeated, as he stepped away from her grasp.

Naala shook her head; small tears started to prick her eyes.

Gini gasped and clutched her tighter.

Chinedu's jaw tightened, his eyes fixated on the ground.

*

The mgbapu, the mad hut, was a small dwelling a little away from the village. It was a place where people were sent when remnant spirits of the magical world plagued their minds. Unlike her grandfather, these people could not be cajoled or controlled. They could not be saved. Naala had only ever known one person in her lifetime who had been sent to the mgbapu: Hanye.

Naala had been a child when he was sent away. She still remembered the piercing screams that filled the village for weeks until, one morning, it was silent. That morning, rather than the usual screams, Naala had only woken to the birds singing alongside the low hum of the cicadas. She had quickly gone to find her grandmother to tell her the news, dragging the old woman away from the yams that she had been peeling. Her grandmother had calmed her before letting her know that he had been sent to the mgbapu.

She had never heard of such a place; in fact, it had only begun to dawn on her that there were other places outside of Igbakwu.

'Éh, he said that he wanted to stay there,' her grandmother had said. 'Being around people was starting to trouble him.'

'He's lost his damn mind,' her uncle had grumbled in the corner.

'Where did his mind go?'

'Somewhere strange . . . and secret, where no one can go . . . to the beyond.'

Naala had scrunched her face; she was even more confused.

'What about his family? Will they go to the beyond too? '

'No, the beyond is the . . . beyond, no one can go there, and he is going to the mgbapu.'

'With his family?'

'No. They will visit him sometimes, until it is time for him to rest forever,' her grandmother had said softly. Naala had not liked this conversation at all; something about it made her sad.

'What's the matter, little one?'

'The mgbapu is a bad place.'

Her grandma had chuckled softly.

'Yes, it is, but, like most things, it is also a good place,' she'd replied. 'Mgbapu is a sanctuary for those with troubled minds. Rather than being disturbed by the triggers of everyday life and work, they can live in peace.'

'But he's all alone,' Naala had said quietly. Her grandmother had turned to look at her briefly before carrying on with her duties around the house as though she had not heard her say a word.

However, Naala was relentless. She'd continued to pester her grandmother about Hanye for months after his departure. Until finally, her grandmother, who was particularly exhausted after a long day, admitted that the mad man had died in the mgbapu. Naala had never brought him up again.

*

Now, Naala scanned the crowd until she saw her grandmother's fear-stricken face as four men slowly approached her. Gini's husband, Tito, gestured hastily to her, until her grip on Naala's arm slowly loosened and she staggered towards him with fat tears streaming down her face.

'I'm not crazy! The army is coming . . . think of the children!' Naala pleaded. She was surrounded by men with sad faces; none of them wanted to be part of this, but it was their duty. In the gaps between their bodies, Naala could see her grandmother struggling in her uncle's arms.

'Esinaala, do not make this harder than it needs to be,' her uncle's voice boomed from within the crowd. 'Go with them.'

'This is a mistake,' Naala shouted, as she was ushered away, her arms held steadily by two of the men who had volunteered to take her to the mad hut. 'They're coming!'

CHAPTER 8

A WALK TO THE SOLDIERS' QUARTERS

City of Nri

Sinai was wandering around the wide, stony halls of the palace. Dull aches suffused her body, and her steps were slow and rigid, but she was pleased. She was finally walking again, after weeks spent nest-ridden with nothing but the sun's slow curve around the earth, and Meekulu's soft chatter, to keep her entertained. It was midday and the sun shone softly through the rows of windows to her left. The sweet, harmonised songs of the nnunu women wafted through the air, as they did every morning in the city of Nri.

There was a time, centuries ago, when the nnunu women were glorious. They were once brilliant bird women who flew for Ekwensu, the god of bargaining and trade. He would use them to send messages around the world and negotiate deals with gods and humans alike. After his departure, the nnunu women lost everything. They lost their ability to talk and to fly; now all they could do was sing beautiful wordless melodies, in the hopes that a stranger would fill their impoverished hands with golden shells. Sinai absentmindedly drew closer to the window to see more of the singing nnunu.

Suddenly, flashbacks of bloodied hands, gripping fear, and Ina's sneer sprang into her mind. She immediately increased her distance from the open windows, drawing closer to the illuminated cream mudstone walls engraved with golden images depicting the various famous *Obis* through the ages.

Sinai paused and took a deep breath before carrying on her path to thank Sergeant Olu, the soldier who had saved her life. She avoided any main hallways, opting to use the many hidden and lesser-known corridors to navigate. These obscure halls were lined with minimalist ọkụ lights, fire flames in the shapes of triangles and simple stars that hovered weightlessly above her head. They paled in comparison to the detailed, extravagant ọkụ shapes found in the well-traversed halls. These modest shapes were no doubt the doings of a trainee flame tamer, who probably dreamt of the days when his work would be featured in grand festivals and hung in the Obis' quarters. For now, his ọkụ flames hung where only few would see them, and even fewer would notice, but Sinai did, and appreciated them.

It would take her twice as long to reach the soldiers' quarters, but she would also significantly reduce her chances of coming across a single person. The prospect of avoiding watchful, pity-filled eyes—or worse: dreary small talk that would inevitably lead back to discussions on her fall—was more than enough to compensate for the additional travelling time.

Besides, Sinai needed to think and strategise. She could no longer ignore Ina's abuse, not when her passiveness could very well lead to her death.

For weeks, a combination of anger and fear had sniffed out her thoughts and pounced on her whenever she was most receptive. However, these emotions—rather than being debilitating, which was usually the case for Sinai—coursed around her body and pushed her to action. Sinai wanted to make it clear to Ina, or anyone else who threatened her life, that the repercussion for such an act would be harrowing pain that even the lost gods would fear. Sinai wanted Ina to feel the same fear that she had felt hanging out of that window. Sinai was desperate to make Ina pay; she just didn't know how.

Sinai had thought about cornering Ina and beating her senseless. Her mouth twitched to a stretched smile whenever she thought of Ina begging for mercy as she herself had done just weeks ago. However, that smile would crumble once she realised that she could not guarantee a win. Ina was much taller than her, and guarded by Lebechi and Ebun at all times. In fact, it would most likely be Sinai who ended up broken and bruised in such a scenario.

Sinai had also briefly flirted with the idea of embarrassing Ina publicly, but that also seemed far-fetched. Ina was not at the centre of the highest social circle in the kingdom by accident. She was calculating and she had always thought quickly on her feet. Sinai had, on a number of occasions, watched Ina spin potentially detrimental situations into gold, right before her eyes. She was certain that the girl would be able to detect any ploy before it came into fruition, likely turning it into something that worked perfectly for her before Sinai could blink. Sinai needed something bigger, something fool-proof and concrete. Something that was completely out of Ina's control.

Sinai paused briefly in the silent stone hall. She was trapped in this dilemma. Sinai took a deep breath and looked out at the bright beckoning sky from the distant window; a new thought suddenly began to flourish in her mind. *Disfigurement?* It was no secret that Ina valued her beauty highly, more so than most. Along with her wit, it was the principal tool she used to snatch and secure her power. If Sinai could take that away from her, she would break the girl completely. Disfiguring Ina could definitely be the answer. It was feasible and effective, yet just as the idea sprang into Sinai's mind, uneasiness settled in the pit of her stomach.

There would be deadly consequences, of course; Ina would be equally, if not more, vengeful than Sinai. It was Ina, after all, who had attempted to kill Sinai unprovoked. Who knew what she would do if given an excuse?

However, that was not what was holding Sinai back. Sinai was sure that she could handle the repercussions of her actions. She would accept death or worse as the price for disfiguring that girl. It was the thought of doing such a thing that disturbed Sinai. The idea had tasted sweet at first, but ultimately left a bad taste in her mouth. For some reason it weighed heavier on her than beating Ina or ruining her socially. Sinai gazed at the Battle of Abam depicted on the wall. Disfiguring felt cruel and sneaky, devoid of the loose integrity practiced in the palace.

I could never do it, Sinai finally admitted to herself.

'But . . .' Sinai suddenly blurted out in the empty hall. *She doesn't have to know that.* Surely the threat of disfigurement was enough to achieve Sinai's ultimate goal: terrify Ina and teach her a lesson about what would happen if she ever crossed Sinai again. She could disfigure a patch on Ina's arm or leg, something that would catch Ina's attention. Sinai could then claim full responsibility, and warn Ina that if anything happened to her, the disfigurement would spread relentlessly over Ina's body.

That's it! Sinai thought, as she jumped up with excitement, causing throbbing pain to explode through her body. She leaned against the wall and caught her breath. Suddenly her smile melted down into a deep frown.

Sinai paused before slowly bringing her hand to her lips.

Something about this plan is not quite right. Sinai couldn't simply threaten Ina with more disfigurements, surely that didn't make sense. Ina would have Sinai killed before she could disfigure her again, and that was assuming that Sinai got close enough to disfigure Ina in the first place.

Her plan was missing something fundamental. It needed to be truly dynamic. Sinai needed to somehow have remote control over the disfigurement. It must be something that Ina would never see coming. Some power that Sinai could flex whenever she needed to. Something like *anwansi*, the ancient practices and spells left by the lost gods. Sinai had heard tales of shadows leaving men, women turning to gold, and children turning to trees. Magical fantastical stories, that some still believed to be true.

Sinai lifted her left arm up to the sunlight and inspected it; it was slightly bruised but functional and straight. She recalled a few weeks back to when this arm was broken and bent out of shape. No one should be able to heal so fast. Sinai was flung out of a *building*—fur blankets or not, she should not have survived that fall, and she was certain that Meekulu was the reason why she had. The old woman was certainly versed in ancient *anwansi*, or, at the very least, knew someone who was. Either way, Sinai was certain that Meekulu could help get her what she needed. Sinai smiled openly; after weeks spent theorising and fretting, she had finally found an idea concrete enough for action.

'What are you doing here, girl?' a hoarse voice boomed. Sinai jumped out of her thoughts and looked up at the armed guard. She had been so lost in her quest for revenge that she had been oblivious to the fact that she had wandered into soldiers' quarters.

The guard was a large man, armoured in gold and red-stained leather plates. He stood sternly before the huge brass doors leading to the soldiers' quarters. She was finally here. The doors were thick and, like many artefacts in the palace, beautifully engraved with stories from the past. These doors whispered the tales of thousands of battles, small and large, throughout the ages. The Battle of Dahomey that took place in Oyo, the Yoruba kingdom, where the Orisha nearly defeated Amadioha, the god of justice. The Battle of Abam where Asilia, the Eze's famously viscous lion, ripped through hundreds of men. Her fur shone softly in the image, illuminated by tiny ọkụ flames.

Sinai's interest began to peak; she would have loved to sit for hours, watching as the engravings jumped to life. While Sinai loved to explore the various sections of the palace, a quiet fear had always held her back from the soldiers' quarters. The raw power of the men and women involved in the Eze's army had never been lost on Sinai; neither had the scent of death that followed each and every one of them. However, now that she stood here, with the remnants of vengeful thoughts still playing idly in her mind, she thirsted for the power and destruction depicted on the doors.

Warmth fluttered through her body and she suddenly felt light and weightless, as though she were seconds away from floating. It slowly dawned on her that her feet were no longer touching the ground.

'Girl!' the man barked again. Sinai's feet abruptly hit the ground, sending a shot of pain up her body. She put her hand out to the wall to stop herself from falling. *What on earth was that?* she thought, but before she could answer, the guard grunted in frustration.

'Did you see that?' she exclaimed, but the brewing anger in the guard's dark eyes, his tensing fists and clenched jaw, told her that he was quickly losing patience.

'Sorry. Never mind,' she murmured. 'I'm looking for Sergeant Olu. He saved my life. I fell a few wee—anyway I'm here to pay my respects.' Sinai tried and failed to keep her voice clear and steady.

'Not here,' the man said sharply, and Sinai's face crumpled in a mixture of disappointment and confusion. While it had been her choice to travel the long way to the soldiers' quarters, she was tired now and ached in pain. The thought of walking all the way back to her quarters filled her with dread, but the thought of walking back empty-handed was almost too much to bear.

'Ozo, please, his name is Sergeant Olu. Please, I was told he would be here,' she tried again.

'He's not here, his platoon has been called out for a disturbance—go!'

'When will he be back?'

'This is the last time, girl,' the guard bellowed. 'Go!'

Sinai took one last look at the impenetrable and intricate doors, before sighing and turning away.

CHAPTER 9

THE EMERALD-EYED SOLDIER

Igbakwu

Naala's head pounded, the thuds reverberating through her soul. She had been left in a tall, spacious and four-walled hut. Large, dark green palm leaves, acting as a ceiling, allowed flutters of light to float weightlessly into the room. Naala had spent some time frantically trying to find a way out. The door that was used to let her into the room seemed to have blended into the wall seamlessly, with no obvious breaks or openings. Naala ran her fingers over the wall, which was made out of series of thick wooden rods, glazed in hardened fish glue and secured to the ground. She pressed against the wall, but it refused to budge; she wouldn't be able to knock it down.

Emerald vines crawled up the walls, and musical instruments lay scattered across the floor along with softened engraving materials and straw. Activities to distract a demented mind. Pressure began to rise in Naala's body, starting in her stomach and ending at her neck. It was becoming hard to breathe. She shouldn't be here. She should be with her family; they should all be escaping. Instead, she was waiting for death to take everything she loved.

Naala had opened her mouth once again, and the thoughts that had been so clear and structured in her mind had appeared rotten and peculiar to the people she loved. She should have been able to convince them. She should have been heard. Should! Should! Should! She hated that word. She hated everything. The pressure that had clenched her throat suddenly built up into something uncontrollable. It exploded into a piercing scream that shook her whole body, as she succumbed to tears.

'Ah ah?!' a high-pitched voice suddenly said, as Naala struggled to catch her breath. Her heart quickened. She looked around the empty room and gasped. As far as she could tell, she was alone. *Where had that voice come from?*

'Who is there?' Naala asked cautiously; part of her was uncertain about whether she had heard a human voice in the first place.

'Be quiet!'

'What! Who said that?!' Naala exclaimed, her voice sounding much more rattled than she cared for it to be.

'Who said that? I said that! Who else? I hope you are happy with yourself; you have officially woken me up,' the voice answered sternly.

Naala didn't reply; she didn't know what to say. Nothing made sense to her anymore. Instead, she followed the sound of the voice to the wall directly across from her.

Kneeling to squint through the cracks in the wooden panels, she could see another room, directly beside her. A shadowy figure paced up and down the room.

'Hanye?' she gasped. The figure stopped and moved towards the wall that Naala knelt beside. Intense fear seized her as she rose and backed away, clutching at her aching heart. Hanye was dead; he had been dead for years. Who or what was this being that took his form?

'*Onyinyo*,' she whispered.

'Onyinyo? So you think that you can abuse me? I'm not a shadow person! You are the onyinyo! Nonsense—who even told you my name, girl?' Hanye called, from the other side of the wall.

Naala forced herself to settle her breathing. His voice sounded real enough, not as eerie and mystical as what she imagined a shadow person's voice would be. He also had not escaped through the wall, or done anything equally otherworldly.

Naala cautiously crept closer to the wall. She looked through the cracks once more and saw a thinner, older version of Hanye pacing up and down a room similar to the one that she was locked in.

'It . . . it's you . . . you're alive?' Naala murmured, as Hanye stopped sharply in his tracks and sauntered closer to the wall.

'Alive? I suppose so . . . and *you* are?'

'Naala—Esinaala—my grandmother is Mama Ugulo. My mother . . . well . . . I'm from Igbakwu,' Naala replied.

Hanye said nothing for a while, before pressing himself closer to the wall. Naala could see a small section of his eye through the cracks, looking her up and down.

'Esinaala? Of course you are Esinaala. Not a word from the usual ghouls; it must be little Esinaala silencing them once again,' Hanye said wistfully.

'I—we all thought you were dead.'

'Hmph. Yes, it's a nice trick that—trick trick trick. But it needed to be done. How else could I stop *those people* from visiting all the time, bringing with them their loud voices? I *need* my peace.'

Naala shifted back uncomfortably. *So he is truly mad,* she thought. Naala's heart sank to her stomach as she settled down slowly.

'We're all going to die.' She sighed.

'Of course, we live because we die,' Hanye replied. She could hear him scraping softly at the wooden walls.

'The army is coming and no one will listen. They will kill us all.'

'No one listens to an army?' Hanye asked.

Naala did not reply. She looked around the room; how long before the army found her here?

Naala could see them now, with cruel mouths, their emerald abaras, unfailing arrows and long sharp spears that yearned to slice through living flesh with the desperation of a thousand starving men. Naala shuddered as she imagined the strange green tinge of the Eze's enchanted weapons smeared with the blood of her village.

Thud! Thud! Thud!

Naala stood up abruptly as a series of loud deafening noises erupted into the air. Her throat closed up as terror invaded her body.

'They have come,' she whispered, backing away to the wall directly opposite. Her body shook with fear, and she searched for a weapon to defend herself with. *Nothing*, she thought in despair; the room was filled with the softest and safest objects that she had encountered; nothing sharp-edged, nothing heavy, nothing that could be turned against a living soul.

Naala closed her eyes and forced herself to breathe; she didn't want to die afraid and alone. Her heart was quickening, and her skin moist with sweat. *But I am alone, and I am so afraid,* she thought hopelessly as heavy tears ran down her face. She wanted so badly to call out to Hanye; speaking to someone, even a mad man, was far better than being alone with her fears. Naala kept her mouth shut. Calling out his name would alert the soldiers to his presence. Naala froze suddenly. *I already have,* she thought. Her heedless screams had surely alerted the men to the fact that living souls dwelled in the abandoned shack. She had killed them both. *How could I be so stupid?* she wondered incredulously.

Naala felt that peculiar sensation once again; the slight tugging at her core, and the earth began to tremble beneath her feet. She looked up as the door suddenly sprang open. Clenching her body and bracing for pain, she was surprised when warm sunshine washed over her face.

'No one listens to the army?' Hanye repeated, as Naala let out a wrenching gasp. She blinked back tears and flinched in the light. It took a while for her to regain her vision, but eventually the clouded blobs of white light formed into a man. A tall thin man with unwavering eyes: Hanye. Two thoughts dawned on her; the first one being that Hanye was alone. The army that she had imagined in her mind, with over a hundred armed, large, and violent men, had disappeared and melted into an old familiar face. The second thought slammed into her, hard, almost knocking her to the ground.

She was free.

The wall was gone; instead, her old neighbour stood before her. Behind him lay the open pasture, beautiful and beckoning. The small thin trees whistled in the light wind, and an amber-coloured stag chewed on yellow leaves as a flock of birds danced in the air.

'Is that what you said? No one listens to an army?'

'How did you get out?' Naala responded, as she stepped out into the midday, not registering Hanye's questions. She looked back at the hut; the wall was now slightly ajar.

'The door, of course. How else?' Hanye replied, as he peered down at Naala with a piercing gaze.

'I tried—the door was locked,' she replied in confusion, as he sighed and walked towards the hut.

'Look,' he said, with his chin pointed to the bottom of the open wall. There was a metal prong, which Naala had no recollection of seeing earlier, latched there. Hanye nudged it down into the ground until it was completely hidden. He then tried to move the door but to no avail. 'See, it cannot move now, but if you lift the spike—' he bent down to lift the metal out of the dark soil '—you still cannot push or pull. If you slide, then the door will move.' Hanye looked at Naala curiously. It was the same look that Naala had given her grandmother over the years when she was seconds away from confessing her wrongdoings. 'This is how I escaped,' he finally said in a rush. 'Then, after that, I left a pool of *rabbit blood* in my place so that they wouldn't try to find me. So that they would finally *give up*.' He chuckled manically to himself.

'Why . . . why would you stay if you could leave?' Naala asked in shock, as Hanye shook his head vehemently and pressed a finger against his temple.

'It's too loud around *people*; the voices get too loud and they scream and claw at my insides.'

'Sorry,' Naala murmured with concern.

'No—not you, the voices have always been quiet with Esinaala.' He smirked, revealing his toothless mouth.

'No one listens to the army?' he asked again, zeroing in on her, as if she were a tool he was inspecting.

'The army . . .' Naala said, and suddenly her curiosity left her like a scared gazelle fleeing from hunters. A sense of urgency washed over her. She didn't want to talk anymore; she wanted to run.

'Yes, the army! We—oh my—we are all in danger, the army is coming to the village, no one will listen but we have to go!'

'Hmm,' Hanye replied, before shaking his head and turning his back on her. 'I was hoping you would say something more . . . *profound.*'

'Profound? We have to go!'

'Perhaps . . . no one listens to the army . . . as powerful as they are, people only move to the death that follows them—ha! Doesn't that sound like something Mohammed Bagayogo would say?' He turned around to face her with glee.

'I . . . we have to go,' Naala pleaded. 'The army is going to—'

'Yes, yes, blood, destruction, blah blah blah—I'm sure you are right.'

'You are?! Great then—'

'However, I am not going anywhere—'

'But y—'

'You, my girl, are free to do what you will, but I'm will not go and meet the voices,' Hanye replied with a shudder.

Naala had already wasted too much time speaking to him. Time was not something that she had the luxury to waste.

'If you do not leave this place, they will kill you, uncle!' she pleaded for the final time, addressing him with a familial term in hopes of breaking down his resistance, but her protests fell on deaf ears. He shook his head as he walked back into his shack. Naala paused for a moment and allowed herself to be washed with a wave of sadness for the man. She kept that moment brief, turned on her heels, and ran towards the village.

Her feet pounded through the dense green forest.

What's the plan? Naala thought, her mind racing faster than her feet. She couldn't repeat the actions that she had taken before, not unless she wanted to waste more time getting locked up. She would have to sneak into the village, and speak to her grandmother. Naala was certain that if they spoke, face-to-face, without the prying eyes of the villagers, she would be able to convince her. She could save her grandmother and the children and—Naala stopped.

Her heart leapt to her throat and her head started to spin. A sickly smell of iron and smoke filled the air and, over the thudding of blood in her ears, she heard screams. Naala doubled over with tears coating her sore eyes; she didn't want to be right. She would have rather been insane. *Please let me be insane*, she pleaded to the ghosts of the gods. Naala staggered towards the village in a trance. A quiet voice told her to run away; *the only thing you will meet there is death,* it whispered harshly. However, her body tugged her towards the people she had loved all her life, and whom she had failed to save.

The jade-green forest thinned out and she was close enough now to see the carnage. Bright splotches of blood and scattered bodies. She could hear a gnarled and disturbing sound. It sounded like a wounded animal; it took her a moment to realise that it was her screams. She walked undisturbed among the dismembered bodies of her neighbours. A combination of disgust, despair, and anger surged through her, the most potent emotion being anger; it swirled through her mind like poison, and she grew dizzier with every step.

She was furious at her village for ignoring her plea. *Look at you now!* she wanted to scream at the top of her lungs. Naala cursed herself. She wanted to claw out of her body and beat herself senselessly. After all, she had *known*; why was she surprised? She had seen what was going to happen, sensed it for weeks. She had truly known about the danger ahead, and she had failed to convey it. She had failed her people, just as they had failed her. She should have tried harder; she should have had a smarter approach; she should have been able to convince them. Once again the word 'should' was dust in her mouth. 'Should' couldn't help anyone now, she thought, as she witnessed the brutal slaughter that had taken place.

Naala continued to walk openly through her village. All around her were the Eze's men, rounding up and hacking away at the remaining few villagers left to kill. They paid her no attention. Naala stepped wordlessly along, just as she had done for years. However, instead of warm smiles and open arms, she was met by disfigured corpses. Her legs were heavy and stiff; she dragged them along like planks of wood. She strolled past the men, with her eyes glazed over and mouth gaping silently. Suddenly her world stopped.

Here lay her grandmother—her small grandmother with leather-soft skin, thin white hair and a strong back, which she had used for decades to beat the fluffiest pounded yam. Her dear grandmother was lifelessly on the dust-red ground. Over her body stood a large man with a long straight scar on the right side of his face, extending from his ear to his chin, and he gripped a red-stained abara. Despite the streaks of wet blood sliding off from the weapon, the abara's jade coating shone brightly. It was strange and vibrant, as though not made out of a solid substance, but rather an almost living liquid, thick like ink, and radiating an unspeakable power.

The soldier had similarly green-snake eyes. Naala had never seen such a thing before. His eyes were bright against his dark black skin, and Naala blinked as something briefly flashed behind them, something warm and familiar, almost like recognition. Quick as a flash, the man moved with purpose towards her.

Naala would have run but she was frozen in place—but not by fear . . . she was far beyond that. She had begun a descent into despair. Her gaze left the monstrous man and found its way back to her grandmother.

She felt her heart collapse into turmoil, and a strange chill took over her body. It started off as the familiar tug that had gripped her stomach in recent days, but spiralled into something far more powerful. An incredible sensation rippled through her body as a high-pitched, eerie scream escaped her mouth. The world eased down into a slow heartbeat. Naala could feel everything and nothing at the same time.

She could feel the earth beneath her come alive. Naala clenched her fists and the ground shook with fury. She raised her arms and the red dust whirled into the air. The soldier stepped away, holding his hand to his head as the dust swarmed around him, choking him with Naala's vengeance. Naala looked down at her hands in shock.

'What am I?' she whispered, as the particles lost their energy and sifted towards the ground. Before she could dwell on that question, the soldier approached again, with the red soaked abara still in hand.

Naala allowed the surge of power to storm through her body, raising her hands towards the soldier. The ground trembled and he lost his balance and fell to the ground. Large waves pulsated through the earth's surface, flinging the people around Naala into the air. They floated as though the air had turned into a substance as dense as water. Naala screamed with her arms outstretched.

Her eyes shone with brilliant gold, her fingers clutching onto the air, whilst energy gushed out of her body.

Boom!

The world exploded. The dead, the emerald-eyed soldier, her village, all melted into nothing. Naala was completely lost. There was only one thing left for her to do.

She entered the black.

CHAPTER 10

THE REQUEST

City of Nri

Sinai tried to wipe the sleep from her face, but she couldn't stop yawning so widely that small tears spurted at the corner of her eyes. The sun crept out of the morning clouds, sending sharp rays across the pink sky; the air was fresh and pleasant, doused with the scent of the fresh frangipanis flowers and sweet bread.

Sinai had woken up especially early, in the same manner that she had been waking up for days. She felt completely consumed by an *airy* feeling, almost as though she had spent the night floating in the air and had suddenly crashed down into her akwa nest. She would clutch at her soft furs or the cold golden rails, gasping for breath. Sinai concluded that these episodes, similar to the one outside of the soldiers' quarters, must have been some kind of side effect from the concoction that Meekulu had given her to assist with her healing. This thought added fire into Sinai's walk to the kitchen. After days of waiting, she was finally getting an audience with Meekulu.

Soon after Sinai had formulated her plan, she rushed to find Meekulu. She had thought that her injuries, though largely healed, would still serve as an excellent excuse for speaking with the old woman, but she quickly learnt that Meekulu's time was in especially high demand. Sinai struggled to even *request* time to see the cook. She had sent several messages through Ozi, her hamerkop messenger bird, but they had all gone unanswered. Even when she'd tried to access the old woman in person, she was stopped at the large doors of the kitchen quarters by someone or other.

'Ehh Meekulu said you should come back later,' the shy kitchen girl said to her when Sinai arrived for the third time in a row.

'That's what she said last time, and I am back later,' Sinai sighed. A soft song from the corner of the hall interrupted her thoughts. Sinai turned to find a nnunu woman crouched on the floor. Sinai had never seen a nnunu up close before; they were not permitted to dwell within the palace walls. The adjacent kitchen quarters were perhaps the closest to the actual palace that they could come to. The nnunu was larger than Sinai had imagined, a little taller than her, in fact. The bird woman's eyes were large and the skin at the top of her face was deep red, as though someone had swept a paintbrush over it. Instead of a nose and mouth, the nnunu had a hard, broad, brown beak. A flurry of brown and black feathers sprouted from her head and clothed her body, as though she was wearing a feathered robe. The nnunu cocked her head and belted out her beautiful song even louder, her hands outstretched for golden shells, that she would no doubt use to petition the Eze for the gift of flight.

'Yes, Lolo, but Meekulu is busy today as well,' the kitchen girl muttered, bringing Sinai out of her thoughts. The young girl let her back leg bend slightly into a short bow.

Lolo: the title given to the noblewomen in the palace. Sinai was rarely ever addressed with such formalities. The girl was too young to decipher how unimportant Sinai actually was. On a normal day, Sinai would have told her to not to bother, she was no Lolo. But Sinai was desperate to see the old woman; perhaps if the girl thought that she was far more powerful that she actually was, it would help her get in front of Meekulu faster.

'Did you tell her it was important?' Sinai asked again, attempting to raise her chin towards the sky, as the senior lord's wives did whenever they asked for things that they already knew they would inevitably obtain.

'Yes, Lolo,' the girl replied hesitantly.

'Okay.' Sinai sighed after a long pause, letting her pretences slide off her body like water. She turned and headed to the nnunu woman, dropping two golden shells into her palm. The nnunu woman nodded, with what seemed like a smile on her beak. If the nnunu received enough shells, she would be able to gain an audience with the Eze, who could then use the Mother's crystal to transform her into a hamerkop messenger bird. The nnunu woman would have to accept a binding servitude to the kingdom, a price all of them begged to pay for the chance to fly again. Sinai had never understood why the Eze would dangle such a prize in front of the desperate nnunus. After all, he had the power to give them the flight they so longed for, so why not transform them unconditionally? As far as she knew, Ekwensu had never had to enslave the nnunus in order for them to send his messages, so why did the Eze? *Why couldn't anything in this city be more straightforward?* she wondered.

'I'll be back tomorrow,' she murmured softly, with her back still turned to the kitchen girl, before walking back to the formidable palace.

A few days later, the same girl knocked at Sinai's door, wide-eyed and filled with excitement.

'Meekulu has requested that you come and visit her,' she said giddily, happy to have good news for once.

'Really?! Oh, finally! Yes, thank you!' Sinai exclaimed, as she began to ready herself to leave for the kitchen, but she was stopped in her tracks by the girl's nervous expression.

'Oh, not now, sorry, Lolo. Tomorrow morning—at sunrise. She can see you before she starts her day.'

'Ahh.' Sinai paused; she was slightly disappointed by the delay, but a smile remained on her lips. 'Thank you . . .?' Sinai continued, slightly ashamed that she did not know the girl's name.

'Oh! Chisi, my name is Chisi.' The girl beamed.

Sinai smiled before waving her off. She finally had a chance to set her plan into motion.

The next morning, Sinai stood outside Meekulu's kitchen; days ago, she had decided what she was going to say. Sinai was going to tell Meekulu the truth. She was going to tell her exactly how she had fallen, the torment that she had suffered over the years at the hands of Ina, and her plans for getting retribution. Sinai thought that her plans, overall, were reasonable. After all, she was not planning on killing the girl. In fact, technically she wasn't even planning on disfiguring her; she was just going to teach her a lesson.

Sinai had even thought of suggesting she should become Meekulu's apprentice, as a means to pay her for her help. It was unheard of, perhaps a little uncouth, but Sinai was desperate for this to work, and what else did she have to offer the famous cook?

A gush of air pushed the heavy wooden door open before Sinai's knuckles had even met its thick frame.

'What took you so long?' the old woman said in a low voice, as Sinai lowered her hand. Facing Sinai, she was seated behind a large wooden table, her wrinkled black hands busy plucking a small mound of dark green leaves. Meekulu was not alone; beside her sat a large soldier. His face was far younger than his imposing body appeared to be.

'Ndewo,' Sinai greeted hesitantly, 'I was told to come at dawn?' She cautiously walked towards the table. She did not want to appear defensive, but she also wanted to make it clear that she would not disrespect the old woman by showing up late. Sinai was also unnerved by the presence of the soldier; she did not want an audience here, and she did not like the way he looked at her.

He stared at her openly, but not as many men before him had done with suggestive whistles and indecent claps. Rather, it seemed as though he was studying her, taking note of the curve of her cheeks and the dips in her nose. Sinai wasn't sure which of the two she hated most; both types of stares made her feel like some sort of animal. She refused to look away in shame. She hated seeing women hide their head in their hands when men leered at them. Sinai was part of the cohort that looked back sternly, either completely ignoring those men's existence or, if the man was being particularly terrible, kissing her teeth and delivering a cold cutting side-eye. She had heard of some women, particularly those of the lower ranks, receiving a slap after doing such things. The thought of that made Sinai's blood boil; she almost wished a man would try that with her. She would kick him so hard that he wouldn't even be able to think of siring a child without receiving pain.

Sinai looked back coolly at the soldier. His strange, emerald eyes lit up his black face and Sinai took note of the large scar that extended down its right side.

'My dear,' Meekulu said. 'Dawn is when I start cooking the royal breakfast; you must arrive before that if you seek my counsel. And you are late so please be on your way—it's also time for you to leave too—both of you.' Meekulu slid off the wooden stool and took the bowl of crushed leaves to the water basin.

'Leave?' Sinai gasped. She quickly lost all interest in the soldier; her entire mission for revenge was at stake!

'No, please, I've waited so long and I really need your help, Meekulu,' Sinai pleaded, as she paced towards Meekulu, dipping her body in a slight, albeit clear, bow. Meekulu may have been a force within the palace, and Sinai may have been an efuọla girl, but Sinai was nonetheless a noble, and Meekulu a servant. Sinai was crossing a very serious line by subjugating to the old woman, but she was desperate. Who knew when Ina would strike next?

Meekulu did not flinch at Sinai's action.

'Stand up straight, child,' she said. 'It's not me you should be bowing to; Sergeant Olu was the one who saved your life.' The old woman chuckled, as she turned to soak her chopped leaves.

Sinai's head spun; she felt as though she was being pulled in ten different directions at once. Part of her wanted to convince Meekulu to hear her out; another part wanted to understand whether or not Meekulu was playing a practical joke; a large part of her wanted to pay her respect and thank the man who allegedly had saved her life; and another part wanted to analyse why she felt so uneasy around him.

You need to get it together, Sinai, a cold voice whispered sternly inside her mind. She took a deep breath and dipped into a sensible bow, low enough to not be viewed as a slight, but not desperate either.

'Thank you so much, Ozo,' Sinai said. 'I'm sorry for taking so long to find you; I was told you had been deployed on a mission. I'm so grateful that you are back safe. Please tell me how I can repay you for saving my life.' Her heart beat ferociously as she uttered those last few words. The man had saved her life, and while it was custom that she offered him something in return, she was apprehensive about what he might ask her to do.

He could demand marriage or, worse, request her as his concubine. How would she get out of that without having to take his life or form some other conniving plan? She was yet to be successful with her plan against Ina. The weight of the palace, and its many cruel rules, pressed against her skin. She wanted to scream out to the heavens. Instead, she forced a small smile and lifted her head slightly, beckoning for a quick response. *Tell me my fate*, she begged in her mind.

'Your smile is all that I need for repayment. Keep safe, little one.' The soldier moved towards the door. 'Meekulu, I'll return soon,' he said. 'Oh and give the girl her counsel before she tries to jump off another window ledge—my back can only take so much.' He winked, before closing the door behind him.

Sinai stared after him curiously; he had set her free from her obligations. She had never known anyone in the palace to do such a thing; perhaps her uneasiness was unwarranted. Sinai had always considered herself to be a good judge of character, but she was not infallible; she could have been wrong about him. His words echoed in her head, and suddenly a deep frown formed on her lips.

'I didn't jump . . .'she muttered. 'I didn't jump, I was pushed,' she called after him, but he was already gone.

Sinai was abruptly reminded of the main reason she was requesting counsel from the old woman.

'Meekulu, I—'

'I know what you want, dear; no need to wait about till I fall into the grave,' Meekulu chuckled, before pausing to face Sinai with a warm smile. 'And I am willing to give it to you on one condition,' Meekulu said, as she turned back to softly kneading the crushed leaves into a thick dough.

'I'm not sure that you know . . .'

'You have been bitten, no?' Meekulu replied, shaking her head as the girl looked down at her bare arms. There were no bumps or blotches that would suggest a bite.

'No, I—'

'I can see the venom running through you. The thirst for

revenge . . . my girl, it is written all over your demeanour, seething in your eyes. Why else would you come to visit me?'

'Well, no—not exactly. There are other reasons to . . . I also wanted to say . . . I think the medicine you have given me has a side effect,' Sinai muttered, as her cheeks became warm with shame.

Meekulu let out a loud cackle as she turned, shaking her head.

'You want me to believe that you bowed to me so that you could tell me about a side effect? What is it, girl? Have you grown a tail?'

'I—' Sinai started. What could she say? *I've been floating? Also I need you to help me disfigure one of the most beloved noblewomen in the palace?* It all sounded strange and peculiar in the light of day; her floating episodes seemed more like an ailment caused by her own mental state than anything Meekulu might have given her. Sinai did not want Meekulu to be put off by her before she had even got to the real crux of what she wanted.

'Okay, fine. That was not the *only* reason,' Sinai tried to explain. 'But still, it's . . . I don't want revenge, not really. I want *protection*. Perhaps you don't understand: Ina tried to kill me—for no reason. She tried to kill me and she will try again. I need protection and I think that you can help. I think you can *do* things that most people cannot do. You healed me, for example.'

Meekulu smiled curiously.

'I'm not even going to hurt her,' Sinai continued. 'Not really—just a threat. You see, I want to disfigure her—not fully, just a slight patch on her arm or leg, and I want to be able to make that disfigurement spread at my whim. So that she knows that if she tries to kill me again, well, I could . . . I could fight back.' Sinai searched Meekulu's face for a reaction. The old woman raised one brow. 'I know it sounds . . . far-fetched,' Sinai added. *Please don't think I am crazy*, she thought, silently thanking the gods that she hadn't told the old woman about her floating episodes.

'Mmm,' Meekulu murmured, with a smile playing on her lips. 'Sinaikuku, you are an interesting young woman.'

'Sinaiku—what?' Sinai interrupted.

'Look, I'll help you with what you need. I don't need to know the ins and outs of your request; the only thing I need in return is another *request* of sorts. When the time comes, you will also do something for me—something to help me.'

'A request? Like helping out in the kitchen?' Sinai asked.

'Perhaps. Or perhaps it will be something far more . . . taxing. I can't say,' the old woman said, her eyes roaming over Sinai's face, reading every movement like a book.

'Okay,' Sinai replied cautiously, 'so you can't give me some kind of clue . . . or indication?'

'I don't know yet, my dear. Not right now anyway, but I will know one day, and on that day you must accept the request, just as I have accepted yours. The choice, my dear, is entirely yours.'

Sinai closed her eyes and slowed her breathing. Something about this did not seem smart. Her heart pounded with excitement, she could taste her freedom at the tip of her tongue, biting like Meekulu's famous pepper soup. Meekulu could help protect her from Ina forever. Sinai would never have to worry about Ina's snide remarks or her more recent attempts on her life.

Sinai wanted nothing more than to claw closer to that thought, embrace it fully and bathe in the satisfaction of knowing that Ina would never be able to cross her again. Sinai took a step closer to Meekulu, *but wait*—a slowly forming, but loud, voice, echoed in her mind—*is it wise to agree to such a thing?* The old woman was strong, respectable, and seemed to genuinely care for people, taking real pride in filling their stomachs and healing their wounds. However, behind her greying eyes, Sinai could sense a strong and brewing power. Sinai had never met a powerful person that wasn't cruel. Sinai sighed and stepped back again, noticing a dull ache in her hip. It wasn't a terrible pain, but it was a reminder. Sinai could hear Ina's sneer once again. She could feel Ina's slipper press against her hand. Sinai could see the blood lust in Ina's eyes and she knew without a shadow of a doubt that Ina would not stop until Sinai was dead.

'I accept,' Sinai replied.

CHAPTER 11

THE SURVIVORS

Furuefu Forest

'She is waking up too slowly, if she doesn't drink some water soon, she'll die.'

'Look at her eyes . . . they are twitching—and her fingers.'

'She hasn't done that before . . . what does that mean, Eni?'

'She is dying.'

'Aii!'

'Eni, are you sure?'

'Yes. She needs to wake up, her body needs water.'

'She's moving more than before.'

'She's waking up'

'Too slowly!'

Naala gasped as she woke to the shock of water slapping her face. She let out another harsh gasp when the water trickled up her nostrils, sending needles of pain through her face. She sprang up hastily, but a wave of disorientation hit her suddenly and she settled back down.

She tried to focus her thoughts, but every attempt was met with a fog that misted over her mind. Moments passed and it slowly dawned on her that she was not alone. She was in a small dim room surrounded by dark figures. Eerie shadows shifted around her, illuminated by pale misty moonlight. The air was dusted with tiny glowing insects, floating weightlessly.

Naala held her breath to stifle a scream. Her mind was moving so slowly that it was hard for her to form a thought, let alone decide on her best course of action. Her eyes darted around the room erratically, but she slowly began to pick out useful details. Empty hands, wide range of ages, nine—no—eight people, women and men; some were smaller than her, no weapons. *Where am I?*

'She hasn't screamed,' a girl from across the room said, sounding worried. 'Is that good? Maybe she's damaged.'

'Or stupid,' another voice added in the distance.

The boy who had thrown the water at her bent down to examine her. His face was sharp and angular and his jaw was so strong that Naala was certain that he was clenching it. Naala's attention slowly drew back towards his eyes. They were blacker than anything she had ever seen; even with the cloak of night, they still stood out dramatically. She thought she could fall into them forever, but his gaze was so focused and unrelenting that Naala's intrigue quickly transformed into unease.

Naala shifted uncomfortably and turned to the other faces in the room. Anxiety crept up her spine; she did not like how little she understood about her current situation.

'You're not—not—' Naala croaked; she could feel the word at the tip of her tongue but she couldn't find it, but then she exhaled sharply— 's-soldiers, so who are you? What am I doing here?'

'We found you in the forest, alone with an injury to your head, and brought you here. You've been out for two days.' The man with the piercing eyes pressed a wooden *iko* filled with water to her mouth. Naala hesitated and he leaned closer.

'You need to drink water; you've gone too long without hydration. You won't survive without it,' he said softly, lifting the iko.

Naala closed her eyes; she needed a moment to think. She felt drops of cold water against her lips and was suddenly aware of the dry scratches inside her parched throat. She opened her mouth and allowed the contents of the iko to pour down her throat.

'The village . . .?' she murmured, before she was hit with a jolt of memories: the wedding, the soldiers, the death, the earthquake, everything cascaded over her. She lifted her hand to her head in despair. 'My village, did you see anyone? My cousin . . . he is small and innocent . . . you must have seen him. Oh, Gini! She's small too, so beautiful and caring—' Naala attempted to get up, but lost her balance almost immediately. She would have fallen, if the large woman beside her hadn't supported her.

'Please don't try to get up,' the dark-eyed man said. 'We suspect you hit your head before you entered your deep sleep. You need time to settle down.'

'More time?' a deep voice from one of the hidden figures said in frustration. 'Eni, we've waited long enough; you said if we moved the girl too much she would not have woken up. We built this hut to protect her from the forest and we've watched her ever since. Now that she has woken, we must go; it's not safe to stay here any longer.'

'I agree,' another voice boomed.

'This girl is a survivor, just like us,' Eni said quietly, yet his words carried effortlessly throughout the room. 'We owe her as much time as we would give to anyone here. Just because *they* have forgotten their humanity does not mean that we should do the same.'

Naala did not understand what was going on; the words and emotions floated around her head, but she had no energy left to grab them. No one had answered her questions about her village people.

'My village . . . please, did you bring anyone else here?' Naala asked.

No one said a word, but Eni's eyes softened with sympathy.

'Tersely,' he said. 'We have seen footprints that have led us to believe that some of your people were lucky enough to escape—I'm sure the earthquake created a distraction—but the majority died at the hands of the Eze's soldiers. You made it out.'

Naala caught her breath and sank lower into the pile of leaves that formed a makeshift nest.

'Among the dead, did you see a—' Naala started, before another faceless voice interjected.

'They . . . they are often hard to recognise . . . those that are left behind.'

Naala's head spun. Black clouds swirled at the corner of her eyes. She felt herself falling backwards, but Eni swiftly caught her and gently held her head.

'She needs food,' he murmured, as he held her in his arms, but Naala pushed him away before he could get a morsel of food into her mouth. She didn't need food; she needed answers.

'Who are you people?' she asked, her voice thick with emotion.

'We are all survivors of the Eze's attack,' Eni said soberly, as he knelt to face her. 'We no longer have our families or homes. We can't even leave the kingdom because the borders are so well guarded by those eager to snap our necks in order to let the army's crimes die with the dead. So we move from place to place, sleeping in the trees to avoid the men who stole our lives. But we have each other and we have a common enemy.'

'We don't even know who she is and already you are blabbing about us,' another unknown voice muttered.

'Relax, Uncle Azu,' a girl, not much older than Naala, said. 'Like it or not, she is now one of us. She is a survivor. My name is Kora,' she added, as she turned to smile brightly at Naala.

Naala did not smile back. All this time her village had thought the attacks were mere rumours.

'Why didn't you warn us?' she sobbed.

The room was silent and thick with guilt.

'We cannot read their minds!' the man called Azu said loudly, as he paced. 'We don't know when the next attack is going to occur – even so, what if we wandered into your village seconds before the soldiers arrived and got caught in that mess again? Don't you dare blame us!'

'Uncle Azu . . . give her a second. Let her grieve,' Kora murmured softly. She could see the fresh pain in Naala's wild eyes and it stirred up memories that Kora had kept locked away for months.

Kora struggled to supress the screams of her own family. When the thick huge men, holding deathly abaras, had rounded up her family and neighbours into the middle of their village, her father had held her tightly. He had begun to shake violently with what she thought was fear, so much so that the two of them had slipped backwards, out of the range of the bloodthirsty soldiers' gaze. Kora had thought she was comforting her father by securely holding onto him; it was only when her father pushed her without warning into the village toilet hole that Kora discovered her father was the greatest person she would ever know. The shock of the fall and the brute stench of the human waste in the hole was nothing compared to the shrill screams and thuds that followed, as her father paid the price for protecting his child.

'Let her grieve,' Kora muttered, as a tear fell down her cheek.

CHAPTER 12

ỌNYE NYOCHA

City of Nri

'So,' Sinai asked carefully, as she dug the sharp *daga* into the ripe plantain. 'Are you ready to tell me the request?' She was back in the stone kitchen, after days spent away. The sticky soft texture of the raw fruit stuck to the palm of her hands, and the steam from the yams boiling in the corner wafted around her. Sinai felt strangely comforted by the large messy kitchen, or perhaps it was the presence of Meekulu that stilled her.

Meekulu was both erratic and calm, eerie and comforting, and as strange as this dynamic was, Sinai had grown to enjoy her brief moments with the old woman. She would show up, several days in a row, eager to get everything started, only to have the old woman say that she was not yet ready. Eventually, Meekulu was forced to tell her not to come back until she was sent for.

'Listen, girl, I better not find you sniffing around here like a lost puppy,' Meekulu had warned just before Sinai turned to head back to the palace. 'You hanging around the kitchen these last days has already begun to garner unwanted attention.'

'What questions? Why should anyone even care where I spend my time?' Sinai had asked as she'd lingered by the door, just as the soldier had done days before. Her trips to the kitchen were far more interesting than her days spent trapped alone in her quarters, and she hated the idea of them stopping.

'You'd be surprised how many people do care. To keep the world we live in running, requires a lot of people with a vested interest in those that step outside the norms. Run along, little one. I will fetch you once I am ready with my request.' Meekulu smiled warmly, before shooing her away and turning back to her cooking.

Sinai had been seconds away from protesting, but she'd bitten her tongue as she'd walked away. The thought of having to wait days, or perhaps even weeks, without a definite answer created tight knots in her stomach, but she could not risk an even bigger setback. Sinai was brutally aware of the fact that Meekulu could pull out of their deal on a whim. If she was ever going to pull this off, Sinai needed to be patient.

Luckily she did not have to wait too long. After two days, Chisi, the kitchen girl, who was now much less shy, came to collect her.

'You must be important,' the girl hummed as they walked to the kitchen quarters.

'I'm really not,' Sinai replied, squinting at the blistering sun; the dry season was relentless this year.

'You must be! Meekulu has invited you to visit so many times now, and your room is so . . . so . . . exquisite,' the young girl replied, as she snuck looks at Sinai from under her eyelashes.

'It's not—I'm really not . . . I'm just . . .' Sinai trailed off, losing the energy to explain how nothing was what it seemed, especially in the palace.

'What is this?' Meekulu asked, as she nudged Sinai aside to inspect the plantain that she had just diced up on the rigid wooden counter. Meekulu turned to look at Sinai with a dubious look. 'You don't know how to cut simple plantain?' she asked incredulously, as she drew closer to Sinai, who gulped nervously, not sure if Meekulu was about to slap her or laugh.

'Well, technically, it was my first time doing. . .'

'Gah!' Meekulu sighed as she threw her wrinkled hands in the air. 'What do they teach you up in the noble quarters?' she muttered, whilst shaking her head; her long braids, which were kept secure by a small red head wrap, shook well after her head had stopped.

'The art of gossiping?' Sinai offered with a small smirk. To her surprise, Meekulu was suppressing a similar smirk. The old woman grabbed one of the fat slabs of plantain that Sinai had butchered, and suddenly her smile grew wider.

'Then again, we could find something useful to do with these monstrous plantain cuts,' she said as she fetched a narrow wooden bowl. 'No waste in my kitchen!'

Sinai took a step back, as Meekulu busied herself on yet another task.

'So . . .' Sinai said, pausing to clear her throat, 'Chisi said that— well, I'm guessing the reason why I was called was for the request?'

'Of course,' Meekulu replied. Sinai waited briefly for another response, but Meekulu acted almost as if she had forgotten that Sinai was here.

'So, what do you need me to do?' Sinai asked. Meekulu dropped the items in her hands, and wiped any remnants of food across her wrapper. She walked to the other side of the room and collected a small white pearl box; its surface was flawed, containing wide crevices and deep dips, but it was beautiful. As Meekulu approached Sinai, she removed the thick lid to reveal a mound of red powder.

'I will take the *ọbara* powder and recite an oath. Then I will blow the powder into your face and you will be bound to the task that I give you.'

'Ọbara powder . . . is this it? Are you asking me to do a ọbara oath? Is that the request?'

'Yes, exactly. I'm glad to see you are paying attention,' Meekulu replied, with a twinkle forming in her eyes. Sinai looked at the old woman incredulously.

'An ọbara oath seems quite extreme,' she finally stated. An ọbara oath would tie Sinai's life to a task; if she failed then the dark forces would take her life as the price.

'As extreme as disfiguring Ina, daughter and first-born of Oba Yemi, King of the Oyo kingdom?'

'I . . .' Sinai began, but she quickly found that she did not know what to say. 'Okay, I see what you are saying, but an ọbara oath is not necessary. Just tell me what you would like me to do and I will do it. I promise you, you can trust me; you don't need to bargain with my life.'

'Trust,' Meekulu muttered, before chuckling lightly. She took Sinai's hands into hers. 'Soft like velvet,' she said wistfully. 'Well, small girl, I can *promise* you that if I told you the task, you would run away with your tail between your legs!'

Sinai opened her mouth to protest, but Meekulu held up her wrinkled hand.

'Ah, ah!' she said. 'You *need* an ọbara oath to keep you clear-minded and determined, to protect against the weak tendencies that seep into you nobles in this castle.'

'I'm not weak; I came to you because I am fighting back. I am disfiguring a girl.'

'A girl that you can't simply face,' Meekulu added, dipping her head low and letting her glasses fall to the end of her nose.

Sinai felt a surge of warm shame, fringed with dark anger.

'It is not that simple,' she said under her breath.

'Then perhaps you agree that the ọbara oath *is*, in fact, necessary,' Meekulu replied. Sinai blinked away her humiliation and took a deep breath before clearing her throat.

'Well, what is my task?' she asked. 'What do I need to do for the ọbara oath?'

'It is best that you do not know.'

'What?' Sinai exclaimed, shaking her head. 'Meekulu, surely that doesn't make any sense. If I am tying my life to a task, I should know what it is.'

'Should you? You and your soft hands say that you require my services to save your life; if you refuse my request, then according to you, you will die. If you accept my request then you could complete my task and live, or fail the task and die. If I tell you what the task is, then fear might grip your heart and in a moment of foolery, you may choose to not go through with the oath, and then what happens?'

'I die,' Sinai said softly.

'Mmm. According to you. So what do you choose, Sinai?'

I don't know, she thought wearily. The old woman was not *normal*, that was for sure, but she also was not bad. Meekulu's heart seemed to emit warmth, a sweet warmth that made Sinai comfortable.

It also made Sinai trust her, something she wasn't used to doing, given her upbringing in the cold palace. Everyone in the palace was hustling for some control, their very own morsel of power, so they could have room to roam some portion of their lives in freedom. The Eze was the beacon, the hub and source of all power; the closer to the Eze you were, the closer to freedom. It was not the least bit surprising for friends to cross friends, people to betray their families and lovers—just to bathe in the Eze's amazing power. Trust was not something that Sinai had come across often, yet with Meekulu, it flowed as easily as a wild river. It simply felt as though she had known the old woman for countless years.

'I trust you, I think. I also don't think you're a witch,' Sinai thought out loud.

'Well, I'm glad to hear that—' Meekulu chuckled with a smile, before studying Sinai's face. '—but what do you choose, my dear?' she finally asked, raising one eyebrow slightly.

'I want to . . . proceed,' Sinai said quietly. When Sinai had decided to go down this path, she had reconciled with the fact that she would do anything to achieve her goal. Sinai was certain that her life depended on it anyway. She'd renewed her resolve every morning, after waking up from the same nightmare, a revolving sequence of her fall coupled with Ina's laugh. A small chill overtook her body.

'Although . . .' Sinai murmured.

'What?'

'I cannot harm anyone who is innocent,' she stated clearly. 'As long as I am not doing that, I'm happy to complete the oath.'

'Very well,' Meekulu said, as she took a handful of the fine red powder, allowing small streams to filter through her wrinkled fingers. Meekulu drew the powder close to her mouth and whispered something in another language. The language was so familiar to Sinai, that for a moment she thought she could understand, but she couldn't grasp the meaning.

'Do you accept?' Meekulu suddenly said. Sinai looked back at her with unease. She had not expected it to go this fast. Sinai suddenly felt stuck. Seconds passed and Sinai could see confusion building up in Meekulu's face.

'I accept, I ju—' Sinai started, until Meekulu blew the red powder into Sinai's face, the shock of the action resulting in a series of chesty coughs. Once Sinai had finally settled down, she rubbed her eyes open to find Meekulu busying herself with items in the kitchen.

'Is that it?' Sinai asked incredulously.

'Ahh yes, the ọbara oath is complete,' Meekulu replied, before returning to the items that she had laid out on the table.

'So . . . shall we discuss everything? The task—my plan for Ina? I'm happy to get started.'

'We discuss tomorrow . . . morning . . . Ina, task . . . Eze . . . Ọnye Nyocha,' Meekulu strained, as she attempted to lift a large bag of rice onto the table. Sinai rushed to help.

'Please, Ma,' she said, as she helped to heave the rice on top of the table. 'Ọnye Nyocha? Spying? For the Eze?' That was a tall task, taller than Sinai had anticipated.

What could she possibly offer in espionage to the all-seeing, all-knowing Eze? In the brief moments she had encountered him, she had felt like a fly, wiggling in the hands of a curious child. She shuddered to think about what he would do if she failed him at this task.

Meekulu may have been the one that presented it, but if she was really tasked to be a spy for the Eze, then surely this request had come directly from him. Perhaps this was all set up by him, her fall, her plot for protection, all set up so that she could be his Ọnye Nyocha? *No, that's ludicrous,* Sinai thought, *and completely pointless*; Sinai's espionage skills certainly did not warrant such an elaborate ruse. Something about this just didn't add up.

'Spy *for* the Eze? No, no.' Meekulu chuckled. 'You will spy *ON* the Eze,' she said, 'not for him.'

Sinai let the bag of rice explode on the floor.

CHAPTER 13

THE GIRL WHO SHOOK THE EARTH

Furuefu Forest

Naala woke up once again to the sounds of multiple people talking. She could hear their voices, high with anxiety and laced with panic. The words were incomprehensible and disjointed; she couldn't seem to make anything out. Until:

'The earth is shaking,' a voice bellowed in her ear. Naala's eyes sprang open and the vibrations through the ground came to an abrupt stop. All around her, frantic people with faces etched with worry, began to calm as they realised that the tremors had indeed stopped.

'Another earthquake,' the girl, who Naala recognised to be Kora, murmured apologetically to her. The moonlight had hidden the collection of raised circle scars across her forehead.

Naala had seen a similar design on a traveller from Kwale before. Her face was flat and soft, and a confused expression suddenly flashed across it; Naala realised that she hadn't formally introduced herself.

'Naala.'

'What?'

'My name . . . it's Naala—Eisnaala.'

'Ah. Ndewo, Naala,' Kora said, as she greeted the girl, her crossed palms moving from her chest towards Naala.

'Ndewo,' Naala replied, performing the same greeting from her position on the ground.

Kora tried to smile back at her, but the strange expression had yet to fully leave her face. 'Your eyes . . .' the girl said, then paused before shrugging. 'Never mind, my mind is still asleep—I'm being silly.' She lowered herself onto the fur mats sprawled across the floor. They were in the same makeshift hut that Naala had woken up to yesterday. The morning sunlight filtered through the rows of thin wooden scraps that bordered the room, filling it with a sandy glow. Naala could see flushed green vegetation through the gaps, swaying in the breeze as the birds began their morning songs.

'It's still quite early; no wonder I'm still frazzled,' Kora continued. 'I would try to get some sleep if I were you. Now that you have recovered, we will be on the move again, and, trust me, you will need your energy.' Kora yawned as she drifted back to sleep. Naala turned on her back and stared up at the straw ceiling lined with wooden rods. *What am I?*

A sense of hopelessness lay heavy on Naala's chest, mixed with guilt, grief, anger, and bewilderment. Out of that brew of emotions, she was unsure about which one she was meant to feel the most, which one deserved her attention. She remembered the feeling of power that had rushed through her in Igbakwu. Naala had felt remnants of that same power when the earth trembled that morning. She knew that the quake was connected somehow to her, which frightened her immensely, because she also knew that that couldn't be true. How could she believe such a thing? Flashbacks of Hanye's bright eyes and rambling words filled her mind. Perhaps she was more like him than she had thought.

Thoughts of Hanye brought with them the stark realisation that her village was gone. What was she supposed to feel? How was one supposed to feel when they were responsible for the massacre of all the people that they held dear in life. Despair? Anger? Or maybe nothing at all. Perhaps everything was supposed to come to a halt after such events. *I should have warned them . . .* she thought.

Shame; that was her most prominent feeling. She wanted to physically shake herself free from it; instead, she sighed and turned her head to the side, only to be met by a pair of dark eyes. It was the man that they called Eni. She raised her head, her heart pounding with guilt, as though she had somehow done something terrible.

'Sorry,' she mumbled quickly. Something about that interaction unsettled her. *Why did I apologise?* Naala thought, *I didn't do anything wrong . . . did I?* She was merely glancing around the room; she wasn't staring rudely at anyone.

He lay at the corner and there were at least three snoring people between them, but she could still feel him staring. She looked back at him cautiously, half expecting to have imagined the whole encounter, but his eyes were still fixed on her.

'I like your name,' he said curtly, before rolling over, leaving Naala gaping at his back.

She said nothing and instead chose to let birdsong pour over her. The delicate tones bounced around her head and the feathery heat embraced her body. Naala couldn't focus. She briefly entertained the idea of standing up from the dusty ground, and facing the day's truth, but she couldn't. A dull pain on her left temple held her down. The thought of being remotely active was more than she could bear. Instead, she allowed the heavy weight of sleep to pull down her eyelids. She felt herself drifting into a dark pool of unconsciousness, until she was overcome with a harsh blow of emotion.

Naala gasped and her eyes flew open. She looked around at the still room filled with sleeping people, snoring softly in the early morning light. Her eyes, now filling with thick tears, flicked quickly towards Eni to inspect whether he had caught sight of her bizarre outburst. His back was still towards her. She exhaled shakily and stared up at the straw ceiling, allowing fat round tears to run down the sides of her face.

Lying here, eyes closed, she had seen them. She had seen her dear grandma, Gini, Eddy, and her uncle. She had seen them sitting down at the oak table that her great-grandfather had built years before her mother had even been born. The wide window had allowed a waft of warm air and muted sunlight into their humble dining room. The room had been filled with love and peace.

Just as Naala had tried to grab hold of the image in her head, it was brutally snatched from her, and suddenly she was left, mouth gaping, in the dark. A crippling pain surged through her body. It was too much for her to bear. She had lost her family. She wanted to scream and punch the air, but instead she lay completely still, staring up at the ceiling. She refused to close her eyes because she knew that if she did, that same beautiful image would fill her mind, only to have reality snatch it away. *Distract yourself*, she thought furiously, her teeth clenched tightly. *Stop thinking of them!*

CHAPTER 14

THE SEVEN OBIS

City of Nri

'Stupid,' Sinai muttered, as she walked towards the crowd of extravagantly dressed people surrounding the Eze. She was in the Elu festival room; it was sandy and decadent, decorated with bright gold and jewels that sparkled in the brilliant ọkụ light. The tall imposing walls filled Sinai with unease as she drew closer to a sea of beautifully laced garments, bursting with vibrant colours and deep rich scents. The palace's elite were gathered; the heads of the seven most prestigious families in the entire kingdom. Collectively they controlled the trade, water supply, finance system, and technology programmes for the entire Kingdom of Nri. They all held their gold and ivory *ọfọ* sticks in their hands, glowing deep within with a green tinge that spoke of the Eze's blessing. The seven Obis stood firm, their heads crowned with locs varying from jet black to almost white-grey, a sacred sign of their power. They all stood slightly bowed as they laughed and entertained the nucleus of the group: the Eze.

'Stupid, stupid, stupid,' Sinai murmured, as she swivelled away from the group, walking instead towards the other end of the festival room, near the platters of food that she had watched Meekulu prepare hours before.

*

'It's impossible,' she gasped for the thousandth time, while Meekulu pounded the softened beans into a thick smooth paste.

'Bah, it's easy. You are a noble, are you not?'

'No, well, yes, but not really . . .'

'Yes, really. We all know that you can enter that room, and listen to the conversations. Impossible? Don't be soft, girl,' Meekulu said, as she wiped her brow before shooing away Sinai's attempt to help.

'It's not that simple, I'm an efuọla child. I'm not . . . established,' she replied with grimace. It didn't feel the right word to describe her station in life, but it was the closest one she had found so far.

In the kingdom, the hierarchy was clear. The Eze was the ruling entity. Next came the Obis, the kingdom's senior lords chosen by the Eze who controlled the kingdom's major sectors. After them came the nobles, considered as cousins or distant blood relatives to the Obis. They were led by a large group of elders and chiefs, who supported the Obis where they could. As Meekulu had noted, the nobles were permitted to interact with the Obis, and even with the Eze himself, under the right circumstances. They were given the right to listen, and even share their opinions of the world that they lived in, but only within reason.

An ambitious chief could even garner enough respect to succeed an elderly Obi, with the blessing of the Eze, of course. However, Sinai had garnered no such respect; in fact, she was barely clinging onto her status as a noble. As an efuọla girl, she technically had the same privileges as anyone born with her blood, but in practice, she was tainted. Her rights, whilst there, were not *established*.

After her, came the palace specialists. They lacked royal blood but were highly respected due to the skills that they learnt from their family trade. Those with skills, like Meekulu's, that were impressive enough to directly serve the Eze, wielded slightly more power and respect within the palace walls. Then there were the palace common folk, like Chisi, who assisted the specialists. After that, came the villagers, the bottom of the sprawling hierarchy that the kingdom prescribed to. They provided the raw materials that fed and clothed the kingdom, and yet they wielded tiny morsels of power.

'Established or not, the task is far from impossible. Even the illegitimate efuọlas can still speak to the Eze,' Meekulu said, before peering at Sinai from behind her crystal glasses. 'Do you know what my name is, child?'

'Meekulu?' Sinai asked cautiously, as the old woman shook her head with a smile forming on her wrinkled lips.

'That is my title. What is my name?' the old woman asked.

'Kaurandua?' Sinai said hesitantly, as Meekulu's smile widened.

'Yes,' she said wistfully. 'Kaurandua—it means *you cannot buy life*, in my language.'

'That's pretty,' Sinai mused.

'It's more than pretty, child, it's true. You cannot buy life, you cannot hide and wait to live it later; you must live and you must live now, because you have no other choice.'

'I am living,' Sinai protested quietly.

'How can you be living if you do not recognise your own power?' Meekulu scoffed. 'You are hiding, all the time, reducing yourself and minimising your power. You *have* power, my dear; everyone, even the tiniest *otomys*, has power. The trouble is we are all too quick to give it away.' The old woman leaned back with a smile. 'The trick is incredibly simple. To know you have power *is* to have power.'

*

'Stupid, stupid, silly girl,' Sinai muttered, as she picked an engraved clay *efere* and loaded it with spiced gizzard meat. *What am I going to do?* she thought. Every time that she attempted to penetrate the Obis' circle, her heart squeezed tight with anxiety.

She had no right to join that discussion, no right whatsoever. Her place was among the hundreds of other nobles around the room, who spoke animatedly about nothing, as they snuck glances at the glittering leaders.

Sinai was supposed to wait patiently within one of those small social clusters for the Eze to make his courteous rounds of the room. He may even pass her group and in that moment she was supposed to be grateful for the fact that he took the time to acknowledge her existence. So far he had only done that four times in her entire life. Yet here she was, imagining that she could walk up to that man and infiltrate his circle of Obis so that she could *spy* on his movements and words. She was stupid to have agreed to such an ọbara oath; there was no way that she would be able to get near the almighty Eze. She had promised her life away.

Sinai watched wistfully as the noble children darted in and out of the Obis' circle. The Eze stopped speaking when one of them barged carelessly into his leg. The room stilled and watched the interaction breathlessly. A woman who, judging by her fear-stricken expression, was the little girl's mother, gaped wordlessly at her child. The Eze bent until he was at eye level with the small girl. A smile formed on his lips.

'I see you are having fun,' he said quietly, but his voice carried across the silent room.

'Yes, Ozo Eze,' the little girl beamed.

The Eze beamed back at her.

'Well, I know something that could make it even better.'

'What?' she said eagerly.

'This,' he said, bringing his palm to face her as he conjured a small, green ǫkụ ball that began to stretch out, creating small, detailed, and intricate swirls until it formed a large and exquisite play ball that glowed brightly. He brought the flame ball towards the child's face and she stepped back, frightened. Her mother made a strangled sound. The Eze chuckled.

'Oh, don't be frightened; I have made this one cool to the touch,' he murmured. 'Come see, place your hand.' And sure enough the girl placed her small hand on the ball, only to leap up and down with joy.

'It's not hot,' she exclaimed. The Eze nodded and smiled as he handed the ball over to her. She squealed like a small pig and proceeded to share her gift with her little friends. The guests looked on in giddy excitement. People could say a lot about the Eze, but he had always favoured the children, for the most part.

'You look well,' a low voice said from behind her, sending a cold chill down her spine. Sinai gripped the clay efere in her hand hard, hard enough to create tiny sprawled cracks up and down it. She placed it back on the decorated table slowly before turning to face Ina. The girl stood before her in two-piece, dark purple attire; the top was tight and cinched at her waist, made of a lace material with tiny patterned holes revealing her dark bronzed skin. The bottom half of her outfit consisted of a beautifully decorated, thick material wrapped tight around her thighs and long enough to drag on the floor. Ina had her head held high and her face was tight, pulled back by an extravagant *gele*. Her long locks sprouted from the nape of her neck and coated her back. Beautiful as she was, a cold and abhorrent scent emitted from her. Sinai's face contorted in disgust.

Sinai was overwhelmed with an intense desire to run. She did not want to be anywhere near the deranged girl. *Don't!* she thought sternly, *be strong; now is not the time to cower and run, be strong!*

Sinai took a deep breath as the small voice in her head turned into a loud siren roar. Sinai let out a deep sigh.

'You will pay for what you did, Ina,' Sinai said quietly, as Lebechi and Ebun sniggered nervously behind Ina. They were not pleased at all to be in such close proximity with Sinai again. After all, they had both witnessed her fall to her death with their own eyes. Yet, here she was, alive and well, with little to no evidence of her deathly fall. How had she possibly survived? Surely she must be some sort of witch. The girls had heard stories of witches before, evil women and men who used the elements of the forgotten magic to benefit themselves as they carried out tasks with ill intent. No one they knew had ever come in contact with such a creature, but the fear of doing so was still present in most people. The idea of unknown forces exerting control over the people was disturbing, particularly since the gods had left the earth. Who, besides the Eze, a lone man, could possibly protect them against a witch?

The two girls stood cautiously back from the exchange, with eyes darting nervously between Ina and Sinai.

Ina hadn't laughed at Sinai's comment; instead she looked at Sinai with a tight expression, her eyes roaming over her face like ants. She starred obsessively at Sinai's dark almond eyes, rich skin, and full lips. The girl was very much alive and Ina's nose flared with hatred.

'You should have died that day,' she said through clenched teeth as she took a step towards Sinai.

'You should have made sure you killed me, because I'm telling you the price you're going to pay for that is high, Ina. You've wanted a fight from me for years; well fine, you've got one.'

'Oh please, you think you can threaten me? You think that I believe a word of those stupid rumours? You're not *powerful*; you're weak and you've always been weak. Don't think I haven't seen you sauntering around the room like a tramp. Listen, girl—I'm not going to warn you again, stay away from Obi Ife, or you will pay for it with your life. Your fall was a warning, but mark my words, the day you speak to him will be your last,' Ina hissed, as Sinai contorted her face in confusion. What did Obi Ife have to do with anything?

Obi Ife was one of the elite Obis. Despite being one of the youngest, he controlled the kingdom's agriculture, its most important economic sector. When his father had died unexpectedly, he had succeeded him, to the surprise of the majority of the people in the palace. People had thought his young age would render him unfit to wield the power passed on to the Obis. It was widely speculated that one of the elder nobles, perhaps Chief Kalu, a close friend to Obi Ife's father, or one of the few nobles consulted by the Obis on complex kingdom dilemmas, would be given the title. However, the Eze had surprised the people by choosing the young boy instead to fill his father's shoes. While his age may have been hard to respect, his blessing from the Eze was not. As disgruntled as the people may have been by his choice, the Eze's word was final.

Sinai knew very little of Obi Ife; as with most of the Obis, she had spoken to him only a handful of times. Strained, forced conversations had left her feeling awkward, and certain that she had somehow said the wrong thing. Sinai looked at the hot anger in Ina's eyes and a bright light suddenly illuminated in her head: Obi Ife was her way in.

'I have power,' Sinai said softly to herself, as a light breeze suddenly wafted through the room. It filled her with elation and provided her with yet another encouraging boost.

'What is she whispering about?' Ina scowled, but all Lebechi and Ebun could do was to squint at the peculiar girl. They both saw a flash of gold shimmer across Sinai's dark irises. They snuck a look at each other before turning back to Sinai, who smiled back at them curtly before pushing past them. She headed towards Obi Ife, who now, thankfully, stood a little further away from the group. He looked up brightly as she approached.

'Nwedo Obi Ife,' Sinai said, bringing her crossed palm to her chest and back towards him.

'Nwedo Sinai,' Obi Ife replied with a smile, repeating the gesture. They stood awkwardly for a moment before Sinai finally spoke.

'I liked the Eze's trick,' she noted, as he nodded.

'Yes, it was very nice,' he replied, but then a painfully long pause halted the conversation. She could see his attention wavering. Suddenly he cleared his throat; he was about to politely pardon himself. She needed to do something to keep him interested, to keep him talking.

'I actually had a question for the Eze; perhaps you could help me to ask him?' she said.

'You should ask him yourself.'

'What?' Sinai choked. 'No, that wouldn't be right. I just meant, perhaps you would tell me your thoughts or you could ask—'

'Nonsense. You saw it yourself; the Eze is far friendlier than gossip suggests.'

'No, please,' Sinai whispered, as he pivoted her towards the tight circle of powerful men. Her heart quickened as she felt the eyes of the room on her. Most of the Obis looked down at her in surprise. Some were clearly disgusted; the Eze, however, was completely expressionless. Sinai scanned the crowd until her eyes landed on the only smile: Obi Ife's.

'Sorry to disturb,' Sinai murmured as she bowed. 'I mean— Nwedo,' she added quickly, as she gestured her greetings. Her heart slammed in her chest. None of them greeted her back. *You have power, you have power, you have power,* she recited in her head, but Meekulu's words now felt like sand in her mouth. They had power, she did not.

'I had a question and my curiosity got the better of me, but now it doesn't seem like a good idea. Please ignore me,' she said hastily. She could barely breathe, as she watched their faces sour.

'No, what is your question?' Obi Ife asked with a wide smile, stepping slightly towards her, as the other senior lords looked from him to the Eze cautiously. The Eze bowed his head slightly, and the crowd gave a slight sigh of relief. Sinai took in a small breath as she racked her mind for something to say.

'I was thinking . . . I was just wondering—how. . .' Sinai trailed off, her face warm and her throat so tight that she struggled for air. She cleared her throat. 'How certain are you about reality?'

'What are you talking about?' Obi Arinze interrupted gruffly, flashing an exasperated glance at the Eze, hoping that he too shared his sentiment, but to his dismay the Eze's focus remained fixed on the girl.

'Reality—what we perceive as real, what we take as fact,' Sinai persisted. 'The fact that we are all here having this conversation . . . how sure are you that any of this is *real?* Isn't it quite possible that all this is an illusion? Or perhaps this is the afterlife? It's just—with the gods gone, where do we even stand? What can we grasp onto that is solid and . . . real?' The crowd looked back at her, perplexed. *What am I saying? What am I saying? What am I saying?* Sinai fretted, before taking another strangled breath.

'I . . . I've . . . it's just something that I've been wondering about for some time, and you all are the greatest minds in the kingdom, so you are my best chance at solving this,' she continued, as she stretched her quivering mouth into a solid smile. Slowly, they began to smile back, warmed by her compliment.

'Well, it is an interesting question,' Obi Ife started, with a bright twinkle in his eye as he felt the beginnings of a good debate brewing. 'I would say that you would need to go to the teachings of Chukwuma Agonon—now he said that we are all the dictators of our reality in our lives and our deaths. Our chis—our souls—are connected to God and through him we can shape everything.'

'You can never know!' Obi Wale suddenly shouted. 'That is the whole point of life, after all: that there is no point!'

'Rubbish. I am standing here, I am real—I say I am here, so I am here.'

Sinai smiled with a nod, as if she were taking in all their responses, her eyes locked on whoever was talking at the moment. But she was not listening. Her mind was racing at an unbearable speed, because at the corner of her eye she could see the Eze. She could feel his still and powerful presence just like scorching heat from the giant sun. She could feel his eyes fixed on her, and she couldn't help but feel like prey, caught in the traps of a skilled hunter.

CHAPTER 15

AN OLD FRIEND

Furuefu Forest

Naala had not slept in days. Her body ached and her mind buzzed with a low sound that made her thoughts slow and troubled. They bounced lazily around her head, a mesh of sporadic ideas and hurt feelings. As aimless as they were, they all seemed to migrate back to the same thing: *I have to warn the others.* Naala had spent some days with the group of travellers; they called themselves the survivors of the Eze's attacks. The group was formed of eight people, no two from the same village. They had found each other haphazardly, and now wandered aimlessly around the dense Furuefu forest. They were terrified of reaching another village; they were all convinced that if they did they would meet death at the hands of the army, waiting patiently for their lost prey.

Naala hated them. A deep and thick pool of anger dwelled within her, working as fuel for her body in the absence of sleep.

She was angry at the group; they were cowards, as far as she could tell. They had all witnessed the atrocities of the army, and yet they hid away like scared mice, not thinking to spread the word to prevent future attacks. She was angry at the army. They were weak; they attacked the innocent with no remorse. They treated death like it was a sport, and they were getting away with it, perhaps even revered and cheered as heroes when they returned to the palace. She was furious at her dead family and friends. They should have listened to her; they should still be alive. She should not have to mourn them all on her own. Most of all, Naala was angry at herself; she had failed all the people that she had loved. She had let that army take everything from her. It was all her fault.

Naala needed to do something. Unlike the self-proclaimed survivors, she could not hide away, knowing that somewhere a village was being attacked. She needed to spread the word and warn the others. Naala rubbed her eyes and climbed out of the woven hammock that she had made with the assistance of Kora soon after she had joined the survivors. The group slept in the trees, using strong vines that they weaved into hammocks and tied between the branches. Naala would be lying if she said that she didn't miss her strong wooden akwa nest, lined with soft beast furs and her grandmother's tightly woven quilts, rich with the smell of sweet cedar wood and *ehuru* spice. That said, she appreciated the soft sways and the safety of her hammock. It allowed her to sleep peacefully without fear of encountering the army or a beast on the ground. Naala had learnt a number of useful survival tips from the group. She had already known how to hunt; her uncle had taught her when she was young.

'Our family doesn't have enough sons,' he'd grumbled once, as they'd marched through the thick, moss green forest one day. It had been during the raining season, and a soft mist had risen from the ground. Bushes of vibrant green leaves had glittered with beads of water soaked up from the air. Naala had felt as though she was floating through a cloud.

'So you will have to pick up the slack; we will not be a burden to the village, you hear me?' he'd said sternly, before breaking into a smile when she'd responded by flexing her muscles to show how strong she was.

Her uncle had taught her how to traverse the forest for hours on end, without falling prey to beasts or poisonous insects. He had taught her how to hunt and gather, but the group had taught her how she could live in the forest. They had taught her how to find the freshwater that Njábá, the river god, had stored in the round, large white *mmiri* flowers. They had taught her how to identify the dull red stems of the poisoned mmiri's left behind by the trickster goddess, Agwu. These spoilt flowers looked exactly like the safe ones, except for their dull red stems.

The survivors had also given her footgear to shield her feet from the forest ground, not the flat thin slippers that she had been used to, but thick crocodile skin, lined with the cool mmiri leaf and tied securely at her ankles with strong vines. They had taught her how to sleep in the woods without fear, how to navigate the terrain. Naala may have hated the survivor's inactivity, but there was no doubt that her time with the group, short as it was, was incredibly valuable.

As soon as she had learnt a new skill, Naala became increasingly anxious about leaving the group and using it. After spending a few days with the survivors, she was convinced that she had more than enough skills to spread the news to the villages. Naala had even begun to formulate a plan; she would start off going to the villages that she knew and then gather new information about obscure villages along the way. Perhaps one of the villages would gift her with a small oxen, which could help her get further on her travels. Naala was not concerned about getting lost. She had always had a good sense of direction; one of the few things that her uncle had been vocally proud of. It was as though she could feel a pull towards wherever she needed to go, even without using the stars or trees to help her navigate. In any case, she was sure that in time her words would serve like ripples in a still lake, travelling far beyond her.

Naala gathered her hammock under her arm before jumping from branch to branch down the tree until she finally hit the ground. She looked out at the vast forest, clustered with towering dark brown trunks engulfed in an army of dense green leaves.

The shimmering light of the morning sun filtered through the giant trees, creating an array of brilliant yellows and striking greens across the scattered vegetation. Silver waters from a narrow stream cut through the trees, and the birds whooshed gracefully in the air.

Naala rested one hand on the huge trunk of the tree she had spent the night in.

'You were supposed to be my freedom,' she said softly to the mute tree, wishing she could go back to a time when marrying Chinedu was her biggest worry.

'Do you often do that?' a voice said behind her, causing her to jump slightly, her hand clasping at her chest as she stifled a scream.

'Why are you always *here?*' she replied, as she gestured to the air in frustration before turning around to face Eni. His personality, like his eyes, was intense. He was constantly watching, focused on the world and its minute details and connections. He knew everything, seemed to be everywhere, relentless and attentive. He dipped his head slightly as he wiped away a smile.

'*Ndewo* to you too,' he said, as he let his crossed palms fall from his chest towards Naala. 'I didn't mean to scare you; I heard you talking to the tree, and I was curious,' he shrugged.

'I wasn't scared. Or talking to the tree,' Naala replied shortly, avoiding his razor-sharp gaze. 'I was just remembering . . . a simpler time.'

He nodded, concluding that this was probably a topic better left alone. Instead, he swept his gaze over the busy forest. Endless shades of green surrounded them, and the air smelt fresh, as the birds whistled in the morning.

Eni took a step closer towards Naala, the new girl that they had discovered only two weeks ago. He had found himself doing that often, as though a thick rope existed between the two of them, tightening every time he took another step closer. Eni could not explain it. Perhaps it was simply her beauty that drew him to her. Even with her eyes darkened from a lack of sleep and her thick lips tightened into a foul scowl, she was breathtaking. Her long intricate braids framed her face perfectly, and her thick sweeping eyelashes created shadows at the corner of her eyes, whilst her rich supple skin shone brilliantly in the sun.

Eni stopped himself from shaking his head as he took another step closer. It wasn't *just* her beauty that drew him. It was something much deeper. He felt as though he had known her before, as though they had always been destined to meet.

'The group is about to eat; will you join us for breakfast this morning?' Eni asked. He asked her this every morning, hoping that one day she would accept. She had been keeping her distance from the group, remaining an outsider and only interacting with them when it was absolutely necessary.

'No,' she replied, aggravated. *People are dying and all you can think about is breakfast*, she thought disgustedly.

'Suit yourself; more tilapia for me, I guess,' Eni said, as he shrugged again, careful not to reveal his disappointment, but his heels dug more forcefully into the thick shrubs as he turned to head towards the group.

'I'm leaving,' Naala suddenly burst out.

Eni halted. He forced his hands to still and attempted to steady his racing heart.

Naala immediately regretted saying anything. She didn't know why she had told him. She had already decided that when she left, she would not say a word to the group. She didn't want to be stopped. She had no desire to even discuss her reasons for leaving. She knew that it would start an argument, and she had no energy for it.

Eni relaxed his hand and turned around, looking back at Naala coldly.

'Goodbye then, and good luck,' he muttered.

'Yeah, thanks—I'll be glad to be actually *doing* something,' Naala replied snarkily. The words had slipped out of her mouth like slugs; she had not wanted to say them, but Eni's comment had irked her.

He took a deep breath before taking another step forward; he refused to let the girl get to him. But she already had. Before she knew it, he had turned and marched towards her.

'We all risked our lives to save yours. You don't have to be grateful, but I will not stand by whilst you accuse us of doing nothing,' he said through clenched teeth. 'What on earth would even possess you to leave? Why does that make sense to—' he stopped mid-sentence and drew back from her as he shook his head '—never mind—just *go*. I shouldn't have to convince you to stay.'

Naala stood stunned for a moment. She had not expected an outburst, least of all from Eni. He always seemed too composed to lose himself to reckless things like anger. She was stuck for words. He thought she was spoilt and ungrateful; she did not like that at all.

'I'm sorry—but, unlike you, I can't wait here safe and sound, while my brothers and sisters die.' Her voice trembled slightly, and she felt weak and silly. She desperately wanted to get her point across, but it seemed trivial and petty in the light of day.

'So what exactly do *you* plan to do?' Eni asked.

'I will warn the others . . . go to the villages one by one, so that they are prepared,' she replied.

'So you plan on navigating the forest on your own.'

'I can survive,' Naala replied quietly.

'You only learnt how to get clean water two days ago; if it wasn't for Gossy, you would be dead by now after eating that black spotted redberry that he had to pry from your hands.'

'Well, I know now, and I will not be eating anything that I don't know from now on—I don't need to explain myself –I know how to hunt, I'm capable, I can do this.'

'You won't. But let's say you do . . . you arrive scruffy, like a madwoman, into the village, yelling that the Eze's army is coming for them. Do you expect them to believe you just like that?' He clicked his two fingers together.

'I—'

'They won't!'

Naala crossed her arms in frustration. *Why did I tell him? Why?!* she inwardly screamed at herself. She didn't need to explain herself to anyone or go over her plans; she was perfectly capable—

'Ow!' Naala cried, as something small and hard hit her forehead. She looked at her feet to find a small papaya fruit lying on the ground. She looked up at Eni in stark shock that quickly turned to a blind rage.

'You little—'

'It wasn't me!' Eni protested with both hands in the air.

'Well, that's rich . . . who else coul-eyahhh!' Naala yelped, as she took a step back in fright, as a small ball of grey fur fell at her feet. She blinked momentarily before breaking into a deep laugh for the first time in weeks. Enwe leapt gleefully into her arms and squeezed at her neck as she snuggled against his grey fur.

'I'm guessing you know this monkey,' Eni murmured, as he took in the warm reunion.

'Yes, it's Enwe. He's from Igbakwu . . . from my village,' Naala replied, her voice sobering as memories of her dead village found their place back in her head. She tapped softly on Enwe's tail and the monkey bounced off from her shoulders and scrambled back into the leafy forest. Naala watched him leave before bending down and picking up the papaya from the soft grass.

'Visitors came to my village countless times, talking about these attacks,' Eni said. 'But no one believed them until it was actually happening. Why would they believe you?'

'It's different,' Naala added, a statement that led to a pregnant pause. It *was* different; she had actually survived an attack. All the visitor stories that she had heard were word of mouth, not one of those visitors said that they had experienced it first-hand.

'It's not,' Eni said eventually. 'But say they do believe you— then what? They pick up and leave . . . to where? They fight? Against the Eze's army? It would be a slaughter.'

'It already *is* a slaughter—I just want to do something,' Naala said, mostly to herself. 'And yes, it might fail but at least I would have tried. What are *you* doing?!'

'But we are doing something . . . we're the only—' Eni started, before blinking hard as if he had just said something that he shouldn't have. 'It doesn't matter, go if you want to go,' he continued sheepishly.

'What do you mean?' Naala replied.

'Go if you want to go,' he said, avoiding eye contact with her for the first time since they'd met.

'You are doing something?'

'We are surviving. Look, if you want to go, then go; if not, then don't. Either way, I'm hungry and I'm not going to waste good fish for an ungrateful girl,' Eni said harshly before walking away, as Naala stared after him, still holding the papaya.

CHAPTER 16

A SERIES OF GAMES

City of Nri

'You're good at this!' Obi Ife said with a clap, as he leaned over the table to better inspect the *mancala* board. Sinai smiled as discreetly as she could, fighting the urge to burst out laughing. She had been holding back the whole time they were playing; she could have beaten him five or so times already, if she hadn't wanted to prolong their encounter. Sinai wasn't there to play games; she was there to gather information.

*

'Fantastic!' Meekulu had said the day before, when Sinai had finally found time to tell the old woman about what had happened at the gathering.

'But I didn't find out anything about *him*,' Sinai replied in a low voice, afraid that the very mention of the Eze's name would conjure him up. She had been initially excited after her encounter with the Obis. She had felt truly powerful and commanding, as though she had been reborn as a new woman. However, with time came subdued thoughts and self-doubt. Now the entire ordeal hung over her like a dark cloud.

Sinai hadn't said a word to the Eze that evening, but she'd caught him looking at her every now and again, his head bobbing around like a deadly snake's, and she had to force herself not to shiver.

'Nothing at all?' the old woman mused.

'Not really.' Sinai frowned. 'Just that he values justice—which everyone who's ever heard the man speak knows, so . . .'

Meekulu dropped the daga that she was using to chop fresh herbs and turned to Sinai.

'Justice?' she murmured low.

Sinai sat up, alerted by the roughness in the old woman's voice.

'Yes, is that important? Obi Ife, he just said—well, I told him I admired the Eze's journey and I asked what would one need to win such a man's favour, and he said that the single most important thing that the Eze cares about is justice.'

Meekulu shook her head.

'Justice,' she said darkly. 'Amadioha and his followers have twisted that concept so much that the word is now obsolete.'

'Amadioha? The god of justice . . .' Sinai shifted uncomfortably in her seat. 'Meekulu, I don't think you should say such things.'

143

Their conversation had become too illicit for her liking, bordering on blasphemous.

Meekulu flashed a hard look at Sinai before her face softened into its usual leathery warmth.

'It seems that I have gotten ahead of myself. Perhaps we will find time to discuss it later, but you are right: now is not the best time. Not the best time at all.' Meekulu smiled, but Sinai couldn't help but notice that it did not reach her eyes. 'I think you have made good progress; you have even formed alliances with people who know him, no?'

Sinai fidgeted uneasily. 'Alliance is definitely too strong a word.'

'Obi Ife—you can speak to him again, yes?'

'I suppose.'

'You can arrange a meeting with him.'

'No . . . maybe . . . perhaps . . .'

'Alone?'

'Ahh, I'm not an *akwuna*, Ma,' Sinai said, as she leapt up from the table.

'My dear, akwuna are some of the bravest women you would ever meet—you should be glad to be considered one of them—but saying that, yes, you are right: you are not an akwuna—you are an Ọnye Nyocha.'

Sinai exhaled loudly; she was becoming increasingly uncomfortable with where the conversation had led. The thought of having to sell her body for this cause unnerved her; truth be told she wasn't entirely prepared to spy on the Eze for the cause either.

As her wounds had healed and the memory of her fall subsided, her desire for retribution had also faded. The thought of gaining some sort of control over Ina still remained attractive, but it was not nearly as pressing as it had been when Sinai had first woken up broken and bruised.

Ina's anger seemed to have burnt white hot until it slowly sizzled into nothing but pale dust. Now, whenever Ina walked past Obi Ife and Sinai, she no longer held any of her previous intensity; it had all melted away into a glazed look of boredom, or a slight curl of her lips.

Ina had always known when it was time to change the game plan. She hated to lose, and so she never did. She simply re-adjusted. If Obi Ife was low enough to fraternise publically with the likes of an efuọla girl, then clearly she must have been wrong about him and his prospects all along.

Now her goal was to find her *true* equal, and she would, and with her by his side, he would be far more powerful than Obi Ife would ever dream of being. Eventually, when she was finally at the level she was destined to be at, she would deal with both of them for this slight, but for now she could no longer afford to waste any more thought on them.

As Ina became increasingly impassive, Sinai grew less sure about the price that she had agreed to pay to protect herself against the girl's supposed wrath. Fear had propelled her into a deadly oath, and with that the fear was subsiding, the reality of what she had chosen to do weighed heavily on her soul. After all, the Eze, as abstract and cold as he seemed, was still the kingdom's ruler. He was still the people's hero.

Sinai had been told the story a million times as a child. Like everyone in the kingdom, she could recite it effortlessly on demand. The story was set in a lost time, hundreds of years ago, when the gods roamed the earth. They were said to be incredibly beautiful, unbelievably strong, and surrounded by auras of brilliant, raw energy.

Ala, the Earth Mother, had given each of the gods a piece of the world to rule. Some were given the physical elements, such as rain and thunder. Some were given the emotional elements like lust and anger, and others were given power over conceptual elements like justice. The gods were said to have walked amongst the humans, tall and outstanding, as they collaborated to help them navigate Ala's elements. The gods grew to love the humans, and the humans worshiped and loved the gods.

Slowly, the Earth Mother grew envious of the love that the humans and gods shared, for neither of them loved her with the same intensity. One day, Ala decided to wipe the humans away, and start again with a new, more gracious form of life. The gods pleaded with her, begging her to reconsider her plans, but her mind was as hard as granite.

The gods loved the people so much that, when it became clear, that pleading would not be enough to save them from the Mother's wrath, they decided to fight. United, humans and gods waged a war against the Mother and her followers. Each side sustained irrevocable losses, but Ala remained unmoved. That was, until one man changed it all. Just as humans and gods alike were at the brink of extinction, he stole Ala's heart, the Ndụ crystal.

Ala's heart was said to resemble a small emerald quartz that could fit easily in the palm of a child's hand. It was said to hold enough energy to sustain countless stars, build infinite worlds, and end all life. When the light touched it, it would spring to dazzling brightness like nothing ever seen before. Ala had kept her heart hidden in one of the caves at Udi, shielded by ancient magic. Only the purest heart, brightest mind, and fullest soul could find it. It was thought to be impossible to steal, but Eze Ochichiri had done just that.

When he snatched the crystal from the cave, the earth screamed in pain. Hurricanes erupted, the land tore itself to pieces, and the rivers burnt with rage. The Earth Mother was dying. One by one, the remaining gods died, until there were none left. They said Ala used her dying breath to kill them, refusing to be the only one to leave the earth.

Soon after, all was still. The sun emerged once again from the blood-red clouds, the rivers settled, flowing with tears of those who mourned, and the land sighed in exhaustion. The Earth Mother was dead.

The earth was broken, but Eze Ochichiri, still armed with Ala's heart, began to repair it. He restored peace and order. He brought back stability and security, and soon enough he was named the Eze of all the kingdoms. While his reign stretched over centuries, his body and wisdom remained preserved by the Ndụ crystal.

This was the being that Sinai had agreed to spy on: Eze Ochichiri, the man who had saved the earth.

'Meekulu, why do I need to spy on the Eze?' Sinai asked for the first time. She had wanted to ask this question ever since Meekulu had given her the details of the ọbara oath, but she had been afraid of anything that could jeopardise her plan, including her very own conscious.

Sinai had been swept up by the notion of doing something as inconceivable and illicit as spying on the Eze. Meekulu had been so nonchalant about the whole operation; her unshakeable faith that Sinai could pull such a thing off had deluded Sinai into thinking the same. However, she was beginning to experience steadying thoughts. The mission was not only dangerous; Sinai feared that it was also wrong.

'He took something from me,' Meekulu replied pointedly.

'I'm sure if you asked . . .'

'It's not the sort of thing one *asks* for,' Meekulu said softly, her eyes saddened by old memories. Sinai had never seen her like this, completely lost in thought. Her heart ached for the old woman. Meekulu was both strong and frail; Sinai was always comforted by the old woman's strength but her fragility pierced Sinai like a shard of glass through the heart.

Sinai wasn't too sure why, but she believed in the old woman's conviction; she believed that there was a reason, a sound, good reason, for all of this.

'And we're not harming anyone innocent?' Sinai asked again, seeking reassurance that any crime she had already undoubtedly committed was as moral as it could be. Sinai was certainly not above delivering justice to those who deserved it, irrespective of what the law said; that was fair. Causing pain or discomfort to those who didn't deserve it, solely for her own gain . . . well, that she could not abide with.

'Absolutely not,' Meekulu scoffed, as her face slowly regained its usual exuberance. The old woman smiled wide, as she stepped closer to Sinai.

'No one innocent will be hurt, but a lot of wrongs must be righted. Sinaikuku, you are such a sweet child—good heart,' she said, as she squeezed Sinai's cheeks softly. 'Most people would have asked me to help them kill that girl, but you don't even want to disfigure her properly.' Meekulu took a step back to look at Sinai.

'Thanks. Also—' Sinai implored, 'Why do you keep calling m—'

'Such a good child,' Meekulu continued, before rushing over to the corner of her kitchen. 'Let's get started on this disfiguring agent, shall we?'

CHAPTER 17

THE THREE PUPPET MASTERS

Furuefu Forest

What are you up to? Naala thought, as she looked out at the group of survivors huddled together under the large looming palm leaves, eating a mix of berries, smoked cod fish, and the coconut fragments that the men had smashed open with a flat stone.

Naala had been conflicted after her conversation with Eni; his words weighed heavy on her, acting like a cord and keeping her chained to the group of wanderers. Naala wasn't entirely sure if she was staying out of curiosity or fear, but either way, she was here and her eyes were wide open.

When Naala had first encountered the group, she'd felt as though she was blocked by a dark mountain of despair. Its presence drove her out of slumber and tormented her waking hours. But that was beginning to change. While the loss of her family and friends still hung over her, she was no longer blocked by the mountain of pain. Instead, she allowed it to melt down into an ocean that washed over her; her head was always bobbing at the surface, but she had yet to drown.

She had started to eat again, and sleep no longer evaded her. Her mind was regaining its former sharpness, and she was astounded by how much detail she had let slip.

She quickly realised that, just as she was watching them, they had always been watching her. Eyes were constantly locked on her as she ate, went for a walk, bathed, or sat in thought. She was never alone. She was overwhelmed with the level of secrecy that existed even within the group. Hidden glances and whispered conversations plagued the group of mixed personalities. Only a select few were privy to portions of these secrets, and one man, Azu, foolishly thought he knew them all. He was convinced that he was the group leader. *He is the eldest,* Naala mused; *perhaps that is why he feels comfortable in this role.*

Azu would moderate any serious conversation and nod stoically before declaring his final conclusion. His booming voice would wake them up in the mornings, and tell them when it was time to retire into their hammocks at night. He would dictate when they moved locations and to where. On certain mornings he would declare that they all needed to 'train'. In a wide clearing with the smell of green wafting through the air, he would walk them through fighting manoeuvres that he guaranteed would help them defend themselves against a chance encounter with the army. Outside of his nonsensical demeanour, he was relatively good at playing the leader. Naala would be lying if she said she had not once believed him. In fact, when she had first joined the group, she was convinced that Azu was a sheep leading a group of lambs aimlessly.

However, when Naala paid closer attention, she soon realised that of the eight people within the group, three of them seemed to be the puppet masters—or, at the very least, knew that the strings existed: Kora, Eni and Madi. From what she could see, all the others were oblivious. These three alone held all the power. They would engineer the conversations with covert but attractive baits that Azu never failed to gleefully pick up. He would then proclaim, with resounding certainty, a conclusion that he had been guided to by the three members. Even his haphazard training sessions were neither haphazard nor his. Every time the fighting sessions occurred, two out of the three members would never fail to be paired together, and during the one-on-one combat Naala would spot them having private conversations.

What could it possibly be? Naala asked herself once again, her legs crossed on the soft grass as she picked up handfuls of stems before throwing them back on the ground. In her lap lay the thick, springy, and deflated mmiri petals that she had just finished suckling for water.

With her thirst quenched, she sat slumped, her eyes glazed over, with a laziness that only the warmest day during the hot season could inspire. Naala had learnt how to look at people without *looking* at people, very early in life. While she may have *appeared* lazy, her mind was not.

As a child, her curiosity had often gotten the best of her. Her grandmother would often scold or smack her softly on the mouth when Naala fired a series of questions out into the world.

'Why does she look like that?'

'What is the real colour of the moon?'

'How many ikos would create a river?'

'Grandma?'

'Nana?!'

Naala had soon learnt to keep her stream of questions locked safely in her mind, and to instead seek the answers with her eyes. Eventually, someone or something would tell her exactly what she needed to hear, and another piece would be slotted into the puzzle.

Naala took a deep breath and sighed with what appeared to be boredom. But Naala was anything but bored.

The group of survivors had taken a small break on their way to a new location in the vast Furuefu forest. Azu had led them to a clearing shrouded by towering branches festooned with dangling vines and large leaves of varying hues. The ground was clustered with dense shrubs, recently grazed by the herd of bushwick that had fled at the sound of the approaching survivors.

Naala watched as the clearing dazzled with greens, yellows, and browns. Shadows cast by the imposing trees cut through the numerous streaks of sunlight. The space comforted her immensely; it was not too difficult for her to feign sleepy boredom as she watched Kora spring up from the ground with strips of fish tucked inside her balled fingers.

Naala twisted her back and stretched as Kora dropped to the ground near a handful of birds, opening her palm and cooing to encourage them to eat. Naala leaned back on her arms while her eyes sauntered over the surroundings; at the corner of her peripheral vision, a black hamerkop bird with a yellow patch on its back dropped into Kora's hand.

Naala's heart tightened as she forced herself not to react. She had only ever known two types of hamerkop birds, the grey ones that the villagers used to send their messages to and fro, and the green ones that were said to reside in the palace, powered by the Mother's crystal to travel long distances. She had never come across a black hamerkop before; it looked strange and awkward amongst the flock of birds competing for scraps of fish meat.

Kora caressed the black bird and coaxed it to open its beak. She gently dropped a strip of fish into its wide mouth, but not before taking something small out of it first. Naala blinked as the girl slipped the small package, discreetly, into her garment. Kora then bounced away from the flock of scrabbling birds, as Naala began to nonchalantly inspect a strand of her own hair, her heart pounding fast as her mind burst into frenzy.

What in goodness name are they up to?

CHAPTER 18

ASILIA WAKES FROM HER SLUMBER

City of Nri

Sinai paused on the polished marble floor of the empty hallway, and watched the bright morning light bounce beautifully off of the white sand pillars, encrusted with golden patterns, the saga of yet another battle. She had found herself, once again, in an obscure section of the palace, somewhere hidden where only those who were lost wandered. The space was deeply calm, inviting, and bathed with a weightless soft light. Unfortunately, Sinai couldn't feel it.

For days now, she had woken to the feeling of heavy pressure on her body. Sinai would clutch at her chest, as she willed herself to take one deep breath. She was finding it increasingly difficult to come to terms with the burden that she had willingly lifted. With each choice, she had walked into her conflicted predicament. Sinai had no one to blame but herself. That thought alone made her restless, desperate to fix the situation or, at the very least, to escape it. So she had started wandering around the palace.

This used to give her a sense of peace. Her mind would dispense all of her endless thoughts, like a soaked *owu* cloth being wrung by strong capable hands. Sinai had spent countless hours walking around the vast palace, learning its obscure crevices and finding rare solitary spots. Sinai would often discover new spaces, people, and artefacts on her walks. However, today she had found nothing. All she had was the same heavy thought that followed her day after day: *I've failed myself.*

A multitude of unanswered questions and fleeting words filled her mind. Ọnye Nyocha . . . was that really what she had become? She didn't feel like one. Sinai felt like a child, taking on a role and acting it out half-heartedly alongside friends that took the play far more seriously. If she was a spy, what did it mean about her mortality, or, worse, her morality? Sinai could very well die on this assignment and, if she did, who would absolve her? Spying was against the law, spying on the Eze was sacrilegious. While these various thoughts circled her mind, one stuck and burnt her at her core.

Why am I even doing this? Sinai finally thought, shaking her head vigorously from side to side. She was tired of asking herself the same questions and, if she was being honest, terrified of knowing the answer.

Grrr . . .

A low and deep inhumane sound materialised behind her, sending a chill through Sinai's body. Her throat closed up and her head felt light. Sinai was terrified to look behind her; whatever had made that sound was not something she wanted to encounter. Sinai turned her head slowly as she clenched her fingers into a tight ball. She looked around the empty hall, shocked to find that there was nothing there. However, she was not at ease. She had felt a shift in the air.

Sinai marched forward. Adrenaline fizzed down her back. She needed to leave, and she needed to leave now. A flurry of movement behind her paralysed her. Sinai felt fear's grip against her throat. She flashed another look behind and shook her head as something caught her eye. Her body reacted far quicker than her mind; her heart quickened and a thick sick feeling dropped in the pit of her stomach. Sinai took a quick breath as she turned to face a large, albeit still, beast. It resembled one of the lions that resided deep in the wild forest; while she had never seen one face-to-face, Sinai had spent many nights reading passages describing the beasts.

It stood large and firm on its four strong legs, and its long slender tail slithered on the marble floor. Locks of beautiful black hair tumbled around its majestic face.

'Lion?' Sinai gasped wordlessly, not entirely sure whether she was calling for help or asking for clarification. The magnificent beast shone in the sunlight, its glossy black coat, unlike anything she had seen on any other of its kind, whispered secrets of wealth and dignity.

Suddenly a strange sensation washed over Sinai; her eyes were locked on the lion and it stared back at her with remarkable focus. It was almost as if the beast was seconds away from opening its mouth to speak to her, its large head cocked to its side and its black round eyes softened with an emotion that resembled understanding.

Sinai's heart pounded in her ears. Her only solace was that everything was completely still; that was, until it wasn't. The beast began to move deliberately. Slowly it placed one paw in front of the other. A ripple flowed through its muscles.

However, that did not last; as the beast grew eager, its pace picked up, until it was almost at a gallop. Sinai's head felt light as a low heavy growl vibrated through the lion's body. Her mind was screaming at her to run, but her body was frozen with fear.

'Asilia!' a voice behind her said, short and snappy, like the finger click that accompanied it. The beast broke its focus, and halted; its large eyes immediately looked towards the direction of the faceless voice. The beast abandoned its pursuit of Sinai and turned abruptly to walk towards the man that summoned it.

Sinai released a wrenching breath, doubled over with her

hands grasping her knees. Her head spun but she forced herself to turn to see who the voice belonged to. As she did, another dose of gut-wrenching fear washed over her . . . the Eze.

He stood before her tall and composed, with the lion rubbing affectionately against his leg. Sinai straightened her back with great unease, her mouth slightly ajar as she searched for words to explain herself . . . before she realised that, in this situation at least, she had done nothing wrong. Displaying guilt would only make her look suspicious which, given what she was involved in, was dangerous. Unsure of what to do, Sinai lowered her eyes to the floor as she brought her crossed palms to her chest cautiously, letting them fall softly towards the Eze. Though her hands shook slightly, she kept them there whilst she bowed.

'Ndewo,' she murmured.

'No need to fear, child, she will not harm you. She only harms the guilty,' the Eze said in a low deep voice, as he ruffled the lion's mane.

Sinai lifted her head and placed her clammy hands by her side. She felt as though she was falling . . . *guilty*: that word was plastered against her head, sewn into her skin, and melted into her blood. *I need to go*, she screamed at her immobile legs. The Eze released a low chuckle as he stepped closer, with Asilia following faithfully by his side.

'So nervous,' he murmured, as he stood over her, his eyes twinkling in delight as though he enjoyed her discomfort. After staring at her for some time, the Eze circled her slowly, increasing the distance between them as he did so.

'I understand. We all have guilt somewhere, over something; even the smallest crimes could make us feel as though we have lost our souls,' he said, trailing off into thought. He stepped towards her abruptly. 'But it's all about balance, see,' he said animatedly, with one finger wagging in the air. 'The impact and reasoning are crucial. To know this, to understand this . . . well, that, my dear, that is to *know* justice.' He paused, searching her face for something, but his eyes darkened when he didn't find it. 'In any case, Asilia is still . . . tired. Ever since she was tasked with delivering justice to Obioma, she has lost herself somewhat.'

Lolo Obioma, Sinai thought frantically. She felt a twinge in her heart as the Eze's heavy words settled on her. What justice did Asillia deliver to the quiet and dutiful queen?

The Eze watched Sinai intently, his eyes brightening as hers widened in horror.

'No one is immune to the call for justice,' he said firmly. 'A price was paid, and my dear Asilia has been spent ever since. In fact, this is the first time I have seen her wandering the palace corridors in decades. She no longer wishes to be *my* overseer of justice,' the Eze murmured distantly. 'Not unless you do something truly gruesome.' He looked back at her, his eyes twinkling once again, his body slightly bent towards Sinai.

Sinai held her breath, afraid that he would be able to smell her fear.

The Eze seemed momentarily lost in thought. 'Well, either that or you happen to have some *ụtọ* plant on you! Nasty business. That's why I banned it from the kingdom; she can be uncontrollable, this girl.' The Eze chuckled as he bent to pat the beast on the head.

Sinai didn't know what to think. In all her time at the palace, she had never actually seen the beast, except in the various artists' depictions scattered around the halls, yet the Eze spoke as though this lion was an old friend that followed him everywhere. She was bursting with questions; after all, this was the most that she had ever spoken to the man in her entire life. *Are you good? Where is the queen? What are your plans? Why did you save us?* But only two words tumbled out of her mouth.

'Thank you.' She wasn't too sure what she was thanking him for: perhaps saving her from the friendly beast, or spending the time to help rationalise her fears, or maybe saving the very existence of humanity.

Whatever it was that she had thanked him for, the Eze seemed to understand. He nodded solemnly before saying, 'You have become more . . . present.' He squinted quizzically. 'Since your fall,' he added.

Sinai was finding it increasingly difficult to breathe. 'Yes, I am present now—more present than before . . . the fall . . . I suppose it . . . well, it woke me up,' Sinai replied, her head pounding as she fought hard to contain the screams within.

The Eze's smooth, deep brown skin revealed neither his countless years on earth, nor his thoughts on Sinai's response. 'Yes,' he replied, nodding. 'You are very lucky.'

Sinai lowered her eyes, terrified of locking gazes with him; she was convinced he could look into her soul.

'Very,' she replied quickly.

'That, or Meekulu is very skilful,' the Eze said quietly.

Unable to stop herself, Sinai's head sprang up at the mention of Meekulu's name. She almost kicked herself right then and there. *Indifferent!* she yelled at herself. *Be indifferent!*

The Eze's eyes lit up once again in amusement.

'Or both,' he suggested, as he walked past her, hands clasped behind his back and Asilia following at his heels.

CHAPTER 19

THE MIDNIGHT MEETING

Furuefu Forest

The group had retired early for the night. They had spent the last two days trying to gain as much distance northwards as they could. After a brief conversation with Eni, Azu had told the group that they needed to move.

'We've been in one spot for too long,' Azu had announced. 'We've become lazy and complacent, moving our camps at a stone's throw from each other. We're leaving trails and evidence, and very soon, just as we lay like sloths, the army will come and wipe us away!'

Eni's words had sounded slightly forced on the big man's tongue, but their effect was still impactful. The group unanimously decided to embark on the journey.

Naala had found herself flirting with the idea of deserting the group for the hundredth time before their departure. But, once again, the allure of discovering the group's secret had kept her tightly bound to the survivors.

She *needed* to know their plan. She suspected that it might be much better than her own. The amount of energy they spent keeping it a secret exceeded anything she had done. If their plan was indeed better, then she wanted to get involved. The urge to be useful in the face of the senseless killings had not left her; rather it had grown stronger with each passing day, and over time it had also become intertwined with her desire to unmask the survivors' secret plans, as though they were one and the same.

As the survivors traversed the lush green forest, the hot sun pounded on their sweat-drenched backs, and their feet throbbed with fatigue, but the fear of encountering the army kept them going. They found some solace as they waded through patches of knee-high, moist grass, with water buds that worked to cool their legs, inflamed with activity and the relentless sun. The wind whistled through the emerald trees, bringing with it the deep smell of damp warm wood coupled with rich soil and sweet flowers.

Bright sunrays pierced the green clouds of leaves and shone brightly in their eyes. But they did not falter. They marched on resolutely. Any fanciful dreams of the strong rhinos or even the sturdy ox that might have helped them were immediately chased away by the knowledge that such large animals would impede their on-going need to be stealthy.

They had only stopped to collect bark from one of Anyanwu's *uchie* trees.

'These trees have not always been like this, you know,' Azu said to Naala, as he placed one of his large hands on the black soot tree trunk.

Naala looked back at him with her eyes squinted in confusion and fatigue. *Surely this man is not going to recite the legend that every child in Igbakwu has learnt after their fourth year?* she thought in exhaustion.

'When the fire goddess still walked the earth they were wreathed in flame constantly—not black and broken as they are now. Imagine the sight of a tree constantly coated with undying flames.' Azu whistled.

Naala had imagined it, countless times, in fact; she had always been fascinated by the fire trees. When the Mother died and the god's vanished from the earth, Anyawu's uchie trees became flameless. The once blood-red trees were now dry and covered in black soot. The Kingdom of Nri soon discovered that it could still obtain its beloved ọkụ flames using the dried bark of the dead uchie trees. Caressing the bark in specific motions would throw ọkụ flames into the air; a small scrap of bark could keep Naala's family going for weeks on end. They would use it to cook, to stay warm, to light up dark nights.

'Yes, uncle, my grandmother actually tol—'

'Not just that,' Azu interrupted, causing Naala's blood to run hot with annoyance. 'But even the ọkụ flames themselves . . . they used to be amazing. You could just gather them at ease and mould them into anything you desired. Anyone could have been a flame tamer. Now we only have these *ye-ye* circles, but back then it was magnificent.'

'Yes, I know; thank you, Uncle,' Naala said, taking a deep breath as Azu rolled his eyes.

'Sure you know, because I just told you,' he sneered, punctuating his statement with a forced laugh that crept up Naala's spine.

She smiled tightly.

'You know,' Naala said nonchalantly. 'The castle still apparently has quite magnificent ọkụ shapes. The flame tamers there can make flames as beautiful as living art, I've been told.' She enjoyed seeing the slight bulge in the big man's eyes.

'No—' he started.

'It's true, Uncle,' she insisted.

'What do you know?' he bellowed.

'More than you, it seems,' Eni chuckled. 'She's right. I travelled to the castle once when I was young. I've seen them; they're quite a sight.' Azu huffed and stormed off. 'Never mind him,' Eni added softly to Naala.

'I never do.' She shrugged as she looked at the broken tree, carefully collecting some of its fragile bark. 'Have you really been to the castle?' she asked curiously. Long before the village attacks, she had always dreamt of going to the city herself, however, even in her dreams, she hadn't imagined a world where she could actually enter the castle itself.

'My cousin is a servant there; he snuck me in one time,' he replied, as she nodded.

'It must have been amazing to see the ọkụ shapes,' Naala said, not knowing why she wanted to carry on the conversation.

'Yes, but it's also sad.'

'Sad?'

'They—the people in the castle—they are all so . . . wasteful. Here, we only use what we need, but *there* they use up what they can. They can use a whole uchie tree, purely for the entertainment of the senior lords. Year after year the people of Nri take scraps from these dead uchie trees that produce no new offspring. It's a finite resource now, yet they're eating away at it as though we still live in a world where Anyawu can simply conjure more. Soon enough there will be none left, and then what will we do?' Eni watched as the survivors carefully broke off and stored pieces of the sacred bark, saying silent prayers to the lost fire goddess as they did so.

'We'll reap the consequences,' Naala replied bitterly, as Eni flashed a look back at her.

'You won't; I'm sure you can get your monkey friend to find some uchie bark for you regardless.' He teased, as Naala looked up to see Enwe swinging through the trees, following the survivors on their new pursuit.

Naala was happy to see her little friend. She had begun to notice that a dialogue of some sort was growing between her and the monkey. Recently, if she pointed or gestured at an object in Enwe's presence, the little monkey would scramble to bring it to her. At times, she wouldn't even have to point at it. It was bizarre, but Naala enjoyed it immensely.

In due time, they had finally put what Azu described as an adequate distance between themselves and their previous camp, and the group released a sigh of relief.

They all slumped down in their new location. Once their aching muscles were given respite, they were reluctant to move. One by one, people gave in, and hooked their hammocks to the nearest trees, before climbing up and falling instantly into a deep sleep.

Naala had never found it so easy to drift into sleep. She dreamt of orange and blue zebras dancing across a blackened sky as a group of elephants sang one of her favourite childhood songs.

An eagle nests in the iroko tree—a rare giant tree!
While other birds bath with glee, glee, glee,
The eagle watches high in the grand iroko tree.
The King of Birds swoops with glee, glee, glee.
A magnificent plumage! Out of the iroko—

One by one the elephants stopped singing. After a brief moment of stillness, they crashed down onto Naala's head and she woke with a jolt, catching herself just before she fell out of her hammock.

She sighed softly in relief. Slightly obscured behind the spread of dark leaves, she could still see the night sky adorned with blinking stars. She allowed her focus to blur and the promise of sleep swept over her; that is, until she heard movements in the hammocks around her.

Naala pressed her eyes shut as she listened to the people moving out of their hammocks and creeping down their tree trunks. Naala felt an intense urge to jump up and point at them accusingly. She knew it! She knew that something was going on. However, rather than blowing her cover, she chose instead to lie completely still. Tonight she was going to discover exactly what they were up to.

Naala lay in silence as she waited for the last of the scuffles to die down, her ears straining to gauge the direction of the fading footsteps.

She crept out of her hammock, climbed down the tree, and stood amongst endless rows of long brown tree trunks, illuminated with the soft yellow lights of glowing insects, which hung in the air like a bejewelled cloud. The ground was soaked with the dim fluorescent green glow of the bulbous *ero* fungus. Clusters of it were scattered between sturdy leaves and throughout the forest. Naala had always been fascinated by the ero, a harmless fungi that was muted and dull during the day, but at night filled the forest with lights. Her uncle had told her that the god, Agwu, had blessed the ero centuries ago, so that the mood of anyone passing by them would alter the colour of their glowing lights. Naala was surrounded by a sea of soft green light, the neutral and natural glow of the ero. Deeper into the forest, Naala spotted a burst of yellow light. *Activity*, she thought, before setting off to follow the trail.

After she'd walked for a few minutes, the ero adjusted back to its sea-green glow. *They've stopped*, she thought.

The trees were becoming increasingly sparse, and Naala could see a small clearing in the forest ahead. Naala squinted before suddenly ducking behind a tree; she had seen them: the three puppet masters, huddled together in an intense discussion.

Naala let her heartbeat settle before looking for a way to get closer without being noticed. She poked her head around the thick tree trunk; they were all looking intently at Kora who was lost in some sort of tale, her hands moving animatedly.

Naala came out into the open and crept towards a closer tree, pressing against its trunk as she listened intently.

'So what is the update?' Eni asked.

'Madi . . .' Kora said carefully.

'No,' Madi warned, as a ruby glow emitted from the ero clusters at his feet.

'He is the only one, Madi—the only one—and he is in the *general's* squad. This is not something we can just overlook . . . please try to understand.'

'Understand? There is nothing to unde—'

'It would be madness to throw away this opportunity.'

'He is not an opportunity. He's my brother and I said no.'

'You have to look at the bigger picture here—we don't have any other options. They have killed off all the villagers who had joined the army before—before all of this. We ca—'

'—and you want to add Emeka to the list now?' Madi fumed.

'Madi,' Eni said quietly, his deep voice solid and final. Madi took a step back and groaned loudly.

'Did you tell them?' Madi said, after a long pause, as he drew his hands away from his face. They remained silent.

'Did you tell them?' Madi repeated, his voice slightly louder.

'Of course she did,' Eni replied sharply. 'Listen, Madi, I understand your pain, but there's no need to blame Kora. She is simply the messenger here.'

'Is she, though? Kora has wanted this from the very beginning. She was the one who told them that Emeka was in the Eze's army. This has been her doing!'

'Madi, we all decided to tell them about Emeka,' Eni noted. 'We all want to see this thing come to an end, we all want justice.'

'I don't know what she writes to those people and neither do you . . . none of us do! This is not a *team*. There is no *we* when it comes to those messages—it's just her and *them*.'

'Madi, the three of us are in this together!' Kora exclaimed, inciting a burst of pale yellow light from the silent ero. 'I'm on *your* side. I'm sorry to say this, but you are really letting your emotions cloud your judgement here. Okay, yes, the plan is not perfect or ideal—but it's all that we have—Emeka is our *only* option. If you could just take a step back and believe that he can do this—because he can, and he will. Do you hear me? Emeka can do this—and when he does, we will all be free from this terror.'

'Stop talking about him like you know him,' Madi snapped. 'You don't know him at all. None of you do. He is not an option—he is my little brother! I know what he is capable of doing. You don't.'

Kora opened her mouth briefly before shrinking back with her arms crossed over her stomach.

'Did you tell them that he is just a child?' Madi implored. 'That he is weak, that he only joined that bloody army to prove something to our father? Did you tell them that when he spared me during our village attack—after watching our father die at the hands of his comrades—it was the bravest thing he had ever done, and even that was out of shame, not honour. You want so badly for this to be a solution that you won't *listen* to me. He can't do this.' His voice was thick with emotion. He paused for a moment, but no one interjected.

Naala, with her back still firmly pressed against the thick tree trunk, slowly turned her head to the right, hoping to catch a glimpse of what was going on. To her frustration, she could not see a thing. She would have to step outside the shield of the large tree to see them, but she couldn't risk getting caught. Naala was starving for more information; she had yet to fully grasp what was going on.

'Madi, with all due respect, that is not for you to say,' Eni eventually said. 'He is your brother and I understand that, but your brother has made a choice—a choice, I would wager, that all of us would make in his position.'

'He is just a child,' Madi added quietly.

'He has reached his fourteenth year, Madi. He is young, yes, but he is no longer a child. He has witnessed, perhaps even participated in, the killing of innocent villagers. He wants to escape, but he also wants to help. He *needs* this . . . he needs to feel absolved of some of the atrocities that he has committed. Wouldn't you?'

'He will die,' Madi said sombrely, as the ever-present mist of floating, glowing insects cast muted shadows on his downcast face.

'He won't. But if he does,' Eni said carefully. 'Surely it would be better than remaining in such a soulless environment.'

'He will not die,' Kora added, her voice sharp and resolute. 'He will steal the key and save us all. Your father's name will be upheld for generations to come. Madi, you need to believe this. They would not have presented us with this option if they thought it was doomed; they would have found another way.'

'We don't even know who *they* are,' Madi sighed, frustrated.

'We know that we would not have survived as long as we have without their help,' Kora pointed out. 'Madi, you know this.'

'What do you *mean* by that? So because they've told us how to collect some food, and given us a map of supposedly safe locations, I should now offer up my brother like a goat ready for the slaughter?'

'No, Madi . . . I'm just saying they're not the bad people.'

'They're not the good people either,' Madi muttered.

Another uncomfortable silence settled over the group and then Madi began to move towards Naala. She held her breath as he unknowingly brushed past her.

The silence continued until Kora whispered, 'What if he's right . . . we would have lost the only contact in the army and Madi . . . would have lost his brother. He would never forgive me.'

'Kora, you told them, didn't you?' Eni asked swiftly. 'You told them that Emeka was young and . . . you told them, right?'

'How could you even ask me that?' Kora responded.

'How could I not? This could be the everything—the difference between our survival or demise. If we get this key, we finally get a chance to fight back—a real chance to avenge our families. I desperately want this to work and I know you do too. If it stood in the way of this mission, I'm not sure I would have told them, which is why I have to ask. Did you?'

Another brief, tense silence fell between them.

'This conversation is over,' Kora suddenly announced. 'I'll see you in the morning.'

Again, Naala heard footsteps coming towards her way. More footsteps than she had heard previously. *They must both be leaving.* She tensed, willing herself to be as still and silent as possible. Naala strained her ears, and closed her eyes. All she could hear was the soothing light symphony of the night's insects, luminous frogs, and restless beasts as they prowled around in the starry midnight.

Naala stared into the night wistfully, as the low light from the glowing insects sparkled around her. She was finally alone with her thoughts but she couldn't begin to process what she had heard.

She had known that the group had a secret, but she had not, in her wildest dreams, imagined it to be to this large. They were planning something, something big, something that could bring down the system that had destroyed her village. Naala could not believe it. She didn't know what to think, other than knowing that, somehow, she needed to get involved; she needed to help. The thought of fighting back and avenging those that had been stolen from her was so powerful that, for the first time in weeks, she felt like herself again. She took a sharp breath and placed her head against the tree. Suddenly a hand cupped her mouth and pulled her backwards before she could scream.

'What are you doing here? Eni growled in her ear.

CHAPTER 20

THE GIRL WHO FOUGHT

City of Nri

The news that Sinai had been waiting on for days, weeks even, finally came knocking at her door.

'Ndewo, Lolo Sinai,' Chisi said, placing her crossed palms over her chest and letting them fall in greeting.

Sinai repeated the gesture back to her, before waiting attentively for her to speak.

'Meekulu said that she has the soup that you requested,' Chisi said, as her eyes darted into Sinai's bare room.

Chisi had taken a liking to collecting Sinai. Sinai knew that the girl was busy with the hundreds of various errands that the kitchen piled on her. She could have easily sent a hamerkop bird in her place with messages from Meekulu, yet Chisi always took the time to fetch her. Sinai often wondered what Chisi was hoping to find, something salacious like a sleeping naked man, or something expensive enough to steal, like a large pretty jewel.

Sinai's curiosity had finally got the best of her. 'Chisi, I'm more than happy to see you, but surely you have better things to do with your time than coming to send me messages?'

Chisi's eyes widened before she looked down in embarrassment.

'Oh, I'm sorry,' Sinai exclaimed. 'I didn't mean—I just feel bad that you have to run up and down on account of me!'

'Lolo Sinai, I really don't mind. I like your room,' Chisi replied, smiling shyly.

'Really? Why?' Sinai pondered. Her room was standard, perhaps even a little subpar for a noble; surely Chisi would have had a glance into one of the other more prestigious rooms on one of her many journeys to fetch her. Chisi bit her lip as though wrestling with something in her mind.

'Well . . . I like . . . I like the air . . . the air dances in your room,' she finally said, darting her eyes from Sinai to the window.

'The air dances?' Sinai replied, as she caught her breath. For a brief moment, Chisi's statement reminded her of the episodes that she had experienced while taking Meekulu's healing serum. Once Sinai had fully recovered and stopped taking the mixture, those *episodes* had subsided. She had since put those thoughts to the back of her mind; after all, she was far more preoccupied with her Ọnye Nyocha assignment. She had yet to even broach the subject with Meekulu, and now that those side-effects had come to a stop, she had little incentive to do so.

Sinai peered at the area by her window that Chisi kept glancing at. Sure enough, small gusts of wind whirled around in light and intricate spirals, but Sinai knew that they were not what they seemed.

Sinai smiled to herself. She lived in the corner of the grand castle, just at the point where the shade and the sun competed for attention. She had read once that the air acted strange at such points where the light and shadows intertwined.

'Oh, Chisi . . . I wouldn't worry about that. It is quite normal for the air to do such things near shaded areas,' Sinai noted.

Chisi nodded but still bit her lip. Sinai could see that the girl still had a lot to say.

'Yes . . .' the girl said carefully. 'But I have not seen anything like that in any other area in the castle.'

'I understand what you are saying, Chisi, but trust me, it's *sayensi*. I'll give you a parchment on it sometime,' Sinai replied, as Chisi's eyes widened slightly in fright at the mention of a parchment. Sinai had seen that same look cross the faces of many servants who had caught her reading. It was a look of fear, caused by encountering something completely unknown, so unknown that dark thoughts would fill the void caused by unanswered questions. Suddenly that thing became something bigger, something shrouded with infinite mystery and dark brewing magic. Sinai suddenly felt bad for offering the parchment; the girl probably couldn't read a single word of Nsibidi.

'Well, since you like the room so much, are you sure you wouldn't like to come in?' Sinai asked for the hundredth time, but Chisi shook her head vigorously.

'Oh no, not at all, I should be getting back,' Chisi repeated as usual; it was the same phrase she had said every time Sinai extended an invite. 'But . . . you are coming? Yes? For the soup?' Chisi edged deeper into the hallway, her slender black arms beckoning Sinai forward.

Sinai's 'soup'—the disfigurement lotion that she had sworn an ọbara oath for—was ready.

'I just need to finish up with some things here; I'll come to meet Meekulu a little later.'

'Oh, but she will be busy later, and the soup will get cold. Are you sure?'

'Yes, I'm sure. I'll be there shortly. Please do not worry,' Sinai said, as she closed the door softly on Chisi's face.

She laid down on her akwa nest, her gaze glued to the high stone ceilings that encased her. She watched as the patterns on the hay-coloured roof began to slowly dance before her eyes. She had spent weeks salivating over the prospect of seeking retribution for her fall, and now that it was here, within her grasp, she was completely unenthused. The social events, the games, the lion, the Eze . . . all of it had drained her.

Stop being stupid, a voice in her mind hissed; *go and collect that concoction!*

If she didn't, she would have become a Ọnye Nyocha for nothing. She would have risked her life, perhaps even her soul, for absolutely no gain.

Sinai sighed and rose from the akwa nest. She could not afford to waste away in a sea of regret and self-indulgent thoughts. As heavy as the results of her choices were, they were still her choices, and the only way she could alleviate the pressure building within her, was to tackle the problems that these choices had created.

Sinai decided that she would carry on with her plan; she would use the disfigurement lotion, and once she had successfully gotten Ina out of the way, she would work to renegotiate her ọbara oath with Meekulu. Her task had been to spy on the Eze, and she had, to some extent, done this. Surely Sinai would not be crossing a line if she asked for further . . . clarification? Perhaps a new clause that would specify a realistic timeframe or goal—something to make this task achievable and finite. Sinai was certain that the old woman would agree; Meekulu was in no way unreasonable.

Sinai rushed out her room and headed towards Meekulu's kitchens. Delighted by a new sense of hope and purpose, she decided to take an alternative route. This route had always filled her with deep warmth because it took her through the gardens.

The palace was grand and beautiful, and left her in awe, but its cold clean pillars and marble floors were no match for the beauty of the wild vegetation that sprawled freely in its gardens.

The palace had five large gardens, where the most wonderful flowers and intricate trees were planted and pruned only by those appointed by the Eze. People would visit the gardens to enter a state of serenity when the pressures of the palace were too much to bear. Musicians would practise sensational melodies, inspired into rich creativity by the colourful petals and fluttering leaves. Students would theorise in whispered discussions about the formation of the stars and the distance between them, drunk on the endless mental nudges that the gardens offered.

Sinai strolled through slowly, her eyes gazing over the bright soft flowers, as the garden breathed in unison with her.

Something is not right, her mind concluded, as she stopped abruptly. She had been so preoccupied with her fall for the past few weeks that she had completely forgotten the dream that had led her to the window in the first place. It came rushing back to her in seconds and, now that she remembered it, she couldn't understand how she could have ever forgotten. The dream was so vivid that she could practically smell the world that it had presented to her.

Sinai could see the depths of its colours, its beauty, and feel its overwhelming sense of home. She couldn't understand it. She had spent her whole life within the grand palace; how could any other place feel more like home than the palace itself?

It seemed to her as though the palace and its garden were merely imitations of what they should be. Sinai started to walk again, her legs moving slowly, her heart still lost in her thoughts. The dream meant something, it felt as real as she did, and yet she couldn't understand it at all. *Perhaps Meekulu would have the answer*, Sinai thought, but something told her that this was likely to be beyond the old woman's capabilities.

Soon enough, Sinai reached the kitchen, but Meekulu was nowhere to be seen. Sinai stood alone in the empty room, among opened bags of powders and spices, mortars with half-ground corn, and a circular ọkụ flame lighting up in the stove. It was clear that Meekulu had begun her preparations for the Eze's breakfast, but for some reason had stopped abruptly and abandoned the meal entirely. Sinai turned to the sundial in one corner, its golden cone coated with markings that gleamed as the small ọkụ ball hovered about it, imitating the sun.

'Hmm,' she said, as she walked over to it. She saw that it was dangerously close to the time that the Eze requested his morning meal.

Sinai looked around nervously.

'Meekulu?' she called, but no one replied. All that she could hear was a light chatter, punctuated by the birds whistling outside, and the brass clangs of pots and pans in the other kitchens.

Sinai stepped out of Meekulu's kitchen and walked along the long hall leading to a number of rooms, where cooks were busy at work. Those who caught a glimpse of her in the door, stared openly, their eyes shining with curiosity and gossip. Sinai stopped at one of the doors and poked her head in. The commotion settled to a stop as the ladies looked back at her incredulously. No noble had ever entered their kitchens before.

'Please, where is Meekulu?' Sinai asked hastily, trying and failing to remain calm. They looked back at her wide-eyed. Not one of them replied. Eventually Sinai moved away to look around the hallway desperately.

Where is Chisi? she thought; surely she would know where the old woman was, or at the very least be able to get clear answers from the women down here.

Sinai had reached the end of the hall and had found neither Chisi nor Meekulu.

She was about to turn away when she heard a small sound, a whimper, coming from one of the resting rooms.

'Hush, my child,' Meekulu's deep soothing voice said out of nowhere.

Sinai nearly jumped out of her skin, before following the voice like a starved animal that had suddenly caught wind of food. Meekulu's voice led her through the last room, a small empty kitchen with a door slightly ajar. Sinai nudged at it and found a small resting room, not at all dissimilar from the room she had recovered in after her fall.

Meekulu sat on a stool by the wooden akwa nest, her hands

rubbing a pungent oil against the temple of the disturbed, young woman who thrashed her bruised limbs. Her garment was torn and stained with blood, her hair dishevelled, and her eyes wild with sorrow. Her long locs draped over the side of the nest and pooled on the ground.

Ina—the beautiful woman who held her head high and spoke with sharp intelligence and unbridled ambition—was unrecognisable.

Sinai stood at the door, motionless. She didn't know what to think or feel. For months now, Ina had been her enemy, the bane of her existence, and one of the principal causes of her discomfort; yet here the girl was, broken and in pain, and Sinai felt an urge to sit and cry with her.

'What happened to her?' Sinai whispered into the room.

Neither of them acknowledged Sinai's question; instead, Meekulu brought a wooden bowl with a bright-blue liquid swimming in it near to Ina's lips.

'Shh shh, be still, child,' Meekulu said softly, as she tipped the bowl into Ina's bruised mouth. 'This will ease the pain.'

Ina let the liquid slide down her throat as streams of tears rolled down her face. Soon enough Ina fell into a deep sleep. The look of anguish and pain had been wiped off her face, but the bruises and cuts remained as a reminder that something terrible had happened.

Sinai took a step forward and stood behind Meekulu, her eyes stinging with emotion that she fought to control.

'Meekulu, what happened?'

'The world is a strange place, Sinai. It can be cruel and brutal, especially if you are a woman.'

'I don't understand,' Sinai said quietly.

'Ina is a strong woman,' Meekulu said, as she wiped Ina's wounds with a white cloth soaked in a medicated concoction. 'In weak men that inspires a need to tear them down. The man uses the closest tool he has in an attempt to break them down.' She paused for a moment, and held the girl's hand, turning it palm up as she leaned closer. After a moment she resumed tending to her wounds.

'She fought. She fought hard,' Meekulu murmured.

Sinai looked at Ina's battered body. *She was always fighting*, she thought sadly.

'I can help her to heal her body, but only she can heal her mind, and that takes incredible strength,' Meekulu said as one tear rolled down her wrinkled cheek.

'Who did this?' Sinai asked, her voice thicker than usual. Enemy or not, Ina had been hurt in an inconceivable way. Any man who could do that to a woman deserved nothing but the worst of outcomes.

'Chief Ojo,' Meekulu muttered, her face darkened with anger as she wrung out the blood-stained cloth into a separate waste bucket.

Chief Ojo was a large loud man who often slammed his fat fist against the table at dinners, sending tremors through the wood. His face constantly shone with grease as though he woke up every morning and smeared palm oil over it. He had taken eight wives, and each one wore the same look of resignation and shame when they were chosen to attend a royal function with him, their hands shaking for fear of upsetting him somehow and sparking his short temper.

Sinai looked at Ina's broken body. He must have asked her to be his ninth wife. Everyone knew that Obi Ife was no longer interested in Ina, so naturally new suitors had come to stake their claim. Ina would have laughed in his face, and why shouldn't she? He might have been a chief, but he was a lowly one, controlling but a small segment of the wheat plantations. He was more than twice her age, a vile man who had a reputation for mistreating his many wives. While Ina, on the other hand, was beautiful, young, and conniving; equipped with a wit strong enough to help her husband reach previously unattainable heights. The fact that he felt he could ask for her hand was an insult in itself. Angered by her rebuttal, he must have sought a way to break her down; perhaps he thought that once rumours started swirling, she would become undesirable to any man, and then would run back to him.

Sinai felt her blood boil. An unfamiliar emotion crept through her body; it felt strange and foreign, but she embraced it all the same. The idea of such a man, of such a notion, made her want to scream. She wanted to curse at the heavens; she wanted to yell out abusive words and shout horrid insults. Instead she simply said, 'Meekulu, where can I obtain the ụtọ plant?'

CHAPTER 21

THE HEAD GENERAL'S KEY

Furuefu Forest

'Speak,' Eni snapped, with his hand still cupped against Naala's mouth. Naala tried to pull away from his iron-firm grasp but found that she could not.

How am I supposed to do that? she thought, exasperated, as her eyes rolled to the starry night. After another failed attempt to free herself, Naala bit down, hard. Eni yelped and backed away.

'What is wrong with you?' Eni muttered as he examined his hand. 'I think you drew blood.'

'You were the one that told me speak!' Naala retorted. 'How did you expect me to do that with your hand over my mouth?'

Her mouth pursed into a scowl and her dark skin glowed in the soft light emitted by the insects.

'Well, now that your mouth is free—speak.'

'What exactly do you want to speak about, Eni?

'What did you hear?'

'What did I hear?'

Eni stalked towards her furiously and pressed her hard against the tree. His thick eyebrows were forced together in a pronounced frown, but behind his eyes she could sense conflict.

'Get off me,' she exclaimed. 'You need to learn how to use your strength responsibly. You're not a small man, Eni, and there's no need to throw me around like a straw doll.'

'I didn't—' he began, as he loosened his grip, only to tighten it as soon as a smile played on Naala's lips. 'This is not a joke, Naala, this is serious—I need you tell me what you heard,' he stressed.

Naala found herself struck by the intensity of his gaze. His slanted eyes with slightly heavy eyelids stood out against his broad face. His prominent cheekbones made him seem as though he was always smiling, even though he rarely did. Least of all now, with flashes of anger within him.

'Why does it matter?' Naala scoffed. 'What do you think I'm going to do? Run off and tell the Eze about your secret plan? That *man* and his army massacred my village. I would die before I got in the way of the abara that could pierce his heart.' Naala pushed Eni away. The ero fungi scattered around them began to glow crimson.

The moon lit up the right side of his face, and his forehead furrowed, creating harsh shadows.

'I suppose so . . .' he said quietly, before taking a step back. He sighed. 'It's sad, isn't it? The lack of trust in this new world, even amongst friends?'

'You think we're friends?' Naala replied, without thinking.

Eni looked amused.

'Well, I was not actually talking about you. I was referring to the group that you were just spying on,' he replied.

'Oh. Well, I didn't mean . . .' Naala began, before clearing her throat, her cheeks hot with shame, 'It—your statement was very confusing . . . I wasn't trying to assume that you and I were friends or anything. I just—'

'I would say that we are friends, despite your biting and eavesdropping,' he said, taking a step towards her.

Naala cleared her throat.

'You mentioned trust . . . well, that is already difficult under the best circumstances. I imagine it's close to impossible when you create a dynamic where everything you do together is shrouded in secrets? Like Azu; what exactly is the point of having him and the others around if you don't want to get them involved?'

The clouds parted and a pale mist of light hovered between them.

'Do you know how many times Azu nearly killed the group?' he suddenly asked.

Naala laughed softly. *What an absurd thing to say*, she thought.

'No, really,' Eni replied with a smile, pulled into Naala's easy chuckle. He stopped abruptly before he could join in. 'It's really not funny. These are dangerous times and people like Azu or those that gravitate towards his loud baseless rhetoric . . . well, they are no longer *safe*. If we abandon them, then they die. If we include them in our plans, then they slow us down, or, worse, jeopardise us.'

Images of her village laughing off her warnings came to Naala's mind. Chinedu's mother, in particular, with her hands on her hips and her piercing eyes. If Naala could have manipulated each and every one of them into following her orders, would she? *Of course*, she realised. Her heart leapt at the thought of it. Imagine, just imagine, if she had somehow managed to save them. If she had not failed. If her message had not been smeared with erratic breaths, dripping sweat and years of wayward behaviour.

'I see,' Naala said softly.

He opened his mouth to say something, but after some cooling thoughts decided against it.

'You should get back to sleep,' he finally said.

'Can you give me more detail of your plan? I doubt that I'd be able to get to bed with all of this just buzzing around in my head!' she exclaimed.

His eyes lingered on her lips as she spoke.

'Fine, yes—but before I do, tell me what you thought about the conversation that you did not hear,' he replied.

'Why?'

'It would be good to discuss it with someone not emotionally involved, someone more objective,' he explained.

Naala's forehead furrowed. Her family had been killed in a vicious attack by the Eze's army; how could she be objective in a conversation about a way to fight back? She felt an urge to argue this point, but she was already so tired. Her prior excitement about the whole situation was steadily dying. Right now all she needed was a goodnight's sleep to settle her thoughts, and sort out her conclusions.

'Your group is going to fall apart when Madi's brother fails,' she noted after a while.

'Who says he is going to fail?'

'Madi—and he has far more insight into his brother's character than any of you.'

'He's afraid of his brother getting hurt. That's understandable.'

'No, he's not. I mean, yes, he might not want his brother to die, but that's not what he's afraid of; he's afraid of his brother dying *without honour*,' Naala replied. 'Those raised marks on his body—' Naala gestured to her forearms, '—they are symbols of the Mpako tribe. We had a guest from there once. Dying with honour is vital for them—it's everything. Death for the Mpako tribe is not a loss, not as you or I would perceive it. The Mpako people believe that if they die with honour then they will be transported to another life, another world, like ours but better. They believe that they will all meet again in this other life, and so death is nothing more than a long trip—as long as the person in question dies with honour. A death without honour results in the ultimate death. The person will never reach their loved ones again. Madi fears that his brother will experience ultimate death; he fears that he will fail.'

'He doesn't know. He can't be certain.'

'My odds are with the man who grew up with the boy. I'd wager that he knows more than you.'

'But he's clouded—'

'No, you are. You are clouded by your need for Madi's brother to succeed.'

'Perhaps, but what if I'm not—we should not let an opportunity like this pass us by. If Madi's brother can get the key, then we have access to the army's weapons—all of them, including those that have been enchanted with the Mother's crystal, no less! We can raid them, leave them defenceless and arm ourselves. The Eze is powerful, yes, but if we have the palace weapons, then we have *something*. If, for some time at least, his army is defenceless, we have a *chance*; surely that's worth taking a risk.'

Naala's eyes widened. *So that's the significance of the key,* she thought.

It was a grand plan, perhaps even foolish. The Eze controlled the all-powerful Ndụ crystal. He could do things that they couldn't even dream about. No one truly knew the extent of his powers, but they were enough to kill the Mother. Who knew what he could do, even with a weapon-less army. Naala's mouth started to water and a sweet dose of adrenaline pounded through her body, as she thought, *But he's not a god, he's not invincible, and even if he was, wasn't he just a man when he defeated the Earth Mother?* Perhaps it could work; either way it certainly offered more of a solution than anything else she had in mind. The ero on the ground gleamed a low, luminous yellow and a flurry of glowing insects swooped towards the brightening fungi.

Naala said, 'I agree; you shouldn't waste this opportunity, especially not by leaving it solely to a boy who you know is doomed to fail. You need to put a better plan in place.'

'Any suggestions?'

'I can't give you all the answers,' Naala said with a sigh, before breaking into a wide yawn. 'Your turn. Tell me everything.'

'I've already told you—'

'You've given me tiny bites; I want to know *everything*.'

'There's too much to say to fit into one short night. I know for a fact that you are just as tired as I am. We should discuss this further, at breakfast.'

'Breakfast? Why not now?' Naala argued. 'Listen, I am no Azu; I will not allow you to keep me ignorant under the pretence of protection.'

'No, you are not Azu,' he murmured softly, his eyes trailing over her face. Naala frowned and he broke into an unabashed smile. 'Azu, for one, is asleep. Please, Naala, I'm telling you that we will discuss this tomorrow.'

Her eyes watering as she tried to suppress yet another yawn. Perhaps one more day wouldn't kill her.

'Okay,' she muttered in irritation.

'Great.' He beamed. 'You shouldn't be so disheartened; there's a rumour that we're having smoked plantain tomorrow. That's two things that you can look forward to.' His dark prying eyes sparkled with delight.

Naala paused and let the idea of plantain ripple through her mind. She hadn't had plantain for weeks, since even before she left home; the patch near her village had been spoiled by pests. She had been waiting patiently for the new crop to ripen.

'I said fine. We can discuss at breakfast,' she said swiftly, before marching back to her hammock, leaving Eni smiling.

CHAPTER 22

THE TIMBUKAN SCHOLAR

City of Nri

Sinai was finding it incredibly painful to move her head. She had smoothed her hair over with a mixture of flaxseed gel and almond oil and then clamped it down with a strong hair band, leaving her hair sleek at the head before it sprouted out into a large, thick, dark cloud. She wore a blue and gold headtie that matched her new garment. It fit tighter than she would have liked, but her aim was to distract people with the shape of her body, so they would pay little attention to what she was doing with her hands. Sinai clutched her bag. She couldn't afford to leave it unattended, but she was terrified of it all the same. The small wild plant hidden within her bag was meant for only one person: Chief Ojo.

Sinai looked around the elegant hall, but could not see him. Her heart skipped a beat as she noted that behind the large bronzed pillars the sky was darkening. A beautiful array of subdued reds, deep indigos and pinks smeared the horizon.

It's getting late, he should have been here by now, Sinai thought frantically. *Unless,* she pondered, as she placed her hand on her chest, *unless he has followed the Eze to the Ofala festival.*

The Ofala festival took place every year, to commemorate the Eze's victory over the Earth Mother. Each year the Obis and their chosen elite guests accompanied the Eze to Udi where years ago he had taken the Ndu crystal. The lower nobles left behind in the palace celebrated the festival all the same. A party was thrown on every Nkwo, the second day of the week, until the Eze returned home to his throne.

Obi Ife had asked Sinai to come as his guest to Ofala; it was the first time that she had been invited, but she had respectfully declined. She had been certain that Chief Ojo would remain in the concrete palace. He was not of high enough rank to warrant an invite himself, and his disturbing reputation preceded him, leaving little chance of someone else extending their invite to him.

With the Eze gone, Sinai had the perfect opportunity to right the wrong done to Ina. Sinai hated what Chief Ojo had done to Ina with a passion that burned as hot as fire. Somewhere underneath that rage, Sinai felt guilt. Wasn't it she who had wished for Ina's downfall? How many times had Sinai been told to be careful about her spoken words. She had been taught that words were the fabric of reality, shaping the world one spell at a time. Perhaps Ina's ill fate had been conjured by Sinai's own venomous words? The guilt ate away at her, and made it easier for her to take up her new role; she was ready to play executioner. In her bag lay her weapon or curse, a ticking bomb waiting for its prey.

*

'Isn't it beautiful?' Meekulu had said to her days before, her thick glasses peering down at the small grey stone that she had just placed in Sinai's hand. It was smooth and oval, coloured different shades of grey.

'I suppose so. A little, ordinary-looking, but yes, I can see the beauty in this . . . I think. So is that the ụtọ plant? I thought it was a flower.' Sinai handed the stone back over to the old woman in an attempt to move Meekulu's small head out of her palm and back into her own space.

'If it were the ụtọ plant, we would both be dead by now, mauled by the Eze's beast—no, no, this is the zoro stone, and its beauty does not reside in its appearance, child; it lies in its very existence. It's a beautiful thing because it does such a unique and beautiful thing,' Meekulu said, as she lifted it to the sky, inspecting it with one eye closed.

'What does it do?'

'Under the right circumstances, this stone can change its state and, poof, it's gone, just like that,' Meekulu said, as she snapped her free hand.

'Change its state? 'Like ice and water?' Sinai asked, recalling the books that she had borrowed from the library.

'Yes, but much more brilliantly. You see, water changes very slowly. Over time the ice will melt, and then the water will turn to steam. Zoro goes from an impenetrable solid to a gas in seconds,' Meekulu said excitedly, as Sinai peered harder at the grey stone.

'So it is like water, but faster?' Sinai asked with her forehead creased in thought.

'Well, water is dependent on its environment to change; zoro's changes occur solely with time.'

'But isn't time . . . relative?'

'Yes, exactly! And yet time is the only thing—which we can measure, anyway—that dictates its changes. Many people have experimented, keeping all elements constant—temperature, pressure, light—and yet time is the only variable that influences it. Here lies the beauty of the zoro stone! It's one of the rare items that defy the laws of the earth, without being godly.'

'How is that possible?' Sinai asked, fully engrossed in Meekulu's words, reaching out to touch the stone.

'I do not know. No one knows.'

'Surely someone must know, perhaps one of the students from Timbuktu?' Sinai suggested. She couldn't imagine that the

Timbukan students, who read and theorised every day, measuring the stars and studying the tides, investigating all the various species of plants and variations of stone, wouldn't know. Surely they would have investigated something so peculiar. They were especially drawn by this type of enigma, where the world of the gods and the rules of the world met to create something plausible and possible.

Meekulu laughed softly. 'No, not even we know the details of such a stone.'

Sinai's head jerked away from the zoro stone, and towards the old woman holding it.

We?

'Meekulu, you were a *student?*'

'I *am* a student,' Meekulu replied with a smile, as she placed the stone back in Sinai's hand. 'One never stops being a Timbukan scholar.'

'But you are a woman, and you cook?' Sinai blurted out, no longer interested in the stone resting on her palm.

Meekulu shrugged. 'Women can be students, and students can cook.'

'I've never come across a female Timbukan student. I didn't even know it was . . . allowed,' Sinai said, as Meekulu's face darkened.

'And what a shame that is,' she said softly. 'But alas this is the way now—but hear this, child: there was a time, when I was young like you, and there were just as many female students as males, no difference whatsoever. All types of people travelled far and wide seeking out wisdom at the University of Timbuktu—but then the world changed, and so I changed.'

Sinai looked at Meekulu in shock, her mouth watering with excitement.

'Surely you don't mean . . . things were different? The world changed?' she asked, gripping Meekulu's hand with the stone still nestled in her palm.

'I've said too much, child. The stone—' Meekulu started, as she shook her head slightly.

'Oh no, please, go on. It's just that I've been having . . . well, I *had* this dream, and the world was so—the colours were so rich and the air was . . . different. It felt like . . . home, but how could it be? I've never known such a place,' Sinai rambled, as she moved closer to Meekulu, searching her face for answers.

Meekulu's eyes sparkled with delight.

'One thing at a time, my dear. You want the ụtọ plant, yes? Well, I have some,' Meekulu noted, as she pulled her glass frames off from her face and wiped them on her apron. 'I have it locked away with the various treasures that I have collected over the years. I can get it but, before I do, I will need to mould the zoro stone. Let's see, it's three days until the next Nkwo party . . . hmm, yes, I will head out there tomorrow then. Chisi can keep the kitchen running. Mmhmm, yes, that's what I will do.'

'Yes . . . that's a wonderful plan. I just . . . if we could quickly—
very quickly, discuss the world? The world changing? Or perhaps
my dream?'

'There's no time for that, dear. Didn't you hear what I said?
We already have so much to do!'

CHAPTER 23

AN IDEA FORMS
AT BREAKFAST

Furuefu Forest

Naala's eyes were glued on the five, thick, boiled plantains skewed over the open ọkụ flame. She sat on the plush green ground in the middle of a small clearing. It was bordered by dense bushes flushed with bright jade leaves, and a cluster of large baobab trees that opened up to a small, shimmering, turquoise lake. The clearing was far more open than any Naala had been used to in recent weeks, but the spirit of the large baobab trees, with their soaring trunks and flat flush of bright green leaves, had calmed the group's nerves.

Azu had said that he could hear the whistle of his ancestors' songs to the lost gods ringing deep within the sturdy trees; he was certain that the Eze's army would not find them there. His comments shocked Naala; it was by far the most profound thing he had ever said in her presence.

The air tasted sweet and smoky as the plantain simmered over the open flames. Naala could not wait to sink her teeth into the soft yellow fruit.

'So . . . can we be friends again?' Kora said, as she plopped by Madi with a wide smile, placing a small collection of flowers at his feet.

'Kora, stop,' Madi replied. His face was deliberately hard and stern, but his eyes were as warm as the softening plantain. 'This is not something one solves with flowers.'

'They are beautiful flowers, though,' Eni murmured, as he lay on the grassy ground with his body propped up by his elbow. His eyes flicked to Naala as he spoke, and she suddenly felt hot and uncomfortable.

'Yes or no, Madi?' Kora replied, pushing the flowers closer to him.

'Stop.' Madi sighed.

'Okay, fine . . . you can have my portion of the plantain?' Kora suggested.

'You don't like plantain,' Madi replied, as he rolled his eyes, but a small smile formed on his lips.

Naala watched them silently, her forehead creasing slightly in confusion. *How can they joke like this?* Just hours ago, Naala had been convinced that they hated each other. The tension had been so thick she could have sunk her teeth into it. It was the type of tension that emitted from a deep hatred. Hatred towards the girl who repeatedly advocated for your brother to be sacrificed, or at a boy who could jeopardise your only chance to deliver justice for your slaughtered family and friends. Yet here they both were, the day after, smiling like lifetime friends. Was it all a charade? A show they were putting on solely for Naala's benefit?

Naala had sat wordlessly by the group that morning, and she had been warmly greeted and embraced. She had waited awkwardly for them to chastise her for eavesdropping, swear her to secrecy, or at the very least speak to her about the events from the night prior. The four of them were at an ideal distance away from the rest of the survivors, where they could comfortably discuss sensitive matters. However, no one had spoken a word on the subject.

Instead, they'd joked about flowers and the weather, stopping every now and again to watch Azu speak enthusiastically. Azu sat yards away with Isioma, an impressionable woman from Nsuka, Gossy, a kind man from Agbo, and Ndidi, a quiet lady from Nnewi. They gathered around Azu, like children by the warm ọkụ flame on a cold dry night, watching his movements and nodding every so often to his booming words. Binyelum, a woman from Ugwutu, who had been found just weeks prior to Naala, was seated away from both groups, her eyes dark with fatigue and her face gaunt. Many people had tried to speak to her that morning, in an attempt to pull her out of the memories that haunted her, but she had refused assistance; today she needed to be on her own.

Naala turned back to the group with whom she was seated. Her gaze drew towards Eni, who had let his elbow drop and was now lying on the grass. He rested his head on his hands sanguinely; a position that emphasised his solid defined arms and exposed a small section of his hard midriff.

Eni had given Naala no indication as to whether he had told the group about her eavesdropping. She had fluctuated between believing that Kora and Madi knew that she had overheard their conversation last night, and being convinced that they had absolutely no clue.

'Why is he no longer your friend?' Naala asked, as she shifted her attention back towards Kora. Naala wanted to seem warm and approachable too, so she attempted a wide smile, but judging by Kora's brief look of confusion, it was anything but pleasant.

'Oh, just the usual lovers' quarrel,' Kora replied, as she flung her hands dismissively in the air, before moving closer to Madi.

'We're not lovers,' Madi insisted, as he swatted off Kora's attempt to pull his face into hers. Eni chuckled from the ground, bringing his hands up to rub his eyes.

'So it's not about Madi's brother?' Naala asked pointedly. She had grown bored and mildly irritated with the hidden messages and games. Naala wanted to have a real conversation. She wanted real answers. Surely she was not the only one bored senseless with this back and forth?

The atmosphere in the group changed instantly. Eni sat up whilst taking a deep breath, Madi's face darkened, and Kora sat back with her arms crossed over her chest.

'The plantain is ready!' Azu suddenly called out. 'Gossy, you can cut them into eight equal pieces and, Isioma, fetch the bean cake and eggs. Now it is time to feast!' A burst of movement erupted from the field as the people rose from the ground.

'Let's discuss this later, shall we?' Eni murmured, as he got up and brushed by Naala, but not before placing one hand gently on her waist to move her aside. Naala's heart fluttered as he mouthed 'Patience,' in her ear.

Eni walked towards Isioma, who had begun handing out the bean cakes and boiled eggs. Kora and Madi follow him.

Was it not he who suggested that we discuss this matter at breakfast? she thought, puzzled, before shrugging and turning towards the small crowd forming around the smoked plantains.

'There you go, Naala,' Gossy said, as he handed her a generous portion wrapped in a large, dark-green leaf.

'All this for me? Thank you so much,' Naala said earnestly.

'Well, we do not typically see you here for breakfast, so today you are a special guest, of sorts. I think it's good, very good, that you are mixing in with the group,' he commented aside. 'The more you do, the easier it is to deal with the pain. Loss is never simple.'

'Yes, thank you, Gossy,' Naala replied with a weaker smile. She felt a slight twinge in her heart, and quickly moved away from him before he could add anything else.

Naala liked Gossy. He seemed like a sweet gentle man; but his comments were precisely why she preferred being on her own. She didn't want to be reminded of her pain, yet everyone here seemed determined to bring it up. Naala had no desire to relive the horrors of her past; she wanted to discuss a solution. After collecting her portion of bean cake and eggs, Naala sat down with the group. The atmosphere was no longer warm; a cool breeze circled the group as memories of the harsh discussion last night bubbled to the surface of their minds. Kora, Eni, and Madi sat at a slight distance from each other, all three completely focused on their food.

'I believe Madi is right,' Naala said after some minutes of strained silence. She had waited for all the survivors to settle down into their previous positions, and when Azu had begun yet another sermon, Naala decided that now would be an ideal time to talk.

'Now is not the time,' Eni interrupted.

'Let her finish,' Kora murmured, as she meshed the bean cake into a ball the size of a mouthful.

'His brother will most likely fail, but, Kora, I think you are also right. We can't afford to throw away this opportunity.'

'If you *really* want my portion of plantain,' Kora exclaimed, as she nudged Madi. 'You need to tell me why you think I am brilliant. I want a debate!'

Naala looked at her in complete shock. *Is this girl mad?* she thought.

'Just a distraction for the group—please carry on,' Madi mentioned, after watching Naala's eyes widen.

'Mmm, yes, well, as I was saying, I think both of you are right,' Naala continued. 'So we need a new plan that prevents Madi's brother from failing, but does not waste this opportunity. Madi's brother needs help to carry off his mission.'

'Help? How?' Kora asked.

'Help with some sort of a distraction, like what Kora just did, so that when he takes the key, he is not taking it from an alert platoon. Or help while he's escaping. Or simply help with his nerve; he just needs help.'

'Yes, he does. We know this. But who can do that? Who can help?'

'Well, you have four able-bodied and willing reinforcements here,' Naala said, as she swirled her finger around to point at the group.

A wave of disappointment washed over their faces.

'We cannot help,' Eni said sadly.

'Why not?'

'For one, we do not know where he is.'

'That can't be true. Someone must know something,' Naala implored. 'How else would he know to collect the key? Someone must have told him, so someone knows.'

'There is a network of people, survivors like us, hidden in the forest,' Kora explained. 'We are all connected via a group of people called the *Amaghị*. We don't know where they are or even *who* they— all we know is they want the killings to stop. They want the Eze's madness to stop. We send them our information, and they piece it together with the other information they receive—just like a puzzle. They are the only ones that see the full picture, so they are the only ones that can make informed decisions. We told them about Madi's brother, someone else told them they had seen the head general's platoon heading for a town, and someone else was instructed to leave a message. We do not know where he is because all of this works by chance. It was pure luck that made it possible for the Amaghị to get that message to Emeka in the first place, but by the time we knew that someone had contacted him, the platoon had moved.'

'He knows that he needs to get the key,' Eni said. 'And he knows where to go when he has succeeded. All we can do now is wait and see.'

'Or send a message to call the whole thing off, before he has the chance to go through with it,' Madi murmured.

Naala stood up in frustration, turning her back on them as she burrowed into her own thoughts.

There must be a way.

The wind whistled through the sun-kissed leaves, carrying with it the songs of the forest: high-pitched clicks, stringy rattles, and the slow gush of the blue-green river.

There must be a way.

Naala's peculiar stance had started to garner unwanted attention, causing Kora to suddenly jump up and join her.

'Okay, fine, no need to get upset,' Kora said, as she gestured for Naala to sit back down. 'You can have my portion.'

'The Ofala festival,' Naala replied, with her eyes brimming in disbelief. She did not know whether she wanted to laugh or cry.

'I—can we sit down?' Kora stressed, looking around at the rest of the survivors with a smile, as she attempted to reassure prying eyes that this outburst was perfectly normal.

Naala let herself be guided to the ground by Kora. 'The Ofala festival!' she emphasised once more, nodding her head in excitement, as Eni creased his forehead in thought, and Madi looked back, clueless.

'The Ofala festival,' Kora added, shaking her head as she spoke. 'Surely that is too dangerous.'

'It's a death trap,' Eni added.

'It's the best solution we have.'

'Can someone explain this to me, please?' Madi hissed in frustration.

'Madi, we know exactly where your brother will be. He will be in Udi for the Ofala festival.'

'With the entire army, and half of the palace,' Nakake said softly.

'And the Eze,' Eni added.

CHAPTER 24

A GIFT FOR INA

City of Nri

'You look very nice today,' Obi Ife said, as his eyes trailed over Sinai's body, and a smile formed on his lips. 'Very nice.'

'What are you . . .? I thought . . . sorry, aren't you supposed to be at the Ofala festival?' Sinai said in annoyance, as she attempted to look past Obi Ife's frame for Chief Ojo.

'Why would I be there, when you, my dear, are right here? Looking so . . . ravishing,' he said, taking one step closer. Sinai caught a whiff of the strong *pito* emitting from his pores and instinctively stepped back. She took a deep breath; her mind swirled in distress as the zoro stone hidden in her bag began to weigh heavily on her soul.

What do I do? What do I do? What do I do? she thought, as she tightened her grip on her bag. She stretched her neck once again, and stood on the balls of her feet with her heels raised from the ground, but Chief Ojo was nowhere to be seen.

Ina, however, was front and centre. She was wearing drapes of long woven raffia cloth, dyed deep red and embroidered with golden lions. The outfit was tailored to suit her body, and topped off with a red feathered *ichie okpu* hat. Ina looked strange, strong, and regal. The parts of her skin that she chose to show looked supple and soft against the glow of the floating ọkụ.

Meekulu had done a marvellous job of clearing up her bruises and wounds, and Ina had concealed what was left with dark-brown body paint. Her lips were darker than usual, lined with dark-red dye, and she had marked her face with white lines; symbols of a warrior. To the unsuspecting world, Ina seemed defiant. She laughed so hard that she had to clutch at her stomach; she talked animatedly with her long arms flinging around. However, Sinai could see glimmers of desperation and fatigue in her eyes, and, on several occasions, Sinai spotted Ina pinching her own hands to stop them from quivering.

Ina was here for a purpose; she was here to save her reputation. If she had succumbed to her pain, missed festivals and locked herself away, questions would start circling. Where is Ina? What happened to Ina? Ina was one of the most sociable women in the palace; she couldn't disappear without spurring on a herd of rumours. Chief Ojo would undoubtedly feed the rumours; he had nothing to lose. Everyone knew that it was women who paid for the crimes that men committed against them. More importantly, he had her reputation to gain. He wouldn't stop until she was completely destroyed, and knowing this, Ina was fighting back.

Ina was clutching desperately at a future that she could control. She was trying to take back her narrative, by remaining consistent, appearing to thrive, so that any rumours that began would be strangled by her resilient demeanour.

Sinai admired her conviction, but she could see it came at a cost. Despite Ina's attempts, Sinai could see the tremors in her hand and the quick glances over her shoulders. Ina too was on the lookout for Chief Ojo.

Sinai had no clue what she would do with the zoro stone if she was unable to find him; she wanted to kick herself for not foreseeing this potential scenario. Chief Ojo had never attended an Ofala festival; he couldn't be *there*. Sinai also couldn't imagine him missing the nobles' celebrations either; he was not the type to shy away from the social events that he was permitted to attend. He tended to show up early, throwing his loud voice and heavy frame around, with a constant stream of alcohol gushing down his throat.

Sinai had not accounted for any variations in this behaviour, an error in judgement that could cost her dearly. The zoro stone was not something that she could simply discard. Once the stone dissolved, the ụtọ plant would be open to the world. Anyone that came into contact with it would meet the wrath of Asilia. If she did nothing, that person would be her. Sinai shivered at the thought of such an encounter.

'What is wrong, my dear?' Obi Ife said softly, his voice sticky and sweet. It irritated her like messy honey stuck between her fingers on a warm day.

'Nothing,' she muttered, turning in case she'd missed anything in the time that she had spent looking away; still no sign. 'Nothing at all.'

'Fine,' Obi Ife noted sceptically. Sinai sighed inwardly and turned her full attention towards him; she needed to remain as close to normal as possible. She smiled and he smiled back warmly. Her fist tightened.

'I actually had a question for you. When the Eze returns I thought that we might . . .' Obi Ife's voice floated away from Sinai as she noticed a commotion at the corner of her eye. She turned her head to find Chief Ojo entering the hall, his hands raised as he chastised two of his wives who he'd brought with him. Sinai watched as the large man plopped down on one of the Obis' seats at the end of the hall. Her heart pounded vigorously.

'Oh, sorry, I'm—well, I—could you excuse me, please?' Sinai said suddenly.

'Sinai, what is the meaning of this?' Obi Ife hissed with narrowing eyes as she darted away from him and towards the large seats at the end of the hall.

The seats were made of a beautiful mahogany and carved with care, cushioned with plump bird feathers, wrapped in soft leopard fur. Only Obis were permitted to sit on them, but in the absence of the majority of the upper class, Chief Ojo had stated his claim. He had sent his two resigned wives to fetch him some food. Sinai's face darkened in anger as she noticed a large dark-purple bruise on one wife's arm, and the slight limp in the walk of the other. Sinai approached his seat and looked down on him before attempting to rearrange her face into a more inviting expression.

'Move out the way, girl,' Chief Ojo said, raising his left hand dismissively as he fanned himself with a large feather fan in his right hand. Large beads of sweat ran across his face and his light mud-brown eyes rolled in disdain.

Sinai was thrown off by his demeanour. She had always been thankful that he had never shown any interest in her, but how was she supposed to get close enough to plant the stone on him if he remained so reproachful?

'I said move then—ah ah,' he huffed, slapping his large hands against his even larger thighs, his garish orange and black clothing creasing.

'You're not supposed to sit there,' Sinai blurted out suddenly, and a look of horror spread across Chief Ojo's face. His eyes bulged before narrowing as he delivered a dirty look, kissing his teeth at her.

'What is the meaning of all this?' he rumbled, as a vein throbbed in his forehead. 'You . . . this efuọla . . . you who can't even open your mouth to talk to me? You are the one telling me where I should sit?'

'This seat is for the Obis . . . *Ozo*,' Sinai replied with a small smile. Her heart pounded so fast that her head became dizzy, but deep down she was enjoying herself. She watched Chief Ojo grow increasingly distressed, his blood boiling and his eyes bulging. And all for what? Because an efuọla girl was telling him what to do? He puffed out his chest in anger.

'Get out of here, bastard,' he replied, as Sinai reached into her bag before charging at him. She used her right arm to tug at his garment, and, as she suspected he would, he responded by flinging her off violently, but not before she could slip the zoro stone into one of the pockets at his hip with her left hand. Chief Ojo stood up, the motion knocking her to the floor. He raised one hand, prepped to deliver a mighty slap. Sinai scrambled up from the floor, her eyes darting between the subtle bulge in his pocket and his thick hand.

'You little—' Chief Ojo spat.

'Hey! What is going on here?' Obi Ife demanded from behind her. Chief Ojo dropped his arm quickly and scanned the room briskly, the hot anger that had been in his eyes cooling, as he remembered where he was.

'Obi Ife, eh, I'm glad you are here. This efuọla—' Chief Ojo began, as he flung his arm at Sinai, who responded by widening her eyes and shaking her head.

'Hey! Hey!' Obi Ife said briskly. 'Don't you ever use that kind of language in this lady's presence. That is not the way of an honourable man.'

'I . . . look, this whore is—' Chief Ojo tried again, before Obi Ife cut him off.

'You better watch yourself, Ozo. You think we all don't know how you carry on?' He gestured towards Chief Ojo's wives at the food table, who turned around instantly when they noticed the new attention bestowed upon them. 'It is *outrageous* behaviour. Keep talking and I'll be forced to have a word with the Eze about all of this.' Chief Ojo pursed his lips in irritation.

'Okay.' Ojo raised both hands. 'The *oga* has spoken,' he snarled, before letting his eyes saunter towards Sinai's chest. 'But don't worry, girl, you now have my attention. I'm sure you've heard of how I deal with disrespect.' He plopped down once more on the seat.

'What has gotten into you?' Obi Ife hissed at her, once he had put some distance between Sinai and Chief Ojo. 'Why would you seek out such a man?'

'Can I step outside, please?' Sinai replied. Her head was reeling. *He has the zoro stone.* Sinai was not entirely sure what emotion was coursing through her blood. It could have been relief or regret, she had no idea, but whatever it was, it left her feeling dazed.

'Yes, that's probably a good idea,' he murmured. Sinai followed Obi Ife's lead through the bronzed thick pillars and into the dark-blue night. They stepped out from the marbled raised floor into the lush vegetation. Sinai felt a wave of warmth softly brush her skin. The air smelt sweet and thick.

'Raining season is coming soon,' Sinai said quietly, almost to herself.

'What?'

'The air . . . nothing,' Sinai attempted, before turning to face Obi Ife.

'Well?' Obi Ife questioned. 'Aren't you going to explain yourself? What exactly were you doing over there?' He was embarrassed at being involved in such an incident, at a noble event, no less. The girl was undeniably beautiful, familiar yet *different*, but it appeared she was also reckless. Obi Ife despised recklessness. Perhaps he had made a mistake by forgoing the Ofala festival to accompany her instead.

'I just . . . I'd heard a . . . *rumour* about him, and I wanted to confirm if it was true,' Sinai said carefully.

Obi Ife looked confused. He began to speak before stopping suddenly, and nodding stoically, as though something had inexplicably clicked in his head. His eyes softened as he approached Sinai slowly. She shifted back uncomfortably.

'Oh dear. Yes, I'm afraid whatever you've *heard* might have been true—which is why it is important that you stay far away from such a man. Things must change—it's difficult—but for now you mustn't worry yourself about such things. I'll speak to the Eze tomorrow, when he's back, and get that *man* sorted.'

'Please don't.' She sighed, already tired of this conversation. She no longer wanted to think of Chief Ojo or the Eze.

'I mean . . . I'm sure that the Eze—and you—are busy with other—'

'Neither of us are too busy to protect a fearful girl from an uncontrollable beast. You are right to be worried; you in particular need of protection. You saw how he acted; it's only a matter of time bef—' Obi Ife began, before he was cut off by loud screams.

Sinai closed her eyes for seconds longer than what was appropriate, her heart thundering, as bloodthirsty cries and gruesome growls filtered through the open night.

Obi Ife looked back into the party hall, straining his eyes slightly to get a better look, before they widened in fear.

'Ehhh! Wait here—you hear me? Wait here!' he said quickly, before scrambling towards the halls. People rushed out of the hall to join Sinai in the gardens, cowering under thick bushes and clutching one another in fright.

Sinai squeezed through the frantic bodies. She stepped back onto the marble floor and witnessed a gruesome scene. Chief Ojo lay slumped on the Obis' seat, beaten and bruised with the cloth around his stomach and groin soaked in bright red blood. Large red paw prints led away from him. One of the two wives he had brought with him held his large head in her lap, whilst the other screamed in a panicked high-pitched voice. Ina stood frozen in front of the three of them. Crowds of people watched in awe; some, afraid that Asilia would make another appearance, edged closer to the nearest exit that they could find.

'I told you to stay in the gardens! This is no place for a Lolo,' Obi Ife said, as he tried to usher her out to the hall.

'What happened?' Sinai asked, before pulling out of his grip.

'I'm not sure; it seems the Eze's lion attacked him.'

'Just him?'

'Yes.'

'Good,' Sinai said swiftly, before she felt Obi Ife's eyes dart across her face, dumbfounded. 'Good that most people are fine . . . relatively speaking.'

'The man will need a doctor. I'll fetch him, but please stay away from here. Go back into the gardens—it's not safe,' he pleaded, as he darted out of the hall.

Sinai did not go back to the gardens. Instead, she walked towards Ina and stood beside her. Ina was so engrossed in the scene that she failed to acknowledge Sinai's presence.

'That was not for *you*; it was *for* you. You are now in my debt. If you don't respect that, respect this: cross me again and next time it will be you, lifeless, on the ground.' Sinai spoke far more quickly than when she had rehearsed the words countless times over the past few days. She hadn't accounted for the huge dose of adrenaline rushing through her body.

Ina turned her head and looked down at Sinai, her eyes glossy with tears that refused to fall, and her mouth slightly ajar. She was in complete and utter shock. Ina blinked, and one tear escaped and rolled down her face, carrying with it smeared white warrior paint.

'Thank you,' she replied in a low raspy voice.

Sinai nodded curtly, before walking out of the hall with her head held high and chest tight.

CHAPTER 25

THE JOURNEY
TO UDI

Furuefu Forest

'It's too dangerous and it's not a solution. The army and the members of the palace, and the Eze . . . he will sense us on sight!' Kora cried, as she threw her hands in the air.

'Not to mention Udi is a long journey away, perhaps even weeks away. Chances are we'd miss the Ofala festival anyway,' Eni added.

Naala argued, 'No, it's no more than eight days from Igbakwu, and we're much closer to it now than I was at home. Also the festival is on the last Nkwo of the month; that's ten days away! We can get there in time if we move now.'

'What would *we* even do when you get there?' Eni asked.

'We would do *something*,' Naala replied excitedly. 'I'm sure we can figure it out. We can go there, inspect the situation from afar, and act accordingly. If the answer is that there is nothing to do, then we turn back, no harm done. But if we can, then we succeed—the point is we have a way to meet Emeka.'

'Meet him in death, you mean,' Kora muttered absentmindedly. Silence fell on the group before she brought her hands to her mouth, realising what she had said.

'Oh, I didn't—' Kora began, as all the scattered ero in the clearing suddenly flushed with a low blue glow. 'I didn't mean it like that, Madi— no, Madi,' Kora called, as she tried to follow after his large frame, but he had already stormed away.

Early the next morning, Madi woke Naala up gently, with a finger pressed against his mouth, signalling for her to not make a sound. She silently followed him down the tree and out of the dwellings of the sleeping survivors, before asking what was going on.

'Kora and Eni are like boulders. Once they have their minds set on something, they won't change,' he said hurriedly. 'And they have their minds set on my brother embarking on this impossible task on his own. No, no they have,' he said, as Naala began to protest. 'It's true, and you know it. I can't stay and wait for them to change their minds—that day will never come—and really, I don't need it to anymore. You know where this festival is, you know where my brother is. I have supplies that will last us . . . spare hammocks in my bag. We can go together and we can *do* something—we don't need them.'

Naala's eyes gleamed with what he could only describe as a flaming fire. But just as quickly as it arrived, that flame dimmed, and he saw doubt creep into her face. Madi prepared for yet another rejection, but to his surprise she said:

'Okay.' And after a short pause, 'Let's go.'

Naala lay on her belly on the dry sun-beaten grass. She squinted her eyes and cupped her hand around her forehead to shield them from the bright light. Madi sat beside her, in a similar fashion; they both looked out over the cliff edge.

The land beneath them looked beautiful; the deep-blue lake sparkled in the sunlight and brushed up against the land, lush with green treetops. Naala watched as a breeze rustled through the tree leaves, and swirled them towards the grand large rocks at Udi. The vast mountain did not move in the calling wind; rather, it stood strong and imposing, like the body of a great dormant grey god. Naala turned away from the mountain and looked back at the white curls of smoke seeping through small sections within the forest leading towards it. Her eyes then swept towards the increasing number of small boats drifting on the lake and towards the shore. The Eze's guests were arriving at the Ofala festival.

'What is this festival for again?' Madi grumbled, as he turned to lie on his back; he pinched the bridge of his nose in exhaustion. The sun's heat, mixed with his anxiety over the wellbeing of his little brother, was taking its toll on him.

Naala was still somewhat shocked at how little Madi knew about the palace and its customs. Ofala was one of the biggest and most exclusive—and therefore most talked about— festivals of the year. But as Madi had noted days ago, the Mpako people lived hidden in the mountainous areas near the north of the kingdom, a far more remote dwelling than any of the other survivors.

Whilst Naala's village typically hosted at least one visitor every other week, the Mkpabo tribe rarely saw more than one visitor a year! Naala's knowledge of the various kingdoms, the palace, the universities, the world, was fleeting at best, formed by patches of conversations from an eclectic group of guests; but Madi's knowledge on the topic was non-existent.

'I'll start from the beginning,' Naala said. 'Are you aware of the gods' war?'

'Yes, of course. The elders would tell us stories as children of the Mother's vengeance on men, and the gods who tried and failed to protect us and the—' Madi paused with a grimace as he turned his head to face Naala, and lowered his voice '—and the Eze who saved the world, and now seeks to destroy it—well, they didn't say the last part, but I'm sure if they were still alive they would have agreed.'

Naala could see his mood shift to one of melancholy. She felt his pain. Mourning the dead was extremely hard when you couldn't justify their passing. She still couldn't answer why the Eze, the great warrior, now sought to destroy the very people he nearly died to protect. It made no sense, which made the deaths of their loved ones senseless.

Naala, however, had no time to dwell on such things. They were here for a reason; she could not get distracted by either her own or Madi's pain.

'How did he save the world?' Naala asked.

'I understand that part—' Madi began.

'Just tell me.'

'He took her heart, the Earth Mother's heart, from that mountain,' Madi said, pointing at Udi.

'Exactly; he took her heart on the last Nkwo day of the eleventh month that the year, and the Mother was dead by the end of that night. So every year, he goes on a pilgrimage back to the mountain to remind himself and his guests of his mighty accomplishment. His guests are the highest class of people in all the top palaces around the world: the Obis—not just from the palace in Nri, but those that reside in various kingdoms far and wide. They all come to pay their respects on that day, and make the journey up the famous mountain, and then they dance and cheer in the spot where the Eze stole the heart. Afterwards, they come down the mountain and spend the night drinking merrily and rejoicing further. I've been told it's quite an occasion.'

'You spoke to someone who went?' Madi asked.

'Well, no. We've had a few servants on sabbaticals who passed by the village. But servants are one of the most reliable sources!'

'According to a servant, I presume?' Madi chuckled, as Naala became increasingly irritated.

'According to people with sense,' Naala retorted, before taking a deep breath, determined not to fall into the trap of Madi's inane teasing.

'Okay, okay—so what is the plan?' Madi asked. 'How do we find Emeka?'

'We join in, of course,' Naala replied, as Madi's eyes widened in shock.

'You can't be serious . . . we would be killed on sight!' Madi replied. He rubbed his hands against his eyes as he recalled Eni and Kora's protests nearly a week ago.

Madi had been so pleased with Naala's willingness to join him on the excursion that he had brushed aside how ill-advised the whole thing was, and how unbalanced a person really needed to be to agree with him at all. He remembered that gleam in Naala's eye, and rather than filling him with hope, it now made him uneasy.

'Oh, don't look at me like that, Madi. Now is not the time to give up. There's a way in, trust me! Look, look at the boats,' Naala said, and Madi followed her gesturing hand.

'Éh, I see them.'

'And they are carrying?'

'People?'

'With?'

'With?' Madi repeated, as a look of confusion swept over his face. Naala took it in with a sigh.

'*With* luggage and clothes and servants—and clothes.'

'I'm not following . . .'

'We can take them—the clothes—from a man and a woman. Look, you see the boats vary in size: some are big and hold groups of people; some smaller boats travel in groups of three or four; and some, well, some are the small boats traveling alone. Those boats typically hold a man and a woman travelling solo. We could easily take the place of the man and the woman,' Naala explained.

'But how would we take their place? Surely someone would notice—we're not *like* them; our mannerisms are different.'

'I can make a mixture that will send them to sleep. My grandma used to make it all the time for Hanye—'

'Who?'

'—never mind. The point is *I* can make something that will send them to sleep for at least two days. All I need are some *ụra* leaves, and I'm certain I saw some on the way here. We could also use tribal marks to disguise ourselves. And just look at how many people are coming to this thing from various parts of the kingdom . . .. It may be an elite event, but it's not small. We could easily get lost in a crowd. Listen, this will work; can't you feel it?! It's a good plan; tonight as they prep for tomorrow, we will sneak into their dwellings, put them to sleep, put on their clothes, and then take their place and find your brother!'

'It's feasible . . . but I don't know,' Madi said pensively.

'What is there not to know?' Naala tried hard to keep the anger that had begun to simmer within her from rising to her voice.

'Giving people ụra leaves? Misusing sacred tribal marks? Stealing their *clothes*? It just doesn't sit right with me; it has no honour,' Madi said, as Naala rolled her eyes.

'So what would you rather we do? Barge in? Fight to the death until someone points us to your brother?' Naala said dryly, her irritation peaking.

'Well, no—'

'Then what?'

'I just don't know if I'm comfortable drugging someone,' Madi replied.

'Then you'll have to get comfortable with losing your brother,' Naala replied sharply. She saw a slither of raw pain flash behind his eyes, before Madi could blink it away.

'I'm sorry. That was unfair. Look, if you have another plan, then I'm happy to listen to it; if not . . . well, I'm happy to turn back too,' Naala said gently. She was lying; she was not at all happy about the idea of turning back, not after what they had been through.

*

The journey that they had embarked on was far more difficult than she had anticipated. Madi was gullible enough to believe her when she had said that she knew the way to Udi; she didn't. All she had was a vague recollection that it was somewhere in the north-east and that it was likely to take five or so days to get there.

Naala had decided to rely on her natural sense of direction to get them there, hoping that if they walked in the right direction, eventually they would see the mountain, and from that point on they wouldn't even need to navigate; they could simply walk towards it. Whilst her time with the survivors had no doubt made her a formidable traveller, her limbs had ached all the same. Naala's feet became sore and blistered, her crocodile footgear had soon become tattered and worn, the mmiri leaves that lined them dried up, and the broken twigs and hard stones tore her flesh. Naala's throat had screamed for more water and her stomach growled constantly.

Naala's heart had lit up five days into their journey, when they spotted a remote village on the way; she dreamt of warm food, fresh water, and villagers who would listen attentively to her warnings about the Eze's attacks. They had found the water, in a disused well. They had found food: cold, spoilt, and abandoned. They had found the villagers: dead from wounds inflicted by the Eze's army.

After a few more days they had finally begun to see Udi in the distance. Naala's heart had sunk deep into her stomach. For some reason, she had never imagined it being so monstrously large.

How on earth will we find the Eze's procession? she had thought, wearily.

But she had refused to let her angst show. The images of the dead villagers still burnt in her mind. *This plan needs to work.* Naala had let a familiar tug in her stomach lead the way. It was the same tug that had led her to countless hidden beautiful areas within Furuefu forest; the same tug that had led her back home in the darkening night after she had spent an hour too long exploring. She trusted that tug to lead her to the Eze's procession now, and it did.

Eventually they had reached an unexceptional hilltop; Naala looked down and saw small royal boats landing on the shore. She had felt called to this place, and was certain that they needed to be here, and that her plan would work. Their journey itself did not explain their arrival; there was no way that they should have reached this place.

Watching the festival preparations from the hilltop, Naala was sure that those tugs that she'd felt were nudges from the old gods guiding her along the way. She was desperate not to turn her back on them now, not after they had brought her so far. And so she had no intention of turning back. She waited impatiently for Madi's response.

Finally he answered, 'I don't have a better plan and I need to help my brother. Turning back is not an option, so I think it's time to pluck some ura leaves. I believe I saw some growing by the wetlands a few cubits away.'

CHAPTER 26

ENIKAN

Furuefu Forest

Eni's eyes narrowed slightly as a strong gust of air flew across the green forest, creating a spiral cloud of dancing dust. He blinked hard, but wasted no time rubbing at his itchy eyes. He couldn't risk the chance of missing her in the scene below. With every glance he took, he willed her to appear. He ran his eyes across the forest, greyed by the onset of the sand storm, but she wasn't there.

Eni had been struck with disbelief when he'd found out that she had left. During her time with the group, she had woken up at sporadic times during the morning—at times she was the first one up; other times they wouldn't see her until after breakfast—so he'd thought nothing of her absence that morning. The day had been young and bright, with the huge ripe sun stretched across the horizon.

'Where's Madi?' Kora had asked absentmindedly, and, for a reason unknown to Eni, a wave of anxiety had broken through his previously calm state. Madi was never late for breakfast.

'I'll get him,' Eni had mumbled, but only Naala's face had flashed bright in his mind. Remnants of her scent, her smiles, and scowls had rippled through his soul and his throat had tightened.

'Why?' Kora had replied, but Eni had already sprung up and was heading towards the trees that the survivors had chosen to sleep in that night. The thick trees had towered over him and showered him with dry multi-coloured leaves as he'd stalked through the forest. Like the leaves swirling around him, fragments of their conversations had fluttered in his head. *The girl is insane but she wouldn't . . . she's not . . .* he'd thought but, deep down inside, he knew he was throwing empty words at an unchangeable reality.

In Naala's dark almond eyes, he'd seen her unshakeable resilience, but had brushed it aside. She had told him on more than one occasion that she was going to leave. He'd thought she had changed her mind; he had been foolish enough to think that the same ache that erupted within him when he thought of parting with Naala also sprouted within her. He should have known that she was simply waiting for a better plan, a better reason to leave.

Now, Eni looked up at the tree that she had slept in the night prior, his throat too dry to call her name. He clambered up the tree faster than he had ever done in his life. He pulled himself up on the branch holding her hammock, and his heart sank as he came to terms with what he already knew. The empty hammocks swayed slightly in the morning gust. They were gone.

CHAPTER 27

THE OBIS' COURT

City of Nri

Sinai had heard, through whispered conversations, that Chief Ojo was still alive. He was maimed, of course. After the attack he was left unable to walk and, given the proximity of the attack to his groin, he would never be able to abuse another woman in the same manner that he had done to Ina.

Apparently Chief Ojo's mind had also changed. His booming voice had softened and now only incoherent mutterings tumbled randomly out of his mouth during the day. His mud eyes were now glazed over and Chief Ojo spent his time in his akwa nest, being dutifully seen to by his eight wives, who now sang songs in harmony with wide smiles spread across their faces and a fresh gleam twinkling in their eyes; they had only dreamed of tasting this type of freedom again.

At first Sinai had been numb to the whole situation, as though her mind had refused to process the events that had occurred at the party. She avoided thinking about it and was adamant about not talking about it either, so much so that she had avoided visiting Meekulu, for she knew that the old woman would certainly have a basket of probing questions that she would be unable to answer.

That said, Sinai's ears sniffed out conversations on Asilia's attack, and followed them like a dog. Sinai would hide in the shadows as people discussed updates on Chief Ojo's condition. The more she learnt, the more pleased she became. Sinai was shocked to find that she felt no guilt. Instead she felt pride; she was pleased that she had corrected such a terrible wrong.

That was, until Ozi came with a parchment from Obi Ife nestled in her beak. Sinai looked at the sage-green hamerkop in despair. Ozi was old and ugly, her pale green feathers ruffled and dull. Unlike the other enchanted hamerkop birds in the palace, who whistled delightfully through Nri, with sharp efficiency and intelligence, Ozi was lazy and often made mistakes. It suited Sinai well. What use would an efuọla have for one of those smart birds? Sinai rarely received or sent messages, and she had always preferred to walk to anyone she needed to speak to. Ozi was more of a familiar, scruffy friend whose soft cooing kept her company during lonely long days. Sinai had spent countless hours staring at the curious bird, imagining what Ozi might have been like as a nnunu woman, an exercise that never failed to amuse her.

However, in that moment, Ozi felt more like poison, bringing slow and timely death to her door. Sinai looked down at the thick grainy paper, soft and frayed with thin wispy remnants of the bark tree, resting between her fingers. The black ink was smooth; it curved along the paper and spelled out a message that caused Sinai's heart to plunge into her stomach.

Lolo Sinai

The council and I request your company in the Court of the Obis at the 8th hour of the day. You have been summoned to trial. This invitation is for you alone. However, if you require defence, we shall provide it for you.

Obi Ife

It wasn't until the parchment slipped out of her fingers that Sinai realised that they were shaking. She looked down at her hands before tightening them into fists.

'Oh no, oh no, oh no,' she muttered, as she paced up and down her room. *How did he know?* she thought.

The Eze's lion had only recently been seen in public; the beast, for the most part, remained a mystery to most. With the Eze gone, Sinai was sure that no one would have been able to connect the ụtọ plant to the lion's attack. Sinai had yet to hear the plant mentioned in the snatches of conversations that she had listened to. As far as she could tell, people assumed that Asilia's attack was an accident. Some had even theorised that it was the lion itself that had targeted Chief Ojo, due to his lifetime of dreadful sins. Some blamed the fact that Chief Ojo dared to sit on the Obis' chair; perhaps that was what angered the beast. As the theories and rumours circulated around the palace, not one person anywhere had suggested any foul play, so why had Sinai been summoned?

Sinai brought her hands to her head as she thought more deeply about that night. She reflected on how she had brazenly looked for Chief Ojo. She recalled being in the middle of the commotion that preceded his attack. She was hardly stealthy at the party, so how could she be surprised now at being a suspect? Sinai took a deep breath and walked towards her window; the sun was still high but gathering clouds had slowly dimmed its light. She walked over to the sundial in the corner of the room; the small ọkụ light hovering above it bobbed excitedly. Sinai peered closely at it before taking another sharp breath and exhaling loudly; it was steadily approaching the eighth hour. After a short pause, she walked out of her room and towards the Obis' court.

Sinai approached the Obis' court doors with her parchment still in her hand. Two large soldiers manned the door and looked down at her blankly as she approached.

'I—I've been summoned,' Sinai stammered; she had wanted so badly to appear calm and strong, but her fear had definitely got the best of her. She had an intense urge to turn around and make a run for it, but she was frozen in place. One of the guards grunted and gestured to the parchment, and in response she stretched out her hand towards him. He snatched the parchment, irritated by her slowness, and glanced at it. After a brief pause, he shoved the parchment back at Sinai before opening the large mahogany door. 'Well, hurry up, girl!' the other guard roared in frustration, causing Sinai to jump slightly, before attempting yet again to compose herself.

'Thank you,' she said quietly, before walking through the entrance. Sinai had never been in the Obis' court before; unlike the general court, which attracted masses of people during high-profile cases, the Obis' court was closed to the public. It was the court where the Eze passed judgement on the Obis themselves, judgement that could not be witnessed by the common folk, lest they think that the highest members of society were also nothing more than flawed humans, a thought that could spark questions about the current distribution of power.

Sinai had no idea why her case would be brought into this court; neither she nor Chief Ojo were of the Obi class. Perhaps it was because she was a woman, a woman who had organised an attack on a man using the Eze's lion as a weapon? Sinai could see how they would want to keep details of that case wrapped up, and then later twist it to place the emphasis, not on Sinai's motivations, but on the repercussions of her actions. Sinai would serve as a lesson, and, with the details hidden, the chances of her becoming a martyr would be slim.

Sinai took a step into the courtroom and let the door close behind her. The room stood out from the rest of the ones within the palace. Sinai was accustomed to wide-open spaces with large airy windows that allowed entangled beams of light and air to dance through the space. She was used to tall ceilings and mud-brick walls. The courtroom had none of these things. It was so dark that it took a minute for Sinai's eyes to adjust. The tiny window in the wall facing her only let a small ray of sunshine through. The room was also smaller than she had imagined; the ceiling hung low and the walls seemed to huddle together. The assortment of wooden benches that lined them, and the large seat in the middle of the room, which Sinai assumed was for the accused, all worked to make the room seem even smaller.

Sinai did not like this tight space; she felt like she couldn't breathe. The four mechanical palm leaf fans at the corners of the room were the only source of ventilation. But it appeared as though only one of them worked; the others stood limp and lifeless. Sinai would have walked over to wind it back up and start its slow cooling waves, but both the obstructions within the room, and her fear of meddling with something that she wasn't meant to touch, kept her away.

Sinai wiped the small beads of sweat forming on her brow as she looked around. Dim light came from a selection of ọkụ flames, small and intricate shapes of floating fire. Their beauty was undeniable. Their geometry was complex, almost incomprehensible, yet they still maintained an elegant simplicity. The flame tamer that drew these up must have spent days, if not weeks, wielding them. Sinai stood in quiet awe as subtle scents of clove and myrrh wafted through the air.

She blinked as her eyes grew even more accustomed to the darkness. Suddenly she began to notice the paintings on the walls. She gasped audibly; she had never seen such paintings before. Rather than the usual engravings depicting the marvellous victories and painful losses of the battles fought through the ages, these paintings were full of life—everyday life.

Sinai took a step forward as she inspected a section of the wall where a small girl was carrying a large bucket of water over to a deep-blue river. Sinai moved closer and followed the river, careful not to hit the bench with her shins. Suddenly, she came across a small crevice in the wall; within it lay a beautiful coral bead necklace, thick and deep orange. She turned her head and noticed that this was not the only crevice; there were at least eight that she could see on this wall alone.

'Ndewo, Sinai,' a deep voice said behind her, plunging her back into reality.

Sinai jumped around, clutching her chest in fright as she stood before Obi Ife. She had almost forgotten why she had been summoned here in the first place.

'I can explain,' Sinai blurted out, as she took a step closer to Obi Ife, her mind racing furiously. She had yet to come up with an excuse.

'Explain what, my dear?' he asked, perplexed. His confused expression created deep shadows on his face. Her principal plan was to deny her involvement in Chief Ojo's maiming, and plead her case with desperation and tears. However, in light of Obi Ife's reaction, she was unsure about how she should proceed.

'Well . . . I'm not entirely sure why I was brought here. I could only assume that . . .?' She paused carefully, as she tried to feel out the situation. Obi Ife looked blankly back. 'Well, honestly, I don't know. I'm sorry, Obi Ife, but I received this parchment; does this not mean that I'm being accused of *something*?'

'Ahh no, that is just silly protocol,' he replied.

'I don't understand.'

'Well, *you*, my dear, are not in the Obi class—not yet, anyway—and so to enter this space you must do so in an official manner. Contrary to popular opinion, Obis are not above the law, but we do have ways to get around some of the inane rules.'

'Okay . . . but why am I *here*?'

'Well, in truth, it is connected to Chief Ojo,' he began, as Sinai's heart repeated its struggled beats. 'Now clearly that was a traumatic experience, not one that a lady like yourself has stomach to witness. I want to make you feel better, Sinai.' Obi Ife paused and brought one finger up to his pursed lips, reflectively.

'Ordinarily I would have showered you with money and the finest clothes and jewellery, but, given how my other gifts have been received, I believe you require something different.'

'Oh,' Sinai said, as a growing discomfort filled her. Sinai was increasingly aware that she was here alone, with this man who had lured her here under false pretences. She cleared her throat as the walls began to close in on her. 'That's . . . thank you, but I'm okay. I'm fine, much better, in fact. I should go . . . I've got so many other—' Sinai mumbled, as she edged back towards the doors.

'No, no—you must stay. Trust me, you'll enjoy this. You are interested in the Eze's history, yes?'

'Oh, well, I wouldn't say *interested*,' Sinai added quickly.

'Ahh, you didn't think I would notice, eh?' Obi Ife replied excitedly. 'I notice these things, and I happen to be in a position that allows me to help you feed those interests of yours.'

'Again, interest is too strong a word. I may have asked—'

'Look around!' Obi Ife exclaimed. 'Look at this room carefully. It contains artefacts from the Eze's history: the ọbara abara that he used slay the god of war who tried to betray the cause. The map to the Ndụ crystal given to him by Mami Wata. So many wonderful artefacts from such a rich history.'

'And he just leaves them out?' Sinai asked curiously, as she looked at gleaming coral beads. Despite her best efforts, she was getting drawn into a conversation with Obi Ife.

While spying on the Eze had been pushed to the back of her mind in recent weeks, she couldn't help but be interested. She had heard stories of the Eze's victories ever since she was a child, and here she was, supposedly, in a room full of objects that had played vital roles.

'Well, why shouldn't he? No one but the Obis enter this room. Even servants are not permitted. Someone of Obi calibre would not dream of taking such precious items and, even if one of us, in a moment of madness, decided to snatch one of them, we would disintegrate before we could leave the room.'

'Disintegrate?' Sinai gasped, as Obi Ife nodded.

'Mmhm; residual old magic that the Eze was able to manipulate using the Ndụ crystal. Anyone who takes any of the items from this room will turn to dust before their feet have crossed through the door. The Eze routinely demonstrates it on Obis who repeatedly break the law,' he said solemnly. 'That's what happened to my father,' he added quietly.

Sinai's head jerked up at that comment, and her heart filled with pity.

'I'm so sorry,' she murmured.

'It was his fault,' Obi Ife replied shortly. 'He accused a man with greater favour than he of robbing him, and when the trial inevitably went in the other man's favour, he then accused the Eze of not being *fair*.' Obi Ife's face turned inward, creating harsh dark shadows. 'As though fairness was ever a given in this world.

He should have kept his mouth shut and developed stronger connections with our leader. His short-sightedness killed him, but it taught me a valuable lesson.'

Sinai cleared her throat. She didn't know what to say. She didn't believe that Obi Ife's father's death was just in any sense of the word, but Obi Ife's venomous tone told her that arguing in a dead man's favour would not end well.

'Well, I'm sorry all the same. And I should be going.'

'But you've barely seen anything.'

'Oh, I have—I had a look before you came. They're all fascinating, thank you.'

'Ahh, you don't like it? I thought that you would like it,' Obi Ife replied in a disappointed tone.

'I do, I just—' Sinai began before—

Touch

Her heart fluttered as *something* called to her. A strong and undeniable *feeling*. It lay in the pit of her stomach. It was similar to the feeling that she felt when she stood at the edge of a tall cliff, with her toes poking out. It reminded her of the feeling that she got when she developed an irrational liking for Adebiyi, a boy she had known as a child, who had left to go study in Timbuktu, and came back looking like a studious sturdy man. She felt a mixture of excitement, fear, happiness, and the urge to run, all at the same time.

Sinai turned away from Obi Ife and walked slowly towards the right corner of the room. Something over there was calling to her. Sinai wandered absentmindedly until she hit a bench; the sharp pain spreading across her shins quickly brought her back to reality.

'I said, are you okay?' Obi Ife said, worried, beside her; she had hardly noticed that he had followed her across the room.

'Ehh yes, what—what is this?' Sinai asked with her eyes fixated on an emerald crystal, which was both rugged and poised at the same time, beautiful and average looking. It gleamed not from the surface, but from within.

'Ahh you have a good eye,' Obi Ife replied knowingly. 'That, my dear, is the Mother's Heart – that is the Ndụ crystal.'

'No,' Sinai gasped. 'I . . . it cannot be . . . no . . .' Obi Ife looked at her with a wide, knowing smile as he nodded heavily.

'It most certainly is.'

'But surely—*the Mother's Heart*—is too . . . too precious to just be *lying here.*'

'Like I said, no one can take it.'

'You don't know that.'

'I think I know more than most,' he said, amused. Then he warned, 'And be careful, because to doubt that it cannot be taken, is to doubt the Eze's judgement.' Sinai glanced back at him before turning back to the Ndụ Crystal.

Suddenly, the pull that she had felt towards the crystal intensified and a chill crept down her spine.

Touch

'I . . . I can't take it . . . but can I touch it?' Sinai asked, as she climbed over the bench and towards the wall, her fingers twitching towards the historic crystal.

'Yes, you can—but really, do not try to leave this room with that thing—don't even take it out of its spot, lest you forget and put it in your garment. That is a mistake that you will end up paying for with your life,' Obi Ife said gravely, as Sinai reached to touch the crystal. Her fingertips merely grazed its cold surface, and suddenly the world changed before her eyes.

*

Sinai was no longer in the dark courtroom; she was no longer standing next to Obi Ife. Sinai was now looking up towards the most spectacular being she had ever witnessed in her entire life. The being snatched her breath away and its beauty brought tears to her eyes.

'The Mother,' she gasped, as she stood in the presence of magnificence. The Earth Mother stood tall, the size of four—no, five men—stood on top of one another. Her skin was a rich, moist dark soil, and as she moved, her soil skin flowed about her, as if it too were alive. Her hair was a thick bush of vegetation ranging through various shades of brown and green. Her eyes were pools of dark-blue water and her lips were full, smooth marble-like rocks. The Mother smiled down at Sinai; her expression was so warm and kind that Sinai felt as though she would melt then and there.

The Earth Mother suddenly turned towards a group of people approaching her. The group consisted of three men and two women. Sinai noted that they all appeared slightly stronger, a little more handsome, than anyone she had seen before. As they drew closer she began to see that, like the Mother, they emitted a radiant mystical glow.

They must be gods, Sinai thought in wonder. *What is this place?* The colours were brighter, the air lighter, and everything seemed *right* somehow.

'Just like my dream,' Sinai muttered quietly.

'Mother! Please! The situation is growing dire by the minute. More so than you could even imagine,' one of the goddesses cried; her carob-coloured skin was so deep that Sinai felt as though she could swim in it. Her hair was wild and scattered around her face, laced with crystal-white streaks. As she spoke, Sinai noticed small sparks erupting around her body.

'Really, Agbala, and I always thought I had a spectacular imagination,' the Mother murmured softly with a low chuckle. Her voice reminded Sinai of what she imagined thick clouds to be: soft; bright; and full of unbelievable comfort.

However, the group was not in the mood to be comforted. Sinai could see worry etched on all their faces.

'And you do. I, for one, have enjoyed many a fruit of your

imagination over the years—but now I think it's time to leverage some of your more *vengeful* skills,' one of the men added, his thick black Afro hair bouncing slightly.

'Yes, you must do *something*. You must kill them—kill them all—every last one of them who even thinks of rebelling, you must—' Agbala blurted, as her sparks grew wilder and less controlled. Her blood boiled with hot anger, but she was not the only angry one. Whilst the others said nothing, they nodded earnestly.

'Agbala, please, be calm. These are your brothers and sisters that you are talking about.'

'No, they are not! They are traitors—as we speak now, Amadioha is rallying a group of corrupt humans to look for your heart crystal, the Ndụ crystal. They mean to . . . this is . . . Ma! This is not the time to be calm!' Agbala screamed, as she stepped forward.

The Mother looked at her for a moment before bending down and cupping her within her large palm.

'You are all so worried,' the Mother replied with a smile. 'It can be entertaining at times, but also draining . . . you, like your brothers and sisters who seek my power, well, all you want is *control*. You want to know how it ends, and control it so that it is in your favour. But child, you must not forget that there is a balance, a beautiful balance. What will be, will be. Chukwu has created a self-correcting realm; your purpose, my dear, as is mine, as is all of ours, is to follow our path as truthfully as we can.'

'Mother, they could kill you,' one of the men said softly, as a tear ran down his cheek.

'Yes. And if that must be, then that will be. All of this has happened for a reason, and it must follow its course. If I click my fingers and end those who speak against me, then what? I've killed the people, but not the idea, so more will rise up, then I kill them, and more will rise up, and before you know it, all my *anxious* children are dead. No, a lesson has to be learned here. If my death is required to teach that lesson, then so be it.'

*

The Mother's voice echoed in Sinai's ears. She was back in the dark courtroom. She gasped and stepped away from the Ndụ crystal in the wall.

'What is it, my dear?' Obi Ife asked.

'Did you see that?' Sinai breathed, as she blinked back tears.

'I— well, yes, it's very impressive . . . the crystal? Is that what you mean?' Obi Ife asked, as a look of confusion spread over his face. He took a step forward just as Sinai took a step back.

'Yes, the crystal,' Sinai murmured, as she placed her palm to her face in an attempt to wipe away some of the heaviness. 'Yes, yes, the crystal . . . please forgive me, Obi, this was a beautiful gift, but I'm finding myself quite overwhelmed with all this.'

'Are you okay?'

'Yes—it's silly. You know us. . . women,' Sinai muttered nervously.

'Mmm, well, let me escort you back to your room, at least.'

'No, no. Please, you've done more than enough. I'll see you soon!' Sinai replied, as she bolted out of the room, leaving a perplexed Obi Ife staring after her.

CHAPTER 28

THE COWARD

Udi

'Madi,' Naala hissed, as she kept her eyes peeled on her surroundings, smiling every now and again at the occasional passer-by. She was standing outside of one of the Ofala guests' tents, which was held up by anchored pre-cut pieces of wood and coated with a large thick piece of *akwete* cloth. Inside the tent she could hear Madi making a commotion.

'What are you doing?' she whispered angrily into the hut. Madi replied with a series of louder noises, which, to Naala's dismay, drew the gazes of concerned eyes. She smiled nervously as she brought out a large colourful fan from her pocket and coughed in an attempt to cover up the commotion.

'Madi, if you don't get out here right now, I'm coming in for you,' she hissed and, after a short pause, she rolled her eyes in disdain before turning around, readying herself to storm into the small hut; only to be confronted by a flustered Madi on his way out.

He stood tall, with a thick extravagant skirt of striped leather wrapped around his waist, and thick white fur bands on his large upper arms and head. A necklace spiked with fangs hung around his neck. His broad chest was bare, save for the red handprints that Naala had placed minutes before, using the red paste that they had found in the couple's luggage. His face was covered in a darker red paste, with bright white symbols sprawled across. Naala's attire matched his, but rather than having handprints on her chest, she wore a large, thick, feathered necklace that came down almost to her navel.

Madi stood flustered at the entrance of the tent, holding one section of the tent cloth in his left hand. Naala could see the dark forms of two bodies lying side by side and propped up against feathered pillows, a far cry from the haphazard position that Madi and Naala had originally found them in.

Naala knocked the cloth out of Madi's hand and let it fall to the ground, shielding the couple that they had drugged the night prior.

'*This* is why you were making all that absurd noise?' she said through gritted teeth. 'Ensuring that they got their beauty sleep?'

'I was just ensuring that they at least kept some dignity. It's not fair what we have done here, Naala. It's very deceptive and sneaky, like a filthy snake coming to poison you in the night, rather than fighting you in the day.'

'Snake bites are not just reserved for the night,' Naala replied drily.

'You know what I mean.'

Crowds of people walked past on their way towards the grand mountain. Madi's eyes scoured the crowds, but he had yet to see his little brother. As distasteful as it was, Madi had to admit that, for the time being anyway, Naala's plan was working excellently.

The day before, Naala had ground up the ụra leaves with an assortment of herbs that she had picked from the nearby shrubbery. Madi had lost track of them after the fourth herb, but he had followed Naala faithfully as she sniffed and inspected them before plucking the ones she wanted.

Naala had put together the mixture that she used to make with her grandmother for Hanye during his particularly restless nights. Depending on how bad the episode was, they would make a mixture that would knock him out for one to three days straight. When he awoke, he would be refreshed and well again; that is, until something else set him off.

That night, Madi, using a makeshift slingshot, had fired pellets of the mixed herbs into the soup pot of a relatively isolated couple that they had identified as most similar to the two of them. Now Madi stood in the midst of the Obis, the generals, and the Eze; disguised and free to find Emeka.

Naala walked up beside him.

'Look towards your right at the far end. The men with the long golden ofo sticks tied to their matching gold belts are in the head general's squad,' Naala muttered. She looked away in an attempt to remain inconspicuous.

'Yes, I recognise their uniform,' Madi said darkly, as he tried to block images of his brother in that same uniform covered in the blood of their neighbours. 'He is not with them.'

Naala scanned the landscape.

'Well, I'm sure they are scattered around the place,' she reassured him quickly. 'There must be more of them. I see only ten men here. I've heard that the general's platoon has at least thirty officers.'

'Yes,' Madi said quietly. 'Okay, let's go.'

An hour later, Madi and Naala found themselves towards the front of the procession of people climbing the base of the Udi mountain. The Eze couldn't have been more than a stone's throw away from them. He stood out with his extravagant attire consisting of a beautiful, rich collar of black fur with two gold-plated oryx horns sprouting at both of his shoulders. On his head sat a large, feathered headdress, on top of his neat uniform locs, tied at the nape of his neck with a gold band. Around his waist he wore a skirt of striped leather and various brilliant furs. This was not the only thing that made him noticeable. His very presence was intoxicating, as though he was radiating a new kind of energy, like light or heat, only far more powerful.

Naala couldn't help but feel drawn to the powerful man. Whilst there was no doubt that she wanted him dead, a growing part of her also wanted to marvel at him, as though he were a long-lost treasure that she could keep safe and locked away forever, only visiting when the urge was too great and she needed to stand in the presence of a god.

He is not a god. He is a murderer, Naala thought bitterly. She hated this man; he and his army had stolen her loved ones. *How on earth could I be drawn to him?*

Naala rummaged through her mind for answers, but found none. Rather than continuing to fret, she decided to push whatever this feeling was to the back of her mind and focus on her ultimate goal: find Emeka.

Naala turned to look at Madi's expression for what seemed like the hundredth time during their journey up the mountain. She was looking for a glimmer of recognition, a sign that he had finally found his brother, but so far all she had caught was his face becoming increasingly sour.

They had started at the back of the parade of people. They would inspect the surrounding faces before increasing their speed and pressing on once it became apparent that Emeka was not in their current section. Madi and Naala had continued this process and edged further and further up the procession. Their feet ached from continuously trying to overtake those around them and their heads were hot and sticky with sweat. They were approaching the front of the group, with no one left to overtake but the Eze himself. Yet Emeka was nowhere in sight.

Naala took a deep breath before turning to Madi once again and tugging at him softly. He brushed her away absentmindedly, and continued to scan the crowd. Naala cleared her throat loudly.

'*Biko*, my leg hurts. Can we pause for a moment?' Naala gestured to one of the crevices on the mountain wall.

'Now?' Madi replied impatiently, his eyes darting back and forth between her and the crowd around.

'Yes, now,' Naala replied coldly, her patience also beginning to wane. Surely he should know by now that his brother was not there.

'Listen to your wife, brother! Trust me, it will save you a headache later down the line,' one man chuckled, as he jovially hit Madi's back and winked at his own wife who smiled.

Madi attempted a smile back, but gave up halfway through. He took one last sweeping look at the group approaching him before sighing and moving towards Naala, who had edged closer to the face of the mountain. She directed them towards a small crevice she had spotted earlier. As they drew closer to it, Naala realised that it was far deeper than she had originally thought; to her surprise the small opening led to a cave.

'Why are you stopping?' he asked quietly, his voice shielded somewhat by a distant stream rushing over what sounded like rocks deep within the cave.

'Madi, he's not here,' Naala said quickly, not wanting to drag out the conversation any longer than it needed to be. She could already see that it was not going to be an easy one.

'Hey, you don't know that for sure. Not yet,' he pleaded, more so with himself than Naala.

'We were among the last people coming up this mountain, and we have travelled up to the front. We've looked through all the people and he's not here,' Naala replied, and, as the words tumbled out of her mouth, a wave of sadness hit her. She had really wanted to find Madi's brother, not solely because of the part he would play in avenging her family, but because she wanted to see them reunited. She wanted to know that the Eze and his army had not completely succeeded in destroying families.

'I could have missed him,' he said softly, as he closed his eyes tightly.

A thick lump formed in her throat and her eyes felt tight and prickly. Naala wanted nothing more than to reassure Madi. She wanted to agree and give him the hope that he desperately needed to cling onto, but before she could say a thing, loud voices rang through the cave. They were not alone.

'What are you two doing in here, eh?' said one of the emerging shadows. As he drew close enough to the light, Naala noticed gold gleaming on his belt: they were men from the general's squad.

'I think it's clear that these lovers were looking for some privacy. Well, don't let us stop you! Heaven knows I've needed a good show,' another resonant voice added, followed by a rumble of deep laughter.

Naala's blood grew hot. She was unsure whether she felt anger or shame; whatever it was, it made her clench her fists and narrow her eyes.

'Oh, no-no-no,' Madi replied cautiously. 'We're just here to take a break from the sun—my poor wife needed a rest.'

'Who said that?' a raspy voice said from the shadows, as Madi looked around, confused.

'Me? Are you talking to me?'

'Yes, who are *you*?' the voice replied, slightly louder as its owner advanced further.

'I'm—well, I'm . . .'

'We are Kamali and Kia, from the Kingdom of Aksum in the far east. We've travelled a long way to come to the Ofala festival; I imagine we are the first of our kind here,' Naala said quickly, attempting to make her accent sound like Madi's. Her village had received a number of visitors from Aksum; each one had been different from the last. Aksum was a region that housed hundreds of different tribes, meaning that, if need be, Naala and Madi could easily create their own.

The man drew closer, slowly materialising out of the shadows. As he came into the light, Naala had to squeeze her fists to stop herself from gasping. He stood tall in a similar, but slightly different attire from the rest of the soldiers. Across his chest he wore a large gold pendant encrusted with brilliant jewels; in the middle of the majestic pendent was an old rusting key.

The head general.

He stared intensely at Madi, before breaking into a hearty laugh and giving him a friendly slap on the back. Madi laughed nervously.

'Young man! You gave me such a fright. Your accent sounds so much like that boy . . . what was his name?' the general asked, as he looked back at his men.

'You mean Emeka? The coward?' another man replied with a low chuckle.

'Yes! Yes! Emeka, I thought I was seeing an onyinyo,' the general said.

Naala blinked and looked back at Madi who was frozen in place; his fists were clenched and his body tense.

'Are you alright?' the general asked cautiously.

'Yes,' Madi replied after a short pause. 'It's just the sun, and the journey.'

'Ahh, give the man some water,' the general ordered, before turning to leave the cave.

Naala quickly stepped in his way, causing him to halt.

'Sorry, Ozo, but who is this man that sounds so much like my husband?' Naala said chattily; her mouth was dry but she forced herself to power through. 'I'd be curious to meet the man. We can tell the people in Aksum that we stumbled across another version of Kamali on the road.'

The general looked down at her with disdain.

'Shouldn't you be tending to your husband? Or are things done so differently in Aksum?'

'I . . . well,' Naala stuttered.

'Please excuse my wife; the women in Aksum are practically famous for their gossiping,' Madi managed to say once he had regained his composure. A chorus of laughter and agreement erupted through the cave as a leather flask was handed to him.

'Although . . .' Madi continued '. . . I too would like to meet this man, who supposedly sounds like me.'

'He is dead! The bloody coward tried to run away in the night and got an arrow in the back. No offence,' he said, turning to Madi pointedly. 'I'm sure you're nothing like him.'

Madi could only nod weakly.

'Well, anyway,' the general said after a brief pause, 'we're falling back—Jayamma and Debare, quickly finish collecting that spring water—the rest of you, let's go!'

Madi and Naala stepped aside as a group of men marched by them. Madi turned to Naala with intense pain and anger simmering in his eyes.

She shook her head in response; she was so very sorry. Soon enough the cave was completely still. Neither Madi nor Naala moved or said a word to each other. Naala's eyes were fixated on Madi's shadowy face as he stared hopelessly at the ground. She had no idea what to say or do.

'I wish they would stop calling that boy a coward,' a voice suddenly said from within the cave. Naala jumped slightly and looked deeper into the cave, but she saw nobody, not even the eerie shadows that she had witnessed when the soldiers were hanging around.

The general ordered two of them to stay; they must be around some sort of bend, Naala thought, near the stream that she could hear but could not see. Naala nudged Madi, signalling that he should remain silent.

Just as Naala and Madi could not see the two men speaking, so the men clearly could not see them either, which could only work to Naala and Madi's advantage, now that the conversation had circled back to Emeka.

'But you know why he is doing that? It is a warning to the rest of us, about what will happen if we step out of line. Death is not enough; your name, your reputation, will be ruined as well.'

'Yes, but it's wrong. That boy did something that we should all do; he stood up to the orders to kill and tried to protect those people. All this senseless killing . . . women, children, the elderly. It's evil, and it is weak. You know the general is still clueless as to why we are being tasked with committing these murders—ask him. That boy stood up for them and paid with his life, and we laugh whilst the general calls him a coward.'

The conversation came to a pause as the heavy words settled onto the dark rocky ground. Naala mourned yet another senseless death, but found solace in the fact that Madi's brother had found redemption. Hopefully Madi would finally be able to rest, knowing that his brother was now at peace in the afterlife.

'You need to be careful, my friend,' a low voice warned. 'You really need to be careful.'

'Careful with what? My life or my soul? Which one do you really think requires more care?' the other man retorted.

'Enough; we've taken too long fetching this water anyhow. Let's finish this off and return— now is not the time for all this,' the other man said authoritatively, as Naala and Madi slowly backed out of the cave.

CHAPTER 29

THE RIGHT QUESTION

City Of Nri

'The Mother!' Sinai exclaimed, as she rushed into Meekulu's kitchen. Sinai couldn't even begin to find the words she needed; her mind was overwhelmed with a chorus of emotions that she struggled to make sense of.

The old woman had white thick powder scattered on her apron and all the way up to her bare elbows. Meekulu lowered her head, her glass frames sliding slightly down her nose as she peered at Sinai intently.

'The Mother?' Meekulu said curiously.

'Yes! No—not the Mother, *the Mother*—she is so much more than this—more than what they say—and he—he . . . what *he* did,' Sinai replied, as she drew closer to the old woman.

Him. The Eze, the hero, the liar. Sinai's mind whirled with thoughts that she had yet to fully process.

The breathtaking Earth Mother. Her beautiful image still burnt fiercely in Sinai's mind; her grace, her *balance*. Slowly those images morphed into the anxiety that filled Sinai whenever she was in the Eze's presence. The bile that had nearly reached her throat when he had smirked over the death of his queen, Lolo Obioma. Unspoken cruelty and harsh rules marked his rule over the kingdom; how could he be the saviour when the Earth Mother had fought for nature itself?

Meekulu raised an eyebrow and continued to search Sinai's face for something untold. Suddenly the old woman broke into a wide smile.

'So you have seen! You have really seen,' Meekulu said wistfully. 'How?'

As Sinai recounted what happened to her in the courtroom, Meekulu's eyes widened further and further. Her powdered hands clamped tightly over Sinai's and her reactive sounds became increasingly animated.

'You saw her, that scene, just with one touch,' Meekulu interjected in shock, as Sinai nodded enthusiastically.

'And you mean to tell me that he let you touch the Ndụ crystal, just like that!' Meekulu exclaimed again, as Sinai continued nodding. 'The folly of man truly knows no bound!' The old woman chuckled delightfully to herself. 'I didn't expect that you would to get close to that thing for months still, years even!'

'You knew that this would happen?'

'I did not *know,* but I most certainly *hoped,* and I worked to create situations that would make such an occurrence likely to take place. Why else would I ask you to spy on the Eze?' Meekulu released Sinai and went over to a bucket to wash her hands.

'Wait, you made me agree to an ọbara oath so that I could touch the crystal?' a baffled Sinai asked, her head still reeling from the revelations about the Mother.

'Yes, and no. I wanted you to spy on the Eze so that you would *know* yourself,' Meekulu said.

'Know myself?'

'Yes, know yourself and develop, grow stronger and wiser, which one only does when faced with threats,' Meekulu said, as she dried her hands and turned towards the girl. Her eyes were slightly lowered, and what Sinai could only perceive as guilt was visible in her leathered face. 'There is one other thing that you should know—the ọbara oath,' Meekulu began, before squinting as she gauged Sinai's temperament.

Sinai's eyes widened. 'Oh no,' she breathed. 'Oh no no, it's been enacted, hasn't it? I'm going to die? But I've been spying on him, and, okay, yes, granted I could have gone to the Ofala festival and spied some more, but—'

'It's not real,' Meekulu interrupted.

'What?!' Sinai choked.

'The ọbara oath and the resulting death and all that nonsense are not real,' the old woman noted, as she walked over to the same cabinet that she had gone to months ago.

'It's not real . . .?' Sinai repeated in a daze.

'Of course not!' Meekulu said, as she dug out the pearl box and opened it. She took a pinch of the red powder and put it on her tongue.

'See, it's just simple cayenne pepper,' she said, as she handed Sinai the box. 'Great for making stews, not so much for cursing! To be honest, I was insulted that you would believe that I would do such things. I have not, and do not, dabble in the ọbara magic, and you better be glad for it. Honestly, child, you are a terrible *onye nyocha*; you didn't find one good piece of information on the Eze. You should be more careful when swearing willy-nilly to oaths that you know nothing about. You would surely be dead by now if that oath had actually been enacted!'

'But why pretend to do so?' Sinai asked, still focused on the fact that very thing she had stressed over for weeks was simple seasoning.

'Well, it worked, didn't it?'

'Well, I don't know. I have no clue what *it* is,' Sinai cried out in frustration.

'You have seen *the Mother*—a mighty gift in its own right, but the *it* you are referring to, is also a lesson into who *you* are.'

'It is?'

'Of course! As with most things in life . . . answer me this: how is it that you were able to see that premonition? How were you able to stand in the past and the present at the same time?'

'I didn't stand in the past and present—'

'You saw a vision of the god's war; was that not in the past?'

'Yeaas, but I was—I am here?'

'Exactly, the past and the present,' Meekulu said firmly.

'Well . . . that . . . it must be a strange side effect of touching the crystal?'

'Many people have touched the crystal, but only *you* have seen the Mother. Only you have been given a mark in the forgotten tongue.'

'I was not marked.'

'Really? What is that then?' Meekulu asked, taking the girl's right hand and turning it. Sinai gasped when she saw symbols that she had never seen before, written on her skin. They stood out, bold and unnerving in a gold ink that shimmered in the sunlight. They resembled the fletching of an arrow overlaid with a cross and a smooth bending line. The symbols were similar to Nsibidi script, yet somehow different, familiar and unrecognisable at the same time. A deep black spark flashed through the markings and Sinai dropped her hand in shock.

'It—I'm sure that it can all be explained, logically. I'm sure the marking is . . . and perhaps the conditions were simply optimal for this sort of thing to happen? The stars? Alignment? The moon? You should know,' Sinai replied; she felt apprehensive about where this conversation was going.

'Or perhaps you are an *mmo*,' Meekulu replied, leaving Sinai speechless.

'It's not possible,' she finally said after a long pause. 'The mmo are gone—all of them gone—they are no longer in this world.'

'Aren't you the same person who, less than an hour ago, believed the Eze saved us from the Mother's wrath?'

The old woman believed what she was saying! She believed that Sinai belonged to the lost mystical folk. She believed that Sinai was a mmo, a spirit that could bend the earth and air elements.

'You are lying,' Sinai whispered.

Meekulu turned up her nose in disgust. 'Why would I do something so *weak*?' she retorted.

'You just said that you lied about the ọbara oath! Who knows what you could be lying about now?' Sinai replied indignantly.

'*Biko*—you'd better relax that tone. I will not tolerate any disrespect in my own kitchen.'

'Sorry,' Sinai said earnestly. 'I didn't mean any disrespect . . . it's just . . . well, there is simply no way. It's crazy that we are even having this conversation. I have never used any kind of *magic*. I have not—I'm not a-a-a—I'm just . . . me,' Sinai tried to explain.

She knew exactly who she was; she had always known. Sinai was unimportant, and she liked that more than she could ever explain. There was a sublime comfort in being unimportant. Sinai enjoyed staying in the background, because it meant that she could watch or dream up extraordinary things without the pressure and pain that came with being involved. Being a mmo, a group of beings that made the Obis—the Eze even—seem obsolete . . . well, there was nothing unimportant about that.

'Yes, you are *you*, and *you* are Sinaikuku, the mmo. Simple as that.'

'That's not my name.'

'Of course it is. What do you think Sinai is short for?'

'It is not short for anything . . . it . . .' Sinai tried to protest but her argument crumbled mid-sentence. Sinai had never known what her name was short for, or what it even meant; she had never cared to ask.

'Mhmm,' Meekulu muttered, as she peered closely at the perplexed girl. 'And one more thing: you have most certainly used magic before.'

'I have not, I—'

'Do you ever use that thing in your brain?' Meekulu sighed, as she pointed vigorously at her own head. 'How many people do you know that survive the mighty fall that you ended up walking away from?'

'But you said the sheets, the fur linen, on afo, you said the cleaners, they . . .'

'I know what I said. I also know what happened! You fell and Sergeant Olu saw you. He ran to inspect the body, but rather than seeing a mangled corpse that he expected, he was met with a bruised and damaged, albeit alive, girl. He brought you to me immediately.'

Sinai slowly took a seat.

'That can't be! You *said* that everyone saw! They would have reported me if they saw. And also, what happened to lying only being for the weak? Apparently you've lied about everything . . .' Sinai's voice trailed off as she became increasingly worried about seeming disrespectful again. 'Meekulu . . .' she added, in the hope that it would soften her words.

Meekulu gave a small smile before swinging her long braids to the side.

'I'm too old to abide by rules, dear, even my own. And yes, everyone saw—they saw exactly what *I* wanted them to see. Do you know which dish I prefer to cook the most?'

'Which one?' Sinai replied tiredly. She had learnt early on that conversations with Meekulu, particularly the serious ones, were bound to be filled with a number of bizarre and unusual diversions. After a series of trials and errors, Sinai now fully understood that it was almost completely futile to try and get the old woman back on track. Meekulu loved to divert and turn about the conversation, so the quickest way to get to the old woman's point was to wait for her to do so.

'Pounded yam! Yes! I love to make the pounded yam; some women say it tires them out, or it is boring, but for me it is fun. Pounding and pounding, you feel like you've really done something,' Meekulu said excitedly, as she squared up to emphasise her strength. 'And the result, the pounded yam—so fluffy and sweet and beautiful—well, it is just like the thing locked in your head . . . your brain. It is so *pliable*. You can reshape it to whatever you want it to be, if you have the time and skill.'

'Okay. . .' Sinai said, as her interest piqued. She suspected that the old woman may be nearing her point.

'The people who witnessed your fall saw *something*, perhaps a dark spot, tumbling down against the bright sun or maybe they heard a scream. They would have squinted at the sun, and blinked as Sergeant Olu emerged from the scene with you in his arms. He rushed off to find me before he could answer any questions, and soon enough stories began to circle around about the fur linen.'

The folds at the corner of the old woman's eyes deepened with her smile.

'Why did he go to you?' Sinai pondered out loud. 'Why not report me to the Eze?'

It was not against the law to be a mmo. As Sinai understood it, mmo were neither bad nor good; they were simply *skilled*. That said, an apparent sighting of a mmo, the first one in decades, centuries even—well, that would have been a remarkable event, one that the head of the kingdom would surely need to know about.

'All the soldiers know to come to me for wounds that are beyond the scope of the palace doctors, for ailments that attack the mind or soul. He knew I would be able to help you, whereas they would have most certainly failed.'

'But . . . but I'm not a soldier. I have no connection to him at all. He had no reason to bring me to you, particularly because his duty was to report me.'

'Duty . . . hmm. Would you have gone to the Eze? Knowing what you know now?' Meekulu asked. 'If you had witnessed what Olu had seen, would you have taken the girl to the Eze or to me?'

'To you,' Sinai replied quietly. She didn't feel as though she necessarily knew anything concrete, but what she did know left her apprehensive and uneasy about the man that they called a hero. After her vision of the Mother, Sinai was certain that something about the history she had been told was wrong.

'Sergeant Olu is a good man that has been led down a very troubled path. He came to me years ago seeking absolution; all I could give him was something to settle his mind, and yet he has been eternally grateful. He trusts my counsel and my judgement. He, like me, seeks change, and so when the opportunity for change came about, it was hardly a surprise that he came to me to help carry it out.'

'And . . . I . . . I am the opportunity for change?' Sinai asked cautiously, unsure as to whether she wanted to hear the answer.

Any trace of the smile that was typically on Meekulu's face, disappeared.

'You are my hope, a fragment of the old real magic—not anwansi that is merely dusty remnants of the vibrant magic that once flowed through the lands. Not *ọbara*, that synthetic disease, bred by greedy men who could never take the time to understand the importance of balance, and instead opt to drain blood, drain life, in exchange for morsels of energy. You are an example of *real magic* and real magic can only be god-given. The one and only, beginning and end: Chukwu. Chukwu has several different names and forms. Some people see Chukwu as the one overseer of the universe, others see Chukwu as several gods with different personalities and functions. Some see him as a Holy Trinity, and some as a force behind the smallest particles within our universe. Either way it is all the same: Chukwu is the reason for it all. The ultimate creator, and the one who brought forth Ala, the Earth Mother. She created a balance within nature and birthed an array of life, from the lost gods to the surviving humans and to the tiny insects that crawl on the ground. We all exist within a system that was created, and not too long ago, managed by the Mother,' Meekulu said, drawing up a stool to sit on, and gesturing at Sinai to do the same.

'Over a hundred years ago, Amadioha, the god of thunder and justice, sought to steal the Mother's power. You see, Amadioha had always been a strange god. He was powerful, very powerful indeed, but whereas most gods influence human behaviour, Amadioha was influenced *by* humans. Our wants and needs, our never-quenching thirst for power, our self-destructive greed—we poisoned him. Justice, the core of Amadioha's power, is and will always be the collective will of the people. The concept started off so pure and genuine, as did its god, but soon the will of the people turned rotten, and with it Amadioha became *new*.

'The people wanted power, and soon he wanted to deliver that power to them. His poisoned mind led him to believe that the people themselves should dictate nature, and have full control over their lives and deaths. This created a divide amongst the gods and the people, between those that sided with the Mother, and those that sided with Amadioha. Amadioha fought cruelly, using his army to spread death and destruction in his pursuit for the Mother's power. She and her loyal children fought to protect and defend; if she had attacked, just once, the war would have ended right then and there. Instead, the war ended when one of the humans working for Amadioha stole the Ndụ crystal.'

'The Eze,' Sinai muttered, as Meekulu nodded solemnly.

'After he stole the heart, the Mother, the gods and the mmo on both sides of the war vanished. The system that the Mother built has kept us going, but our connection to nature, to Chukwu, to meaningful life, is broken. Instead, injustice and negativity flow through every waking day—and they are growing day by day.'

'Can I help? Can I do *something* somehow? If I am what you say, if I am a mmo, can I help right this wrong?' Sinai asked, as Meekulu's story ended.

'Now that you know the right question to ask,' Meekulu replied with a gleam in her eyes. 'We can seek the answer.'

CHAPTER 30

ASHES TO ASHES

Udi

Naala and Madi re-joined the procession without saying a word to one another. They kept their heads lowered as they walked slowly among the cheerful crowd. The energy that had propelled them to the front of the procession earlier that day had deserted them, and soon enough they found themselves trailing at the back of the long line. Sounds of the deep-based drums, grainy *shekeres*, and windy *algaitas* danced vigorously through the warm air as the procession drew closer to the famous site.

Naala looked cautiously at Madi. She was desperate to discuss next steps, but her concern for both Madi's grief, and the threat of being overheard, had kept her quiet.

In due time, the latter was becoming increasingly obsolete as the music grew louder and the distance between the two of them and the crowd grew further and further apart.

'I'm sorry about your brother,' Naala said quietly, once the last two people in the crowd—a brawny boy who carried an elderly man, presumably his grandfather, on his back—were now far ahead of them. Madi looked at her briefly.

'Don't be sorry. He died with honour. He is well,' Madi replied stiffly, as he allowed a small smile to form on his lips.

'He did. Yes, he did,' Naala replied, unsure of what to say next. After a brief pause she added carefully, 'I'm really happy that you got to hear that. I wasn't too sure if you had fully appreciated what the soldiers said . . . it still feels as though you have a lot of pain hanging over you.'

Naala was wary about overstepping her boundaries. She was also not entirely comfortable about delving into a conversation about senseless murders, with the memories of her village still resting heavily on her soul. But Madi was in pain, and she felt he was the type of person that benefited from such conversations.

'No, I'm not in pain.' He stopped for a moment, loudly clearing his throat. 'It would have been nice to see him once again—alive, that is—but he suffered . . . he suffered in his life, and so I can only be happy that he found peace and honour in death. He is fine now. Who am I to be upset?'

'You're his elder brother and a lot has happened, to you and your family,' Naala replied softly. 'It is okay to be upset, even if you're happy for him.' Emeka might have died honourably, but not in the sense that Madi was accustomed to. For the most part, dying honourably in Mkpabo meant closing your eyes to sleep in old age after using your body to protect, love, and nurture your family. On a rare occasion it meant protecting your village in a war or from a wild beast, and it would be followed by stories of love and admiration from those who witnessed or recorded the death. Instead, all Madi had were hushed words from pitying soldiers working against the harsh words from the general. It was hardly a cause for a celebration.

'My concern now is with that necklace around that serpent's neck,' Madi's face soured.

'You still want to get the key?' Naala gasped.

'You don't?' Madi replied.

'I do, no. I do—I just thought, given that Emeka is no longer with us, we would . . .' Naala trailed off, as she searched Madi's face. For Naala, the mission had become impossible the moment Emeka's death was revealed. How could they steal the head general's key? Even with their disguises, they were still outsiders.

'We would do what?' Madi replied. 'Go back? Back to where?'

'Not back,' Naala murmured. It was the first time she had truly considered what their next steps were. 'I'm just not too sure what *forward* looks like. I don't see how we could get close to the general as we are,' Naala said, gesturing to her attire. As elegant as it was, there was no way that they could receive clearance to get near the head general of the Eze's army.

'We were pretty close to him just a few minutes ago.'

'Yes, but I couldn't have reached out to grab that key from his neck, and I'm guessing neither could you.'

'Well, couldn't we do what we did before? Put pellets in his food, then grab it at night?'

'He is the *head* general of the Eze's army, not some plush royal. He has been trained since he was a child to catch those antics before we can even think of them.'

'What about Enwe?' Madi asked suddenly.

'What about him?' Naala replied, unnerved. She didn't want to discuss further plans; she could see where Madi was going with this and she do not like it at all. She wanted Enwe to be left out of all of this. Madi's eyes narrowed with frustration.

'He could grab the key,' he replied with emphasis, throwing his arms wide.

Naala looked around cautiously to see if anyone had been drawn into their conversation by Madi's outburst. He also had a quick look around before taking a step closer to Naala.

'He could grab the key,' he repeated in a quieter voice.

'He . . . can't; he's just . . .' Naala answered doubtfully.

'I have seen him snatch many *things* for you, and it is not by chance. I know you use gestures—he can certainly steal a key.'

'No. Sorry, Madi, I just . . . I don't think this will work,' Naala replied tightly. 'He steals the key, hands it over to me and then what? I get trampled on by the army?'

That's a lie, she admitted to herself, *you taught him how to hide away items for later when you were spying on the group.*

'We could make a replica of the key? And when he hands it to you, you drop the new one?' Madi added.

'A replica? Now you're really reaching. How will we make a *replica* of that jewelled pendant? With what metal? What time? Do you know how to weld? Do you have some spare jewels lying around? Because I certainly do not?' Naala retorted. Her face felt warm and her throat tight. Enwe was her only piece of home and the thought of losing yet another piece of herself ate away at her soul. *Tell him about the other way.* 'No, just no,' Naala said finally. 'It won't work.'

'Because you don't want it to. You don't even want it to work because of that stupid *monkey?* Are you seriously placing that animal before hundreds, maybe even thousands, of lives?'

'I—' Naala started. She didn't know what to say. He was wrong, she knew he was wrong. That's not how she felt at all, except that, for a brief moment, it was. She didn't want to place Enwe in unnecessary danger; she didn't want him anywhere near the general.

'Why did you even come here? You don't care about Emeka; you don't care about me. I don't even think you cared about your village. If you did, this wouldn't even be a question.'

'Don't you dare bring up my village,' Naala replied darkly, as thick rage swirled within her heart, her fists tightened into balls, and her jaw stiffened.

'I'm sorry,' Madi said. 'Maybe we should just leave . . . try and find the group again.' He was trying to convince himself, more than anything.

Naala took a long deep breath, before snapping her fingers twice. In a matter of moments Enwe swooshed down in a ball of grey fur. He snatched the spiked necklace from Madi's neck. The little monkey scurried off as quickly as he came, hidden by the green leaves waving in the breeze.

'It can work,' Naala said wearily, her eyes gazing over to the last spot that she had seen the joyous procession, just before it curved around the side of the large mountain.

Naala released a shrill whistle. Madi's necklace suddenly fell out of the sky, before landing with a clang in Naala's hands. Enwe leapt onto her shoulder with his tail curling affectionately around her neck as she raised her right hand to rub his back.

'Yes, I can see . . .' Madi eventually replied, his eyebrows furrowed deeply in thought. 'So you were the one that stole my mangos,' he added, as Naala tried and failed to control the wicked smile spreading across her face.

'On what occasion?' she replied smugly.

'I knew it!' Madi replied, congratulating himself with a loud clap.

'Okay, okay! We can do this, so let's . . . just do it,' Naala said, as her heart quickened. She dropped her hand away from Enwe's warm soft fur and tapped his tail before he leapt away and melted into the trees.

'He will be fine,' Madi said.

'Yes,' she replied, as she handed over his heavy necklace.

'So what should we do? Catch up with the procession again, get close to the general and then wait for a big distracting event—so you can snap or whistle? You know, do the thing that will draw that thieving monkey.'

'Sounds like a plan,' Naala replied, before sprinting towards the procession.

The procession came to a sudden stop. The people had spent a large part of the morning hiking up the towering mountain, and yet the peak still loomed above them, hidden in the distant clouds.

Unlike the other, more knowledgeable, people in the crowd, Naala and Madi had not brought any snacks. Neither one of them had anticipated that they would be spending hours following after the Eze and those privileged enough to dance before him.

Naala was mortified. No matter how hard she tried, she could not will her stomach to stop its awful gurgling. Eventually she settled for simply crossing her hands around it, trying to muffle the increasingly embarrassing sounds. Madi suddenly gave her a slight nudge.

'I know, I know. I'm just hungry, okay?' she hissed defensively. His eyes widened expressively before signalling towards the centre of a slowly forming huddle. Naala followed his gaze and found the Eze at the centre of it, surrounded by eager-looking spectators, including the head general of his army. Naala blinked hard as the gold pendent shot a reflected sunbeam into her eyes.

'So we have arrived,' the Eze boomed to the crowd. 'To the same trail that I came to years ago, when the world had entered a deadly turmoil and needed someone to stand up.' His words carried over the wind and were punctuated by the sounds of the deep drums. Naala glanced at Madi, who flashed a look back at her. *Now?* she thought nervously. Any plan that they had formed earlier now seemed too open, too risky, and too dangerous. Naala watched the golden pendant twinkle as the sun beat down on the general's chest. The air tasted dry and cold, not rich and vibrant like the air closer to ground, closer to the trees and beautiful flowers. High up the mountain, Naala felt chilled and afraid.

'Let this be a lesson to you. Justice will always prevail. The true winners, the true victors, they all serve justice, and justice is why we prevailed!'

Click – click.

The sound of Naala snapping her fingers together was covered by the loud applause. Naala held her breath in anticipation when she saw Enwe swiftly swooping down towards the head general.

Naala watched, frozen. She had not decided to click her fingers. She had not yet made that decision in her head, and yet her body had acted. Her heart beat loudly in her ears, as her little friend scrambled up to the general's neck, dodging each and every one of his blows before yanking the necklace off. Just as Enwe turned to leap away, a loud frightening sound exploded through the air, and Enwe puffed into grey ash right before Naala's eyes. Slow, misty fragments of silver dust floated in the air. Enwe, Naala's little friend, was gone, and the necklace, imbedded with the key that she had made him steal, lay on the dark ground. The general moved to pick it up, just as a swarm of men, his platoon, gathered around him. All of them stood in the warriors' stance, and scanned the crowd with squinted serious eyes.

Naala's heart skipped a beat and her mouth suddenly went dry. Not only because Enwe had been destroyed right before her eyes, not because they had failed to retrieve the key, but because among the soldiers stood a man with a large scar across his face. The same man who had stood over her grandmother during the massacre. The same man with bright green eyes who had looked at her squarely that day, and was looking at her now, with that same expression of recognition.

'We have to go,' Naala murmured, as she backed away, still facing the soldier, whilst tugging discreetly at Madi.

'I don't think that's a good—' Madi started, as he looked cautiously at the people around him. Now was not the time to draw attention to themselves by attempting to escape. A crime had just been committed and running away would only expose them as the perpetrators.

Naala did not hear a single word of what he said. Instead her heart seized as the soldier took a step towards her.

'No, we have to go *now*,' Naala said, before turning and bolting out of the procession. Madi gasped; he had no choice but to follow her. They barged through the crowd of confused elites. The two of them, no longer bothered to uphold any pretence of decorum, moved with a raw, unbridled quest for survival.

'Hey! Hey!' a voice yelled, as they broke free from the crowd, picking up speed as they dashed down the slope of the mountain.

Naala heard whooshing sounds around her.

'Arrows! No-no-no-no,' Madi yelled in fright. Naala turned back to check if he was okay, but instead she got swept into a terrifying scene. Behind Madi, eight large men with bulging muscles and weapons at hand were pursuing them. Naala had imagined that she and Madi had put a suitable distance between themselves and the soldiers. She was wrong. They were catching up at an incredible pace, like cheetahs plummeting towards injured prey.

Naala's heart leapt out of her throat, and abandoned her body entirely.

A strange, yet familiar, sensation overtook her body. A deep cold shook her to her core. Naala wanted to scream, but the earth was breaking away faster than she could react. The ground dropped from under her, and she found herself completely lost. The black came for her once again, and Naala succumbed to it before she could breathe, let alone think.

CHAPTER 31

MEEKULU'S CAVE

City of Nri

'Hurry up, child!' Meekulu called from several cubits ahead of Sinai, as she traversed up the hillside. The hills around were patched with varying shades of green, from a deep dark seaweed colour to a bright lime. The old woman's waxed braids dragged weightlessly on the cushioned ground, as her small body bounced forward.

'How are you so fast?' Sinai breathed heavily. 'You're at least three . . . maybe even four times my age,' she added in a quiet breathless murmur.

'Much more than that, dear,' Meekulu cried out.

'Huh . . . really? Good ears too, fascinating,' Sinai wheezed, her chest tightening with fatigue. 'One moment,' she mouthed wordlessly, as she bent over with her hands clasped around her knees. Sinai was not used to climbing up and down so many steep hills. 'Sorry . . . I must still be . . . oh dear . . . recovering . . . from the . . . fall.'

Meekulu replied with a loud snort.

'No, my dear; you are just lazy and unfit. I guess one can hardly blame you given that you've spent the better part of your life lounging and partying. But now hurry up, girl—we are almost there,' Meekulu said as she climbed further.

Sinai looked up in pain as the old woman walked through the gathering mist, remnants of the morning's heavy rainfall now slowly drying and disappearing back into the heavens.

Sinai forced herself to carry on and place one foot in front of the other, though try as she may, she couldn't stop her back from hunching in defeat. It was only when she began to hear a loud gushing noise that she lifted her heavy head to see a magnificent waterfall.

'Wow,' she sighed, once she had taken a moment to restore her lost breath. Her chest was sore, her legs ached, and her stomach throbbed with a dull cramp, but for that one moment, she didn't think of any of that. All she could take in was the beautiful scene, the frothy white water falling beautifully over the lush green vegetation. The sky looked sweeter and the air was fresh.

'Meekulu, this is just—wow!' Sinai added, as Meekulu nodded in agreement, a wide knowing smile crossing over her face.

'Come on,' she said, as she marched towards the waterfall with Sinai following wordlessly.

*

That morning, Ozi had crashed unceremoniously into her room with two invitations clamped in her beak, one from Meekulu and the other from Obi Ife.

Sinai had shuddered at the thought of interacting with Obi Ife again. She had immediately discarded the parchment, without even reading it. While he certainly was not the worst man amongst the Obis, he was still stifling, overbearing, and entitled. Now that she was no longer tasked with spying on the Eze, she could rid herself of acquaintances like Obi Ife and focus on far more important matters.

Meekulu's message had been short and brief:

Meet me at the palace entrance. Bring comfortable slippers.

Given their previous conversation, whatever Meekulu had planned for the day was likely to help Sinai figure out what exactly she needed to do to help the Mother.

Sinai had clung on to that thought as she pushed her aching heavy legs over the ground. Mist from the splashing waterfall coated Sinai's face and the warm ripples swept her ankles as Meekulu led them through the shallow bay and closer to the large waterfall.

Sinai clambered across the round rocks and boulders. She looked up momentarily, only to find Meekulu passing through a thin gap in the waterfall. Sinai's eyes widened as the old woman disappeared behind the frothy water. Without stopping to think,

Sinai scrambled after Meekulu and followed her through the torrents.

Sinai had expected the water to beat heavily against her head and back, but instead it caressed her breezily, like a flurry of feathers. She wiped her eyes, but, just as she did, trickles of water from her soaked hair drizzled down her face. Sinai wore her hair up, with golden clasps clutching sections of her ponytail. She sighed at the thought of having to detangle her black moss-like hair once she got back home.

Sinai found that she was in a hidden cove. The dark wet sand looked smooth and untouched, and the rocky walls that surrounded her stood strong and imposing. Sinai turned to look back. She could no longer see the rocky boulders and distant green hills that she had come from; instead, she was met with a bright, wide, frothy wall of water.

Meekulu strode further into the cave with Sinai following. As they moved away from the bright waterfall, they slowly descended into darkness. Sinai took a sharp breath when she could no longer see nor feel for Meekulu. She would have called out her name, if she wasn't so overcome with fright. Sinai felt lost and alone, and she didn't like it at all.

Fortunately she could still hear Meekulu's movement as she shuffled around with what seemed like various strange items. Without warning, a large, bright yellow ọkụ flame lit up the cave and Sinai's eyes slowly adjusted to it.

289

'This is where I keep all my treasures,' Meekulu explained.

'Oh . . .' Sinai replied, as she looked around. 'I . . . I don't see anything.' She was confused; all she saw were grey rocky walls and the bare sandy floor.

'Well, I couldn't make it that easy for prying eyes!' Meekulu cackled, before reaching out her wrinkled hands and tugging at the wall. To Sinai's surprise, the rock creased as easily as dried leaves, revealing a wide gap opening.

Sinai stepped closer and inspected the peculiar wall. She quickly realised that it was not a wall at all. It was nothing more than a stiff thin cloth, made to look like hard rock in the dim light.

'Mmm, clever,' Sinai murmured, as Meekulu strolled into the large crevice that was lined with trinket-filled shelves. The old woman frowned momentarily as Sinai raised a foot to enter the room.

'Wait! The wall is not the only protection that I have set up. Before you cross into this room, you need to focus your mind. It can be on anything at all, an object, a person, but whatever it is, it must have the power to keep your attention completely for as long as you are inside this room,' Meekulu warned.

Sinai nodded. *Focus, focus . . . on what?* Sinai thought desperately. *The Mother's crystal!*

Sinai thought hard about the emerald crystal as she stepped into the room: its rigid—no smooth—exterior; the exchange with the Mother and the gods and goddesses that—that—.

Sinai's mind went pitch-black. Suddenly a sweet song, the most beautiful song in the world, pierced cleanly through her thoughts. Her mouth watered and her heart leapt into her throat. Sinai took a step back and turned towards her left. She hadn't noticed it before, but now it was all that she could think of. Just a few steps ahead of her stood a smooth marble statue, propped against the wall.

Sinai hurried towards the marble statue. It stood large, almost the size of Sinai herself. As she drew closer, she could see that it was a replica of a strange being. The marble creature's hair was braided in long single plaits, its chest was bare and plump, and, instead of legs, the creature stood on a long thick tail, similar to that of a fish's.

The statue was beautiful, perhaps the most beautiful thing that Sinai had ever seen. It filled her with endless promises and dreams. Silent whispers echoed through the cave, and suddenly Sinai knew that she had to follow the statue. If she did, Sinai would be able to drink the purest, coldest, most satisfying water; crystallised water made for the gods themselves. Sinai brought her hand to her throat; she hadn't realised how thirsty she was. Her throat felt dry and sandy. She was dying from thirst. She had to follow the statue.

'Sinaikuku!' a voice from nowhere rang in her head, as she felt a sharp smack against her cheek. Sinai blinked before taking a deep ragged breath, as though she had just broken to the surface of a deep ocean. She looked down at Meekulu who fought hard to keep hold of Sinai's gaze.

'Hey! Focus on me! Resist! Resist! It's not real!' Meekulu exclaimed, as the haze lifted from Sinai's mind. Sinai let Meekulu nudge her away from the statue as a chill trembled through her body.

'What was that?' Sinai finally said.

'That, my dear, is a *mami wata*, one of the spirits of the water,' Meekulu replied.

'A mami wata? Didn't they perish when the Mother died?' Sinai interjected, as she shook off the strange feeling that her mind was not her own.

'They did not die; they *changed*. Their spirits marbleised into these rock statues. Those spirits, whilst trapped and weakened, are still very much alive, something that I'm guessing you can now attest to,' Meekulu said, as she inspected Sinai carefully. 'I told you to focus, girl. If you had not broken out of that trance, you would have sat at the feet of the statue for days, unable to move, or talk. Only when you died of hunger and thirst would you have been able to escape.'

'I did—I thought I was . . . *focusing*,' Sinai replied.

'Hmph,' Meekulu said. 'Well, let's get going.'

This time Meekulu made Sinai step into the room first. Once Sinai had entered, the old woman followed, letting the material fall and form, once again, a makeshift wall.

Sinai blinked wordlessly as she entered what appeared to be a large cave. She had never seen anything like it. Rock stalactites dripped from the ceiling, basking in the glow of the numerous balls of gleaming ọkụ light scattered across the room. The ọkụ balls appeared to be simple at first glance, but they were in fact made of a series of small delicate lines.

'*Nsibidi*?' Sinai gasped, whilst Meekulu nodded approvingly.

'Yes, they are prayers of sorts,' the old woman said.

Sinai had seen many breathtaking ọkụ formations, but she had never seen this level of detail in the fiery balls. They hung weightlessly in the air, beautiful marks of pure genius.

The walls were lined with endless rows of shelves, each stacked with strange artefacts, but Sinai was preoccupied with the most extravagant of them all. In the centre of the cave, a stream of silent silvery water fell out of the ceiling and formed a hollow circle as tall and wide as she was. The water streamed down in a straight line and then followed the curve of a circle before travelling back up to somewhere Sinai could not see.

She couldn't work out what was holding the liquid structure up. The water flowed rigidly as though it was encased within an invisible tube, but Sinai could see that no such tube existed. She drew closer to it and realised that it was not silent at all; the stream was singing: a light and rhythmic sound, similar to the sweet melodies played on the lyre.

'What is this place?' Sinai said softly, as she gazed around the cave.

Meekulu beamed behind her. 'It's home,' she replied with a smile.

Sinai's heart filled with delight.

'What is this—' Sinai added, frowning slightly; she couldn't find words magnificent enough to describe such a structure. '— this water fountain?'

'It's an *ọnụ ụzọ*,' Meekulu said, and laughed heartily at Sinai's perplexed expression. 'A gate that I use sparingly to go places I have no business being and obtain things I have no right to have.'

Meekulu scurried towards one of the many shelves, searching excitedly for something. Soon enough, she came to a sudden stop. Sinai stood on her toes and craned her neck to see what Meekulu was staring at, but it took the old woman turning around for her to fully see.

Within Meekulu's hands lay two small golden globes that emitted a golden misty light.

'But this, my dear, this is the true treasure.'

'Another plant?' Sinai joked, smiling as she thought back to her mix-up with the ụtọ plant and the zoro stone.

'No. It is an oracle's eye,' Meekulu replied.

'Oh, I was just jok—a *what?*' Sinai gasped.

'An oracle's eye. They were one of the rarest, most beautiful creatures to inhabit the planet. As you can imagine, it is one of my most prized possessions.'

'An oracle? I don't think I know what that is.'

'Mmm. Well, you should. After your vision of the Mother, I've had suspicions that you might be somewhat akin to these beings,' Meekulu murmured, as she gazed softly at the golden globes.

An oracle? A mmo? Which one am I, Sinai thought, careful not to share her frustrations with Meekulu, lest the old woman finally lost patience with her.

'An oracle is a truth teller,' Meekulu continued. 'She knows what is, what was, and what will be. Her eyes are a major source of her power.'

'. . . and you have its—her . . . eyes . . . just in your hand,' Sinai replied in disgust and awe.

'Isn't it wonderful? This world, this life, even in the midst of its horror, delivers you such beautiful gifts.'

'Mmm,' Sinai replied, fixated on the oracle's eyes. 'What is, what was, and what will become,' she repeated. 'That is . . . overwhelming, isn't it? No, I don't think I am an oracle— I barely know anything.'

'Perhaps,' Meekulu replied with a small smile. 'And, yes, of course it is overwhelming; that, my dear, is the nature of life. Unmasking what you need in order to discover your divine purpose will always be overwhelming.'

'Will they tell me everything? Everything that has happened and will happen?' Sinai murmured, as she reached out to touch them. *Will they tell me if I really have these powers? Who my parents are? How I will die? How I will fail?* she thought, as she drew her hand back.

'They will tell you only what you need to know,' Meekulu said.

'Are you sure we should be doing this? Sometimes things are better left unsaid.'

'Are you mad? You have a gift! And if you saw the Earth Mother after touching Ndụ once, then it is a far greater gift than I originally thought. You must also have a mission, and it is connected to the Mother—this much I know. How can you throw away an opportunity to figure it all out?'

Sinai didn't have an answer; instead she looked at the golden globes uncomfortably.

'Sit down,' Meekulu said firmly.

'On the ground?'

'No, on my head!' Meekulu said in annoyance, as she lowered herself to the floor. 'What is wrong with you today, Sinai? Please, I need you alert.'

Sinai assisted her, before falling on the cold rock floor herself.

'You take one eye and I'll take the other,' Meekulu said, as she placed the cold metallic ball in Sinai's quivering hand. 'Now close your eyes.'

'Okay, my eyes are closed and the eye is in my hand. What now?'

'We wait,' Meekulu said. 'Calm your thoughts and let them pass through you with ease. Let her eyes guide them to what was, what is, and what will be.'

Sinai nodded and waited. She could hear echoes flowing

around her. The light melody of the ọnụ ụzọ, the flicker of the ọkụ lights, the sound of strong wings flapping in the cave. She attempted to tune them out but then realised that the floor was incredibly uncomfortable. She shifted position so that she wouldn't be distracted by the aching pangs, while she waited. She waited and waited, but nothing happened.

'So . . . how long do we usually have to wait . . . roughly?'

'Shhh!' Meekulu replied. 'Who knows! Minutes, hours, days—there's no rule to this.'

'Days!' Sinai exclaimed, feeling pangs now in the depth of her stomach, as well as her buttocks.

'It will take longer if you don't stop chattering!' Meekulu scolded. 'Close your eyes, shut your mouth, focus, and wait.'

Sinai did so. As time passed, her thoughts wandered into the wilds of her imagination. She thought about the Mother, the Eze, Obi Ife, even the mami wata. She thought about what she might eat tonight for dinner. She thought about the cave, and its wild bats. Her mind wandered completely until it reached a sharp stop.

Esinaala

A woman's voice whispered the name in her ear. The woman sounded breathless and familiar. Sinai's heart panged almost as though it missed someone, someone she had never known, but missed nonetheless. Suddenly a wash of sickening dread overcame her. They were chasing her! *Who?*

We need to run! Madi, move!

Sinai's eyes sprang open and she looked behind her, half expecting the person who had screamed in her head to emerge from the shadows. Meekulu's eyes were closed tightly and a look of discomfort spread across her face, but no surprise or shock. If she too had heard the voice, she wasn't showing it at all.

Sinai looked down at the golden ball in her hand. The voice was in her head, but she was certain that it did not belong to her. She recognised the voice, but she had never heard it before. Sinai let the golden ball slip through her fingers and drop softly on the floor as she let out a slow and steady breath. She didn't know what she had heard, but she knew that she didn't want to hear it ever again.

CHAPTER 32

TAKEN

City of Nri

Meekulu walked slowly by Sinai's side as they headed towards the palace. Sinai had expected Meekulu to scold her severely when she had finally opened her eyes to find Sinai sleeping on the ground with her oracle's eye abandoned beside her. The old woman had not said a word. They had picked themselves up and wordlessly headed home.

'I'm really sorry, Meekulu; it's just I heard a voice and it . . . scared me . . . we can go back and do the whole exercise again, if you would like,' Sinai said eventually. She was pained by the old woman's silence; she would have much preferred her to shout. Sinai could handle anger, but disappointment was much harder to swallow.

Meekulu did not say a word; she just moved ahead, watching the sky cool into a dark-blue evening, against the distant palace's tall beige walls.

'Meekulu?' Sinai tried again, as senseless tears pricked her eyes. 'Did you hear me? I said I was sorry—Ma?'

'What?' Meekulu blinked, as she looked at Sinai's face for the first time since leaving the cave.

'Have you been listening to me?' Sinai mumbled uncomfortably. 'Are you . . . okay?'

'Yes, yes—I'm fine. I am blessed, in fact, to be here, to have followed my path, to be who I am. . . but you see, one often forgets that when pesky things like pain come to distract.'

'Are you in pain?' Sinai asked, relieved that Meekulu was speaking again, but concerned with *how* she was speaking. The energy that usually fuelled the old woman's vibrant words was gone, replaced with thick heavy sadness that slowed her words and pulled down at Sinai's heart. Sinai took the old woman by her shoulders.

'I don't think you are okay. Just tell me what it is, what do I need to do? Should we go back to the cave?' Sinai implored.

The old woman's smile dropped away from her face as something caught her eye over Sinai's shoulders. 'Listen to me, Sinai. We don't have much time. I thought we did, I thought I could teach you, but I was wrong.'

'Meekulu—'

'You have to be strong. Do you hear me? You *are* strong, you must know this—you have a tall task ahead of you, but the two of you can succeed as long as you *know* you can succeed—but you have to remain strong and focused. Forces may work against you, but you have the power to make them work *for you*.'

'I don't understan—'

'Hey, step away now!' a voice thundered behind Sinai, causing her to jump and swivel around.

Sinai's heart dropped as she saw three soldiers, armed with glowing abaras, standing in front of her. Sinai was accustomed to soldiers patrolling the palace, their weapons present, but now something in their stern faces and cold voices raised the small hairs at the nape of her neck. The weapons were not there just for show; they were meant for her.

'We haven't done a-anything. I don't under—'

'Get her, quickly! The Eze is waiting!' The soldier who had spoken earlier shouted at the two men behind him.

'No!' Sinai said, closing her eyes as she anticipated strong hands around her neck and arms. Her heart thudded loudly as she heard movement all around her, but she felt nothing. She slowly opened her eyes, and saw Meekulu being marched away by the three large soldiers.

'No! Leave her! No!' she screamed, as she scrambled desperately after them.

CHAPTER 33

SHARP ARROWS AND SOFT HEARTS

Furuefu Forest

Naala was floating through the air when she felt a muted jolt flow through her body. Her head felt heavy and almost detached from her shoulders, loose and free as though she was upside down. In fact, she was upside down, but she wasn't afraid of falling. The air was warm and humid, carrying the scent of flowers and rich soil. Another jolt ran through her body, and Naala lifted her heavy eyelids in response. At first, all she could see was a splatter of brown and green smudges, but slowly it formed into a full and vibrant forest.

What? she thought in bewilderment. Suddenly adrenaline hit her. She wasn't floating. Someone was carrying her. She jerked her body up, and her captor lost his grip in shock. Naala took advantage of the opportunity and forcefully slithered down his body, slamming her fists violently against his flesh.

'Naala, stop!' a voice cried. A strange sense of familiarity suddenly came over her, causing her to pause briefly. *Madi?* His hands were held up in surrender, his eyes widened in shock, and he looked wearier than she had remembered, but it was definitely him.

'Well! What were you doing carrying me? Sorry! I just . . . you shouldn't have been carrying me!' Naala snapped.

'Sorry, I didn't mean to—' Madi mumbled, as he rubbed at the areas of his body that she had hit.

'Oh, don't apologise! I'm the one that . . . sorry.'

'It's fine,' he said, after a brief pause. 'You're very strong . . . and heavier than you look . . . and about . . . carrying you—I want you to know—I had to, you . . . were not in the right state of mind to walk around.'

'What?' Naala replied, before gasping in fright. Flashbacks of their encounter with the general's army ran through her mind, as she looked left to right, expecting the men to come charging through the forest. It slowly dawned on her that, not only were there no armed soldiers ready to attack, but the two of them were no longer in the same area.

Udi was no longer in sight; instead she was surrounded by a thick forest. Huge looming trees enclosed her, a mass of green, dusted with bright flowers. Greens, yellows and browns bled seamlessly into one another. Naala was incredibly confused, particularly because some part of her recognised this place.

'Do you remember?' Madi asked cautiously.

'I remember Enwe . . . he . . . he's gone. I saw the soldier with the scar . . . we ran away and . . . and . . .' she trailed off.

'And . . .?' Madi prompted.

'And . . . darkness,' Naala said quietly.

'Mmm,' Madi replied, as he looked intently at Naala's face, before taking a deep breath. 'I don't think you are . . . normal, Naala. I mean, I knew you were never *normal*, but I . . . I don't think you are normal.'

'I . . .' Naala started, but she quickly realised she didn't know what to say. A mixture of anger and fear rippled through her. She didn't want to know what he was going to say, but she also couldn't stop herself from listening. Tears pricked the corners of her eyes, but she had no intention of crying, so she blinked them away as fast as they came.

'But it's good—' Madi added quickly, sensing the rising tension between the two of them. 'I think . . . you—what you did, it got us out of there, it saved our lives. I owe you my life. The soldiers were gaining on us so fast, and they wanted blood, but then you moved the ground and brought us here.'

'The ground moved, but I didn't . . .' Naala shook her head in disbelief.

'You did, it was you, it was definitely you. I felt you pull me towards you. Your eyes shone, bright like the sun; I've never seen anything like it before. The earth opened up from below you and pulled us in. We were moving so fast through the darkness, until we were released back into the air. I was shaken, but I was fine, I could get up and walk . . . but you couldn't. I feared that you had . . . maybe even . . . but you were fine, you were breathing at least—so then I picked you up and carried on moving.'

Naala turned away and let her gaze run over the deep greens of the growing vegetation, peppered with blossoming flowers and fluttering insects. Strong thick vines slithered down tree bark, like snakes too lazy to attack. That sense of familiarity grew into an overwhelming feeling. *I've been here before.*

'Do you think they'll still be here?' Naala said quietly.

'Who?' Madi replied, confused.

'The group. That is why you brought us here, right? To find the group.' The place looked familiar because it was their last resting place with the group of survivors before they began their expedition to find Emeka. *How long have I been out? Surely Madi couldn't have carried me all the way back?*

'Oh, I didn't . . . it wasn't me who . . . I've just been walking in circles . . . you were the one that brought us here. I have no idea how, but it is truly amazing.'

'Right . . . okay, well, let's keep moving,' Naala said firmly. 'They might have left a clue for us about where they were going.'

Naala wished desperately to move the conversation away from anything that related to what she had supposedly done. She had no doubt that the group had left. Eni would have never let them stay; he was too smart for that.

They trodded softly through the supple forest, the humid air parting around them, carrying with it colourful butterflies and hissing insects.

A silky black jaguar cub started to follow them, weaving between them and the trees. Naala enjoyed its strong and silent presence so much that she almost called out to it, but before she could, it quickly lost interest and darted off into the thick forest. She watched it go and, as she looked ahead, she saw a shadowy figure in a distant tree. The figure was crouched and holding something in its hands. She locked eyes with the shaded figure; even with the distance between them, its piercing eyes drew her into them. *Eni*, she thought, as an arrow was let loose into the air with Naala as its target. She froze as it passed by her ear, so close that she heard it humming.

Seconds later, Madi pushed her forcefully to the ground.

'It's Eni,' Naala said, dazed.

Madi searched her face and then rose slowly from the ground. His arms were raised in surrender.

'Eni! Brother! It's me . . . it's Madi and Naala,' Madi boomed, as the figure bolted towards them.

'There's no need to alert him; he knows exactly who we are,'

Naala said coldly, as she lifted herself up from the ground, allowing the dried leaves and soil to fall off her body.

Eni slowed as he approached and stopped momentarily when he came face-to-face with Naala, before stepping past to pick up his arrow.

Eni turned back to Naala silently, before brushing his long fingers lightly against her jaw. His eyes scoured the side of her face that the arrow had flown past, searching for any tears or scratches. Eni's eyes softened when he found none; a mixture of emotions—so raw they caused Naala to hold her breath—surged out of his black eyes. Suddenly a blank expression swept over his face and Eni dropped his hand.

'Disappointed that you missed?' Naala murmured, as anger, distress, and something that felt strangely like excitement welled up within her. Underneath her fiery rage, Naala was glad to see him again.

Eni didn't reply and an awkward silence blossomed. Luckily Madi was there to intervene.

'It's really good to see you, Eni,' Madi said carefully, as Eni slipped the arrow back into his quiver.

'I wish I could say the same . . . what you two did . . .' Eni sighed in frustration. 'Reckless. What were you even thinking? You risked everything on a doomed expedition.'

While his words appeared to include Madi, he kept his gaze locked on Naala. It was very clear they were directed towards her alone.

'It was not doomed, we're back here . . . alive,' she said defensively.

'You have the key?'

'We have answers to questions, a better understanding. We are in a better place, and we haven't lost anything,' Naala retorted, as she suppressed the image of her poor little Enwe.

'You don't know that yet!' Eni fumed. 'You don't know the damage you've caused. You could have led the general's army right back here.'

'That's impossible, Naala was—' Madi started.

'We were very careful,' Naala interrupted. She had no intention of discussing the events that had occurred with anyone, especially not Eni, not until she had made sense of them herself.

'Where are the others?' she asked.

'They've moved on,' Eni replied.

'What do you mean?' Madi asked, his face screwed up in confusion.

'It was too dangerous for them to stay with you two gone. What if you had been taken by the army and forced to reveal our whereabouts?'

'We wouldn't have done that.'

'You don't know that, but that is the risk you decided to take, not only for yourselves but for us too,' Eni chastised.

The Eze had made Enwe disappear into thin air without lifting a finger. Eni was right; if they had been captured, who knew what those people could have done? Naala felt a trickle of shame dripping through her body; she had never really considered the implication of her actions on the group. She had accepted the risk of death for herself. She had accepted Madi's consent as his acceptance of that same risk, but she had failed to gather the permission of the group. She had gambled with their lives without any form of consent.

'But if they are gone, then why are you here?' Madi said quietly, after a moment of reflection. At this, Naala looked up, only to catch Eni staring at her. His gaze dropped nervously, which felt odd to her; after all, it was usually she who was forced to look away from him. She watched him closely as he turned to Madi to respond.

'Kora . . . she wouldn't let us leave. She wanted to stay here on her own, but we couldn't let her do that . . . anyway, it was decided that I would stay for a few days before re-joining the group,' Eni said smoothly. His words made sense and his delivery appeared honest, but Naala had a feeling that he was lying.

'Why are you here?' she echoed.

'I'm not playing these games with you, Naala. I've said what I said and that's how I'm leaving it,' Eni said.

'How about we re-join the group?' Madi offered cautiously.

'In those outfits? You look so. . . ' Eni smirked, before turning back to Naala, his eyes softening with something that made Naala shift uncomfortably. 'You look . . .' He cleared his throat. 'I'll just—I'll get something more suitable. Both of you can wait here for me.' He dashed into the dense forest. Naala stared after him, her breath still caught in her throat.

CHAPTER 34

THE BASEMENTS

City of Nri

Sinai paced on the uneven limestone floor with bare feet; her leather slippers lay discarded in the corner of the wide short room. She was in the dark basement of the palace, and the only light was the soft glow of the ọkụ flames lined across the corridor where the armed guards patrolled. Sinai had never been to the basements before.

They were used sparingly to hold those who had committed a crime against another person, long enough to decide what the victim needed as compensation. The perpetrator would stay in the room, unable to run away or hide their prized possessions, and they would only return back to society when the victim had been compensated. Sometimes that meant surrendering a herd of cows, or cubits of cloth, or, if the crime was serious enough, the perpetrator's life.

After Meekulu was taken, Sinai had run after the soldiers. She had thrashed them with her slippers, demanding that they release the old woman.

'Hush child, must you be such a bother?' Meekulu had murmured with the usual twinkle in her eyes.

'No! They can't just take you like this! You have done nothing wrong!' Sinai had exclaimed before being shoved harshly to the ground. 'Please, just listen; you've made a mistake. This is Meekulu, she is the *head* chef, the Eze's cook; you must unhand her now!' she had cried as she scrambled to her feet and attempted once more to claw away the soldier's grasp on the old woman.

'Uduike, take this girl away. I've had enough of these antics,' one of the soldiers had said and Sinai was picked up and dragged away with her arms outstretched towards Meekulu Amainata.

'Remember what I told you, child,' Meekulu had called, as Sinai continued to struggle in the soldier's grasp.

Now, in the basement, Sinai stopped mid-pace. She heard movement rippling through the empty rooms. She walked to the rusty iron bars separating her room from the lit hallway. Sinai held the bars in her hands, whilst pressing her face against their cold surface. For several hours now, she had heard nothing but the periodic shuffling of her door guards. She was desperate to speak to someone who could speak back to her. She was desperate for clarity about the whole situation.

Sinai watched as a dark figure descended the hallway. The

soldiers straightened. Whoever was walking towards her cell must wield significant power. As the figure drew closer into the light, Sinai felt her stomach drop in disappointment.

Obi Ife.

'You've gotten yourself wrapped up in some serious mess,' he said despondently, as he looked around her new dwellings in disgust. 'First the nonsense at the party, and now this—fighting soldiers! This is no way for an Obi's wife to act.'

Sinai wanted nothing more than to scream at him, but, before she could, logic kicked in. Obi Ife had power. He had the Eze's ear, and he most likely knew where Meekulu had been taken. Sinai took a deep breath.

'I . . . I know. But Obi Ife, I think you would agree that Meekulu, the Eze's most highly regarded cook, should not be manhandled by those . . . those men. I lost my temper, and reacted in a way that is . . . beneath me. Maybe you could teach me a better way to act when something this unjust takes place?'

'Yes, I have many things to teach you. First and foremost, always, and I mean always, abide by what I say; had you simply come to meet me as I requested this morning, none of this would be taking place right now.'

'What do you mean?' Sinai asked cautiously, releasing the bars and taking a step back. She felt as though she had just been punched in the stomach. Obi Ife looked at her indignantly.

'I *mean* you would have been with *me*, not here shamefully locked away like a mad woman,' he spat. 'I will try and get you out of here, Sinai, but all of this must stop, do you hear me? It must all stop.'

'Stop *what*? I haven't done . . . we were just walking back to the palace, just walking, and we were apprehended . . . I don't know what is even going on or where she is. She is an old woman—an elder. We all should be protecting her, and they were *dragging* her away.' Sinai's voice rose in volume as her repressed anger rose to the surface of her skin. 'This—none of this is right! Where is she? Where is Meekulu? Do not shake your head—I know you know— please, just tell me what is going on?!' Sinai shouted desperately.

'You would do well to leave that *witch* woman alone. This has nothing to do with you, but you keep inserting yourself into the matter, attacking guards like a mad woman. It's no wonde—'

'Stop! You are *wasting* time—just tell me where she is! Tell me what is going on!' Sinai cried.

Obi Ife looked at Sinai sternly, before taking a step closer to the bars.

'I'm warning you now, stop this behaviour. You are quickly losing favour with me, and once lost, you will never be able to regain it,' he hissed, before stepping back and taking a deep breath. 'It looks like you need this time in the basement to regain control of yourself. Take that time—but once this has all settled, you better return to normal,' Obi Ife murmured, before storming down the hallway, leaving Sinai sobbing in frustration.

CHAPTER 35

AKWỤNA

City Of Nri

Sinai's eyes were closed but her mind raced with images of Meekulu laughing in her kitchen, Chisi bowing at her door, Chief Ojo screaming as Asilia tore at his stomach, Ina lying broken in the small nest. The memories were disjointed and jagged like broken pieces of glass scattered on a dirty floor.

In the midst of her sleep, Sinai heard slow heavy footsteps descending the hallway. Her eyes sprang open, and the thick blackness that surrounded her sent a chill down her spine. Whether belonging to friend or foe, the footsteps drew closer, bringing a low but growing light with them. Finally they drew towards the bars, and Sinai lifted herself, once more, from her small akwa. Her heart sprang when she heard keys clanging against iron. Was she being freed? It seemed unlikely that the guards would have processed a release at this time of night.

Sinai clenched her hands in anticipation, but then slowly released them when she saw Sergeant Olu, the soldier who had brought her to Meekulu after her fall.

'Wh—' Sinai began, but he rushed to her and gestured for her to remain silent. Once he was certain that she wouldn't make a sound, he waved for her to follow him out the open door. Sinai did not think twice before she breezed through the room, walking right past her slippers, leaving the cell barefoot and washed with relief. She gasped quietly when she entered the hallway and caught sight of one of her guards, wide-awake and armed. Sinai turned swiftly to Sergeant Olu, but he only nodded at the guard before striding down the hallway. Sinai looked at the guard cautiously, but he didn't acknowledge her at all.

Sinai followed the broad stairs up and out of the basement, and was struck by how light it was outside.

She had imagined it was midnight, but the dark orange and purple sky suggested that it was the early hours of the morning. Sinai followed Sergeant Olu through the pillared bright corridors of the palace, winding back and forth before they came to a section that was all too familiar to her; the noble women's quarters. Sinai stopped suddenly.

'No, I . . . please take me to Meekulu,' she blurted.

Sergeant Olu looked at her sternly. Only his jade eyes betrayed traces of sympathy.

'We can't do this here,' he said deliberately.

'I'm not going back to my room to sleep. I need to find her now,' Sinai replied, louder and firmer, causing Sergeant Olu to look around cautiously before grasping her shoulders.

'If you want to help her, the best thing you can do is get to the safety of your room, and form an action plan. Shouting up and down the corridors will only land you back in the basement—with me along with you,' Sergeant Olu said seriously.

Sinai succumbed with a sigh. She was so tired. She was still clueless as to what was going on. She felt as though she was losing her mind, and Sergeant Olu was the closest thing that she had to answers. She did not have the energy to go against him, so she let him lead her to her room.

He swung her door open, revealing Ina sitting soberly on Sinai's akwa nest. Sinai gasped before turning to Sergeant Olu who remained in her corridor. Ina sat up, her locs drapping over her arms.

'Good. You were able to procure her,' Ina said, as she stood stiffly and stepped out of the golden nest frame.

'What are you doing here?' Sinai said. She felt increasingly frustrated with how little she understood about her present situation. A dark feeling had weighed heavily on her shoulders ever since she had been dragged away from Meekulu at the entrance of the palace. The old woman was in danger and Sinai had failed to protect her. The chilling coldness in the eyes of the soldiers that took her had placed a shard of glass in Sinai's heart, which twisted every time she thought of them. Sinai knew exactly what that coldness was. Those soldiers were detaching themselves from the task at hand, dissociating the body that housed Meekulu from the woman who had fed them, laughed with them, and at times even healed their wounds. They were reducing Meekulu to nothing more than flesh and bones that could be slaughtered at the Eze's whim. Sinai felt completely powerless and stuck. She knew nothing, so she could do nothing, and, as she meandered up and down the palace, instead of gaining more information, she had simply become more confused.

'Pleasant as always,' Ina said drily.

'Pleasant? I . . . you pushed me out of a window!' Sinai replied incredulously.

'I did not *push* you, and I think we have bigger things to worry about at the moment. You are not the only one that cares for Meekulu,' Ina replied, before turning to Sergeant Olu in annoyance. 'And why in heaven's name are you hanging in the doorway?'

'Well, I have not been invited into Sinai's room,' he said quietly and Ina rolled her eyes.

'We do not have time for these formalities,' Ina replied shortly. 'With someone as respected as Meekulu, they push for an immediate sentence. Sinai, please.'

'Sentence? I . . . you can come in—someone tell me what is going on. Where is Meekulu?'

'Meekulu has been charged with witchcraft and the brutal assault of Chief Ojo,' Sergeant Olu said, as he walked into her room, closing the wooden door behind him. Sinai felt the air rush out of her lungs as Sergeant Olu's words hit her squarely in the chest.

'Okay . . .' she breathed slowly. 'Okay . . . okay . . . so who do I need to confess to?'

'Confess?' Sergeant Olu repeated, perplexed.

'Yes. Confess,' Sinai replied sharply, her heart beating so fast she could hear it in her ears. 'I did it. It was me, I maimed him. Meekulu can attest to it, and Ina . . . she can too. So who do I need to confess to?'

'I don't think you understand,' Sergeant Olu said, as he took a step towards Sinai, a look of concern spreading across his face. She took a step back whilst shaking her head viciously.

'No-no, I really do. Meekulu has been charged for a crime that I, and I alone, committed, so now I need to confess and she will be released.'

'It is as though you have never lived in this palace,' Ina replied coldly. 'It won't make a difference if you confess. You think they couldn't figure out who maimed *that man*? You think Meekulu is the most plausible suspect here? I was wearing a garment imprinted with lions, for heaven's sake. They charged her because they *wanted* to charge her, not because that they think she is guilty.' She turned away from Sinai.

'Ina is right; confessing will just get you put back in the basement, so that they can charge her in peace,' Sergeant Olu added.

Sinai stared in complete bewilderment. 'But why? *Why?* She has done nothing . . . *nothing,*' she said despairingly.

Sergeant Olu replied, 'I don't know.'

'Cruelty is always senseless and never far away in this city,' Ina added quietly.

'For years there have been rumours that Meekulu is a witch, but no one has ever taken them seriously. At best, people just regard her as quirky—but the Eze has been . . . *unsettled* lately. After the Ofala festival, he has just been on a rampage. It simply took one complaint from Obi Ife to set this whole thing in motion.'

'I'm sorry . . . Obi Ife? What does he have to do with anything?' Sinai interrupted.

'He complained about Meekulu getting in the way of him meeting someone, doing something? I can't be sure—' Sergeant Olu replied.

'Meeting me,' Sinai said quietly.

Shocked, Ina opened her mouth to say something, but closed it before any words came out.

'H-he wanted to meet me and I ignored him,' Sinai said, as she scrambled through her room, pausing only when she found the discarded invitation. She tore it open and read.

Sweet Sinai,

I have arranged a lunch in the Gburugburu room at noon, with the Eze and a few select Obis and their wives. I look forward to seeing you.

Obi Ife

Sinai read and re-read the short message until she couldn't see the words anymore through her tears. She threw it on the ground and let out a strangled cry. 'He wanted to meet me! He took her because of me!'

Sergeant Olu marched towards her and hastily covered her mouth. 'I know you are upset, but now is not the time for this. If you draw too much attention to yourself, I cannot guarantee your safety,' he hissed in her ear.

'You did nothing wrong, Sinai,' Ina said firmly, as she walked slowly towards the both of them. 'You are *allowed* to ignore parchments, you are allowed to move and walk around without having to accommodate these *men*. You know this, you *know* this— that is why you did what you did to Ojo. You saved me from that monster, but now you need to be strong again. Do not take this blame, do not let him do this to you.' Ina gestured for Sergeant Olu to remove his hand. He did so cautiously, as Sinai blinked away her tears.

'What can I do?' she said hoarsely.

'You need to appeal to the Eze,' Ina replied.

'No, she cannot go to him in this state,' Sergeant Olu warned. Ina's eyes remained fixed on Sinai.

'No, she cannot,' Ina said softly, before turning around and scanning Sinai's room. Her gaze fell on Sinai's wardrobe where she kept her garments. 'She needs to splash some water on her face, and change her clothes.' Ina marched to the wardrobe and opened it, rummaging until she pulled out a black garment that Sinai used sparingly to sleep in.

'She cannot wear that to meet the Eze, she's not an akwụna!' Sergeant Olu exclaimed, visibly distressed. Sinai stared at the garment before shifting her gaze up at Ina's hardened face.

'Sinai needs to appeal to the Eze. The elite world works through exchanges. Exchanges of land, wisdom, assets—all of it is centred on exchange. Women have only one thing to offer as an exchange: themselves.' Ina straightened her neck, before taking a few steps closer to Sinai. A tense pause ensued. 'I would go myself,' she whispered, blinking away tears. 'But alas, I am out of favour. The Eze would consider it an insult; me, a shamed woman, offered as a prize. But he might listen to you. I've seen the way he watches you. I think you have a real chance at saving her.'

'You must be out of your mind,' Sergeant Olu began. 'No. Absolutely not. Sinai is not cattle. Not all men are *like* that. The Eze is not like that—'

'He is a man,' Ina snapped. 'And, if she succeeds, Sinai would not be the first woman to offer herself to him in exchange for mercy, this I know for a fact.'

Sergeant Olu's mouth gaped before he collected himself.

She softly touched the mark that the Mother's crystal had left on her hand.

'Listen, you don't—' he began.

'They burn witches,' Sinai interrupted. Sergeant Olu fell silent. The kingdom did burn those found guilty of witchcraft. The hot flames scorched their skin as the smoke filled their nose. They could not let that be Meekulu's fate. They all loved the old woman too much to let her burn before the masses. Sergeant Olu could not fight against the Eze's wishes. The only option they had was to appeal to the Eze, and Sinai had the most clout.

'I'll make the appeal,' Sinai said.

CHAPTER 36

THE ÌHÈ COURTYARD

City of Nri

Sinai wore a silk cloak over her scanty night piece as she walked through the empty hallways. The rich indigo sky was filled with splashes of red. It was still far too early for anyone to be awake. The only beings that kept Sinai company were the kestrel birds, which called at the budding sun.

For once, Sinai's head was completely empty. She took steps towards the Obis' quarter and watched as the palace decor became increasingly rich. The marbled floor glistened with small crystals and the gold and bronzed ornaments placed by the walls were far more extravagant than the wooden pieces that she was accustomed to. The heavy stones and glittering gold weighed on her chest. She felt trapped by the large pillars emblematic of duty and formality. The weight of the hall, the weight of what she was going to do, was crushing her soul.

Sinai took in a strangled breath before pausing abruptly.

She cocked her head and strained to hear the faint sound that had stopped her in her tracks. In that moment all she could hear was light wind. *Wait.* She looked around frantically and moved closer to the phantom sound. She stumbled away from the Obis' quarters and inched towards one of the large windows. A distant scream echoed on the light breeze.

Meekulu? Sinai thought manically, before kicking up her heels and sprinting down the halls towards the faraway screams. Sinai's feet slapped against the cold floor. The distant yells were becoming increasingly loud, and soon Sinai could distinguish tortured words.

'Death meets . . . me as death, death, death . . . will meet you!'

'Meekulu!' Sinai screamed into the morning air. The old woman's words were suddenly muffled crackling fire. Sinai crashed to the ground as she tried to turn a corner. Doors cracking open behind her but she scrambled to her feet and dashed on.

'Eze, Aljaneṣu-ojọọ, the fraud, the serpent, the thief, the murderer
She will come again and she will come in two.'

'No, no, no!' Sinai cried, as a sickening waft of burnt flesh curled around her.

'But death will meet me as it will meet you!
No life, no hope, no days to come

But it is how it was always to be done.'

The hallway split into two corridors and Sinai couldn't distinguish which side the screams came from.

'Justice rotten and cruel will be reborn through you
Through your ashes my ashes more ashes.'

Tears ran down Sinai's face as she impulsively skidded down the right-hand hallway. But to her dismay, Meekulu's screams quietened.

'Noooo!' Sinai screamed, jumping up and down violently in rage. She had chosen the wrong corridor. She spun on her heels and rushed towards the hall junction, before curving around to the corridor on the left side. Sinai dashed through the hallway, but stopped abruptly as something bright caught the corner of her eye. She scrambled back towards the wide window, and convulsed with horror; her whole body shook. Far below in the Ìhè courtyard, Meekulu was engulfed in angry red flames.

'We burn, I burn, I breathe and will breathe forever and always, I live for
I love and they love forever and always.

'Meekulu!!' Sinai screamed so hard that her voice broke, her arms outstretched to the old woman. Sinai jumped onto the ledge of the window, just as a burst of flames swallowed Meekulu, silencing her forever.

Hot lava coursed through Sinai's body. She screamed at the top of her lungs as gathering winds whipped her hair and garments violently around her. Her eyes shone bright and golden. She was filled with a rage so powerful it almost blinded her. Sinai threw her hands to the heavens as she abandoned all hope and all control. She succumbed to the sensation that rocked her body at its core. Thick black curls of smoke bled through her palms and spread through the hall. Sinai found herself completely lost.

Boom!

A thick intoxicating blackness coated her body in brilliance; she could see the palace crumble before her and she revelled in its destruction. She wanted all of them to crumble beneath her inconsolable pain. They had killed Meekulu, her friend.

Sinai could taste powerful rage; she was bathed in a thunderous hate and, at last, she entered the black.

CHAPTER 37

NEW ARRIVALS

Furuefu Forest

'You like him,' Kora said, as she pulled out a handful of bright green *ugu* leaves, still wet from the recent downpour, and placed them in her small woven basket, ready to be chopped for tonight's stew. The pale yellow afternoon sky hung above them, shrouded by a mist of thick clouds threatening even more rain. Naala and Kora stood in the middle of the dense viridescent forest, shaded by a flurry of vibrant green and amber leaves. They were surrounded by trees with drooping birds' nests hanging like fat rain drops at the end of broad leaves. The birds whirled around the two girls, bringing with them the moist scent of sweet flowers and ripe fruit.

Naala did not reply. The comment irritated her slightly, and any curiosity she had was overpowered by her certainty that this was not a topic that she wanted to explore. She hoped that by not saying anything the conversation would carry off into the wind, but Kora had other plans.

'I think he likes you too,' Kora noted, as Naala inspected the viability of a browning leaf. 'But given the current situation, I would advise both of you to keep away from each other. At least until things settle down; a baby—'

'Okay, stop talking now,' Naala snapped suddenly, as a smile spread across Kora's face. She held her hands up in surrender.

'Don't be such a prude; this conversation is necessary.'

'No, it is not. Quite frankly, it's just irritating.'

'Look, it doesn't do well to bottle everything in, and after what I saw last night, we need to set boundaries before any unwanted surprises take place,' Kora continued relentlessly.

When Naala and Madi had been led back to the group, they were met with warmth and excitement. Kora had burst into tears and jumped between Madi and Naala like a small excitable dog. Between Kora's yelps, the other members of the group came to hug and pat them on the backs. Naala had felt a small twinge in her heart; the glow in their faces and the warmth of their hugs reminded her of her fallen village.

'We thought you were dead!'

'Lost in the woods.'

'Did you run into the Eze's army?'

'Where have you been?'

Naala had taken a step back as questions were hurled at her. Madi, on the other hand, had moved closer towards the growing huddle with a chuckle erupting from deep in his throat.

Madi had said smoothly, 'We simply went to farm for more fish at one of the distant lakes, hoping to find a more varied selection, but without our trusted navigator, Kora, we got lost on our way back. We spent these past weeks wandering around trying to find all of you. I guess it's a good thing, though. Shows that our hiding tactics are top-notch.' Madi had winked at Azu, who soaked up his lies and smiled with a glow of deep pride.

A few hours later, the novelty of Naala and Madi's return had worn off, and it was as if they had never left. Soon after, the night hurried the sun away and the group retired to their hammocks. Naala was looking forward to her first night of solid sleep in weeks, but the three puppet masters had different plans. She found herself being woken in the middle of the night and escorted to the same field in which she had been caught eavesdropping months ago.

'Okay, let's have the real story,' Kora had said hurriedly.

Naala and Madi had looked at each other apprehensively before diving into the tale of their exploits over the past weeks. As the story drew towards their inexplicable escape, their voices had quietened until they were completely mute.

'So how did you escape?' Eni had asked; his piercing gaze had remained transfixed on Naala for the entirety of the retelling of their story. Naala had forgotten how hard it was to breathe when Eni looked at her that way; she felt exposed and raw. She had the urge to push his face away and scream at him to never look at her again, but beneath that lay a far greater desire to move close to him, close enough for her to become completely lost in the deep of his coal-black eyes.

Stop this foolishness! she had berated herself, before clearing her throat. She wasn't ready to expose what had happened at the Udi mountain. She wasn't ready to think too deeply about the rush of power she had felt, or the fact that she had felt it before; the day her village had been completely destroyed. The ero fungi scattered around the group had flickered white as fear crept over Naala.

'There was . . . an earthquake,' she had said finally. 'It acted as a . . . distraction and we were able to flee.'

'Another earthquake. What is happening to this world?' Kora had muttered in despair.

'How did you get back to us so quickly?' Eni had probed.

Naala had opened her mouth and closed it as the words died on her lips.

'I think we should carry on this conversation another day,' Madi had quickly noted, as Eni and Kora looked to him in confusion. 'I don't know about Naala, but I'm exhausted from these travels, and everything has become a blur. I can't even decipher how long we were away for, months, days—they're all meshed together.'

'But Madi, surely we need to discuss next steps,' Kora had protested.

'But we have—in essence, at least. Kora, you have the details of our stories. I'm assuming you will share it with *them* and we will await their instructions,' Madi had continued.

Kora had opened her mouth to say something, but stopped herself and turned to Eni instead. He looked back at her and then let his eyes roam around the group, before they settled on Naala.

'I think that sounds like a good idea, Kora?' Eni had said, as he turned back to Kora. She nodded slowly in response.

'Okay, we can all get some rest. I'll send a message tomorrow. But listen, this is not the time to be complacent. Our first plan may have failed, but we will find a new one, and we will succeed,' Kora had said determinedly.

As they had moved to leave the field, Naala felt a light brush against her hand. She had turned to find herself face-to-face with Eni, so close that she could feel the warmth from his body graze her skin. She had turned to watch Kora and Madi melt into the forest night before shifting her attention back towards Eni. *What do you want?* Naala had planned to say, but she was stopped by the look on Eni's face.

'I'm sorry about the arrow,' he had said suddenly, as he brushed her hair aside with his fingers.

'It's fine. I did not—it did not hurt me at all,' Naala had replied, her heart racing as her ears tingled with the electricity of his touch.

The ero fungi had begun to bleed with a light lilac glow; the soft, beautiful light drifted through the dark night. Naala had looked at the ground; she had never seen the ero turn that colour before.

'No, it's not.' he had said quietly. 'I was reckless, and you could have been killed. I just—' he paused, his eyes roaming her face as the fire beneath his pupils grew '—I really want you to know that I wasn't trying to shoot you or hurt you. I was just shocked. I couldn't believe that it was actually you, and then I let go of the string thoughtlessly.'

'Okay,' Naala had replied, unsure what to say. They stood silently in the brilliance of the moonlight. Naala looked down and was surprised to see that her hand was within his. She didn't know whether she wanted to fling his hand away or draw him closer. A loud crack brought Naala back to earth. She jerked towards the sound, to find a wide-eyed Kora standing before them.

'Sorry, I just wanted to make sure you two were okay,' Kora had said hurriedly, as Naala snatched her hand away from Eni.

'Yes, yes—just heading back now,' Naala had replied, as she walked past Kora and back towards the hammock. Kora watched her go before turning back to Eni with a smile on her lips and a twinkle in her eye.

Now Naala stood in the bushes with one eye looking out for potential snakes lurking in the shades of green, and the other waiting for Kora's response.

'I guess you could always take the herbs that the village doctors give to reduce the chances of you falling pregnant but those things are never fool proof—the best thing is to stay away.'

'I am not having this conversation with you,' Naala replied coldly

'It is important that you and Eni know where you stand—it just makes it easier for the whole group, trust me! One time Isioma and I . . . well, we—' Kora started.

'There is nothing going on between me and Eni. I don't . . . I'm not . . . we're not having this conversation.'

Kora lowered the spinach bundle she was collecting and turned to examine Naala.

'Oh no,' she whispered with bright knowing eyes.

'What?' Naala cried in frustration.

'It's worse than I thought. You *can't* stay away, can you? Well, I guess a little baby in the group wouldn't be so bad—we already have Azu to take care of. I don't see a baby being any more work.' She gave a hearty laugh; Naala couldn't help joining in.

'It's nice to see you smile and laugh,' Kora said, as they settled down. 'Now you're in a good mood, you won't mind me saying,' Kora noted, as she bit her lips guilty.

'What?'

'Your braids . . .'

'What about them?' Naala asked, as she tugged at one of her plaits.

334

'They are sooo old! You've had them in since you joined the group! They're nice, but they are worn out! Please let me redo them!' Kora exclaimed, as Naala grimaced. She hated the process of braiding her hair. The ache in her neck, the countless hours spent doing it, the sore feeling around her buttocks for sitting for too long.

'No. I'd rather cut it off like you have done,' Naala replied, but Kora pulled a face.

'No offence, but not everyone can pull this look off. Besides, I love playing with my friends' hair! Pleeease,' Kora cried, as she jumped up and down.

Naala was slightly taken aback by her comment; she hadn't realised that Kora had considered her a friend.

'Fine,' Naala murmured, as Kora leapt in the air.

'Yes! Yes! Yes,' she screeched. Naala let out a sigh of frustration just as a drop of heavy rain smacked her head.

'Whoops! Even more great news!' Kora shouted. 'If it rains now, it will be dry by the evening and we won't be woken up by the torrential rain tonight!'

Naala picked up her basket of plants and balanced it on her head before she followed the crazed girl back to the settlement. They rushed through the rain. Soon enough, they reached the makeshift hut the survivors had made out of palm thatch propped up on tall thick branches to provide shelter from the rain.

Naala took the basket off from her head and settled it on the floor. Their entrance had attracted the attention of many eyes, including two pairs that Naala had not seen before. A short middle-aged woman and a tall slim man stood next to Azu and Eni. They turned to look at her with a gleam in their eyes that made Naala uneasy.

CHAPTER 38

NO LIGHT

City of Nri

Sinai woke with a start in a pitch-black room. As her heavy panting subsided, memories of what had happened flooded her mind and she let her head fall on her pillow, as a fresh wave of sorrow overcame her. Sinai did not know what day it was; didn't even know if it was night or day. Some time ago she had dragged her wardrobe over to the window in her room, so that it now blocked all signs of the treacherous sun.

Since the old woman had died, light has ceased to be a source of peace. It now not only hurt her sore red eyes, but pierced her soul, taunting her with a time when a new day provided her with exciting hope. Sinai felt empty and cold.

They had found Sinai, knocked to the ground, amongst the rubble of the destroyed south-eastern wing of the palace. Some attributed the damage to a viscous storm. Others said that it was Meekulu's soul crashing against the palace in a last attack. Some whispered that it was a punishment from the lost gods, for taking away a life as innocent as Meekulu's. People fretted silently over the deep sorrow that had swept through the city; the nnunu women had ceased their singing; the palace food had lost its prior appeal, and heavy dark clouds remained perpetually in the sky.

Sinai thought nothing. She did nothing. She ate nothing. She stayed in her akwa nest all day and all night, clutching at her fur and crashing her fists against her head when the memory of her loss became too much to bear.

It is all your fault, you might as well have lit the match yourself, her thoughts poked out of her mind like bloody jagged knives cutting at whim and breaking her down into nothing.

Sinai had never known her family; she had never had friends. Meekulu was the first person who had felt familiar to her. The only person whom she trusted. *Just like poison, I crept into her life and left the old woman for dead.* Sinai tugged at her hair as she willed her mind to stay silent.

Time passed and the door creaked open. A hidden figure stood at the foot of Sinai's akwa nest, watching her closely before speaking.

'You have to get it together,' Ina hissed, her voice strained with anger and sorrow. 'You are not the only one in pain; you are not the only one who loved her. If you do not pick yourself up and get on with it, you will be next, Sinai.'

Sinai closed her eyes as Ina sighed and walked away, slamming the door shut behind her.

Time passed and Chisi came in, along with the smell of fresh pepper soup and warm sweet bread. Sinai felt bile rising up her throat, but she suppressed it before she could make a mess.

'Take it away,' she croaked.

'Please, Lolo Sinai, if you don't eat, you will die,' Chisi sniffed.

'Take. It. Away,' Sinai said, before drifting back to sleep.

Time passed and the door opened and closed again. The person who entered stood by the door for a while, until Sinai almost forgot that they were there.

'You have a kind heart, and I applaud it. I too did not anticipate things transpiring as they did . . . I did not want Meekulu to die but the Eze—' Obi Ife began, before something hard hit him in the chest and cracked open on the floor.

'Get out! Get out! Get out!' Sinai screamed with the little strength she had, throwing more artefacts at the door, long after Obi Ife had scurried out of it. Sinai collapsed on her akwa nest and erupted into a stream of tears, drowning herself in endless sorrow.

CHAPTER 39

BORN OF BLACK AND GOLD

Furuefu Forest

'Can I not have one good night of sleep?' Madi yawned into the darkness, illuminated by clusters of small gleaming insects, creating a soft wavering glow. The survivors had entered their usual spot for their midnight discussions.

'Why are you complaining? No one forced you to go on your *adventure*,' Kora retorted, as she poked his stomach mid-yawn, causing him to bring his outstretched arms over it to prevent any more incoming attacks.

Naala had expected any mention of their recent travels, and by proxy, the death of Madi's brother, to spark a much darker reaction. Naala breathed a sigh of relief when she saw that the topic did not bother Madi. Instead, he chuckled at Kora's comment with a sense of humour that Naala had only just begun to notice. In fact, since they had returned from their trip, Madi was not nearly as withdrawn or prone to raging outbursts as he had been prior to them leaving. Instead of waking up with a scowl that could only be smoothed with a warm breakfast, Madi now spent his mornings praying to the spirits of his ancestors, no longer plagued by the fear that his brother would never reach that point of enlightenment.

'*We* happened to sleep very well while you were gone,' Kora continued with a smile. 'At least I did. Eni was too busy pining over—'

'Everyone,' Eni said firmly, as he walked into the field; the ero by his feet blushed with a low orange colour. 'We are lucky to have special guests here today.' He gestured over to two shadows emerging from the dark trees: Bayo and his wife, Lato, the tall man and short woman who had joined the group days prior. Naala tensed.

When they had arrived, Bayo, a supposed priest, had told the group that they too were survivors. He'd recounted how they had been travelling to see Lato's father in Oka, not knowing that they would arrive to the aftermath of a deadly massacre. They had left, distraught and broken, only to arrive back home to the same blood and gore. With nowhere else to go, they had fled into the forest, where they had been wandering ever since.

Naala hadn't believed a word of that story as it tumbled out of Bayo's well-polished mouth. Something about the way he had spoken, slowly and deliberately as though reading a script in his head, had filled her with unease. She had found him on more than one occasion inspecting her with a glimmer in his eye.

'Ndewo,' Bayo said, as the group performed variations of their palm greeting, accompanying it with a slight bow, a sign of respect to their elders. 'I too am not thrilled with meeting at such an ungodly hour but, after my brief introduction to Azu, I understand the reasons why.' Lato smiled blankly at the four of them. 'Well,' he noted with a clap. 'I have no time to beat around the bush, so here it is. While this is the first time we have been properly introduced, this is not the first time we have been in contact. Lato and I are from the *Amaghi*,' he announced.

Kora and Madi released loud gasps. Naala's forehead creased apprehensively. *What are they doing here?*

'Wait, no wait, wait—the Amaghi? As in *the* Amaghi! How . . .?' Kora began, before a look of shock spread over her face as a thought settled in her head. 'Why didn't you tell us? I'm the one that has been corresponding with them.' Kora rushed over to slap Eni across the shoulders.

'I didn't get the chance,' Eni shrugged, while Kora threw her hands in the air.

'Well . . . ndewo . . . welcome again, I guess! This is so *exciting*, I can't tell you how grateful I am—we are—for your help and your guidance over the past months. This is—I just, I never expected to see you here! Just here, right in front of us. Oh my goodness! You're here for another mission, aren't you? Is there another mission?' Kora exclaimed with glee, as Bayo's nose flared in irritation at her open display of emotion.

'If you would let me finish, perhaps I would get to that point,' Bayo said curtly, as Kora opened her mouth apologetically to say something else, before deciding against it.

'The short answer is *maybe* . . . there may be a new plan. At least, that is what we are here to determine, the viability of such a plan,' he continued, before directing his gaze toward Naala. She shifted uncomfortably under the prolonged inspection, and turned to Eni who looked away with a hardened jaw.

'What do you mean?' Naala asked.

'There have been rumours that the powers of the mmo have been re-awakened,' he replied, as Naala's heart quickened.

'The power of the mu-what?' Madi asked with a scrunched-up face.

'It is as if you grew up under a rock!' Kora exclaimed, as she threw up her arms.

'Well, technically . . .' Madi murmured.

'The mmo were spiritual beings—' Bayo began.

'I'm sorry to interrupt—again—but with Madi, it's best to start from the very beginning,' Kora stressed, as Madi scowled silently. Bayo glared coldly at Kora before clearing his throat.

Bayo explained, 'Chukwu, the supreme spirit, the alpha and omega, created the universe, the stars, the earth, and the sky.

343

Chukwu created the Mother, who then birthed life on earth, the great gods, and the passionate humans. In between the humans and the gods, are the mmos. Some of them appeared to be human but they had the power to control earthly things, impact the weather, move items; some could even move the earth itself. Some were just simply spirits as light as mist. Like humans, they could be good or bad; unlike humans they could access the black and gold realm: the power realm. This is where they draw their remarkable powers.'

Naala felt Madi's eyes flicking towards her as Bayo's words hovered in the night air. *Stop it*, she wanted to yell, *he's not talking about me*, but images of the earth crumbling beneath her feet at Udi silenced her thoughts.

'What could she, the mmo, use her . . .or *their* powers, to do? Steal the key somehow? But isn't it . . . won't it kill anything that tries to steal it?' Madi blurted, as the image of Enwe turning to dust before his eyes flashed in the back of his mind.

Bayo continued, 'Yes, we recently discovered that the Eze has used the Ndụ crystal to enchant the key and various other artefacts. The enchantment means that anyone born from the dust will return to dust if they steal it—but mmo are born from the black, and that enchantment can never touch them. With a mmo on our side, we can get the key, but we won't have to— because with a mmo on our side we could get the one thing that powers the Eze—'

'You can't mean—?' Kora whispered.

'Yes, the Mother's crystal. We can finally reclaim and transfer that power into more capable hands.'

'It should be destroyed,' Eni added. 'It is the cause of all these problems. The Mother used it to persecute us, and now the Eze has started to do the same. Who's to say the next appointed leader will not continue to do so?' he concluded, as Bayo regarded him slowly.

'Perhaps, ' he murmured. 'Either way, that crystal needs to be separated from the Eze. As long as he controls it, he has the power to give and destroy life at his fingertips. He is the one determiner, the one executioner—but that power cannot rest with a man who has proven himself to be unjust.' Bayo took a deep breath. 'You are all too young to even imagine it—you see the Eze as the almighty ruler because that is all you have known. I lived during the period where he had to *prove* it. When hundreds of warriors were wiped out in seconds, simply because he had that crystal. His army, his enchanted weapons, are simply decorations. He mocks us all when he purges the villages using them. He is laughing at us when he leaves it unguarded in his court. He knows he has already won, he knows he cannot be stopped, but he does not know that a mmo has been reborn.'

'Wait . . . sorry but . . . you said . . . and you're here—you really think there's a mmo? Here? Around our dwellings?' Kora asked in shock. No one replied. Slowly, Bayo, Lato, Madi and

Eni's eyes drifted towards Naala. Moments passed and Naala stopped breathing.

Kora looked around in confusion. Her eyes soon settled on the bright red glow of the ero scattered around Naala. She gasped.

'You think Naala is a . . .? No, that can't be!' Kora exclaimed

'She just might be, and if she is, we may have a real chance to win this fight,' Bayo murmured.

CHAPTER 40

DANCING LEAVES

Furuefu Forest

Naala was seconds away from punching Bayo in the face. She gritted her teeth as she thought longingly about slamming her fists squarely into his forehead, just as he rolled his eyes to the heavens in disdain.

'You're not even trying,' he murmured, as she clenched her fists so tightly, her nails dug into her palms. Heat crept up her back and the dense green forest started to feel heavy and tight around her.

'Yes, I am. *You* are the one who is not *teaching*,' she replied sharply, causing him to rap his cane against her sore ear.

Naala despised Bayo. He was completely useless. He'd spent the whole session telling her to *feel* her power, to *visualise* the magic, but he had yet to tell her how.

Now he said, 'No one can *teach* this to you, girl. This is not

Nsibidi with set rules and letters to learn. This is your connection with your chi, your soul—it will be different for everyone, so you and only you can learn to recognise it.'

Naala rolled her eyes.

'I have felt it, more than once. In fact—I've felt it but I still can't—'

'No. You did not *feel* it, you used it. You were thrust into it, your emotions—your instinct—took over, but now you must take a step back and recognise it, understand what it feels like to you, what it tastes like. Only then can you master it. The more you call on it, the more you flex it, the greater control you will have.'

Naala looked up at Bayo's thin frame with a scowl; his words tumbled over her like dead leaves. She watched as the large palm trees behind him rustled in the warm afternoon air and sighed. 'Try. Again,' he ordered, gesturing for her to sweep back up the green leaves on the ground.

Every day Naala followed Bayo deeper into the woods for lessons on what Azu and the like considered to be spiritual healing.

'Spiritual healing?' Azu had asked when Bayo had first mentioned it, his eyes squinting at Naala as he looked her up and down. 'What is wrong with her?'

'The girl is not well—not strong of mind. Not everyone can carry the burden of loss. I'm sure you must have noticed it too,' Bayo had noted, as Azu looked confused. 'Oh no? Funny, I thought you had an aura about you of someone with *the eye* for these sorts of things.'

'Oh! I do! Yes, yes, of course I've noticed the girl . . . her problems. In fact—there are others too that may be in need of this *spiritual healing*,' Azu had whispered, as he glanced over to Kora and Eni.

'Mmm perhaps—but the healing is most effective during one-on-one sessions. Why don't you watch over the group and take note of any other *peculiar* behaviours? I see that I can trust your judgement. I will use what you say to determine the next candidate.'

Azu's eyes had widened with glee, as he was intoxicated with the idea of his own expertise. Little did he know that Bayo would not listen to a word of his advice; he was here to help Naala, and Naala alone.

Now, staring at the palm fronds, Naala sighed and thought, *Mmo powers*. She still couldn't believe that she was corroborating with all of this. Not long ago, she would have laughed at the notion of attempting to call upon powers she didn't have, to protect herself in an impossible battle against the almighty Eze. Yet here she was, sitting in the middle of a lively forest, attempting to make a handful of leaves move with nothing but her mind.

If she wasn't so desperate, if she wasn't so angry, if she couldn't still taste the intense power that had flowed through her soul in what Bayo called the black and gold realm, Naala might have slammed her fists into Bayo's face days ago, and left all talk of magic locked firmly in his broken mouth. But she *was* desperate.

Ever since the Eze's army had marched through her village, she had been losing things. She had lost her family, her friends, her home, and now Enwe. Naala *needed* to win. She needed to find a purpose amidst the sorrow. Naala had spent countless hours fretting about ways to avenge her family, protect the remaining villagers, or do something meaningful to honour those that were left. However, all those ideas felt impossible, hollow and pointless, as they churned in her head; failing before they had even begun. Stealing the Mother's crystal was another impossible idea, but it was neither hollow nor pointless and, as absurd as it seemed, Naala couldn't fight the feeling deep down that told her she could pull it off.

'It's been days; clearly I don't have mmo powers,' Naala finally said, dropping the rubbery leaves onto the thick grassy ground once again as she began to stand up. She had only got to her knees when the wooden cane stung against her raw ear.

'Can you please stop that? I'm not a child!' Naala exclaimed.

'No? You are petulant, rude, and certainly not my age, so if you are not a child, then what are you?' Bayo replied.

'Not the person you were looking for,' Naala muttered, as she rose to her feet, dodging another incoming blow. 'We just need to stop. We both know that I can't make those leaves move. It is clear that you, or they or whoever, might have got the wrong person.'

'Perhaps,' Bayo replied coldly. 'Or perhaps you need to focus.'

Naala sighed in protest whilst he picked the scattered leaves up from the ground and pressed them into her palms. 'Just *visualise* it! Your mind is your tool; visualise the black and gold realm, and draw power from that.'

'I don't know *how* to draw any power from it . . . last time . . . at Udi . . . I just kind of fell into it . . . also I don't really remember any gold, just black, pitch-black.'

'Good. You've finally admitted that you've done this before. Now you need to remember the details properly.'

'I did. I told you I fell—'

'No, you didn't. One cannot simply fall into a black and gold realm and come out unscathed, or at all. Once you are in the realm, that's it; the energy required to leave the realm is greater than you can imagine—greater than the force you need to move a mountain, lift up all the oceans—even the world or the sun! It is more energy than you can even quantity; it's—'

'Hard?'

'It's impossible, not even the Mother could do such a thing.'

'Well, I . . .' Naala began, but she was lost for words. She recalled the extraordinary power that had rushed through her soul when she had fallen into the black, but what if it was a hoax? Just a figment of her imagination that she had magnified into a realm of magic and awe?

'Maybe it was just an earthquake then?' she murmured quietly, as Bayo sighed again in frustration.

'It was not an earthquake,' he exhaled with flared nostrils, the long cane quivering in his hand.

'You don't know that!' Naala muttered, and, to her surprise, Bayo chuckled. It was the first time that he had shown any sort of positive emotion around her, and she didn't know how to take it.

'My dear, I know,' he said finally.

'No, you don't,' Naala insisted through clenched teeth. *If you did then you would know that I can't do this!*

'Listen, girl—you are a mmo,' Bayo said sharply, as a deep scowl settled on his face. 'I can see the power emitting off you as clear as day. It was even strong enough to leave a trail that we could follow and that is how I *know* that you are deliberately refusing to use it.'

Naala opened her mouth to protest, but before she could, something Bayo said hit her in the chest.

'You can see it?' Naala asked, swivelling around frantically, before stopping suddenly as something else dawned on her. 'A . . . a trail? You followed a *trail?* I'm leaving a trail.' Naala gasped, as she pictured the Eze riding towards her with an abara outstretched in his hand and murder glinting in his eyes.

'Yes, but there's no need to be *dramatic*. Only *dibias* can see power.'

'Dibias?' Naala asked, as Bayo sighed.

Bayo replied, 'Dibias are people who can see and feel magic—they may even be touched by magic and live longer than the average person—but they cannot possess it. For years, these abilities have been useless. The Mother's death closed all portals to the black and gold realm of magic, and so dibias like me have seen nothing but dreary nights and uninspiring days. But something has *changed*, little bursts of magic have begun to bloom here and there—and the magic is *growing*. You need to grasp this *now*, because for the first time in centuries we have an advantage! But we won't for long. Soon a dibia, one who is loyal to the Eze, will also detect these instances and if he gets to it first, we're done for.'

Naala's heart leapt to her throat as he spoke. She looked down at the leaves in her hands, closed her eyes, gritted her teeth, and willed the black and gold realm to take over her.

'Please,' she whispered, but after a few painful minutes, they both knew nothing was going to happen. Naala opened her eyes again, her face was awash with shame as Bayo glared at her with disappointment. Naala turned and looked deep into the forest for relief. She nearly caught her breath when she spotted Eni walking past the trees, one of his long arms brushing away vines whilst the other held a basket of fruit for the group. He stopped briefly and tensed before turning his head to look in her direction. His eyes locked with hers, his body relaxed, and a small smile formed on his lips.

Naala felt a light twinge in her chest and found herself smiling back. Eni's gaze drifted over to Bayo; in a flash, his expression hardened and he quickly turned away and walked on.

He had been against the idea of Naala's supposed powers being used to fight the Eze. Her abilities seemed to rile something up within him. If Naala thought hard about it, she would have said it repulsed him. When she had agreed to train, Eni had pulled back from her notably. He no longer waited for her in the mornings, or sat next to her during meals; the majority of their interactions were now isolated to these moments when he forgot himself and smiled when their eyes met.

Naala took in a deep breath before turning to Bayo. She was shocked to see a smile had also formed on his lips. His eyes were completely focused on her palms. Naala looked down and nearly screamed when she saw the green leaves dancing vigorously above her hands.

CHAPTER 41

STRAINED LUNCHES

City of Nri

Ina's eyes roamed over Sinai's haunted face, and her heart squeezed tightly. Sinai was a shadow of her former self, her once luscious brown skin dry and rough, and her bright eyes so dimmed that it was hard to detect even the slightest flicker of life behind them. Ina felt anger and concern flare within her. *Just get it together, damn you,* Ina wanted to scream at the sad girl.

Not long ago, Ina would have been overjoyed to see Sinai in this state, completely broken, a threat to no one with a pulse. However, much had transpired between the two girls in recent months, and Ina could not deny nor forget the fact that the girl had given her the greatest gift she had ever received: justice.

If it wasn't for Sinai, Ina would still be plagued by the fear of Chief Ojo cornering her one day in a dark room, her mouth filling with bile at his repulsive odour, her hands quivering at his voice.

Sinai was the last person that Ina had thought would free her from that torment. When Ojo's rumours about their encounter had begun to circulate amongst the nobles, Lebechi and Ebun were amongst the first to discard her, as though she were nothing but a gnawed bone, sucked dry by ravenous dogs.

Ina had been disappointed, but not all that surprised; she had always known them to be outstandingly weak. Instead of letting such things keep her down, Ina had clenched her fists and held her head high, and prepared to face the court on her own. She was ready to claw back to her former position in society, and climb higher still if she could. She was prepared to do it all on her own; damn the rumours and damn the whispers. However, when she had stepped into the hall that day, she was not prepared for the overwhelming sense of doom that overcame her when she had seen Ojo sneering at her. Ina had known in that moment that, not only did Ojo not feel any remorse, he was certain to attack her again. Moments later Asilia had torn him apart before her eyes. The sense of relief that had overpowered her was almost too much to bear. Ina took her first real breath since Ojo had first attacked her, all because of Sinai, her unexpected supporter.

Ina was hoping to return the favour to Sinai, but this was proving difficult. All she wanted to do was shake and slap the weeping girl. Ina was desperate for Sinai to wake up from her dreamlike state, and accept life for what it was: a journey punctuated by pain, which could only be escaped by being lived through. Ina had quickly found that pushing the girl was a futile process. As was everything else that she had tried. Ina had attempted various tactics over the past few weeks; anger, cajoling, sadness, disappointment, pretence, happiness—not one of them worked.

Eventually, Ina had settled for simply being there, being present. Ina would visit Sinai at least once a day. She would ensure that her nest furs were routinely cleaned, and that Sinai had washed and eaten. Whilst she visited, Ina would often recount the ins and outs of her day. Ina was used to talking about herself without needing prompting or interjections from those around her, so it suited her quite well. She had even begun to imagine that Sinai was improving. Sinai had started responding to her comments every now and again, her crying had quietened down, and she had stopped smashing her head against her pillows.

However, in the bright daylight, the full extent of Sinai's pain was exposed for all to see. *She is still not ready to be out in court yet*, Ina thought frantically, as she bit her lips.

'Are you sure you want to be here?' Ina asked cautiously. Sinai shuddered slightly, and for a moment Ina was afraid that the girl would burst into tears right in the middle of the Obis' gardens.

'Obi Ife summoned me, did he not? We know what happens when I refuse his demands,' Sinai finally said. She spat out his name like it was something vulgar and obscene on the tip of her tongue. It was true; days ago the Obi had cornered Ina in the hallway, and asked about Sinai. He was adamant about seeing the girl, despite Ina's protests.

'I cannot go to her room and have her screaming again; it will start ungodly rumours. You should know,' Obi Ife had said, as Ina's heartbeat had thudded violently in her ears. *Breathe*, she'd told herself as he'd continued, 'If you could tell her to meet me in public in the gardens near the Obis' quarters, perhaps we can clear this all up. Tell her she doesn't have to come alone, if she's not yet comfortable—she can bring a friend—she can bring you,' Obi Ife suggested.

Ina had said that she would try to arrange a meeting, but in reality she did not see or want such a meeting to ever come to pass. After what Obi Ife had caused, Ina did not want the man anywhere near herself or Sinai. She did not even know why she had mentioned it to the girl in the first place. The words had tumbled aimlessly out her mouth whilst she was pruning the flowers that she had brought for Sinai's room. Ina had almost choked when the girl had insisted on going, but how could she say no? For weeks Sinai had refuted all attempts get her to leave her room; how could Ina stand in her way now? However, looking at the dead darkness swirling in Sinai's eyes now, she wished that she had.

'I think it's best we should go—,' Ina began.

'Sinai, Ina, it's so nice to see you out and looking so . . . well,'

Obi Ife exclaimed behind her. Ina turned around and gaped absentmindedly at the Obi before she remembered her manners.

'Eh yes, lovely to see you too. Thank you for inviting us,' Ina said smoothly, as Obi Ife gestured them towards a small table in the midst of extravagant flowers. It was a truly breathtaking spot in the garden, reserved for the most favoured Obis.

There was a time, not too long ago, when Ina would have been ecstatic to be sitting there. She would have relished every envious glance from passers-by, she would have leaned towards Obi Ife enticingly and soaked in the glorious feeling of superiority. But Obi Ife now carried some blame over Meekulu's death, and that fact hit her like cold water every time she laid eyes on him. The Eze may have given the orders, but Obi Ife's weakness and short-sightedness had led the lion to its victim. His presence now repulsed her.

Yet, she sat down and engaged in conversation, offering witty comebacks and nodding along to his statements. Whenever he tried to engage Sinai, the Obi was met with a cold silence, and Ina would interject and carry the conversation forward. It came too easily to her, playing the game, pretending to be happy, engaged and sane; she almost wished it didn't. She wished that she too could sink into her grief, only she wasn't sure that, if she did, she could ever come back out.

In a flash, something bright caught the corner of Ina's eyes.

'Oh!' she gasped, as she slammed both hands on the table, one clasped tightly on the daga within Sinai's hand. Ina's heart

359

pounded with terror as Obi Ife looked confused, completely oblivious to the struggle taking place.

Ina was also confused; she had acted before she could think, but had seen the glint of the daga angling deliberately towards the man across the table. Judging by how much Sinai was resisting, Ina was certain that the daga's intended path was towards Obe Ife's throat.

Ina dragged both the daga and Sinai's fist under the table. The girl put up a solid resistance despite her weakened state. Ina felt a sting in her palm as the daga sliced her skin. *You can't do this, you can't stab him*, Ina screamed in her head, willing the girl to somehow understand. *They will burn you too—just get it together!*

'What is wrong with you?' Obi Ife asked, visibly perturbed and unable to decipher the cause for the sudden commotion.

'I—I'm sorry, I feel very, very, very unwell—I—Sinai, can you help me back?' Ina said, as she lifted herself and Sinai up from her seat. Sinai's hand was still clasped around the daga, which Ina struggled to angle towards her back.

Suddenly Sinai's grip slackened. The fire in the girl's eyes smouldered out, as they travelled towards the small pellets of blood spouting from Ina's hands. Fresh tears threatened to enter Sinai's tired eyes; she had given up.

'I can help—' Obi Ife said with a frown, as he took stock of Sinai's pained expression and Ina's desperation.

'No! Please, you stay here,' Ina exclaimed, holding her free hand up as she signalled for him to remain in his seat. 'I—I . . . it wouldn't be . . . *proper*,' Ina eventually offered, before backing away slowly, angling her body to cover the bloody daga, and pushing Sinai's limp body along. Ina used a fold of her garment to further shield the weapon before turning and rushing out of the garden, dragging a tearful Sinai, and hoping no one would see the trail of blood that was left behind them.

CHAPTER 42

FOUR FRIENDS

Furuefu Forest

Naala felt warm as she traversed the green forest alongside Kora, Eni, and Madi. They climbed over a series of moss-covered boulders and darted between the tall twisted trees dusted with tiny lime-green leaves, rustling in the light wind. Naala looked out at the boundless expanse of deep greens and exhaled.

It had been a while since the four of them had been together. Naala refused to admit it, but she had begun to miss the others. Despite her best efforts to remain detached, she had grown accustomed to their company.

She had even started to miss their midnight meetings, which had come to an abrupt stop. While Naala was pleased to get more sleep, she couldn't shake the feeling that Eni was deliberately cancelling the meetings in order to avoid her. This notion left a sick feeling in the pit of her stomach.

When Naala had seen Eni and Madi heading towards the lakes

to gather the mmiri flowers filled with freshwater, she couldn't help calling out, 'Kora and I will help you.'

'We will?' Kora had responded, not bothering to hide her displeasure. She had always made it clear that collecting mmiri flowers was her least favourite chore; their large swollen white petals disgusted her, and squeezing the freshwater out of them was a tiresome and thankless task. Kora had done well to avoid it for weeks now.

'Yes, we should help,' Naala had replied, as she took hold of Kora's hand and rushed after the boys.

Now that she was here, she felt as though she may have made a mistake. While on the surface the conversation flowed smoothly enough, a thick undeniable tension between herself and Eni made it impossible for Naala to relax. She felt as though she was standing over a still, flat river, wanting nothing more than to dive in, but paralysed by the fear of the huge boulders just beneath the surface. Naala sighed as she fell back a little more, increasing the distance between the two of them, terrified that Eni would realise that she was too close and be disgusted.

'You're quiet, Naala,' Kora said, cutting through her sombre thoughts.

'Mmm,' Naala murmured; she had little desire to follow up with a more detailed response.

'What does that mean? Don't you want to tell us all about your *mystic enchantress* powers?' Kora asked jokingly.

Naala stopped as she blinked back at Kora, before sweeping her eyes over to Eni. He still had his back turned, but she could see the tension in his shoulders rising. *So this is what they all think? That I'm a witch? That I'm evil?* Naala thought frantically.

'I'm not evil,' she said firmly; her tone prompted Kora to look confused.

'What? No, Naala, of course you're not a-a *witch!* I didn't mean that *at all.* I just meant that—you know . . . I mean, you're a *mmo,* an *actual* mmo. That's . . . well that's *big*—but you haven't said anything, we haven't discussed it . . . at all,' Kora explained.

'We don't need to talk about it,' Naala replied sharply; she hated to admit it, but she was hurt by their reactions to all of this, particularly Eni's.

Naala had yet to come to terms with how she felt about being a mmo. As her sessions with Bayo progressed, she was beginning to gain a better understanding about what he had meant when he asked her to *feel* for her power. She was beginning to recognise the black and gold realm, a deep feeling within her that she could mould and even call upon. Her control of it was fragile at best, but at least now she knew what it was. However, the more she knew, the more she didn't want to know.

Naala only thought of her supposed powers in the context of how she was going to use them to defeat the Eze. She had not processed what being a mmo really meant to her, but she felt as though Eni had already disrupted that process, with his growing distance and deepening frowns conveying.

'You never tell us anything, Naala . . . I understand it . . . but . . . it's good to open up and talk about these things. Aren't you afraid of going crazy?'

'I don't want to upset anyone, I imagine it is not an easy thing to hear,' Naala offered, as Kora shook her head.

'What are you talking about? No one is upset,' Madi frowned, as he slowed down to Naala's pace.

'Well. . .' Kora started, as her eyes trailed towards Eni's back.

'Eni?' Madi replied.

'It doesn't seem as though he likes it,' Naala murmured; *me*, she corrected in her head.

Eni turned around. 'Why would I *like* it?' he said finally, as he looked at Naala square in the face. She felt her stomach twist.

'It's . . . I'm not . . . I just want to stop the killings, that's all,' Naala whispered, as she tried to keep her voice steady, she could feel sharp pricks on the surface of her eyes. *Don't you dare cry*, she warned herself.

'I want to stop them too—but not at your expense,' he said quietly, as he approached her. 'These powers have put a target on your back. You are now a pawn; the most valuable pawn out there. They are going to put you right at the front of this fight— and I know you're strong and capable and powerful—but you *can* die, even with your mmo abilities. You can bleed, and—you don't

365

even know what you are up against.' He shook his head. 'The platoons that they sent to the villages are *nothing* compared to the whole army—*a thousandth* at best. Not only that, but the Eze will also have magic in his arsenal, old magic from the Mother's crystal that he has honed for *years*. And now, because of these powers, you are going to face all of that on your own. I—how could *I like* that? How could you like that? Why aren't you refusing? Why do you want so desperately to embark on these suicide missions?' Eni's voice was slightly louder than he intended it to be. He hadn't expected to say all that, but this was the first time he had been so close to Naala in days, and her presence was intoxicating. It disturbed him that he was so affected by this one girl, who seemed to draw towards death like a moth to a flame. Eni turned away, fearful he would say something else that he'd regret.

'She will be fine,' Kora said after a pause, her voice quiet and muffled as though she were really speaking to herself rather than Eni.

'She won't even be fighting,' Madi added. 'She'll still be safe . . . she'll be fine.'

As Bayo had explained it, the whole mission should be relatively straightforward. Months ago the Amaghi had discovered a safe way into the palace, through a merchant who traded gold and fabric in the court.

The merchant had traded for years, and was supposedly on a first-name basis with all the guards who patrolled the palace walls.

He was so close to them that they had not performed a proper inspection on his cargo cart for years. The man was tried and tested, and the Amaghị had used him to bring spies in and out of the city for weeks now, without any issue.

The plan was for Naala to sneak into the palace, hidden within the merchant's cart. Once inside, she would be led to a room where the Eze supposedly left all his enchanted treasures. She would then get the crystal, the description of which Bayo had bored in her head for the last few days:

> *It is located on the same wall as the door of the room. When you enter, follow the wall towards the end of the room. The crystal is located within one of the holes in the wall, and you will find it at eye level. The crystal itself is emerald, with a subtle but powerful beauty.*

Once she had taken the crystal, she would be brought out of the palace. She could cripple the Eze without even having to face him.

Doubt suddenly spread across Naala's face as she thought, *But what if I fail? Then what?* She had failed to return with Emeka or the key. She had failed to save her village. Who was to say she wouldn't fail this time? Who would stop the Eze and the endless killing?

'. . . and she won't be alone,' Eni added, interrupting her thought. Naala looked up to find Eni looking straight in her eyes; she felt herself falling into his gaze and took a step closer to him.

'What do you mean?' Naala replied.

'I'm going with you. You should not have to do this on your own, mmo or not, you need protection, you need support.'

'You can't—'

'I've made up my mind. I'm going,' he said firmly, stepping so close that she felt the warmth of his body.

'Ahem,' Kora noted, as she stepped between them with a knowing smile. '*We* will all come with you!' She took Naala's hand in hers.

'You . . . you can't mean that. We can't all go; we will all be caught before we reach the palace wall,' Naala said quietly.

'No, we won't,' Madi said softly with a smile. 'We can all be brought into the palace via the merchant. You and Eni will be escorted through the palace, and Kora and I can trail you—and if something goes wrong and you need a distraction, we will assist. We will all protect you.'

'It's not safe,' Naala murmured. She did not like the idea of putting any of her new friends in harm's way. The thought of all of them entering into this fight just to support her felt wrong . . . like a waste of life.

'You're not the only one who wants to destroy that stupid goat of a man,' Kora responded with a smile.

'It is better that we all go; it will increase our chances,' Madi added.

'We're going,' Eni said.

Naala said, 'So . . . you don't despise me? For being a . . . for having these *powers*?'

'*Despise* you?' Madi exclaimed. 'Certainly not! Are you kidding? It's amazing!'

'I—we just want to protect you,' Eni replied, and Naala felt a chill. Suddenly a huge flurry of leaves lifted from the ground and encircled them all in a dance before settling again. Naala laughed at the shock and delight that spread across all their faces.

'Hate to break it to you, Eni,' Kora exclaimed. 'But I'm pretty sure she'll be the one protecting us! But at least we'll there to cheer her on.'

CHAPTER 43

THE NZUZO GARDENS

City of Nri

Sinai lay still in the pitch-black room, her eyes closed and her body heavy with fatigue. Her thoughts lay still in a thick pool, and complete nothingness consumed her. She could not recall where she was or even what she was; all she knew was that she needed to sleep. Suddenly a thin light cut through the room and familiar sounds bounced across the walls. A girl spoke, her voice hushed and filled with sadness and angst. Moments later, a woman's face appeared. Even though her features were largely hidden behind the velvet darkness, Sinai knew the girl to be Ina.

I'm sorry, Sinai tried to say, but all that escaped her mouth was a series of croaks. Sinai was sorry for cutting Ina's hand, she was sorry for causing Meekulu's death, she was sorry for being weak.

Most of all, she was sorry that it was not her that the soldiers had taken away outside the palace walls. Just as the thoughts rushed into her head, they rushed out and Sinai was left again with nothingness.

A sudden jolt unnerved her. Was she moving?

Sinai could not feel her feet against the ground, but she could feel cool air brushing her cheeks. It slowly dawned on her that there was a tightening sensation around her body, almost as though she was being hugged. *No carried, I'm being carried*, she thought, before drifting back into nothingness.

I'm being carried? Sinai opened her eyes. The faded grey moonlight hazed her vision momentarily, but soon enough figures materialised. She *was* being carried, and was no longer in her room. Sergeant Olu held her in his strong arms, whilst Ina led them through the sleeping palace. Before Sinai could process how she felt about this, her body gave up and drifted back into nothingness.

Ina looked back nervously at Sinai as she lay lifelessly within Sergeant Olu's arms. The girl looked so small against Sergeant Olu's solid frame, like a broken bird nestled in the crook of a tree, waiting to die. *Please let this work*, Ina prayed, as she quickened her pace towards the Nzuzo garden.

After Meekulu's burning, Ina was shocked to find that the site had not been cleared. Typically, after a burning, servants would clear away the ashes and charred wood, and give the remains to the family or state to bury. However, days after Meekulu's death, the site remained untouched and abandoned.

Numerous times, Ina had demanded that someone clear the site, but the servants were either too distraught or frightened to touch it. Meekulu had been an incredible force; both her life and death stirred up intense feelings within the people of the palace.

Frustrated at the inactivity, Ina had decided one day that she would clear the site herself. She'd rushed down to it, determined, only to find that one of the kitchen girls had beat her there. The small girl had sniffed back tears as she swept ashes into one of Meekulu's large mortars.

'Here, let me help you,' Ina had said, as she bent before her. The girl had been shocked.

'No, that's okay, Lolo, I can do it, I should have . . . but I . . . sorry—' she began, before dissolving into a flood of tears. Ina watched her uncomfortably before resting her palm on her shoulder.

Emotions swirled deep within Ina's soul as she stood beside the weeping girl and the old woman's ashes. Ina was reminded how cruel life could be, and it filled her with an uncontrollable rage. She didn't know if she wanted to cry or scream.

Suddenly Nzuzo gardens flashed in her mind, and Ina instantly felt calm.

'I know a beautiful place where we can lay her to rest,' she said quietly.

The Nzuzo gardens had been her secret for as long as she could remember. She had discovered it as a child, a hidden wilderness within the palace walls. Up until that point, she had always known there to be just five gardens within the palace. All five were beautiful, pruned, and always full of people.

Nzuzo was different. It was wild, with overgrown shrubs, imperfect trees, and an indescribable harmony. The place filled her with ease, and she found herself sneaking off to it during moments when she couldn't silence the loud cutting voice in her head. Nzuzo was unknown to most, if not all, of the people in the palace. Ina had yet to hear anyone refer to the sixth garden, nor had she ever encountered a single soul there.

That is exactly where Meekulu should be buried, she had thought; somewhere beautiful, wild, and protected. Ina had taken the kitchen girl to her secret place, and together they'd clawed open a small area of ground and buried the old woman's remains.

Ina had not thought about that day or Meekulu's burial ground for weeks after. It was not until Sinai had almost sliced Obi Ife's throat that she had an urge to visit the hidden garden.

Ina had felt emotionally drained and the sides of her head were tight with fatigue. She was in desperate need of respite, and so she'd rushed to her favourite place in the world. Ina had almost screamed when she arrived in the garden and found a huge flame tree at its centre, where just weeks ago she and the kitchen girl had buried Meekulu's ashes.

The tree stood large and majestic; its bundles of bright-red flowers whistled in the air, illuminated by a soft glow. The same kitchen girl who had helped her bury the ashes stood before the tree. She'd turned with a full beautiful smile.

'It's amazing,' she had said.

'Yes,' Ina had agreed softly. 'It is just what she needs.'

CHAPTER 44

THE FLAME TREE

City of Nri

Sinai felt herself sinking into the black: a thunderous ink-black darkness that caressed her skin and pulled her into an ocean, deep within another realm. The last time that she had encountered this realm, she had felt electrified and charged. She had been in total chaos and had yet retained full control. She had felt as though she could soar far above the skies and touch the sun. However, this time she felt slow and heavy, weighed down by a blanket of death. Sinai knew that the black realm would take her and would not give her back. The forces lured her further and further in. Her breathing slowed, her body felt numb, and all she could see was complete darkness. She sank deeper and deeper.

Until suddenly it all stopped, as though the invisible ropes dragging her down had suddenly snapped, and unravelled, to slither off her body. Sinai heard a distant but clear voice.

'Forces may work against you, but you have the power to make them work for you— wake up!'

Meekulu?

Sinai felt herself rising to the surface of the black realm, as rich energising power surged through her bones. She blinked her eyes open, and looked around.

She was in a garden, one that she had not been in before. From the look of it, no one else had been in it for a while.

There was none of the usual order customary in other perfectly-groomed palace gardens. Instead, it was filled with complete mayhem and unbridled beauty, with wild feather grass tossing its plumes. A large flame tree stood in the middle of the garden, its branches flushed with glowing, ruby-red flowers that touched both sides of the cream palace walls that framed the garden. There was no ceiling, so the bright moonlight showered the majestic tree in shimmering white rays.

A vivid image of Meekulu, her red wax braids and white puffs of curly hair, burned fiercely in Sinai's mind. Sinai could smell the old woman's scent of rose, lavender, and myrrh oil, and she instantly felt *awake*. She felt more awake than she had been in weeks.

Sinai realised she was cradled in Sergeant Olu's arms with Ina nearby, and she was overcome with the urge to move. Sinai pushed herself out of Sergeant Olu's arms, as a warm glow strengthened her body.

'Sinai—' Sergeant Olu protested, but Ina silenced him by placing her palm against his shoulder, her gaze transfixed on the girl.

Sinai stepped out from his grasp and walked toward the grand tree, and a wave of memories poured through her mind.

'Don't be soft, girl.'

'You don't know how to cut simple plantain?'

'But then the world changed, and so I changed.'

'You are strong, you must know this.'

Meekulu's voice ruffled Sinai's thick hair and her loud cackling laugh pierced her heart.

'She's here,' Sinai whispered, as she moved closer to the tree, looking back at Ina and Sergeant Olu. Her heart flipped in delight as a rush of joy flooded her broken body.

'Do you feel it?' Sinai said louder. 'She's here—you *must* feel it.'

She couldn't explain it. Sinai was certain that she was not mad. She knew that she had a full grasp on her senses. She felt clear-headed, clearer than she had felt in months, if not years. Sinai knew that she was looking at a grand flame tree, and yet she also knew that she was looking at Meekulu. She *knew* that Meekulu's spirit dwelled within the dark-brown branches and crimson leaves.

Sinai took another step forward and tears of joy filled her heart and sprang to her eyes, as more images poured through her mind. Meekulu climbing the stool to fetch the supposed ọbara powder,

Meekulu bouncing up the hill on their expedition, Meekulu tugging at her cheeks with a wide, warm smile on her face. Sinai looked up at the tree, and a ripple of life flew through its leaves. Its trunk bent back and forth, as though it were dancing.

Sinai was filled with a beautiful sense of peace that tingled from the pit of her stomach to the tips of her fingers. She wanted to laugh and dance and sing and cry for joy. Never had she felt so happy to be alive, and to find true joy amidst heart-wrenching sorrow. She felt connected to everything and everyone, and as though she had discovered a truth she hadn't known she needed. She was blessed to have felt a love so strong that it tore her apart, and to witness the beauty of eternal peace.

'*Chukwu Di Mma,*' she said, as she gazed at the beautiful tree with tears running down her cheeks. She let that statement sink into her soul, realising she had never felt such gratitude before. '*Chukwu Di Mma!*' she cried out to the heavens, her head thrown back as she erupted into laughter.

Seconds later, a massive rush of petals flew up into the air and swirled around the garden, creating intricate beautiful shapes as they weaved in and out. Ina and Sergeant Olu watched with shocked amazement as the red petals brushed lovingly against their cheeks. Sinai leapt into the air and danced alongside the flowing petals with her arms outstretched.

'She's here!' Sinai proclaimed, as she turned to Sergeant Olu and Ina with an infectious smile.

Ina looked back at her with a similarly wide smile, and small tears in her eyes, 'she's here,' she whispered back, before breaking into a laugh.

CHAPTER 45

A NIGHT'S DANCE

Furuefu Forest

Naala thought that the sky looked particularly beautiful. Its highest point was a dark navy colour that slowly melted into a lustrous turquoise closer to earth. It was lined with soft pink clouds and twinkling with stars that couldn't wait to emerge into the night.

The low rumble of Bayo's talking drum hit her in waves that were perfectly intertwined with Leto's light voice, as she sang old tales of the gods. It was the first time that Naala had heard Leto make a sound, and yet the usually quiet and timid woman sang so wonderfully that Naala wondered why she didn't do it all the time. Wispy clusters of small radiant insects illuminated her in a beautiful glow as they swayed to her delicately beautiful voice.

The group of survivors circled an ọkụ flame. It was shaped as a circle lined with small triangles, similar to artists' renderings of the sun. It was the most intricate ọkụ shape that Naala had ever witnessed. Bayo, it turned out, was a skilled flame tamer. He and Binyelum also provided some music for the occasion; as they performed, the rest of the survivors clapped and danced with their feet lighter than Naala had ever seen before. The ground shone with deep yellow, orange, and green light from the vibrant ero fungi. The survivors were all fuelled by a new unnamed and invigorating energy that had been sparked by fear of all things.

That afternoon Bayo had revealed that the merchant would be crossing their paths the next evening. That realisation hit Naala as hard as a boulder; hours later, she was still struggling to get out from under its sombre weight.

Naala could not understand what was holding her back. After all, she had agreed to get involved with the fight; in fact she had sought it out. Naala still wanted to avenge her loved ones and protect those left. She wanted to believe that she could do it—but she did not.

Naala had never mulled over decisions; she had always preferred to act first and think later, an approach that had landed her in many tricky situations, but had nonetheless always propelled her forward. Now, for the first time, she felt stuck. A strange feeling stirred within her, as though she was missing something, something vital, and its absence might be her downfall.

Naala had said nothing when Bayo told her that her mission would start tomorrow. She had also said nothing when Bayo attempted to dissuade Madi, Eni, and Kora from joining her.

He'd growled, 'I won't allow it—you people will ruin the whole mission. We already have strong people, trained spies and assassins placed along the way and in the palace to assist Naala. All you can provide is a distraction!' To his annoyance, he had been met by an unrelenting team and their new plan. Madi had stalked him, Eni threatened, and Kora attempted to bribe him.

Finally, Madi had said, 'Naala said that if we don't go, she won't.' She had said no such thing, and yet when Bayo looked back at her with terrified eyes, she hadn't repudiated Madi's statement. She had stared back at him wordlessly.

In truth, Naala had actually agreed with Bayo's arguments, but the fear of going to the city of Nri all on her own kept her silent.

Eventually, Bayo had sighed and conceded.

'Fine. If you want to go to your funeral, that's fine, but know this: my people are there to protect the girl and the crystal, and them alone—if you get in the way, you *will* be taken out.'

After that, everything was set. All they had to do was wait until the next day. Suddenly the whole mission to the palace, and its dangers, felt real and tangible, and a wave of sadness flowed through each of them. It dawned on them that it was very possible that not all of them would make it back. Kora, in the face of such doom, insisted on throwing a party. Some sort of celebration to ease the mood and ensure that, regardless of the outcome, they enjoyed what could be their last night together.

Naala tried to step out of herself and enjoy the festivities. Madi brought out a batch of palm wine that he had retrieved from a tree he had sapped on their journey. Other than Kora, all the women had re-braided their hair. It felt like a true party.

Yet Naala found herself sitting alone, watching orange flames dance in the darkening night. Her mind wandered to her lost family, her sweet grandmother, her little cousin and her . . . uncle. Suddenly a thick fog of shame clogged her throat. She couldn't picture him. She couldn't picture her uncle's face anymore. She could hear his loud voice, she could even recall his woody scent, and whilst she might have been able to describe them, she couldn't pinpoint his features.

'Heartless girl,' she muttered, a phrase that her uncle had used to describe her cold attitude many times. She had always thought it was a joke, but all along he had been right. She could not remember her family and she was allowing her new friends to follow her on a suicide mission. *What type of person am I?*

Naala jumped out of her thoughts momentarily when she found Eni looking at her from the other side of the fire. His piercing eyes cut through her soul, and in that moment she realised that he knew exactly what she was.

Naala suddenly felt exposed. Sickening shame curdled her gut.

Why can't he just leave me alone? she thought, as she turned to one of her favourite emotions: rage. Hot anger burned away any remnants of her shame. Naala could not stand to remain in the party any longer. She stood and stormed out of the area.

As she walked through the forest, her anger seeped away, replaced by a slow trickle of guilt. She paused momentarily. The party was supposed to raise the group's spirits, and she had let her mood drag it down. Kora, Eni, and Madi were risking their lives to help her, and she couldn't even muster up the strength to be happy?

Naala heard a branch break and she turned to face Eni.

'Go away,' she said, before she could think. He paused before nodding slowly and turning to leave. *Good,* Naala thought, but she didn't feel it. She felt empty and alone. Suddenly, she stormed after him.

'You need to leave me alone,' she blurted, and he looked confused.

'I will—I am—look, I'm sorry. I just wanted to check if you were fine. You seemed upset earlier, but if you don't want me here then I'll go.'

'Of course I'm upset! We all *know* what's going to happen tomorrow,' Naala said agitatedly, as the ero fungi radiated red and white. *I'm going to die,* she added in her thoughts. 'And I can't

384

remember their faces, and you keep *looking* at me—everywhere I turn, you are *looking* at me. It's . . . it's too much.'

Eni's stern face exposed his self-doubt and vulnerability for the first time. The glowing insects floating around him worked to further soften his face. Just as quickly as the soft expression came, it was replaced with Eni's usual hardness. His jaw tightened.

'You look at me too,' he finally said.

'Sorry?'

'You *look* at me too. It's not just me,' Eni replied; his eyes searched her face for some acknowledgement.

Naala kept her expression blank.

Eni sighed.

'Fine,' he breathed. 'I look at you. I . . .' he hesitated, before dropping his gaze. 'I . . . I think of you. I think of you all the time, Esinaala. I can't explain it—I'm sorry.' He looked back at her nervously. 'I'm sorry if I've made you feel uncomfortable. I'll stop, I will, but you . . . you look at me too.' Although his voice had softened, his expression remained hard, as though challenging her to refute his words.

Naala didn't. Her heart quickened as she became increasingly aware of how close he was. The ground lit up with a deep royal-purple colour; it illuminated Eni's face and drew Naala into his brightening eyes. He smelt of warm vanilla and pine, and it was making her dizzy. *Focus*, she thought, appraising his full lips and strong jaw. Naala did not know what to say. As time crept between them, disappointment and doubt spread across Eni's face; he had exposed himself and she was leaving him out to dry. She simply didn't know what to say.

'I—' Naala started, and his expression was expectant, but her words died on her tongue. 'I . . . do you think that I'm going to die?' she said eventually. Naala had wanted that comment to seem light-hearted and carefree, like something Kora might have said to pivot the conversation into something more digestible, but on her lips it was sombre and sad.

'I won't let you,' Eni murmured; something in his voice made her heart leap to her throat. It was as if he had just sworn an oath to the gods and Naala knew that he meant it.

'I won't let you die either,' she said, and the warmth of his smile spread through her entire body.

Naala took a step closer without thinking. Eni drew her to him with one arm around her waist. Naala relaxed. He brought one of his palms towards her face, cupping the back of her head with his hands, his fingers tangled in her coarse hair. A burst of electricity exploded within Naala, and yet she felt completely at peace. She raised her face as he leaned towards her; when she closed her eyes, he paused to watch her dark skin glisten in the moonlight.

'You are so beautiful,' he said suddenly, his voice heavy with wonder, as though he had never witnessed anything like her before. Before she could say anything, Eni's mouth found hers.

The world stopped. Naala clutched his back as his weight engulfed her with a force that made her gasp. Thick, sweet adrenaline and desire rushed through her body, tingling every place that Eni touched her. His hands roamed her body; he caressed her buttocks, and clutched her closer. Naala grasped at Eni with desperation for more, she couldn't breathe, she couldn't think, she—

'How can they say that small Gossy dances better than me? It is jealousy!' Azu's thundering voice pierced between Naala and Eni. They pulled away from each other in fright, gasping for air as they looked around the evening forest. 'I know it, Gossy is so stiff—only jealousy of the highest degree would make anyone say that he can out-dance me.'

Azu's voice carried through the forest, but his body was nowhere in sight. Naala spotted rustling leaves as Azu stormed off, accompanied by Isioma, using a quieter voice to reassure him that no one was against him.

Naala blinked as the forest settled down into its usual low hum. She could still feel the pressure of Eni's mouth against hers. A dose of reality seeped into her. *What am I doing?*

'I should g-go,' Naala murmured quietly, afraid to look up at him.

'Are you okay?' Eni said, his voice laced with concern.

'Yes, I'm fine,' Naala replied quickly, before flashing a smile. When his face relaxed, a fresh trickle of desire shivered up her back.

'Okay, goodnight!' Naala blurted, before dashing to the hammocks before Eni could reply.

CHAPTER 46

A PARCHMENT FROM THE EZE

City of Nri

Sinai sat with her deep brown legs dangling freely over the pale window ledge. The wind rushed against her toes and she breathed in the fresh morning air. The nnunu women had begun to sing again; their soft deep voices filled the city with a sad, desperately hopeful song. She looked over the waking city, just as she had done months ago when she had almost plunged to her death. Sinai was not afraid; she now knew what death tasted like, and its cold metallic pull was nowhere nearby. Sinai remained still as she heard movement stirring behind her.

'Heavens, have you not learned your lesson? What is your obsession with these high windows?' Ina scolded before approaching Sinai cautiously. 'You're . . . you're not thinking of jumping, are you?'

Sinai laughed heartily, tickled by the concern in Ina's voice.

'No, I'm not! Besides, why waste the energy when I can get you to knock me off?' Sinai joked, making Ina roll her eyes.

'Well, I . . . could you just get down from there, please?' Ina pleaded, as Sinai laughed, a sound that still stirred wonder within her after the weeks of painful gloom.

'Okay, okay,' Sinai finally said, before swivelling her feet inside the palace walls.

'I'm sorry for that,' Ina murmured quietly, as Sinai hopped down.

Sinai was about to ask what she was sorry for but, as guilt streaked across Ina's face, the memory of her fall flashed through her mind. Sinai shook head as a small smile formed on her lips.

'That was a horrible thing to do, but it was also a lifetime ago. You were so *different* then . . . I was so different then,' Sinai said as she shrugged.

'I was jealous. Incredibly jealous,' Ina said.

Sinai nearly choked.

'Jealous? Jealous of what?' Sinai asked. In had rich skin, bright eyes, and perfect locs; she was stunningly beautiful, and Sinai was perplexed.

'Of you!' Ina replied, rolling her eyes at Sinai's shock.

'But you're *Ina*—you have everything, you're beautiful?'

'Yes, I know I am,' Ina replied in irritation. 'But it's not enough, it's never enough. Eyes still wandered from my face to yours and

I hated it. I tried so hard to be *better*, to rise above my station. I wanted to be the wife of an Obi, but it felt like every time that I had one on the hook, his eyes would wander to you.' Sinai listened pensively. She had always thought Ina despised her because she was an efuọla; she never dreamed it was due to jealousy.

Sinai had always felt that Ina's life was so easy. She had the entire court at her beck and call. She had always been surrounded by a sea of admirers.

'And is that what you still want?' Sinai asked.

'Well, that was a lifetime ago; I'm different now,' Ina replied with a smirk, as she threw her hands dismissively in the air, and then they both erupted in laughter.

As they settled down, Ina said, 'I'm glad that you're okay now.' Sinai took in her statement. It was true, she was okay. While Meekulu's death had scarred her heart, Sinai had finally found peace with it.

'I'm glad to—' Sinai stopped as a servant approached; a boy who often delivered messages for the Eze.

Sinai's heart rate quickened. Curled around the parchment, the boy's hands shook with nerves.

Sinai had gotten this response from people more often than she liked. In the space of a few short months she had gone from being invisible, to having a solid social grounding, to being a pariah. Rumours had spread about Sinai's manic behaviour following Meekulu's death, and soon the palace was convinced that Sinai was cursed or infected by madness. Despite her recovery, they were afraid of catching the mystery ailment too, if they got too close to her.

'Oh, for heaven's sake, hand it over, will you?' Ina said. The boy's mouth gaped before he dropped the parchment into her hand and scurried off.

Ina kissed her teeth in frustration before she opened the parchment. As she began to read it, her eyes bulged dramatically and she looked at Sinai with such pure terror it caused the girl to shiver.

'What? Don't tell me that you also think that I am cursed,' Sinai asked jokingly, but her smile didn't carry to her eyes.

'He wants to see you, the Eze wants to see you,' Ina whispered.

Sinai snatched the parchment out of Ina's hand.

Meet me at in my quarters. Come alone – Eze Ochichiri

'You don't have to go,' Ina whispered. 'That boy didn't put the note in your hand and he left before we read it. We could discard it, and we could get you out of the palace immediately.'

'No,' Sinai replied.

'We can, there are ways—trust me, I know.'

'Ina, it's the Eze. You don't think he will find me? Even if he doesn't, you don't think he won't take out his vengeance on anyone I've ever talked to? You, Sergeant Olu, even little Chisi. He will torture and kill you all,' Sinai said calmly, as Ina's eyes darkened.

'If you go, he will kill you,' she finally said. Sinai knew that Ina was probably right. She also knew that she would spend her last hours alive trying to kill him first; even if she were somehow able to scratch him, that would be enough, for she too had a vengeful soul.

CHAPTER 47

WOODEN BOXES

Furuefu Forest

Naala woke with her fingers grazing her lips as the memory of Eni lingered on her tongue. *Curse him,* she thought. She couldn't stop replaying their kiss from the night before, over and over. Her heart leapt to her throat when she saw him an hour later at breakfast. She quickly diverted her gaze towards Kora and plunged into an enthusiastic conversation about her new braids, while he lingered in the background for a moment before stepping away. Kora's eyes jumped between the two of them after that, and her mouth seemed curved in a permanent smirk. *Curse him,* she thought again, as the four of them, led by Bayo, travelled out of the forest.

The trees became increasingly sparse, and soon the group reached an open road for the first time in months. They were greeted by a small stout merchant with a smile almost as wide as his well-used cart, which was pulled by a group of four strong large oxen. Bayo repeated his instructions for what seemed like the hundredth time; Naala heard nothing that was said. All she could think about was Eni and that all-consuming kiss. That is, until she entered the box.

Everyone winced when they saw the shockingly small size of the wooden boxes that would house them as they travelled towards the guarded palace walls.

'Surely you can't be serious,' Kora gasped, when the merchant told them to hop into the most suitable box.

'Yeaaah, I wouldn't want to get in those boxes either,' the merchant said with a chuckle. 'But that's exactly what *you* are going to do. You are going to get in, stay quiet and be still. If you do, you'll get into the palace without getting yourself, or any of these fine people, killed.' The merchant's accent was a strange mixture of ones from different places.

'Assuming we don't suffocate first,' Kora muttered, as she poked around her box. 'You just can't be serious.'

But the merchant was serious. Naala lay with her knees pressed to her stomach. She was consumed with the desire to stretch out her aching legs and release the tight knots in her lower back. She had never felt so uncomfortable in her whole life; fanciful thoughts of screaming at the top of her lungs tugged at her. She wanted it to end, and if a swift arrow or guard's blade was the only way, then so be it.

They travelled non-stop through the night and well into the following day. Naala had had enough. Her only respite came when the cart jolted suddenly and sporadically on the bumpy road, sending a sharp pain through her body, a welcomed distraction from the aches that plagued her joints.

Suddenly the cart stopped moving and Naala heard distant voices. She turned her head to try and make out what was said, but all she achieved was to create a small creaking sound. Naala bit her bottom lip as she willed herself to remain still and silent. Without warning, a wash of pale light entered the cart, and Naala blinked as the rays filtered through the small holes in the wooden box. *Someone must have opened up the cart doors, but who?* Naala thought. No one was supposed to open the cart until they had arrived safely in the merchant's home in the city of Nri.

Naala was certain that they had yet to arrive there. The merchant lived within the heart of the city, at the foot of the Eze's palace. Wherever they were, it was far too quiet to be the bustling and busy city of Nri. But then, who had opened the door?

Perhaps the merchant was simply checking on them, or maybe they were being robbed, or, worse, caught by palace guards. Naala's head swam with the endless scenarios and deaths that could occur before they had even stepped foot into the palace. Naala took a slow steady breath as she reminded herself to remain calm; regardless of whom it was, the merchant had made it clear: no one should draw attention to themselves until their box had been cracked open.

'The cart is very full today,' a deep voice said, as Naala's heart pounded. So it was an inspector. *We're dead,* she thought, as her heart sank into a dark hole. There is no way that they could pass an inspection; one decent look at the various boxes stuffed with random artefacts and four villagers, and they were done for.

'Haha, well, I said it, didn't I? Why do you think I'm in such a hurry to offload all of this! Once all of this has been sold off, I will be eating sweet for weeks, if not months.' The merchant chuckled.

'All this from Abyssinia?'

'Eh-he, yes now. You were too busy doing this new kin' inspection that you didn't let me tell you the gist.'

'Look at this guy—so you're back with one of your stories?'

'Listen, in Abyssinia, I have this girl—very, very, very fine girl—'

'There's always a fine girl!' the guard chuckled.

'No, this one is different, she's not any kin' fine—she is *fine:* skin smooth, body . . . just wow—anyway, her *oga* died suddenly.'

'Wait, her oga? She has a husband?'

'*Had*—he died—open your ears and listen.'

'O' Chinaka, you're bad man,' the guard laughed.

'Bad, good, up, down—is it not all the same in the end?'

'Mmmm. So the guy died.'

'He died and so all his riches were just sitting there gathering dust. He wasn't a nice man; he had a lot of enemies, even amongst his friends. She wanted safe passage out of town, and in return she handed me over all these beautiful artefacts.'

'Mmhmm. So you mean to tell me that she just gave you all of this, just like that?'

'Yes, now, she turned to me and said that I should quickly carry them and go.'

'Carry them and go? What kind of nonsense is that?'

'It's true! She was afraid that if she stayed there, all his enemies would come and kill her. If she asked one of her neighbours to take her, they could sell her out to his enemies too. Me, I don't know any enemies or neighbours; all I know is that the girl is fine.'

The guard chuckled. 'Wonders will never end.'

'Bunke! Hurry up with that inspection, it's time for the guard rotation and I'm starving!' another voice called from a distance.

'Yes, almost done!' the guard yelled back.

'Hmm, well, if you're really going to inspect all of this, I better help you take them out. Trust me, I nearly blew my back out trying to load these boxes.'

'Mmm,' the guard grunted. 'Listen, you know the checks—no weapons, no poisons, and no ụtọ?'

'Can you repeat the third one? Haha! You are becoming too serious. Yes, of course I know all the rules. I have traded for over thirty years. I'd wager that I know them far better than you do,' the merchant laughed.

'I'm being serious. The Eze is getting . . . *firmer* about this; if there's any trouble that would be both our heads on the stake.'

'Bunke, what are you doing?' the other guard roared.

'Listen, if you are worried, feel free to check. Like I said, as old as I am, I can even help you if needs be, but I'm certain the cargo is completely fine, as usual.'

'Bunke!'

'I'm done!' the guard shouted, as he shut the cart door and plunged Naala back into darkness.

CHAPTER 48

THE GOLDEN DOORS

City of Nri

Sinai slowed to a stop as she approached the same spot that she had stood in when she first heard Meekulu's deathly screams. She took a deep breath and looked ahead at the opulent hall. This time, she could at least say that she matched the regal decorations. She had decided to wear the green and gold akwete cloth, wrapped around her body in the latest style, keeping her right arm bare.

The cloth had been gifted to her by the ladies in court for her coming-of-age ceremony. Every year the girls who had begun their transition into womanhood were celebrated at the coming-of-age festival, an event that was strictly restricted to the women in the city. Tales were told, music and food was abundant, and the women danced freely.

Sinai cherished the cloth dearly; not only was it the richest cloth that she owned, but it reminded her of her most loving moments in the palace.

As at all major festivals, the attendees were expected to dress their best; this was never more true than at a coming-of-age festival. The girls were expected to wear new and premium garments, crested with sparkling jewellery.

Typically it was the mothers that styled their daughters, draping them in the finest cloth that the family could afford. The motherless efuọla girls typically made do with gifts from friends, but Sinai had none. So she would have to fend for herself; she had imagined herself wearing one of her dated party garments to the festival.

She had prepared herself for the snide remarks and sideward glances, but she was not prepared to find this beautiful cloth sprawled over her akwa nest the night before the party, with a note that read,

A coming-of-age is a blessing. Cherish this gift — the mothers of the court.

Sinai had cried at such generosity, and spent that evening smiling and talking to everyone who walked past her. It had been a wonderful night. The following day, however, she was met with the usual coldness and detachment. It seemed as though things had gone back to normal. Nonetheless, Sinai basked in the glow of that night for months after.

The rich, gold and green garment was the first outfit that came to her mind when she thought of what she would chose to die in.

Sinai's hair also looked regal, intricately plaited, thanks to Ina and Chisi's skilful hands. Ina had also lent Sinai one of her coral headdresses. Sinai had never felt so majestic in her life. She hugged Ina and Chisi as they saw her out.

'You look . . . presentable,' Ina had said stiffly.

'Thank you,' Sinai had replied, as she blinked away tears.

She took another sharp breath, turned away from the view of the spot where Meeluku had died, and continued down the mesmerising hallway. Finally she approached a pair of large luxurious golden doors; she had never seen an entrance as extravagant. *This must be the Eze's quarters,* she thought wistfully.

No guards, she mused, before falling into the immense beauty of the doors. They were carved with various scenes from the gods' war: Ikenga's fall; the burning of the city of Igwe Ojii; Agwu's double-cross, and, at the centre, a large triumphant Eze stood with the Mother's crystal raised high above his head. *The coward didn't bother to put the Mother's image on his pompous wall,* she thought. Suddenly a loud crack sounded, and Sinai took a step back as the golden doors sprang open.

Sinai gasped. She was seconds away from turning on her heels and dashing off. Something held her back.

'Ndewo Sinai,' came the Eze's resounding voice as he beckoned her to enter his quarters. Before she could reply, a strong force

401

dragged her inside. Sinai struggled with no avail, she tried to fling her arms but they didn't move, she tried to kick her legs but they remained limp. Her eyes were pinned on the open doors, as she willed herself to escape, to run as far as she could from the Eze.

I shouldn't be here, she thought desperately, as she stood frozen in place, watching the golden doors shut firmly behind her.

CHAPTER 49

THE HIDDEN VILLAGERS

City of Nri

The city of Nri seeped through the cart and into the tight box that held Naala's aching body. The ringing voices of street sellers haggling for higher prices, the high-pitched sounds of what seemed to be armies of children laughing freely, the scent of live animals, flavoured spices, a chorus of drums, carts, bells—they all rushed through Naala.

Though Naala couldn't yet see the city, her imagination was rich with an arsenal of images derived from years of listening attentively to guests. She could visualise the cobbled streets, the rows of open markets, the stacks of houses leading up the grand palace. Naala had dreamt of exploring Nri for as long as she could remember. She had seen herself picking out the exotic spices in the market, climbing the mighty wall that encircled the city, and dancing the night away at the famed street festivals. She had not imagined being brought through the city locked within a tight wooden box, as she prepared herself to steal the Eze's most treasured asset.

The cart came to another sudden stop, and Naala held her breath. *Not again*, she thought.

'Ayy Chinaka, is that you? Welcome!'

'Quick, Soki, help me with these boxes.'

'So you cannot even say a simple ndewo first. Chinaka, it's been weeks since I saw you last.'

'Ndewo Soki,' Chinaka said, as he paused to cross his palms over this chest. 'Now, please, help me with these boxes.'

'Oh my, it's so heavy! We need to call the children. Ijemma, call your brothers and sisters to help with these boxes.'

Naala's heart pounded with anticipation. The closer she came to being released, the more desperate she felt. *Get me out of here!* she wanted to scream, but all she could do was press her fists against the rigid planks. Soon enough, she felt a lightness in her stomach as the box lifted into the air and a new warm light bled through the wood. Without warning, the box was dropped harshly on the ground and Naala bit her lip to stop herself from yelping in pain.

Naala heard heavy footsteps walking away from her and her heart skipped a beat as the sound of a daga hacking away at her cage became increasingly apparent. She pushed against the wood to hasten the process.

'If you don't put them hands away, this daga will slice right through them,' a woman's voice cautioned. However, Naala did not care. If it meant that she could escape her cage just a second earlier, she would have gleefully sacrificed both her hands.

A sharp clang resonated through the floor as the daga was dropped in haste.

'I told you, girl!' the woman warned. Naala gripped her fists tightly. *You need hands for the task at hand,* she told herself. Naala waited for the frayed lid to burst open. Finally a wave of light showered over her and Naala could finally stretch her arm. The relief of being able to move was met with a painful twinge as her locked muscles awoke.

Another pair of hands clawed at the wooden lid and helped Naala draw back the planks. Once there was enough room to allow it, the stranger's hands pulled her out of the box. Naala cried in a mixture of pain and relief; tears ran down her face as she stretched out her aching back.

The woman scuttled over with a bowl of a thick waxy substance. She dipped her hand in the wax and began to spread it on Naala's joints. Naala didn't object because the wax cooled against her skin and soothed the aches in her muscles.

'Thank you,' Naala murmured, as the woman handed the wax to Eni who was stretching.

Naala watched as Eni's toned muscles flexed underneath his pecan brown skin; his body shook slightly and Naala's heart fluttered. She looked up to find him staring at her.

'Are you okay?' he asked, his eyes roaming over her with concern.

'Yes,' Naala said sharply, as she broke his gaze and looked at her surroundings.

They were in a small living area. The wall behind her was filled with an array of beautiful and colourful artefacts, and to the right was an open window. Naala looked out at the buzzing street, with the grand palace brooding in the background.

'So this is the city,' Naala murmured.

'A bit of it,' the merchant said. 'The crappy bit,' he added with a chuckle, as the woman that Naala assumed to be his wife slapped his arm.

The merchant's smile was bright and settled on his face easily. His eyes sparkled with stories and jokes. His brown-leathered skin was sun-beaten, and he stood with a slouch. He was designed to be likable, to filter in and out of different groups with ease. Naala didn't like it. His smooth transition with the guards, charming rapport with his wife despite his apparent promiscuity—this was not a man to be trusted. Yet here they all stood, in his home with their lives planted firmly in his hands.

'So what exactly is the plan? You said that you would give us more detail here?' Naala asked firmly. The merchant responded with yet another easy smile.

'In a hurry to save the world, eh?' he chuckled, before turning to his wife. 'Soki, please get the clothes, the ones from Abyssinia. After some slight adjustments we will have a group of travelling nobles in our home.'

'We're posing as nobles again.' Madi sighed, nervousness spreading across his face; the mission had become real.

'How else will you get near the Eze's court?' the merchant asked with an easy laugh, before inspecting them. 'Soki,' he called loudly. 'Get the hooded cape for the impatient girl, her hair would not match their style at all.'

'Just one hood?' his wife called from the other room.

'Two,' Eni suddenly said, causing everyone to look confused. The merchant glanced at Kora.

'No, the other girl's hair will do, even her tribal scars are fine too; I've seen some of their women adopt that style.'

'We'll have two hoods please, not for Kora—for me . . . I'd prefer to wear a hood also,' Eni added.

The merchant smirked. 'Very well,' he murmured. 'Two hoods, Soki.'

The woman brought colourful garments piled in her arms. She handed them out one by one, and after some inspection, they all began to get into their new attire.

'Soki, what of the scented oils?'

'What about it? You did not tell me to get any scents,' the woman scowled.

'Soki, I said they are dressing as Abyssinian nobles. When have you ever seen an Abyssinia noble without a cloud of sweet smells?'

'Chinaka, you know those are the only things I like in all the rubbish you bring back. My bottle is almost empty; I told you to pick one up during your last trip but you refused and now you want to give what is left to them?'

'Soki, what are you saying? Is it my fault that your natural scent is so ravishing? Am I the one that you should blame? Come boy—abeg you smell this woman, and tell me if you would bastardise that sweet scent with nonsense oils!' The merchant attempted to pull a hesitant Madi over to his wife.

'Chinaka, you are trouble-o!' Soki cried, as she tried and failed to hide her smile.

'Please, my love, get that scent now so that we can send these people off and I can have what I've been missing for weeks,' the merchant pleaded, as his wife hushed him before skipping out of the room.

The merchant eyes squinted as he continued his final inspection.

'Good; you all look good. Once you have the scented oils, you will be ready,' he muttered, turning his head towards the door. 'Soki,' he called.

'I'm coming, I'm coming,' Soki said, as she strolled in with a dark bottle in her hands. She handed it reluctantly over to Chinaka who proceeded to rub each of them heavily with the oil; it smelt of jasmine, rose, and a spice that Naala didn't know. Kora sneezed loudly in response.

'What now?' Naala asked.

The merchant walked to the window, 'I have a cart that will escort you to the palace; from there you will meet with Okeke, another member of the akwụna. He will pose as your palace guide, and take you to the Obis' court, the home of some of the greatest artefacts that man has known.' The merchant peered outside. 'No one but the mmo girl should touch that crystal. Do you hear me? Only she can take it out of that room. Once you have the crystal, you will be escorted back here—you must return by nightfall at the latest. Any later than that and you will be on your own. Soki, the kids and I, will be gone, and you will have no way out of this palace.'

'Why are you doing this?' Naala couldn't help but ask. 'You've risked your life; you have to move your entire family: why?' The more the words tumbled out of her mouth, the more suspicious she felt.

The merchant's face was sombre. Raising his arms and allowing his sleeves to fall, he revealed deep burns across both forearms. He then made his right hand into a fist and hit softly against his left breast three times, a gesture that Naala had only seen once from a visitor from a village in Osisi, one of the first rumoured to fall to the Eze's wrath. The people of that village marked rings around their arms for each year that they were born. Naala looked at the merchant's burned arms, a brutal cover-up to protect his village origins. He blinked tears away before lowering his hands.

'Just get here with the crystal before nightfall,' he said softly, before falling into one of his easy smiles, his face completely rid of all its former pain.

CHAPTER 50

WOODEN DARTS

City of Nri

Naala was thankful for her hood as she walked through the majestic palace. She was certain that the shock and awe, imprinted on her face since she walked into the palace, would give her away instantly. Naala marvelled at the craftsmanship and beauty that exuded from every wall. Even the floors were paved with sparkling marble. Naala had only ever seen that material in Chief Ofo's stick; here it was so common that people walked on it.

Naala was completely astounded, but also perplexed. The Eze walked around this palace knowing that it was completely his. The soldiers came back to the palace as gods, staying in the most pristine living quarters. How could they, in the midst of all this beauty, still choose to commit such heinous crimes? How could they slaughter innocent people, and then return to bask in this splendour?

Naala turned to Eni, curious what he thought of the palace, but that curiosity faded. Something was wrong. Eni had shifted his hood back and he looked around questioningly.

'What's wrong?' Naala asked, trying to spot what was making him uneasy.

'We're going the wrong way,' Eni murmured, before he marched towards Okeke, the large round man, who was posing as their guide. Okeke had greeted them enthusiastically at the entrance, bowing low and showering them with compliments. He had taken them around the palace, explaining the extravagant paintings and carvings with a passion that made Naala question if he indeed knew that they were here to steal back the Mother's crystal, and not learn about the artists' depictions of the many battles fought over the years.

Naala watched curiously as Eni spoke to Okeke. The large man had a worried look that soon melted into one of relief as Eni gestured at the halls behind them.

'Yes, yes of course, I always miss that turn! Thank you, young man, that's a good eye you have there. I definitely need to drink more herbal tea, my age is catching up to me!' he replied, before turning to the group. 'Sorry, sorry, I missed a turning—please, can we all just turn here, yes—sorry, it won't happen again, I am awake now!' The man laughed nervously as he bowed apologetically before hurrying ahead leading them through yet another network of halls.

'How did you know?' Naala asked, as she caught up with Eni.

'I didn't know—it just felt like the wrong way,' he replied, as Naala frowned. *What did that mean?* He added, 'I've heard this route described over and over again, and it felt like we were going the wrong way.'

Naala opened her mouth to protest, but fell silent when two nobles past them. She was not at all satisfied with his response, but did not have time to get to grips with it now. Naala instead focused on getting the Mother's crystal out of the palace, and addressing Eni and his bizarre behaviour when they were out of harm's way.

Before long, they approached a large impressive set of doors with two guards, decked with the royal attire, standing in front. Naala's heart quickened as she noted the gleaming abaras at their sides. The sight of those green glowing weapons filled her with dread, as the voices of dead villagers echoed in her ears.

'Ndewo, ndewo,' Okeke said with a slight bow, as he brought his palms towards his chest and let them fall towards the guards. 'I'm here with some members of the Tsega family. Nobles from Abyssinia. They have requested to see the famous Obi court,' Okeke exclaimed pridefully.

'Get out of here, swindler. You are not a member of the official tour guide. You should not be guiding anyone,' one of the guards said dismissively, causing Naala's stomach to flip with fright. *It's all over*, she thought. *What now?*

'Ozo, I am not a swindler. Yes, I am not an official guide yet—but I am a highly regarded server, so much so that these fine people requested me, and me specifically. They have come over here and they should be able to see the room. I can wait outside with you, if you please, but please do not punish these people because they chose to bless me with the honour of guiding them.'

'Get away from here,' the guard said sternly.

'I—I have a parchment, an official parchment signed by the head of the *official* tour guides, giving me access to the court. Please, Ozo,' Okeke pleaded, as he scrambled in his garment and pulled out a parchment before handing it to the guard. He grabbed it and tore it to pieces.

'I'm not going to ask you again,' the other guard said, as he shoved Okeke back and placed his hand on the hilt of his abara.

'Why do you have to make this so difficult?' Okeke sighed, before snapping his fingers twice. Suddenly, wooden darts whistled through the air and hit both guards in the neck. Naala, Kora, Madi, and Eni stepped back, shielding their heads in anticipation of an air attack, but no more darts followed. Okeke pulled Naala forcefully towards the door where the two guards lay slumped. Eni pushed Okeke's hand away, and stood between the two of them protectively.

'We don't have time,' Okeke hissed at Eni. 'We need to be quick—they will wake in the next fifteen minutes and alert the army, and the palace will shut down.'

'Shut down? How will we leave?' Madi asked, his eyes glued cautiously to the sleeping guards.

'It doesn't matter—we have a fall guy in place, the whole thing will be resolved in the next hour but you must go,' Okeke said.

'Okay, but you keep your hands off her,' Eni warned before Naala shoved him out of the way.

'Let's just go,' she said hurriedly, as she stepped over the guards and pushed the door open.

The room was darker than she had expected, and she blinked before she found her bearings.

'Where is it?' Kora whispered behind her. Naala turned her head to her left; Bayo's instructions sung in the back of her head, but she didn't need them.

'There,' Naala murmured, as she walked towards the artefact that tugged at her the most.

'Yes, yes, that's it! Now take it so that we can go,' Okeke hissed from the door, as Naala bumped into a wooden low bench on the ground, and cursed in pain.

'Hurry up,' Okeke said, as a fresh wave of anger coursed through Naala. She didn't answer; instead, she grabbed the crystal and suddenly her anger dissipated. In its place she felt a rush of intense power.

Naala stood astounded as black marks appeared on her left hand. Strange markings that she couldn't place. *Nsibidi*? No, this was something else. *Something magical,* she thought, as the markings

415

settled on her hand. Before she could think, the black and gold realm suddenly appeared before her, circling her like a large snake. She was coiled in its thick smoky mist, like the dust clouds she used to create in her village, but black with speckles of bright gold—just as Bayo had said.

'Let's go,' Eni said, breaking her from her thoughts, causing the black and gold mist to vanish.

The five of them walked through the halls on high alert. The urge to run was so strong, but it would only lead to even more suspicion. All they could do was walk, a slow torturous pace that was synonymous with the rich, lazy nobles that they were pretending to be.

He's going to kill me! I shouldn't be here.

Naala stopped dead in her tracks and gasped. Her hand went to her heart as an unknown but familiar voice rang in her head. She felt a rush of emotions: fear, anger, and despair all at once. That voice wrapped around Naala's heart and tugged her towards it. She couldn't leave, she needed to find it, she needed to save *her*. Naala had never felt an urge as great as this before; she felt as though she would die if she did not follow it.

'What's wrong?' Eni asked, as he turned to find Naala bent over with her hands on her knees.

'I need to go to her,' Naala breathed; every second she resisted the pull towards the voice, she felt a tightening pressure against her heart.

'Who?' Eni asked, as cold fear ran up his back.

'I need to go,' Naala gasped, before dashing away from the group and towards the nameless voice.

'No, no, no, no, no! Where is she going? She has the crystal,' Okeke cried, before sounds of a commotion broke out.

Naala whipped her head around to see Eni knocking the daga that Okeke had aimed towards her, out of his hand, while Madi pushed away a passer-by who suddenly started to charge at Eni. Kora watched, stunned.

More wooden darts whistled through the air, but this time Naala raised her hand in and drew power from the black realm. The darts stopped in their flight and clattered to the floor, as Naala turned a corner.

CHAPTER 51

THE NDỤ CRYSTAL

City of Nri

Sinai wanted to scream, but she couldn't make a sound. Her back was pressed against the Eze's walls, and her arms pinned above her head. She watched as the Eze circled the large stone table in the middle of his room. The table held five tiny people made from sand, brought to life by the Eze's hand. One of the people broke away from the group and ran off the edge of the table before exploding back into a small pile of sand on the floor.

The Eze let out a cruel laugh as he watched.

'Yes, little one, bring me back Ndụ,' he muttered, before turning slowly back to Sinai.

'So Ala's supposed daughters have come at last!' he exclaimed, throwing his arms in the air and beating at his chest. A manic look flashed across his face, but vanished quickly, and the Eze's profile was expressionless again. He let his arms fall to his sides before stalking towards her. 'I'm sure you expected me to be afraid?'

Sinai tried again to move, but all she could manage were small shuffles within her invisible chains. The Eze stroked her cheek, and Sinai roared silently within herself. His touch felt like scorching flames. Tears rolled down her cheeks, and her breathing increased into rapid short bursts, but she remained stuck to the wall.

The Eze smirked.

'Admittedly one might have said that . . . at one point anyway . . . that I was . . . *afraid*.' He spat the word as though it was poison. 'Can you believe it, *me*—a whole Eze—as great as I am, as weak as you are—*I* was afraid, of what? A whore's prophecy!' He looked at her with pure hatred.

'For years all I could think about was the two of you coming to hunt me down in the dead of the night. Until one day I decided to take matters into my hands. You see, the whore said that you would come as twins. So I made sure that every twin born in Nri was slaughtered.

'That settled me for some time, but then, whilst on a visit, I spotted two boys with the same face in one of those *villages*. You see, people in the cities are easy to track, everything is recorded, everything is monitored— but in the villages . . .' he swivelled around and faced her, his eyes burning with fury.

'They are all *treacherous*. Can you imagine it? Keeping secrets, disobeying my law. After everything I did for all of them. I saved every single one of them. Me! I *sacrificed* my *soul*—and what did they do? Betray me,' he snarled through clenched teeth, before taking in a deep breath and draining all emotion from his face.

'You see the problem is, there are too many of them. Too many people roaming the earth, causing trouble, creating ripples everywhere they go. The more people, the wider the net, the lower chances of *complete control*,' he noted, as he swivelled a finger lightly on the edge of the table. 'Some of them *have* to go. These remote villages are where the problems always start. So one by one I am wiping them all out,' he said, as he flung the sand off the table.

'I embarked on creating yet another new order. A kingdom with less people to track, a kingdom without any villages. Just a nucleus of the best, most loyal people. And why not? Am I not *the* Eze of Nri? The people's champion? Am I not the Mother's slayer? I can provide all the food and material that the cities need with the Ndụ crystal. So what do I need villages for? I have never *needed* those villages—they are no use—and since the villagers refuse to obey me, what else is there left to do but to wipe them out?' The Eze mused, as he dusted his hands. A sickening smirk crept again over his face.

'But you,' he said, drawing closer to her. 'You wormed your way out of my grasp—an efuọla! Hiding right under my nose. I should have known,' he murmured, as his nose flared and he poked his finger repeatedly into his head. 'But I found out! I always find out! I discovered *you* and *her*—I bet you thought that stunt at the mountain was clever! All it did was confirm the suspicions that I already had!

'Mmos! That witch had me believe that you were actually born of Ala! You are nothing more than mere mmos, HA! What could a mmo do against me?' he hissed. 'I have had the Ndụ crystal for centuries; its power has filtered into my soul for *centuries*. I am a master of the black realm. How could *you* possibly kill *me?*' the Eze screamed, as his eyes searched Sinai's face desperately. Sinai willed herself away from him.

The Eze turned from her in disgust. 'Weak, that's what you are. That's what I have been afraid of! Can you imagine? I even gave you fuel for your fire,' he continued incredulously. 'After Udi, I could have come back here and killed you straight away. But alas, I am merciful, I am fair. I gave you the chance to face me at your full potential. I wanted *you* to come to *me*. I wanted to feel your wrath—I wanted you at your peak when I crushed you alive. So I killed your treacherous mentor. I handed it over to you—all the pain that you needed to access your full potential, and even then all you could muster was a little bit of wind.' The Eze flung his hand dismissively in the air and a gust of wind whipped through the room, gathering all the grains of sand before settling them back on the table. The Eze broke into another manic laugh before turning back to Sinai.

'This is who she sent to kill me!' the Eze roared. The room fell into a deathly silence as the Eze stalked towards Sinai, his eyes thundered with rage. Sinai's body filled with dread. She needed to run. She needed to scream so loudly that her throat bled raw. But all she could do was wait. The Eze cupped a hand around her throat. A blind and all-consuming pain coursed through Sinai's body. In that moment, all she was, all she knew, was hot, unrelenting agony. The Eze lifted her in the air, not with his hands alone, but with a strange, charged, green, lightning substance.

Sinai couldn't breathe.

She did not want to breathe. She longed for the comfort of a sweet, dark death that would release her from the Eze's torment. In due time, the pain lessened somewhat and Sinai began her descent. She closed her eyes and succumbed to the deep beyond. Seconds later her body slackened lifelessly.

With a flick of his wrist, the Eze flung her vacant body behind him. He straightened his isiagu and wiped sweat from his brow. He stood for several minutes, waiting for the door to fling open. When it did, he smiled.

Naala stumbled into the room breathlessly. The large, exquisite space was almost dizzying, filled with bright gold ornaments, encrusted with sparkling stones; gleaming marbles and polished woods. It took Naala a moment to come to grips with what was happening.

When she did, it hit her like a punch in the stomach. A large powerful man watched her from the right side of the room, like a beast stalking a new prey. She looked at him wordlessly as he strode towards the centre of the room, the thick furs on his shoulders ruffling.

The Eze.

Naala gulped as he stood squarely before her; behind him a figure lay slumped on the floor.

Naala's heart contracted, but not solely from fear. Naala had accepted her fear long ago; she wore it like a scar that she could do nothing else with. However, she was surprised to find sorrow also coursing through her veins. Deep sorrow for whomever lay lifelessly on the floor. The person that she was called to save. Once again she had failed, but this time, somehow, it felt so much worse.

'So here is the *other* one,' the Eze said darkly, as he flicked his wrists twice. Naala's heart skipped a beat as she felt the Mother's crystal breaking out of her tight clasp.

No! she screamed silently, as she tried desperately to keep hold of the Ndụ crystal. But try as she might, she could not stop it from nudging out of her quivering fingers, cutting across her skin until finally it pulled away from her grasp. The emerald crystal zoomed through the air with the same determination as a bloodthirsty hawk zeroing in on its prey. The crystal reached the Eze's hand.

Then it flew past it.

His face contorted with violent wrath as he looked incredulously at his empty hand. He swivelled to find the crystal hovering over Sinai's lifeless body.

423

The Eze let out a vicious snarl and edged towards the fallen girl. Naala looked from the Eze to the girl lying on the floor and then back towards the crystal. *He can't get it,* she thought desperately, before springing towards him and leaping on his back. Naala caught the Eze by surprise. She called on loose pieces of wood, lying unburned in a fireplace nearby, to bind his hands. The wood formed chains as she dug her fingers into his eyes. His piercing roar shook Naala to her core, but she refused to waver. *He can't get it!*

Sinai's body began to lift weightlessly into the air. Her head and feet dangled as her torso drew closer and closer to the illuminated crystal. The index finger on her right hand suddenly twitched. With her eyes closed and her throat breathless, Sinai's right arm reached up blindly towards the crystal. As soon as the tips of her fingers brushed against the surface of the powerful crystal, Sinai let out a loud and strangled breath. She cupped the crystal in her hand as she crashed unceremoniously to the floor.

Naala and the Eze ceased their struggle momentarily. The Eze roared as Sinai scrambled up from the floor, the Ndụ crystal gleaming in her hand. He jerked his body violently and Naala tumbled to the tiles in front of him, just a hair's breadth away from her sister. She sprang up defensively.

'So you are going to make this a little more interesting, I see—that's fine,' the Eze rasped. Naala's wooden chains burst unceremoniously from his hands as he raised them, and curls of green smoke coiled his palms. 'You will both die by my hand and that curse will be broken forever. The Mother will die forever and Amadioha's rule will never end.' He narrowed his eyes, curling his left hand into a fist.

Sinai stumbled forward as the crystal in her hand nudged towards the Eze.

'No!' she shrieked. Naala watched the scene with horror. Seconds later, she instinctively drew her left hand towards the Mother's crystal. She placed her hand over Sinai's and the fingers that had once pressed against Ezinne's stomach all that time ago, now extended over one another for the first time in years.

A deep red colour suddenly bled into the Mother's crystal, as bright and potent as fresh blood.

In that moment, everything changed.

Something inexplicably powerful exploded between both of them. The room erupted in a golden bright light. Suddenly a burst of deep black mist, speckled with gold dust, engulfed both Naala and Sinai. Their eyes filled with a golden glow as they looked at the red crystal in their hands.

The Eze looked on in shock, before roaring in anger as he rushed towards the girls.

Without warning, the black and gold mist exploded with a resounding force throughout the room. The various artefacts and furniture, used to decorate the elaborate chamber, suddenly shattered into tiny pieces.

The Eze blinked wordlessly, his jaw clenching, and his muscles tensed. He stumbled towards the two girls, the light dimming behind his frozen eyes, but before he could reach them, he crumbled to the floor and burst into a cloud of grey dust.

The mighty Eze was gone.

CHAPTER 52

THE DAUGHTERS OF NRI

City of Nri

Naala and Sinai breathed out simultaneously as though an unseen force had suddenly let go of its iron grip on their throats. They released each other's hands slowly. The Mother's crystal hovered weightlessly between them.

Sinai looked at the girl who had just helped her to defeat Eze Ochichiri.

Esinaala

A light, almost musical, voice whispered delicately in her mind. Sinai blinked as her heart raced furiously. She was pleased to find that she was not afraid. Unlike the voice she had heard in Meekulu's cave that had left her feeling uncertain and nervous, this voice made Sinai feel completely at peace. She knew something phenomenal was happening. Sinai accepted that she did not understand it and she knew that she was exactly where she needed to be. The face of the other girl was so recognisable, so familiar, that she could have sworn that she had known her for years.

'I know you,' she whispered incredulously.

'The Eze is dead,' Naala murmured back in a daze. She too felt that something about the other girl, her face, her voice, her scent, felt exactly like *home*. Naala couldn't even begin to comprehend it. She couldn't comprehend any of it.

The Eze is dead, she thought. Grey dust floated weightlessly in wispy beams of bright yellow sunlight. Her family was finally avenged and the threat of the Eze's rule was gone. Yet she did not feel at peace. She felt as though she had suddenly been thrust into a new world. A world full of uncertainties, hidden demons, and bitter consequences. Naala closed her eyes and took a deep breath in.

'Esinaala, I know you,' Sinai repeated, as she watched the girl carefully. A flash of shock rippled through Naala. It jolted her awake and her mind churned. *How does this girl know my name?* The question pounded through Naala's head as she opened her eyes and settled them on Sinai.

The other girl was utterly serene. Her eyes gleamed with something bright and magical, something Naala had only seen in her forgotten dreams. A sense of recognition leapt between the girls, and Naala's heart suddenly felt full.

'Who are you?' Naala asked softly.

'I don't know,' Sinai replied with a laugh, as one tear gleamed in her eye. 'I'm looking at a girl with my face; I've just helped to do the impossible, and I don't know *who* that makes me.' Sinai did not understand how she could be standing here right now. How she could have helped to defeat the Eze. How she could access a power that felt as though it could tear her apart and bring her back to life at the same time. She didn't understand how she could be standing in front of a complete stranger, and yet know, without a doubt, that she was destined to exist alongside her. 'But I know you.' She smiled warmly.

Naala found herself smiling back. She took a step closer and, without thinking, embraced Sinai for the first time since they were both nestled safely within Ezinne's warm womb. Naala was overcome with an incomprehensible joy that swirled gently around her heart before engulfing it whole. Her eyes watered, but she refused to blink away the tears.

'I know you too,' Naala whispered.

Neither one of them noticed the light winds stirring around the room. Nor did they did see the fierce gust that chased the heavy clouds from the sky, invigorating the birds that swept through the air with unbridled jubilation. They did not notice the sudden and inexplicable blooming of lustrous plants shooting up throughout the kingdom. All they could see, all they could feel, was each other.

The End.

*Naala and Sinai will return in Book 2 of
The Return Of The Earth Mother series.*

ACKNOWLEDGEMENTS

Firstly, I want to thank you so much for taking the time to read Daughters of Nri. This story is incredibly close to my heart. It began as a form of therapy but soon grew into a beautiful world that I could escape into; a world where the magical, strong and *real* black women in my life were finally the focal points. A world where their beauty was a fact and their power undeniable. A world where they were given room to have flaws and space to grow. A world where the weight of slavery and oppression was non-existent and in its place a look into the complexity of black female relationships, internal conflict and a true expression of what it is to be human.

Unfortunately, we are not all currently given the freedom to be *human* in this present world. Black women shoulder immense burdens and we endure far too much pain. But change is coming. We are taking up our space in this world. We are demanding love, respect and the care that we deserve. We will change the world.

In the meantime, I hope this book gave you a break and provided an escape into a world where you didn't have to fight to be seen; a world created entirely for you.

I want to give a special thanks to my sisters, by blood, Amar and Simi, and by fate, Mariam. We've undergone a hard but incredibly rewarding journey with this book. Thank you for supporting me every step of the way. Thank you for giving me the confidence to share my story with the world. Thank you for telling me how much you loved it and thank you for being fiercely honest with the improvements that needed to be made. Thank you for staying up several nights with me to make book boxes and other miscellaneous things that helped to bring this story to the world. I can't tell you how much I appreciate the work that you have all put into Daughters of Nri. This book, this experience, wouldn't be what it is without you. Thank you especially, Mariam, for dedicating your time and patience to help publish this book. You are my angel.

Thank you to Ade, for constantly reassuring me and being there for me to vent. Thank you for letting me bounce ideas around with you and for always providing a safe space for me. Thank you to my Mum and Dad for telling me stories about home that helped shape the world in this book. Thank you for telling me that I deserved everything the world had to offer. Thank you for supporting me through this journey and for your unbridled excitement through every step of the way. Thank you, AJ for

ACKNOWLEDGEMENTS

being so eager to help and get involved. Thank you Aunty Chichi for allowing me to consult you about the wonderful Igbo words that helped to make this book magical.

I'd also like to thank Donna, Alice and Troon, my brilliant editors, and every single person who has helped to shape this book.

Thank you once again to the reader. I hope you enjoyed the magic of this world; I can't wait to share more with you.

DICTIONARY OF WORDS

Word (Pronounciation)
Language
Meaning

Abara (Ahh-baa-rah)
Igbo
A double-edged sword, originally used by the Ika people of Delta State, Nigeria

Afọ (Ahh-for)
Igbo
3rd day of the Igbo week system

Agbala (Ag-bah-la)
Igbo
Priestess of Ala; She is in charge of executing punishments against individuals who commit immoral acts

Agwu (Ahhg-kwoo)
Igbo
God of health and divination; the trickster deity, who enjoys confusing human beings

Ajo-nmuo (Ahh-gee-ohn-moh)
Igbo
Demon

Akara (Ahh-cah-rah)
Igbo
Tainted; Marked

Akwa (Ahh-kwa)
Igbo
Nest

Akwa Akwete (Ahh-kwa Ak-wet-tay)
Igbo
A unique handwoven fabric of Igbo women of Akwete in Abia State, Nigeria. Akwete cloth weaving is said to be as old as the Igbo nation.

Akwụkwọ (Ahh-kwu-kwoh)
Igbo
Green leaf

Akwụna (Ahh-kwu-nah)
Igbo
Prostitute

Ala (Ahh-la)
Igbo
Earth Goddess; female diety of the earth, fertility, creativity and morality

Algaita (Al-hai-ta)
Hausa
A woodwind instrument with double reed in the Northwest African savannah; also known as algaitu

Alijanesu-ojoo (Ahh-li-jah-neh-su-o-joh)
Nsinri
Demon

Amadioha (Am-ahh-dee-owm-ha)
Igbo
God of justice; Metaphysically, Amadioha represents the collective will of the people; he speaks and strikes through thunder

Amaghi (Ama-yee)
Igbo
Mysterious; unknown

Anwansi (Ann-wan-zy)
Igbo
Magic

Biko (Bee-co)
Igbo
Please

Chi (Ch-ee)
Igbo
Chi, the spirit believed to inhabit each individual; soul

Chukwu (Choo-kwu)
Igbo
God

Chukwu Di Mma (Choo-kwu dee-ma)
Igbo
God is good; good God

Dada (Dah-dah)
Yoruba
A child born with naturally mattted or locked hair that cannot be combed

Daga (Dah-gah)
Igbo
Knife

Dambe (Dem-bay)
Hausa
Dambe is a form of boxing associated with the Hausa people of West Africa

Dibia (Deeb-pee-yah)
Igbo
Mediators between the human world and the spirit world

Efere (Eh-fair-reh)
Igbo
Plate

Efuolas (Eh-fu-oh-lah)
Nsinri
Illegitimate

Ehuru (Eh-oo-rue)
Igbo
A spice similar to nutmeg

Eke (Eh-kay)
Igbo
1st day of the Igbo week system

Ekwensu (Eh-kwen-zoh)
Igbo
God of bargaining and war; ruled over the wicked spirits and the chaotic forces of nature

Elu (Eh-lu)
Igbo
High

Ero (Eh-ro)
Igbo
Fungi

Gawa (Gah-wah)
Igbo
Move; go

Gburugburu (Goh-bu-rue)
Igbo
Round

Ikenga (Ee-ken-gah)
Igbo
Literal meaning "place of strength"; a horned deity; personal god of human endeavor, achievement, success, and victor

Lolo (Louw-louw)
Igbo
Lady; revered woman

Mami wata (Mah-me woh-ta)
Pidgin
Water spirit; mermaid

Mgbapu (Mm-ng-bah-pu)
Igbo
Going away; leaving; running away

Mmiri (Mm-ee-ree)
Igbo
Water

Mmo (Mm-moh)
Igbo
Spirit

Ndewo (Nn-de-oh)
Igbo
Greeting; welcome

Ndụ (Nn-du)
Igbo
Life

Nkwọ (Nn-kwo)
Igbo
4th day of the Igbo week system

Nkwobi (N-wkoh-bee)
Igbo
A delicious dish consisting of cooked cow foot mixed in spicy palm oil paste

Nnunu (Nn-nu-nu)
Igbo
Bird

Nwunye (Nn-wun-ye)
Igbo
Wife

Nzuzuo (Nn-zuh-zwo)
Nsinri
Secret

Ọbara (Oh-bah-rah)
Igbo
Blood

Obi (Oh-bee)
Igbo
An aristocratic title, meaning either elder in the first instance or chief in the second; also symbollically meaning heart

Ofo (Oh-for)
Igbo
A staff carried by selected Igbo elder men

Oga (O-ga)
Pidgin
Boss; master

Ọkụ (O-ku)
Igbo
Fire

Ọnụ ụzọ (Onour uh-zoh)
Igbo
Entrance; portal

Ọnwa (Oh-wah)
Igbo
Moonlight

Ọnye Nyocha (On-yay Ny-oh-cha)
Igbo
Reporter; someone who reports; spy

Onyinyo (Oh-nin-yo)
Igbo
Shadow

Orie (Oh-rey)
Igbo
2nd day of the Igbo week system

Osigwu (Osi-gu)
Nsinri
Midwife

Otjize (Oht-jeeze)
Herero
A mixture of butterfat and ochre pigment used by the Himba people of
Namibia to protect themselves from the harsh desert climate

Otomy (Oh-toh-me)
Nsinri
Atoms; miniscule particles

Ozo (Oh-zoh)
Igbo
Sir; revered man

Sayensi (Sigh-en-see)
Nsinri
Science

Shekeres (Sheh-ke-reh)
Yoruba
A percussion instrument consisting of a dried gourd with beads or cowries woven into a net covering the gourd

Uchie (Oo-chee)
Igbo
A delta region; Uchie tree, flame trees originating from Uchie

Ugu (Oo-gu)
Igbo
Pumpkin

Umu ada ogu (Uh-moo ahh-dah oh-gu)
Nsinri
Warrior goddess

Ụtọ (Uh-toh)
Igbo
Sweet

Zoro (Zoh-roh)
Nsinri
A grey material that can change its state instantly

Udara (Uh-dah-rah)
Igbo
An African cherry fruit with a chewable, edible skin that ranges from green to orange depending on its ripeness